THE PARADISE WAR

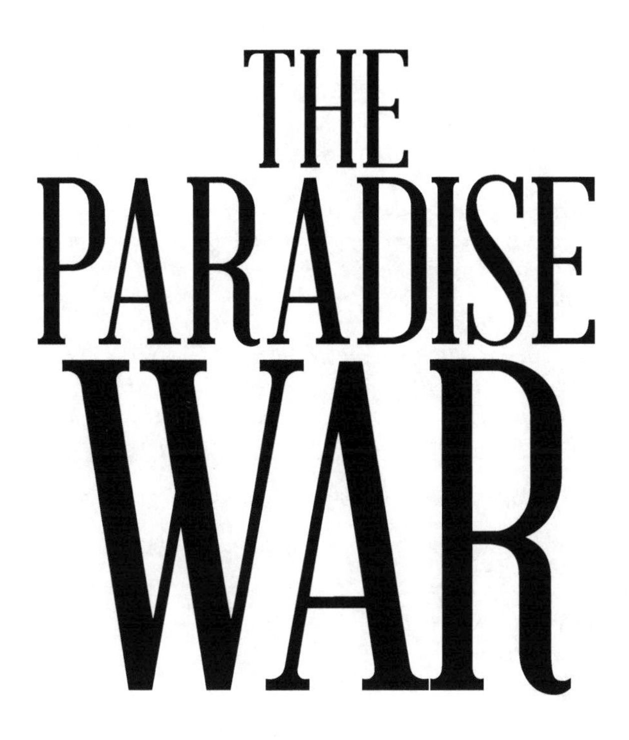

World War II
in the
Caribbean

JACK MATTIS

THE PARADISE WAR
WORLD WAR II IN THE CARIBBEAN

iUniverse books may be ordered through booksellers or by contacting:

iUniverse
1663 Liberty Drive
Bloomington, IN 47403
www.iuniverse.com
844-349-9409

ISBN: 978-1-6632-0092-1 (sc)
ISBN: 978-1-6632-0091-4 (e)

Library of Congress Control Number: 2020909046

Print information available on the last page.

iUniverse rev. date: 07/24/2020

For Nancy

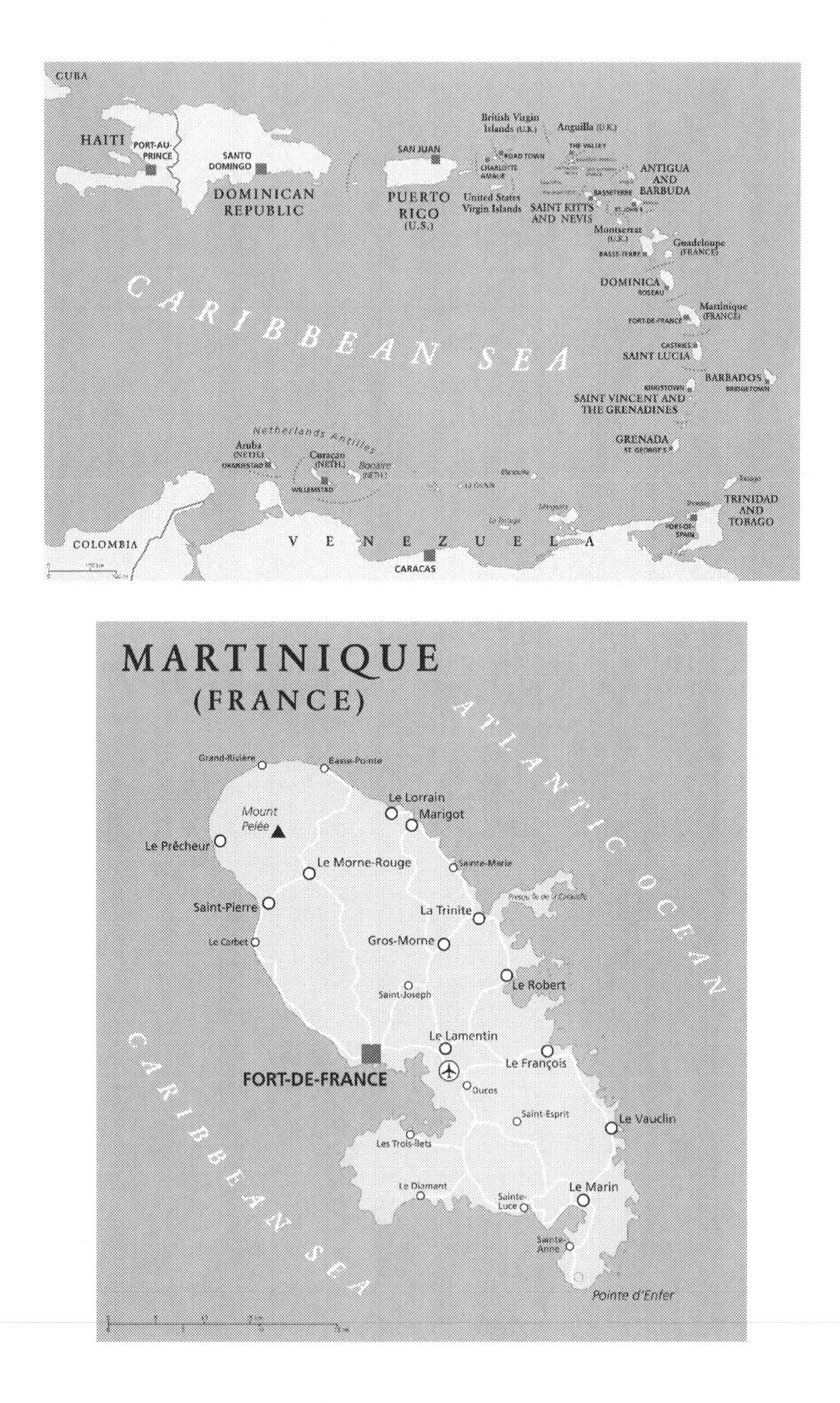
CUBA
HAITI
PORT-AU-PRINCE
SANTO DOMINGO
DOMINICAN REPUBLIC
SAN JUAN
PUERTO RICO (U.S.)
British Virgin Islands (U.K.)
ROAD TOWN
CHARLOTTE AMALIE
United States Virgin Islands
Anguilla (U.K.)
THE VALLEY
ANTIGUA AND BARBUDA
BASSETERRE
SAINT KITTS AND NEVIS
Montserrat (U.K.)
Guadeloupe (FRANCE)
BASSE-TERRE
DOMINICA
ROSEAU
Martinique (FRANCE)
FORT-DE-FRANCE
CASTRIES
SAINT LUCIA
BARBADOS
BRIDGETOWN
KINGSTOWN
SAINT VINCENT AND THE GRENADINES
GRENADA
ST. GEORGE'S
CARIBBEAN SEA
Netherlands Antilles
Aruba (NETH.)
ORANJESTAD
Curaçao (NETH.)
WILLEMSTAD
Bonaire (NETH.)
TRINIDAD AND TOBAGO
Tobago
PORT-OF-SPAIN
COLOMBIA
VENEZUELA
CARACAS
MARTINIQUE (FRANCE)
ATLANTIC OCEAN
CARIBBEAN SEA
Grand-Rivière
Basse-Pointe
Le Lorrain
Marigot
Mount Peléé
Le Prêcheur
Le Morne-Rouge
Sainte-Marie
Saint-Pierre
La Trinite
Le Carbet
Gros-Morne
Le Robert
Saint-Joseph
Le Lamentin
FORT-DE-FRANCE
Le François
Ducos
Saint-Esprit
Le Vauclin
Les Trois-Ilets
Le Diamant
Sainte-Luce
Le Marin
Sainte-Anne
Pointe d'Enfer

PROLOGUE

June 1940

Running without lights and with engines at flank speed, the French man-of-war EMILE BERTIN steamed a southerly course through the Atlantic night. In the hours before dawn the seas were running and a mist was forming off the Newfoundland Banks. In the soft blue lights of the combat bridge, Rear Admiral Robert Battet stood braced against the thrust of the turbines. Behind him a crew of hand-picked officers was manning their posts, their faces anemic in the glow of the battle lanterns, their eyes shifting anxiously between the darkness beyond and the man who commanded their fate. High above the main deck the throb of the engines and the hum of the ventilators offered the prospect of serenity, but the air was taut with expectation. Battet could feel the men behind him watching: watching the instruments, watching the night, watching him.

With painstaking precision he swept heavy binoculars to the limit of their vision. To his flanks and dead ahead, the infra-red lenses revealed a horizon rose-hued and sharp.

The admiral swung the glasses aft.

Three spidery masts.

He handed the binoculars to his executive officer. "Destroyers, Louis. They are in our wake."

The young Commander gauged the distance to the pursuing ships. "We can outrun them, Admiral."

"Perhaps. But we are heavily burdened. They know our cargo. Like sharks, they can smell it. Order thirty degrees starboard."

The executive officer sensed the anticipation that ran through the bridge. For the first time in his career he ventured a comment on the judgment of a senior officer. "The shoals, Admiral...we'll be cutting it close..."

"The fox relies on more than speed, Louis. God has provided. Steer for the fog."

As the cruiser heeled grudgingly toward the mist, the Admiral felt the vibration in the deck plates, the uncharacteristic sluggishness of the response. Heavily burdened, indeed. In the labyrinth below, on every deck, in every hold, in every compartment and companionway, in every storage locker, utility locker and magazine, in the galley and infirmary, in the officer's mess, and even in the Admiral's stateroom itself, was stored row upon row of canvas sacks, each stenciled with the numeral 35, each containing thirty-five kilos of gold, a total of 350 tons in all.

As the sleek warship nosed perilously close to the North American coastline, the embattled French admiral peered anxiously through the windscreen, his mind on the pursuing destroyers, his eyes in search of the first elusive beads of mist.

PART ONE

FIFTY-SEVEN YEARS LATER

1997

THE ISLAND OF MARTINIQUE

FRENCH WEST INDIES

Where dead men meet on lips
of living men....

LE DIAMANT, MARTINIQUE

Rear Admiral Sean Whitely stepped barefoot onto the beach. Though it was nearing midnight, the sand felt warm beneath his feet. Behind him the lamps of Diamant were strung against the cove like the lanterns of a fishing fleet. The village was preparing for sleep; screens had been latched over the sides of fruit stands, and fires were banked in the grills of beachfront cafes. A single pair of headlights swung slowly onto the coast road, leaving his rented Peugeot the sole remaining vehicle in the seaside parking lot.

Taking a bearing on some nets drying on poles, the Admiral headed north. Ahead stretched a crescent of sand, long and white beneath a buoyant moon. If Madame Paquet knew her beach, the wreck should be somewhere beyond the point. If the madame knew her husband, the fisherman would be somewhere near the wreck.

Their hut on the flank of the rain forest had been modest, a roof of corrugated tin, windows lacking glass, a dilapidated couch and some cane-backed chairs. Frayed rush mats cushioned an earthen floor.

"He be taking d'fish," Madame Paquet had said, a kerosene lamp etching shadows on her face. In a niche in the wall a crude Madonna was drawing life from a wick burning serenely in a saucer of coconut oil. Her homespun *chapelle* boasted an offering of orchids in a broken cup. "Fish or no fish," she said, drawing lightly on a thin black cigar, "he be takin' d'drink."

The Admiral trudged steadily up the strand. The beach was fringed with palms, their trunks arched seaward by the westerly Trades. A fleet of *gommiers* lay blue-shadowed beneath the fronds, their prows pointing stoutly out to sea, the names on their sides a litany of saints. He was surprised to find surf on this side of the island; not the booming breakers of the Atlantic coast, but a gentle swell that silvered as it arched and slithered to a frothy death at the edge of the tide line. In the distance he could see the snout of the headland; beyond that the offshore outcropping the Martiniquais called *Rocher du Diamant*.

The Captain had noted it in his dairy:

.. Rocher Diamant...a volcanic formation
off Martinique's Caribbean coast
near the fishing village of Diamant...
...ideal cover for a submarine...

To tourists it was known as Diamond Rock, a miniature mountain that served as the western sentinel to Diamant Bay. The British had another name for it, Whitely knew. On the Admiralty charts it was carried as HMS Diamond Rock...to commemorate a battle in Nelson's day, when, to safeguard the southwest passage to the capital city of Forte de France, British seamen carried ammunition to the crest of the ridge and held out against French artillery for eighteen hellish months. To this day, Her Majesty's warships dipped their colors when passing the hallowed spot.

Admiral Whitely picked up the pace. In build he was lean but wiry, a physique well-suited to the constraints of a cockpit. He walked with long loping strides, the kind that had outpaced a Viet Cong patrol after a flameout over the jungle. On the flight from Washington the night before, he had worn tropical khakis. After a morning meeting with a group of French naval veterans, he had changed to jeans and a T-shirt. The jeans were rolled to his calves. In the style of the old Navy, he had folded a pack of Camel cigarettes into a sleeve of the shirt. With his hair blowing freely in the wind he looked a decade younger than his fifty-four years. From here on out he would pursue his ghosts incognito, much like The Captain had done more than half a century before.

The sand was yielding, the going slow. To quicken the pace he angled to the tide line. The water temperature was in equilibrium with the air, the run-up warm between his toes. He found his stride on a hard-packed ridge and replayed the anonymous telephone call he had received at his hotel room that afternoon.

"To learn more about the bullion, monsieur, cast your net at the hut of the fisherman Paquet."

Had he mentioned at his morning meeting that he was staying at the Meridien? He couldn't recall. The session in the bowels of the fort had lasted the entire morning. In explaining his visit to the assemblage of French naval veterans, he had focused on the gold. It was as good a place to begin as any. Despite the fifty-year interval, it was something they would remember. As he expected, their recollections had varied with their vantage points. In the spring of 1942 some had been billeted aboard ships in the harbor, others at encampments around the island. A few had been stationed at one of the three main forts. Fifty years put a strain on the best of memories. Through the prism of time, the skirmish in the islands took on the proportions of the siege of Troy.

But on certain facts they agreed:

...the gold had arrived on the cruiser EMILE BERTIN in June of 1940...("*...beaucoup lingot, monsieur...*)

...throughout the war the gold was stored at Fort Desaix, the sprawling encampment on the heights above Forte de France...

...at the cessation of hostilities the gold was shipped back to France...

"All of it? he had asked.

"But of course, monsieur."

As he expected, he knew more about it than they did.

But then, he had The Captain's diary.

And Casey's letters.

Through his interpreter, he had asked if any of the veterans had run across an American civilian on the island in 1942. They had not. Nor had he expected them to. With the exception of a U.S. Naval Observer and a few consulate personnel, Americans were *personae non gratae* on the island during the early years of the war. Besides, The Captain had been under cover.

So what to make of the anonymous tipster? Why would someone wait until he had returned to his hotel to direct him to the fisherman Paquet? Less than twenty-eight hours on the island and already the questions were piling up.

He was nearing the point, a sandy beak of land that hooked sharply out to sea. Behind him the lights of Diamant cast a hazy glow over the jungle of palms. The breeze shifted fractionally and he caught the scent of cooking. The odors were spicy and exotic. Fishermen's huts were scattered around the dunes; the soft glow of oil lamps seeped dimly through the trees.

Even if nothing came of the fisherman, it had been a productive first day. After meeting with the veterans he had driven to the plantation where the Buffaloes lay buried. The Captain had waxed poetic on the Buffaloes:

...one hundred and six dive bombers in all,
beached on an island without an airstrip,
warbirds that never left the nest,
eagles that never flexed a talon..."

The Buffaloes' burying ground was now a forest of banana trees, the stalks blue-bagged and ready for picking.

The Captain had been Whitely's grandfather. His recollection of the man was vague...a tall suntanned stranger who, when Whitely was three, had given him a model airplane. He remembered, or at least he thought he did, the braided gold bars on the shoulder boards and the scrambled eggs on the officer's cap. Now that he was on the island, he felt it important to retrace The Captain's every step. Not that he doubted his accuracy. The Navy had put great store in The Captain's accuracy. But though the island's contours remained the same...mountains, inlets, mornes, valleys... much had changed in the intervening years. There was no telling where one might stumble across a piece of the puzzle.

He had thirty days.

Thirty days to bridge fifty years.

Thirty days to re-assemble the fragments of his past.

High above the island the sky was extravagant with stars. On the horizon a meteor fell as silent as a snowflake. He was beginning to wonder if he had misunderstood the madame's Frenchified creole when he spotted the wreck. It lay at the edge of the tideline, its backbone mired in sand, its ribs salt-bleached and gaunt like the bones of some long-starved sea monster. The prow had a peculiar shape to it, like the skull of a serpent peering blindly out to sea. He was reaching for his cigarettes when a match flared near the base of the keel. The flame moved, then brightened, and the ribs flexed eerily as though the monster had managed a breath. A figure was squatting in the shadows. When the flame softened, he could make out the framework of a lantern. It rose from the sand and the glow fell on the face of a man. He was wearing a battered straw hat and a sleeveless sweatshirt. Like Whitely's, his pants were rolled to his knees and his feet were bare. The man raised the lantern to eye level and Whitely could see he was a native, stooped with age and squinting into the darkness like a refugee from a pirate ship.

"Pardon the interruption," Whitely said, feeling a trifle foolish at the banality of the remark. "Is your name Paquet? Sedonie Paquet?"

"No interruption," the man said. Beneath the hat his eyes reflected the glow of the lantern. "I be fishin'."

Whitely saw a pole angling from the sand, a line beaded with droplets where it stretched to the sea.

"Your wife told me I would find you here. Are you having any luck?"

The fisherman lowered the lantern and crooked a finger toward an empty bucket.

Whitely approached the ribs of the wreck. "I'm touring the island," he said. He pointed to The Rock. "Among other things, I have come to see Diamant."

The fisherman raised the lantern to eye level. Whitely could see that he was old indeed, old and gaunt, with prominent cheekbones and eyes that seemed clouded by cataracts. He had thin ropy arms and hands as crooked as roots. Coiled around his waist was a belt at least three sizes too large. The skin on his face was as rough as parchment, shriveled and taut. When he spoke, there was a gap where his front teeth had been.

"Your name came up in a meeting I attended," Whitely said. "In Fort de France. Someone said you have lived here all your life. On Martinique, I mean."

The fisherman planted the lantern, and shadows danced along the ribs of the wreck. "Seventy, eighty year."

Whitely noted that he displayed no interest in whoever might have volunteered his name.

"Then you were here during the war. In the forties, I mean."

The fisherman looked out to sea, as though the answer lay beyond the horizon. Whitely noticed a small circular seashell hanging from the lobe of one ear.

"D'war. I be here." His Creole patois was thickened by the loss of teeth. He set the lantern on the sand and produced a colorless bottle from the ribs of the wreck.

"Do you remember much about the war?" Whitely asked. "Do you remember the fighting ships at Forte de France?"

The fisherman yanked the cork and offered the bottle without comment.

Fighting an impulse to swipe a sleeve against the rim, Whitely tilted the bottle and swallowed deeply. As the liquid coursed his esophagus, he felt the fire of immature rum. He handed the bottle back and the fisherman dabbed the mouthpiece against his shirt.

"D'big boats," Paquet said, tilting the rum and catching the moon in the bottle. "In d'harbor. Daht be true. Many boats dere were..." He smacked his lips and took a long slow swig of the rum.

"Was there much excitement then? Were people afraid?"

Paquet seemed to ponder this a moment. He corked the bottle and returned it to its niche in the wreck; then squatting on his haunches, he fidgeted with some bait.

"Some be afraid, I tink. Mostly d'French. D'French be afraid of d'French."

Whitely remembered reading of defections; of Frenchmen favoring De Gaulle ferrying in the night to the neighboring island of St. Lucia; of other Frenchmen trying to stop them, to hunt them down and detain them. Or worse. It was a bitter time for Frenchmen. The penalty for defection was death.

"Did you stay here during the war? On this southern end of the island, I mean?"

"Me womahn live here," the fisherman said. "I go to d'harbor for work."

Whitely ran a hand over a rib of the wreck. It was pitted and damp, scoured by the sea. "Tell me what you remember about the war. What do you remember about working at the harbor?"

"I remember d'boats," Paquet said, eyeing the tautness of the line. "And d'soldiers. And d'lights dat be put out in case d'bombing comes. Outrageous dark, it was. I remember dat...."

Whitely glanced at the serpent-headed bowsprit. Someone had painted an eye on the seaward profile. It had the look of Vikings. It was late. The fisherman seemed intent on his bait. Remembering he still had a bit of a drive, he decided to come directly to the point.

"Do you remember meeting any Americans during the war? At the harbor? Here in Diamant? Or anywhere else on the island?"

The fisherman pondered a moment, squatting near the pole and studying his line as though anticipating a twitch.

Whitely thought he might not have heard him. "Someone said you could tell me about an American. An American who was here during the war."

The fisherman scratched a leg. "'Merican. Be true. 'Merican be here. Even on dis very beach. When dey bring d'gold. I remember dat. I remember it good."

There it was again. And this time he had not brought it up.

"The gold?" Whitely asked.

"From d'fort. I be here my own self when dey bring it."

"Here? Where? Where did they bring it?"

Dey bring it dere," Paquet said. He pointed to a slash in the the coastline. "To da cove. To take it away."

Whitely followed the line of his finger to a dark indent in the treeline a few hundred yards up the beach. In the spill of the moon all he could make out was a wall of feathery palms. "Away?" he asked.

“In d’ship. D’ship dat sail under d’sea.”

“A submarine?”

“Submachine. Dat be it,” the fisherman said. “I do recall. Dey take d’gold away.”

Whitely knew the Caribbean had been swarming with submarines in the early forties. American. French. German. Italian. Despite the heat, he felt a shiver of anticipation. He remembered the telephone call he had received from Paris before leaving Washington:

“...Admiral Whitely? Jean-Luc here. As you requested,
I have checked with French Intelligence.
Three hundred and fifty tons of bullion had been
shipped to Martinique in 1940.
When the gold was returned to France
after the war, a ton was missing.
On arrival in France, some of the crates
contained sand. An investigation ensued.
Since the sand was of the type found on the Normandy coast,
the switch was presumed to have been made
on the mainland.
When the Nazis pulled out of Paris there was
mass confusion.. .records destroyed,
personnel missing...local infighting over who got what....
The missing ton was never accounted for...”

Whitely extracted the cigarettes from the sleeve of his T-shirt. He shook a Camel out of the pack and held it out to the fisherman. Paquet plucked it neatly between bony fingertips and wedged it tightly behind an ear. Whitely struck a friction match against a rib of the wreck and let it flare between cupped fingers.

“There in that cove, you say? A submarine carried gold away?” He lit his cigarette and flipped the match into the sea.

“Certain I am of it, mon. It be one big secret. D’Merican. He see d’boxes. Dey be like d’boxes at d’fort.... Now lemme see...” He squatted on his haunches and scribed the numerals ‘35’ in the sand. "1 remember it, mon. Yessir, I remember it good. Big secret. Big trouble. When d'Merican leave, I tell me womahn. She say I'm drunk. Twas a long time ago, mon. But I remember dat night. I be seein' it wid me own eyes. Trucks on d'beach. Outrageous shootin' and yellin'. I run away. I hide on d'mountain."

Whitely looked back at the cove, a sheltered inlet with a sandy beach and lush vegetation.

Were you in that cove, Captain? And the German? Was he there too? He turned back to the fisherman. "So they didn't believe you?"

"For true. Dey don't believe me. But d'lady know. She keep d' secret."

"The lady? You mean your wife'

The fisherman suffered a short catarrhal cough. He swiped his mouth with his hand and brushed it against a pant leg. "Not me wife," he said, gathering his breath. "D'doctor lady. She know. D'fact is, she be dere. She be dere wit d'Merican and d'mahn in d'white suit."

Confident he knew the answer, Whitely asked the question that had brought him to this southern tip of the island. "Is this doctor lady on Martinique? Is she still alive?"

Paquet plucked the cigarette from behind his ear. He wet it with his tongue and raised the hood of the lantern. "She be much alive," he said, drawing the flame to the tobacco. "She be at d'clinique."

"And you know her name?"

"Only one doctor lady. She be d'one."

"Where is this clinic?"

The fisherman crooked a finger south. "'Bout five mile."

Whitely had already booked a room at Ste-Anne. "And you don't know her name."

"Dere be but one."

Whitely noticed a tightening of the fishing line. When the pole arched slightly to seaward, Paquet touched a finger to the line.

"The man in the white suit?" Whitely asked. "Is he still on the island?"

The fisherman offered the bottle again. "He be gone, I tink."

Whitely ventured a more generous sip of the rum. This time it went down easier, the heat less searing. "And you? Do you fish here often?"

"Me womahn, she trow d'bottle out d'house. I take d'rum. I catch d'fish."

Whitely thought back to Madame Paquet. Was she asleep by now, or was she dozing, rheumy eyes aglint, in the sanctum of her chapel? From his wallet he dug out one of the cards he had taken from the hotel's reception desk.

"If you remember anything more about that night, the night you saw the American and the submarine, I'll be at Point du Bout for another two weeks. Hotel Meridien. I'd be grateful for your call."

The fisherman took the card without comment.

Certain he'd never call, Whitely thanked him for his time.

The slog back up the beach seemed tougher on the legs. The sand was less supportive now, the breeze a touch less congenial. As he rounded the point, he glanced back at the wreck. The skull of the serpent was cutting a death mask across the face of the moon.

***

The village of Ste-Anne sat with its feet in the bay and a shoulder against the mountain. What passed for a commercial area consisted of a cobbled lane, a tree-lined square, and a compact grid of sidestreets that angled into the hills.

It was well after midnight when Whitely pulled onto the grounds of L'HIBISCUS. The hotel was built directly on the beach, a tidy encampment of whitewashed buildings and flowered walkways that could have been plucked from any of the Antilles venues. A bar off the lobby was catering to a handful of tourists, the breed unwilling or unable to suffer the high-season tariffs. On an elevated bandstand, three bare-chested musicians were tapping gaudy steel drums in a mellifluous tribute to some obscure island ballad.

Despite the flight from Washington the day before, with the

usual island-hopping delays followed by a fitful night's sleep, Whitely felt energized and awake. The fisherman's story had invigorated him, filled him with a renewed sense of mission. The hollow resonance of the drums beckoned, so he left his gripsack with the desk clerk and ordered a rum punch at the bar. He remembered reading somewhere that steel bands were a throwback to World War Two, when oil drums were awash on every island in the Caribbean. Though he had been born on St. Thomas, he had left the West Indies as a lad and returned only once, as a tourist some thirty years later. The Navy had shipped him around the world, but despite his origins a billet in the islands had eluded him. Still, the memories were deep-rooted: the perfume-scented blossoms, the incandescent stars, the warm moist breath of the Trades. As he sipped the rum, the encounter with the fisherman nagged. With every step he took, the gold loomed larger in the equation. If it were not so late he would seek out the lady doctor now. The village was compact. She could not be more than a few hundred yards from where he sat. He would lay odds she was the "SJ" mentioned in The Captain's diary.

You were on the wire, weren't you, Captain? Someone was at your heels.

He downed the drink and jogged a short flight of steps to his second floor apartment. It was a gaudily-appointed suite with an adequate bathroom and a compact sitting room. As soon as he'd unpacked, he tapped the Rhum Clement he had purchased on landing. He poured a healthy measure over a glass of ice and set it on the dresser. To remind him he was in the tropics, the ice melted away before he could strip for a shower.

Clad only in shorts and sandals, he wrapped the bottle in a clean wet towel and placed it beside a lounger on the terrace. The lights of Ste-Anne reflected serenely off the bay. Certain he couldn't sleep if he tried, he slipped a packet from his briefcase and propped reading glasses on the bridge of his nose. He had been over it a dozen times in the past two weeks, pored over every word until he had it all but memorized. But here on the island it would take on new meaning. This was where it had all begun. This was the crucible in which the fate of The Captain had been forged. It could well be where he would uncover his own fate, a fate that until recently had seemed as predictable as sunrise.

The plain manila envelope was as he had discovered it among his mother's papers the evening after her funeral. A note she had addressed to him shortly before she died was stapled to an outside corner. The Captain's diary and letters were within. Though he could recite the note by heart, there was something in the cursive script that drew him to the words...something in the symmetry of the stroke, the tremulous scrawl, that revived the memory of loving hands and caring fingers. With a heavy heart he fought off the memory of those final agonizing minutes when the hands had lost their strength, the fingers their ability to function.

He read the note again.

MY BELOVED SEAN

Enclosed is a letter I wrote to you when
you were seventeen. I wrote it doubting
I could find the courage to release it,
and, indeed, I did not. It seemed the right
decision at the time. I hope these many
years later you will deem it so.
I have decided to pass it on
at this late hour in the hope that you will
understand the reasons for my
procrastination. More important, I pray you
can find it in your heart to accept what the
letter reveals in the spirit in which it was written.
I love you, Sean. With so much of my being did I invest
that love that it may have tainted my judgment.
The decision must rest with you now.
It's your burden to carry.
May you do so in peace.

She had signed it, Casey.

Casey. It was an intimacy they had shared, their own private endearment. Once he reached the age of reason he had stopped calling her mother. She looked too young to be called mother, he had said, too beautiful. He had only been seven, and she had hugged him tenderly and kissed his cheek.

The stationery was pale violet; the handwriting, from a healthier time, assertive and decorous. He was a teenager when his mother had set the words to paper. He wondered how he would have reacted had she shared them with him then.

June 6, 1956

My dearest Sean

I write this as you are on the brink of manhood,
on the eve of your graduation from high school.
While I'm bursting at your academic
achievement and looking forward to your fulfilling
your dream of entering the Academy, I find myself
weeping at the loss of my companion of seventeen years.
I watch with an ambivalent heart as you prepare for your
new life as a Naval officer. Infant and child,
boy and man, you have been the core of my life, my baby,
and I release you but grudgingly to an
indifferent world.
This will be a most difficult letter for me
to write, Sean; so difficult that, having
written it, I'm not yet certain I can release it
for fear of muddling what to now has been your
clear and unfettered path.
Since there is no easy way to say this,
let me thrust it upon you in a single, untidy burst.
The man you believed to have been
your father all these years, the man whose name
you bear, was not you natural father.
There! I've said it! So painful is it
for me to confide that my hand
is trembling as I write it. Please forgive me

for not telling you sooner, Sean. All things considered,
I could not. If you will bear with me through
a brief explanation, perhaps it will ease
the blow somewhat.

Whitely's fingers brushed a stain on the paper. It was as unyielding as ever. He sipped the rum and turned the page.

You were conceived on the island of
St. Thomas in 1938, Sean, three years before America
entered the war. Your father was not
Kevin Whitely, as you have been led to believe.
I did not meet Kevin until Dec. 6, 1941,
the day before the Japanese attacked Pearl Harbor,
the day before America entered the war..
For a time while we were courting, I withheld
the identity of your natural father even from Kevin.
Then, as events unfolded and Kevin and I decided
to marry, I could procrastinate no longer. Kevin, too,
thought it best to wait until you were older
before telling you of your real father.
Sadly, he never got the opportunity.
In the short time you knew him, you were
devoted to Kevin, Sean. You loved him as much
as any son could love a father. And he
could have been no prouder of you were
you his natural-born son. When he was killed in 1943, a piece
of both of us went with him to his grave. Had you known him,
Sean, you would have loved him as I did, without reserve,
with all your heart. But that is beyond
us now. Now we must deal with things
as they are, as difficult as they are.
Now to your real father. For years I've
agonized over telling you, so terribly important
is it to me that the bond we share be not diminished
by some veil that may descend between us. Even as I write

these words in the enlightened year of 1956, a stigma attaches
to birth out of wedlock. In 1938 it was positively
not spoken of. Not on a small island like St. Thomas.
Part of my retaining this secret had to do with your
youth, part with my own pride, but most, I confess,
to my fear of losing your respect. Having put that
at risk, all I can hope for now is your trust and
understanding. I love you, Sean, more than life itself.
If I have been less than candid with you,
you must believe that it was more to protect
you than to gloss over any indiscretion on my part.
Even now it is difficult to proceed; even now,
when the memory of the war is fading and your generation
has relegated it to the perspective of history.
You see, I still find myself hesitating...
I will delay no longer.
Your real father's name is, was...he may be dead
by now, I have no way of knowing...Reinmann...
Viktor Reinmann. When Viktor and I met early in 1938,
he was, he told me, a German student on a sailing
holiday in the islands. I was seventeen, Sean.
A child myself. Viktor came into my life for a few short
weeks then disappeared as abruptly as he had arrived.
When next I saw him, in December of 1941, he was
a German naval officer. He had returned to the islands
on a special mission, something to do with
submarines. He dropped in unexpectedly.
You were three, Sean. He saw you. He knew you
were my son, but I never admitted
he was your father. The next day America entered
the war and I never saw him again.
Are you piecing it together, Sean?
You were three when the incident with the
submarine occurred. I have often wondered how much you
remember of those wartime years.
How much does a three-year-old recall?

At three, most everyone is a stranger,
every happening a new experience.
Does a child of three distinguish the ordinary
from the bizarre? If you do recall the
incident with the submarine, Sean, it was Viktor,
your father, who provoked it, I'm sure of it.
Enough. You must be numb.
If I find the courage to release this letter,
we'll talk, Sean. You'll have questions, I'm sure.
I want you to know the truth. It's been a pox
on my conscience all these years. For once I want to look
in your eyes and know that you're seeing me as I am.
You're strong, Sean. Driven. Collected.
I hesitate to divert you,
but without this confession
I could find no peace.
So now, as I struggle with the decision to
release this letter, we'll see
if that strength redounds to me.
I'll pray it does.
Your loving mother,
Casey.

There was a footnote:

Enclosed you'll find some letters from
your grandfather......the Captain......as you knew him.
He sent them before he disappeared.
I have also enclosed his diary. His last
mission was on the island of Martinique. After he
disappeared I was visited by an officer
from Naval Intelligence. He questioned
me about your grandfather's mission.
Later, when we returned to the States after the war,
I was questioned by the FBI and some people
from French Intelligence. They wanted to know if your

grandfather had ever mentioned anything about
his assignment on Martinique, but they never told me why...

Whitely refolded the notepaper and slipped it into the envelope. The moon had set and the sky was thick with stars. Ste-Anne's bay was outlined by a slender ribbon of surf. From beneath the balcony came the soft melodic rhythms of the steel drums. He poured a measure of rum over a fistful of ice.

They had never talked about it. The letter his mother had written when he was seventeen had remained sealed until the day after her funeral. Even in her final hours she had apparently failed to muster the will to discuss her confession face to face. His mother had been right. There were questions he would have liked to ask. Her letter had come as a shock, a jolt so harsh that it had sent him reeling for days.

A German. His father had been a German naval officer. In 1942. The heart of World War II.

Yes, Mother. There were questions.

...something to do with submarines...

No Reinmann had ever commanded a U-Boat; he had checked the records......re-checked with the German Admiralty. And no Reinmann had been listed as a crew member. Had his father been a Nazi? What was he doing in the Caribbean? Where had he been born? Who were his parents? Did he have other children? Brothers? Sisters? None that Sean had been able to locate. But he had only been on the problem for a few short weeks. Germany was a large country.

If it wasn't so shocking, it would be amusing, he thought. Sean Kevin Whitely, Annapolis graduate, Rear Admiral, United States Navy. Mother, Casey Olivia O'Shea, widowed schoolteacher born in the Caribbean of Danish-Italian parents. Father-of-record, Kevin Sean Whitely, deceased pilot, United States Navy, Irish-English. Wife, Jessica Whitely (nee Romanoff), the daughter of Russian Jews.

The son of a Nazi.

And what of his grandfather? Why would French and U.S.Naval

Intelligence question his mother about the Captain's mission on Martinique?

He reflected on the incident with the submarine. On that, his mother had been right. It was shadows and phantoms. A ship, slender and long. Scorching hot sun on a wooden hot deck. Barechested men singing and laughing in a strange language. Then suddenly the clanging of bells, harsh and insistent. The men scrambling below. A period of darkness. Silence....

Shadows and phantoms.

A week after his mother's funeral he had embarked on a project to trace his origins, to track down the man called Viktor Reinmann. So far the search for his natural father had led him in a circle, back to, of all people, his own grandfather. Through a colleague in Berlin, a German naval officer with whom he had shared a billet in the Philippines, he had learned that one Kapitanleutnant Viktor Reinmann had been reported missing in action in the spring of 1942 in the eastern Caribbean. Whitely's grandfather, U.S. Navy Captain Dante O'Shea, had been reported missing in May of the same year, somewhere off the island of Martinique. Captain O'Shea had been on special assignment for Naval Intelligence. The German's presence in the West Indies was unexplained. Neither body had been found, both were presumed dead.

His father, a German seaman.

His grandfather, an American airman.

Both reported missing in the same quadrant of the Caribbean within days of one another.

Neither body recovered.

Coincidence?

Oddity of war?

Perhaps.

Were it not for The Captain's diary.

Were it not for his mother's letters.

And mysteriously, the gold. Whenever he inquired about his grandfather's mission, he ran smack into the gold.

He sipped the rum. Beyond Ste-Anne's bay, the peak of a mountain defined the island from the surrounding night. On the spine of a ridge he could make out a scattering of lights. He remembered the old fisherman, the massive outcropping that was Diamond Rock.

...ideal cover for a submarine...

A week before leaving for Martinique, while researching the World War II Command Files in Washington, he had come across a communique in the archives.

TOP SECRET
CMDR. TENTH NAVAL DIST. TO CINCLANT
April 6, 1942
...a U-Boat lurking in the vicinity
of Martinique torpedoed the
passenger liner LADY NELSON
while it lay at anchor
in the harbor of Castries
off the island of St. Lucia...
...thirty civilians killed...

Whitely looked out at the serene black waters. St. Lucia lay off the southern tip of Martinique, less than thirty miles from where he sat. He tried to envision a passenger liner at anchor, the frothy wake of a torpedo...gouts of flame against the blue-black sky...

Were you on that U-Boat, Herr Reinmann? Were you part of that massacre?

And what of the lady doctor? What was her role in all of this, if any? Would she remember anything? It was fifty-odd years. She would be seventy-five, at least. Older, more likely.

As he sat there sipping the rum, one by one the lights on the mountain flickered and died. When he retired to the bedroom, the stars were quivering in the heavy air and the drums had fallen silent.

He awakened in the night to a brief squall. Rain was beating like gravel against the windows and he could hear the palms thrashing on the beach. He sat up in bed. On the balcony the leaves on the hibiscus were twitching like ducks in a shooting gallery.

After dozing off again, he dreamed of pigeons pecking puddles of rainwater.

In the morning he awakened to birdsong. He pushed back the shutters and the village of St-Anne lay sparkling in sunlight. Beneath a scrubbed blue sky, the bay stretched serenely to the horizon. Just off the beach a solitary sailboat lay at anchor looking small and impotent beneath a naked mast. Near the mouth of the bay some native schooners were beating their way steadily out to sea. He recalled his conversation with the fisherman Paquet. Had his memory survived the fifty years, or was his story the rum-soaked dregs of a fertile imagination?

He took breakfast on a porch that lay open to the sea, *cafe au lait* and a flaky *croissant.* A bird with golden eyes and sleek black feathers alighted nimbly on a nearby table. While Whitely ate, the bird snitched breadcrumbs from a wicker basket.

Whitely inquired at the desk about the lady doctor. A delightfully charming Creole girl, all smiles and proud of her tourist-sufficient English, directed him to an office on the square. The doctor's name was Rollet. Nikole Rollet. Yes, the cheery clerk confirmed, Docteur Rollet had been in St-Anne as long as anyone could remember. She had lived there longer than the clerk's own mother, who was approaching sixty.

Nikole Rollet did not compute with the cryptic "SJ" in The Captain's diary, but his grandfather had displayed an affinity for code names.

Whitely left his car at the hotel and walked the two blocks to the small town square. The village was built just centimeters above sea level. From a white sandy beach, cobbled lanes climbed gently-terraced foothills to mimosa-draped heights. The square was shaded by tamarind trees, its perimeter flanked by a variety of shops, none higher than two stories, their balconies fretted with iron scrollwork. The streets were clean, the buildings in good repair. The top of the square was dominated by a centuries-old church. At the foot of the square a barefoot lad in tattered cutoffs was sweeping rain gutters with a broom of twigs. A sparrow was bathing in the dust beneath a wooden wheelbarrow. Whitely tried to imagine what the village might have looked like in 1942. With only a handful of cars on the narrow lanes and the pastel buildings retaining a touch of senescence, he supposed it had changed very little.

He found the doctor's office sandwiched between a dress shop and a pharmacy. A small bronze plaque identified the office as belonging to one *N.Rollet*, Médicin. He tried the knob, but the door was locked. There was no sign indicating office hours, and he was about to turn away when the sweeper strode across the square pointing his broom in the direction of the church.

Le docteur est dan l'eglise.

The church was small, more like a chapel, with a high-shouldered belfry and a tall graceful spire. Once through the heavy wooden doors, he paused to let his eyes adjust to the dimness. The nave was lit by a few guttering candles. There were two people inside. One, a native girl, was dusting the main altar and dabbing a cloth between bowls of flowers. She was humming what sounded to Whitely like a rock tune, her thin falsetto echoing clearly through the vaulted chamber. In a forward pew, bathed in iridescent rays from a stained-glassed window, knelt an old woman. She was slight and stooped and wore a sheer linen scarf draped over silver-gray hair. She looked deep in prayer, so Whitely slipped into the rearmost pew and sat quietly against the hard wooden bench.

The broad center aisle was paved with diamond-shaped stones meticulously painted to simulate marble. Pews of warm-colored wood bore the nameplates of parishoners. At the rear of the pews stood a stone confessional, the sides unshuttered and open to the nave. Between high arched windows were hung the Stations of the Cross.

The old lady crossed herself and sighed as if shedding some minor burden. When she stepped to the aisle and genuflected, she looked considerably taller than she had at prayer.

Whitely stepped out of the pew as she approached the vestibule. She saw him and prepared a smile, the kind reserved for patients, he supposed.

Doctor Rollet?"

She stopped and squandered the smile. "Yes."

Forgive me, Doctor. My name is Whitely. Sean Whitely. Could you spare me a moment? I think you may have known my grandfather.

She studied his face, took in the sharply pressed chinos, the highly-polished loafers, the loose-fitting sport shirt. With a gesture toward the square, she said, "Everyone seems in good health this morning. My cottage is but a few paces from here. You're American, are you not?"

Her English was measured, with a slight French lilt.

"Yes," he said. "American."

She dipped a finger in the stoup and crossed herself with holy water. She gestured to the door and he followed her into the sunlight.

Her cottage was larger than it looked from the road, a two-story dwelling in the colonial style perched smartly on a hillside with a magnificent view of the bay. She led him beyond the verandah to a clipped green lawn dominated by a giant red mimosa. The garden was lush with hibiscus and bougainvillea. As she draped her rosary beads over a coat hook near a doorway, he took the occasion to study her profile. Time had stamped its imprint, but age had not diminished her well-proportioned features. Delicate cheekbones, an imperious set of the chin, a mouth bearing the residue of a permanent smile. Though the features were serene, her eyes retained the spark of sagacity. Each crease in her face seemed to hide some cherished memory or abandoned hope.

Was this the woman who had been at the cove that night with his grandfather?

They entered the garden and she motioned him to a chair. The furniture was wicker, the cushions a lusterless print. Beyond the garden the sweep of the bay was framed by the leaves of a tamarind tree. While he surveyed his surroundings, she walked to a doorway and spoke to someone within. She returned and took a seat opposite him in a high-backed rocker.

"Forgive the intrusion," he said. "I'm researching some articles set during the war. In 1942 to be precise. I thought you might share a memory or two." It was a small lie, intended to relax her, to break the ice, but he suffered a twinge of guilt.

At the mention of the war her eyes hardened a bit, but her smile held firm. She settled herself into the rocker. An elderly Martiniquais with cottony white hair backed carefully through a door bearing tea on a tray. He was tall and slender, his skin the color of burnished oak. His features were shaded by a wide-brimmed hat, but the eyes were alert, the smile amiable. He set the tray on a table and bowed fractionally. As he turned to leave, Whitely thought he looked familiar. Had he seen him the previous morning at the meeting with the naval veterans? Throughout the morning men from the fort had wandered in and out of the cavernous meeting room, an alcove of which had housed the communal coffee pot.

As Madame Rollet waited for the tea to draw, Whitely studied her further. Thinning gray hair pulled tightly behind her ears, a pair of spectacles suspended from a chain around her neck. Her eyes were watery blue. Compassionate, he thought, as though they had absorbed their share of pain. When she poured the tea he noticed her long slender fingers, spotted by age but as deft and elegant as though fashioned from the flanks of Carrara.

"You mentioned your grandfather," she said, taking him in as though measuring him against some mnemonic template.

"Yes. He was here during the war. In 1942 to be exact. He was on assignment for Naval Intelligence. I have his diary and some letters he wrote to my mother. He mentions a lady doctor, but not her name. Though he would probably have used an alias for cover, his real name was O'Shea. Captain Dante O'Shea."

He studied her reaction. The eyes held steady, but where she gripped the teapot her knuckles seemed to whiten perceptibly. For a moment she seemed to leave him. Then she returned, her attention re-focused.

"And you have chosen me."

"I did some checking. As best I can tell, there were three women doctors on Martinique in the early 1940's, a nun at Forte de France, a missionary in Ste-Pierre, now deceased, and yourself."

She measured him with speculative eyes. "I see." She stirred her tea, though, Whitely noticed, she had added nothing to it.

"Did you know my grandfather, Doctor Rollet? Do you remember an American on Martinique in 1942?"

Again she seemed to leave him. He caught a faint reflexive reaction somewhere in her eyes, an infintesimal quickening. Was she sifting memories or weighing her response?

"It was a long time ago," she said. "There were many names. Many faces."

She was buying time. He decided to press a bit. "My grandfather was in love with this woman, Doctor Rollet."

He held her gaze. She seemed distracted. His comment lay on the table between them for a long time.

"Your articles," she asked, finally. "Was there any particular aspect of the war you had in mind?"

He ignored the change of subject, decided to be direct. "The gold," he said, watching her eyes. "The night they moved the gold."

This time the eyes betrayed her, the pupils locking on his before darting quickly away. As though the answer lay in the sapphire shoals, she glanced abstractly out to sea again. She seemed flustered, her reserve as shattered as if he had uttered an obscenity. A hectic flush invaded her cheeks and she set cup against saucer without testing the tea.

"I know nothing about moving any gold."

"Surely you were aware of the gold at Fort Desaix."

"Of course," she said, on firmer footing now. "The entire island was aware. One could barely pass a day without some rumor of the gold. The gold had been stolen. The Americans were coming for the gold. The British were planning to confiscate the gold. The Germans were sending ships for the gold. DeGaulle himself was sailing for the gold. All very entertaining. All very vacuous. In the end, the gold was returned to France."

"All of it?"

She studied her teacup. "The Government did not honor me with an accounting, monsieur."

Either she knew or she didn't. He decided to push harder. "But you were on the beach that night. A witness has put you there when the gold was being moved. You and an American. And a man in a white suit."

She fingered her bodice as though drawing an invisible stole around her shoulders. Almost imperceptibly, she began to sway in the rocker.

"You have talked to him?"

Whitely felt a glimmer of reassurance. The man in the white suit was alive. At least she thought he was. He decided to play it out. To press his advantage.

"There's little to be gained by equivocation, Doctor Rollet. I have my grandfather's diary. A witness has come forward. The story is out. Now it's merely a question of detail."

She was put out of countenance, her poise evaporating like the steam from her cup. "Out, you say. Do you mean you have discussed this with others?"

"Not yet. But eventually. Unless, of course, there is some reason to remain silent. To judge that, I would need the entire story."

He was bullying her. But she knew more than she was letting on. He was certain of it.

She drew a barely perceptible breath. She looked trapped. In a quandary. "I'll need some time. A day or so to collect my thoughts."

He had pushed her far enough. Nothing was to be gained by an inquisition. It had, after all, been fifty years. If she had been his grandfather's lover, his arrival must come as quite a shock. Better she should relate the story after sifting her memories. Her memories might be his best hope. Perhaps his only hope.

"I'm at the Meridien on Point du Bout," he said. "I'm booked for a fortnight. I can return whenever you choose."

Though her mind seemed elsewhere, she nodded. "Very well. I'll need..." she hesitated, as though calculating..." ...a week...a week from today."

"At noon?"

"At noon," she repeated.

He stood and took her hand. Her fingers were wafer thin, her wrist as limp as though the tendons had dissolved. On an impulse he raised the fingers and touched them to his lips.

She looked at him warily, a crust of uncertainty clouding her eyes. Confusion mingled with consternation. But something else was coloring her countenance, something beyond confusion, beyond frustration. Beneath her perplexity he detected a flicker of excitement. He held her gaze to be sure. Her agitation seemed coupled with relief. And then it dawned on him. She wanted to tell this story. She'd been sitting on it for half a century, and now she could be free of it.

But she had to check with someone first.

The man in the white suit?

He'd bet a third star on it.

He was back at Pointe du Bout by noon. The Meridien had disgorged its guests. From his balcony he could see thatched umbrellas along the beach, bathers in the turquoise lagoon, novices on sailboards. On a staggered line of beach chairs lay a bevy of sun worshippers, some oiled, some bronzed, the newer arrivals pale or pink. Most of the women were topless, extracting their money's worth from the magnanimous sun. A bulbous-sailed catamaran was departing the pier, its ship's company a gaggle of slim-bodied, scantily-clad teenagers.

A large motor launch rounded the headland, the passenger ferry that shuttled between the resort hotels and the capital. Far beyond its wake he could make out the city of Forte de France. It lay slumbering at the base of a mountain, the pastel facades of its shops huddled along the quayside like a painting in a Paris musuem. He could distinguish the tall burnished spire of St-Louis Cathedral, the park that bordered the quay, the seawall at Fort St-Louis. In the foothills above the city sprawled Desaix, the fort where the gold had been stored, the wartime repository of the wealth of France. Far to the north soared the volcanic Pelée, its peak a tiara of mist, it skirts a hazy gray-green.

From the kitchen below drifted the piquance of a Creole buffet. He changed to bathing trunks and a loose-fitting tropical shirt.

The meeting with Madame Rollet had brought him a step closer to the core of the mystery. The nearer he came to his grandfather, the more he learned of the gold. The more he learned of the gold, the closer he came to the German. He could not yet think of him as "father". The thought of a Nazi submariner as his progenitor was so alien as to be fantasy. He preferred to think of him as Herr Reinmann; to keep him bottled away like a frog in formaldehyde, not wishing to examine him too closely, yet knowing that someday he must pin him to a table and dissect him.

They were linked, The Captain and Herr Reinmann. He was sure of it.

And the gold? Was that linked too?

For now he would concentrate on his grandfather. There were people here who remembered him. People who had known him in his final days. Nikole Rollet was the key to The Captain. Was the Captain the key to the German?

He seated himself at the small writing desk and unsheathed a tape recorder from a leather carrying case. He had replayed the interview before leaving the States, but here, like The Captain's diary and his mother's letters, the words would take on new meaning. Fast-forwarding past the introductions, he pressed the PLAY button. In an instant he was back on the Virginia estate of Commodore J.J. Harding, USN, Retired, a colt frolicking in the paddock, the Commodore spicing their coffee with a generous dollop of Jack Daniels. The Commodore's drawl came through thick and metallic.

"...a man among men, your grandfather. Even among his fellow officers he was a legend of sorts. Fresh out of the Academy, Dante looked a certainty to make admiral. Had an affinity for languages and a genius for command. A gutsy aviator, too...grit clean through. And a master tactician before they nailed him to a desk. If anything, his wit was his worst enemy, Sean. It is Sean, isn't it Admiral ....?"

"Sean, yes Commodore."

"...yes...well, as I was saying, Sean, his worst enemy. So articulate was he, so proficient in French, that the Navy assigned him to our embassy in Paris. But his heart was with the fleet, at sea and in the air. When his wife died...did you know your grandmother, Admiral?..."

"No. She died before I was born."

"...well, when Caroline died, Dante stumbled a bit. Fell prey to the Creature, as he liked to put it. It didn't diminish his skills as an officer, but it did plant some doubt as to his ability to command, dampened his chances for promotion. Then the war broke out, and...well, the rest is history..."

"Did you know his daughter, Commodore? My mother?"

"Casey? Yes. I met her once. Pretty thing, like her mother. I'm not sure Dante was always there for his daughter. But that had as much to do with his travelling as anything. Goes with the job, the globetrotting, months at sea. Toward the end they were close. In all things important, I'd say he was recapturing his balance near the end..."

"What was my grandfather doing on Martinique, Commodore?"

"Planning an invasion. The Brits had a plan, and we had a plan. Martinique was the eye of the hurricane down there in '42, the Gibraltar of the Caribbean. When France surrendered to the Germans in 1940, French warships in this hemisphere scurried for the West Indies. In the spring of '42 the best of 'em were bottled up in the harbor at Forte de France. The Brits didn't want them breaking out to join the Krauts, and the Germans didn't want them commandeered by the British. Then the Brits got busy defending their home shores and we set up our own Caribbean patrols. Roosevelt was keen on keeping an eye on our southern flank. A French admiral ran the show down there on Martinique. Admiral Robert, as I recall. Had his hands full, did Admiral Robert..."

"So my grandfather was surveying the island?"

"Among other things. He was a true Francophile...had a working knowledge of the French and he loved the culture. When the Germans were blitzkrieging the Lowlands, he was with the American legation in Paris. As the Wehrmacht swept through France, he kept tabs on the French naval contingent. They fled to Vichy with the rest of the Government. After France accepted Germany's terms for an armistice, Dante returned to the fleet."

"And that's when Naval Intelligence picked him up."

"Right. He knew the Caribbean and could 'parlez vous' like a Parisian, so they worked him into the Martinique situation. All kinds of rumors were rife back then: U-Boats refueling in the Antilles, Nazi agents reporting on Allied shipping, Frenchmen defecting to neighboring islands. Axis submarines were clobbering our oil tankers down there. And not only U-Boats. The Italians sent some subs over too. Old Admiral Robert was thought to be cozy with the Krauts. He took his orders from Vichy, and Vichy was under the thumb of the Germans. We needed a handle on Martinique; unofficially, of course. Your grandfather was a natural for the job..."

"That was early in 1942, wasn't it? A few months after we entered the war?"

"Right. Another thing. The French had a mountain of gold stashed down there. In some fort up in the hills. Now that I think of it, I did hear from you mother after Dante was reported missing. It was a few months after the end of the war. She rang me up from... somewhere...New Jersey, I believe. Wanted to know if her father had gotten into hot water with the Navy before he disappeared."

"Hot water?"

"It seems Naval Intelligence had sent some agents to interview her. Asked her if Dante had ever mentioned anything about his assignment on Martinique. She was worried he might have been in some sort of trouble. Said her son would be a naval officer someday. She was concerned about Dante's reputation being tainted by conjecture."

"And?..."

"Well...I retired shortly after that. That was the last I heard of it."

"Was there anything else, Commodore? Anyone who might remember what went on down there?

There was a pause in the tape. Whitely recalled the Commodore pouring more bourbon, this time without the coffee.

"Well, it's probably not germane, but there was a woman..."

"A woman?"

"I remember it because Dante was pretty shaken up when his wife...your grandmother...died. A real tragedy, that; a boating accident as I recall. He went to the booze and I thought he'd never connect with another woman. The last time I saw him, we tied one on in San Juan. Dante got reeling drunk. Told me about a lady he'd met on Martinique. A French widow, as I recall. Classy, he said. A doctor or somesuch. I think he found something with her...."

Whitely thumbed off the tape.

Nikole Rollet. Doctor Nikole Rollet. She'd gone chalk white when he'd mentioned his grandfather's name. And she'd foundered when he brought up the gold.

So what did happen in that cove fifty years ago? Was his grandfather involved? The German?

Officially, the record seemed clear. Three-hundred-and-fifty tons of gold had been transported from France to Halifax, Nova Scotia, in June of 1940 aboard the cruiser EMILE BERTIN. When France fell a few days later, the British threatened to intern the ship for the duration. The French admiral commanding the EMILE BERTIN made a run for Martinique, the largest French port in the Caribbean. While the home country writhed under the grip of the Nazis, the gold was stored at Fort Desaix on the heights above Forte de France. At war's end, the gold was shipped back to France. Some of the crates contained sand. A ton of gold was missing. An investigation was launched, but it was kept secret. Everyone involved was questioned, including the skipper of the EMILE BERTIN and the High Commissioner on Martinique, but no one could explain the missing ton. The discrepancy was never resolved; officially it was never publicized. By the time the war ended personnel had disappeared, records had been destroyed, and confusion was the order of the day. The gold could have been taken at any point along the line, beginning with its original transfer from the vaults in France to its transshipment to ports of embarkation to Halifax to storage at the fort on Martinique to its return to France after the war.

There were loose ends. Unanswered questions.

If the old fisherman was right, what was the gold doing in a cove thirty miles south of Forte de France in May of 1942? Why did none of the French naval veterans on Martinique remember the gold being moved from the fort? For that matter no one on the entire island recalled the gold being moved from Fort Desaix, nor was it recorded in any official records. And what of the missing ton? If the fisherman Paquet could be believed, there had been gunfire in the cove that night. And a submarine.

And what of the lady doctor? She knew more than she was telling. The man in the white suit? Was he still alive? According to the fisherman, he too had been in the cove that night.

Whitely dug through the folder containing his mother's letters. He extracted a copy of a memo he had come across in Washington's archives a full eight days after his mother's funeral, a memo from the Office of Naval Intelligence files. The document was addressed to Tenth Naval District Headquarters on San Juan, stamped TOP SECRET, and dated April, 1942. The memo was, in effect, an addendum to an invasion plan, a contingency plan for American forces to invade Martinique should the French not agree to American demands.

But the plan was secondary. What had caught his eye was a footnote, a paragraph scratched in longhand at the bottom of the typewritten page. It read, in part:

> ...though the French agree the gold
> will not be moved as part of said
> agreement, my sources report a plan
> is afoot whereby hostile parties
> will attempt to seize the gold...

The communique was authored by one Dante O'Shea, Captain, USN. The footnote was initialed "DO" in the same lefthanded scrawl that marked his grandfather's letters to his mother.

When he returned to Ste-Anne a week later, there were three of them. Madame Rollet had been joined by two men. Whitely was ushered into the garden by the cotton-haired Creole. The trio were sitting on the flagged patio, their backs to the sea, their silence the reserve of conspirators. Both men looked to be in their seventies. One was a dapper sort, Whitely noticed, clean shaven with iron grey hair and swarthy Mediterranean features. His tailored silk suit was European-cut, his shoes the buttery leather of the Via Veneto. Expensive shirt. Muted necktie. Cufflinks to match the glitter of his watch. Despite his Mediterranean features, he was not tanned; his skin had a sallow cast, as though jaundiced by some illness. Whitely assumed he had just flown in from the Continent.

The other he guessed to be French. He sported a trim white beard and dark-rimmed glasses and looked to be an academic or professional type. His pale straw Panama hat and crumpled linen jacket were a bit on the casual side, more in tune with the dress code of the island. For a man his age he was strikingly handsome. Had his hair been darker and his shoulders less stooped, he could be mistaken for a far younger man.

As Whitely stepped onto the veranda, the men pushed slowly to their feet. Unlike his previous meeting with Madame Rollet, when he had dressed as a civilian, Whitely had opted for summer tans. With his hair slicked back and his cap at a jaunty angle, he bore a striking resemblance to the figure in the photo on his mother's dresser. As Madame Rollet stepped forward to greet him, she seemed to falter a bit. She clutched her chair and stared at him for an instant as though transfixed. When she regained her composure, she introduced the dapper one first.

"Admiral Whitely, may I present Monsieur LeBaron."

They shook hands. Despite the man's age, Whitely noted his grip was firm, not the handshake of a clerk. LeBaron nodded indifferently and sat down.

"And Mr. Harris."

The bearded one's eyes betrayed a flicker of hostility, but he put nothing special into his handshake.

"Admiral Whitely is researching some articles on the war," the Madam said. "The war in these islands."

They stared as though awaiting some reply. He removed his cap and handed it to the Creole, who nodded amiably and retreated to the cottage. There was an uneasy silence while Whitely looked about the grounds.

"A veritable paradise you have here, Dr. Rollet; it's hard to believe there could ever have been a war out here."

"It seems another lifetime," she said, her eyes softening. "You must tell us why you are here, Admiral. Surely there can be no interest in what transpired in this backwater of the war."

To the contrary, Madame. I came here to learn firsthand what happened the night the gold was moved from Fort Desaix. Much of the story has been pieced together, but I'm lacking some details. No mention of such an incident is to be found in any official history, either American or French. I have begun, therefore, a preliminary investigation which I will pursue, if necessary, to the shores of France or wherever else it leads."

He made no mention of his grandfather or his affair with a lady doctor. Had the three of them discussed it? Or was there no need?

They were seated around a white wicker table. The bearded one motioned him to a chair. When he settled in, the man called LeBaron took up the questioning.

"And if such a story is true, Monsieur, you intend to publish your findings?"

Whitely could not pinpoint his accent. European, to be sure, but eroded by years in the islands. "Possibly. That depends on the story."

Glances were exchanged around the table. They had obviously discussed their options prior to his arrival. He was inclined to believe a decision had already been reached. He wondered which, if either, was the man in white. Finally, the man called Harris broke his silence. From his delivery, Whitely concluded he was French educated, if not born. Despite his cold exterior, he maintained a polite neutrality.

"What of proof, Admiral Whitely? What if this story you are pursuing is not verifiable?"

"Then a magazine article, perhaps, treating of the missing pieces. Some inquiries in the island newspapers, veterans' publications in France; a review of the official record, a screening of others on Martinique. With enough stirring, perhaps others will come forward."

"Who would bother?" the Madame asked. "Of what importance would it be to anyone if the gold were moved? It was accounted for in the end."

"If that were the case," Whitely said, "perhaps no one will come forth. But frankly, that is not the case, and I think you are as aware of that as I am."

It was a long shot. He fully expected them to call his bluff. But no one flinched, though the dapper one scrutinized him with a touch more interest.

They exchanged glances again. Madame Rollet remained on edge. The bearded one eyed him calmly. The dapper man looked to be weighing his credibility, his tenacity.

The bearded one leaned forward and fixed him with a not-unfriendly stare. "Some things are best left undisturbed, my dear Admiral."

"Perhaps," Whitely countered. "But if so, there must be a reason. If indeed the gold was moved, why would anyone want to deny the fact?"

The man called Harris offered a disclaiming shrug. "We have discussed it at length, Admiral. My preference was to let you cast for phantoms. But my colleagues fear you might uncover enough to re-open old wounds without realizing the consequences that might ensue. They think it wiser, therefore, that we relate some of the history of that period and let you decide for yourself."

"Fair enough," Whitely said.

The man called Harris pushed slowly to his feet. He turned from the table and looked beyond the garden to the bay. With his back to the others, he asked, "How much time do you have?"

"I've taken thirty days leave. But my schedule is flexible. I'll go where the facts lead me. I'm prepared to see this through no matter how long it takes."

Harris turned to LeBaron. He responded with an all but imperceptible nod of the head.

"Good," Madame Rollet said. "It's a lovely afternoon. We can dine on the patio."

Seated on the flagstone terrace under a broad umbrella, the man called LeBaron started the story. The picture he painted was of paradise gone awry. But the story had started before that. It had started in the winter of 1941, when Nazi jackboots echoed sharply on the streets of Paris.

PARIS

November 1941

Oberleutnant zur See Viktor Reinmann stood at the window of the third floor apartment and watched his breath collect visibly against the glass. The room was hot; someone had been overly generous with the logs in the fireplace. Reinmann cranked the window and felt a rush of cold air. Beyond the balcony a coal barge labored ponderously up the Seine. Swollen by winter rains, the river was filling its banks, and minutes before it had begun to snow.

Reinmann pressed a hand against the icy casement and drew in lungfulls of cold damp air. A gust blew snowflakes against his face; he felt them melting against the ridge of his eyebrows. He watched the snow swirl gracefully up the river, all but obscuring the bookstalls on the opposite bank. In the fading winter light the Seine was shimmering like silk. Below him on the Quai d'Orsay a taxi rattled to a stop at a traffic light. Even in the raw November chill the boulevards exuded an unyielding charm. Paris was a coquette, Reinmann conceded; a coquette slipping quietly into an ermine wrap; a lady to be seduced, not taken roughly like some streetwalker. He was glad the French had declared it an open city. What a shame to have it reduced to rubble. This was real victory, conquest without ashes.

It was nearing dusk and the streets of the 7th arrondissement were quiet. What little traffic there was felt hushed by the snow. A handful of Parisians were pedaling bicycles, their tires carving narrow-gauged tracks on the snow-dusted pavement. Across the boulevard an elderly woman was trudging the embankment.

Bundled against the cold, she cradled the ubiquitous baguette of bread under an armpit.

To shield her from the snow she unfurled a slender red umbrella.

Near the Pont des Invalides, a middle-aged Frenchman stood bending over a brazier. Reinmann could see steam rising from the slow-roasting chestnuts. The man was of the vanquished French Army. In the grey bitterness of defeat, he had torn the buttons from his tunic to confirm he had become a civilian. Still, he bore a red Legion of Honor on his lapel. The city was littered with them, a breed Reinmann could neither understand nor respect. Day after day Parisians watched silently as the Wehrmacht's Guard's Regiment marched ceremoniously from the Place de la Concorde to the Arc de Triomphe in a stiff-necked display of German might. With the tables reversed, he was certain he could not withstand the humiliation of watching occupying French troops parading the Linderstrasse in Berlin.

He turned back to the room, a high-ceilinged chamber with ornate moldings and expensive carpets. In the foyer the marble floors gleamed like water. He dabbed a handkerchief against his eyebrows and caught his reflection in the window; straw blonde hair, close-cropped and freshly trimmed, a skiers tan, the dark blue uniform of the U-Boatwaffe. He flicked a snowflake from the insignia on his collar. Pacing the carpet, he wondered at the secrecy of it all.

Why was he here? Why had he been summoned? Was he to be transferred to Paris? As tempting as the prospect seemed, he hoped that would not be the case. He was thirsting for action. While his shipmates in the fleet were pinning Iron Crosses to their tunics, he was generating public relations reports from the Admiralty Building in Berlin.

Still, he was enjoying his sojourn in Paris. The city had suffered virtually no damage. Cafes were catering to their conquerors as though they were tourists. Before midnight, when the curfew began, theaters and cabarets were accommodating both French and German patrons alike. For well-heeled collaborators and ranking Wehrmacht officers, champagne flowed at the better clubs and the cuisine was as artful as in peacetime. All the parks and museums were open, and on weekends the thoroughbreds drew conqueror and conquered alike to racetracks at Longchamp or Auteuil.

Viktor had sent perfume and lingerie to his mother. As far as he knew she never used perfume, and the lingerie would create a scandal in their Black Forest village. But the gifts were symbolic of conquest, a sign that he was safe and that victory had been achieved. For his father he had included a bottle of cognac and some coffee beans. To his sister Elsbeth he had sent chocolates with a liqueur filling. He had wrapped the chocolates in a pair of silk stockings. Did nuns wear silk? If not, Elsbeth would appreciate the humor.

A scent lingered deliciously on his handkerchief. He recalled the evening before, at the chateau on the outskirts of Versailles. The girl had been Norwegian, selected like all the volunteers of Himmler's "Lebensborn" project for her Aryan features. She was sixteen, she had said, and proud, like many in the occupied territories to bear a child for the Fuehrer. Reinmann had participated in the Lebensborn project before. An SS aquaintance had set him up at an officer's club near Berlin, an estate formerly owned by a Jewish banker. Thousands of teenage girls in Germany were volunteering for the project. As a result of the 1917 war and the million or more homosexuals in Germany, females outnumbered males five to one. Did the women of the Reich not deserve the chance to serve the Fatherland? To nurture the seeds of a superior race? They had the choice of raising the children themselves or putting them up for adoption by an SS family. Whatever they decided, they could be proud to stiffen the backbone of the thousand-year Reich.

Viktor had played his part well. Though his ability to procreate was in doubt, he could still manage an erection. Not to partake of the Lebensborn ladies was unthinkable. Who would want a eunuch for a commanding officer? He had been fortunate to be stricken while on leave. And his family doctor had vowed to keep his secret. Mumps, of all things. And at the ripe old age of twenty-four. There were some things even the U-Boatwaffe did not have to know.

And tonight? French women were volunteering in surprising

numbers. At the Versailles villa his Norwegian consort had introduced him to an eager young mademoiselle. Tonight he would see if the Frenchies lived up to their reputation.

Enough, he told himself. There were other lusts to be satisfied. He had been out of action since Narvik. Of late the Admiralty had been using him to educate his Wehrmacht and Luftwaffe counterparts on the value of the submarine. A public relations job; necessary, no doubt, but for an officer of his ambition an assignment of limited potential. He would push for combat. Insist on it. He deserved it.

The door opened and Reinmann stiffened. Now the mystery would be solved; the questions answered.

The figure that strode into the room was instantly familiar; the Kriegsmarine greatcoat, the braided gold shoulder boards, the slender erect carriage. Responding to the alert appraising eyes, Reinmann snapped to attention.

Rear Admiral Karl Doenitz popped his gloves against his thigh and touched a baton to the peak of his cap. The Admiral handed his hat to the same bespectacled corporal who had escorted Viktor to the room a scant few minutes before. Viktor noticed the Admiral's cheeks were flushed. An open car, Viktor remembered. Rain, sleet, sun, or snow, the Admiral would insist on an open car.

The corporal removed the admiral's greatcoat, and Doenitz massaged his hands at the fire. When he turned to face the room, Viktor thought his eyes looked a touch weary. The strain was taking its toll.

"So, Lieutenant. It has been some time."

"Two years, Herr Admiral." Viktor remembered a cold rainy morning at the submarine base at Wilhelmshaven. It had been his twenty-second birthday. The then *Kapitan zur See* Doenitz had braved a sou'wester to welcome Viktor's submarine back from a trial run, a run at which they had broken the depth record. They were daring times, those days before the victory over Poland. Exciting days. All very secret. All very exhilarating.

The Admiral motioned him to a chair. The aide re-entered with a tray and poured the Admiral's coffee. When he started to pour for Viktor, the Admiral placed a hand over the delicate porcelain cup.

"Herr Reinmann isn't overly fond of coffee," he said, holding Viktor's eye. "A sailor who doesn't savor the juice of the bean. An individualist, indeed."

Viktor was flattered. With all the Admiral had on his mind, with his wolf packs engaging the British in the Atlantic, with the struggle to secure more U-Boats from the infantry-oriented Hitler, he had remembered.

"A brandy, perhaps." The Admiral motioned to the sideboard. "It's a trifle early for me," he said, "but youth knows no limits."

Viktor read the approval in the Admiral's eyes. He nodded and the corporal poured brandy into a snifter. He placed it at Viktor's elbow and left the room.

Doenitz sampled the coffee with obvious approval. "Paris," he said. "A long way from *der Nordenmeer,* Herr Reinmann."

Viktor caught the gleam of reminiscence. The Admiral was back on the sodden North Sea beaches, with sleet coating the rigging and ice clogging the minor channels. Doenitz had been a U-Boat commander in the 1917 war. For a time, he had been a prisoner of the British; and after the war, he had helped to circumvent the Versailles ban and rebuild the U-Boat fleet. Since submarines were prohibited, he had used torpedo boats to simulate submarine surface attacks. 'After all,' he told his colleagues, 'a surfaced submarine is merely a slow-paced torpedo boat.' During the final years of the buildup, Doenitz had worked side by side with his men in the field. It was common knowledge that he preferred the deck of a ship to a desk in some landlocked office. Noticing the weariness in the Admiral's eyes again, Viktor wondered if he wouldn't prefer some inclement outpost to this warm Parisian apartment.

"Vienna. Warsaw. Amsterdam. Paris. The head spins at the velocity of it, Admiral."

Doenitz fingered the dainty cup. Viktor noticed it looked fragile in his long, lean fingers, fingers that clamped like steel on the handles of a periscope.

"There's no denying it, Reinmann, the wheel is grinding at a furious pace. In a few short weeks the Panzers have overrun the Low Countries and the Wehrmacht has conquered France."

Viktor raised his glass. "Thanks to the Fuehrer and men like the Admiral."

Doenitz touched a finger to his brow. Viktor noticed his thinning hair, the wisps combed laterally over a balding pate. He fought back an urge for a cigarette and sipped the cognac.

"The French still make an exceptional brandy, Admiral."

"And the women?"

Viktor felt the color rise to his neck.

The Admiral allowed an uncharacteristic wink; there was a barely perceptible softening in the steel blue eyes. From a man with a reputation for being cold, stiff, and correct, it was a rare display of emotion.

"It's good to see some modesty survives, Herr Reinmann. Our fortunes have been such that we might count ourselves supermen. We must guard against overconfidence. There is much to be done. England has refused to collapse under the weight of the Luftwaffe, and now that we face the Russians on our eastern flank, an invasion of Britain is improbable. We will have to starve the British out. Isolate them. For that we need more boats. Bigger and better boats."

The amenities over, Viktor suffered a letdown. More public relations work? He could argue his case up to a point. But with the head of the U-Boatwaffe? Impossible.

"And the British are only part of the problem," the Admiral continued. "The French are still kicking under the shroud. Surrender or no, armistice or no, French forces continue to resist in the colonies."

Viktor had heard that a captain named De Gaulle was amassing a force of so-called Free French in West Africa, but rumor had it that Frenchmen in the outposts were irreconcilably split.

"And that brings us to the reason for this little meeting, Herr Lieutenant. You have been languishing in the Admiralty. You are a young and promising officer. I intend to put some color in those cheeks of yours, color of a different stripe than I detected a minute ago."

As Doenitz sipped the coffee, Viktor felt the blood collecting hotly beneath his collar.

Combat! He was going to see combat!

"There is important work to be done, Reinmann. For the Reich. For the Kriegsmarine. For the U-Boatwaffe. We must isolate the British. And we have a surprise or two left for the French."

Viktor met the Admiral's eyes. What could a mere lieutenant do that would warrant so urgent a meeting with the commander of the submarine fleet in the bowels of the fallen French capitol?

"Your task has two parts," Doenitz said. "Oil is the lifeblood of the British fleet. Without oil their war machine will seize up and grind to a halt. A critical percentage of that oil originates in South America. We have tried to cut the supply in mid-Atlantic, but the area is far too vast; our wolf packs are spread too thin. We must strike them nearer the source."

Viktor was beginning to piece it together. The trips before the war, the Caribbean sailing junket he had been encouraged to take at the expense of the party, the mapping of uncharted islands.

"The Caribbean is the neck of the funnel, Viktor. Much of the oil the British rely on is shipped from the fields of South America to refineries in the Caribbean. From there it is tankered to England. I intend to send a handful of boats down there, mostly to upset British shipping. But it will not be enough. We must increase our activity in those waters. Throw a cat among the pigeons, so to speak. You know the islands. Your charting expeditions were more than simple mapping exercises."

Viktor's collar was growing too tight for his neck. He could feel the veins swelling against his tunic. It was better than he could have hoped. A submarine. Perhaps even, someday, a command.

"You'll have to be careful," the Admiral resumed. "American interests abound in that part of the world. We're not yet ready to prod that tiger. Initially, your task will be surveillance."

Viktor reddened again, this time in anger.

The Admiral caught the flash of temper and ignored it. "Our

agents have infiltrated the area. They're setting up radio networks and recruiting collaborators. We want to know everything that goes on down there. Convoys. Harbor defenses. The American buildup. As for the French, some of their warships are bottled up at Martinique. The British have an eye on those vessels, but they must not get them."

Viktor decided to be frank. "I had hoped for a combat assignment, Admiral. One of the newer boats, perhaps."

Doenitz smiled. "Don't look so forlorn, Herr Reinmann. You'll have action enough to suit you. When you hear the second part of your assignment you'll have more than a mere torpedo run to set your juices flowing. It might even whet your appetite for the assignation you have scheduled this evening."

Viktor lowered his eyes. He felt foolish. Naive. The Admiral knew of the night before. Of his plans for tonight.

The Admiral leaned across the table. "Relax, Herr Reinmann. Even Admirals feel the need for diversion."

Viktor breathed easier.

The Admiral removed a map from an inner pocket. He spread it lengthwise across the table and smoothed its edges. As the head of the Nazi U-Boat command laid out the details of his assignment, the young lieutenant's eyes narrowed, then widened, then glazed. When the Admiral began refolding the map, Viktor was looking at him but not seeing, listening but not hearing. This will do, he told himself. This will more than do. This will bring an Iron Cross. He felt humbled that the Admiral had singled him out. Proud. It could be the lynchpin of his career. More. Of his life. Yet try as he might to avoid it, a vagrant thought came creeping through. He envisioned a beach, white powdery sand rimmed by coconut palms and waters as warm as the baths at Baden. And a girl, suntanned and long-legged and heartbreakingly beautiful. Was it possible he might return? Was she still there? Could they recapture the magic?

The Admiral downed the last of his coffee and pushed from his chair. Viktor stood and snapped rigidly to attention.

Without doubt, he thought, an Iron Cross.

Perhaps a Knight's Cross as well.

ONE MONTH LATER

DEC. 6, 1941

THE WINDWARD ISLANDS

EASTERN CARIBBEAN

Captain Dante O'Shea banked the twin-engined flying boat a few degrees to starboard and the island of Martinique rose gently beneath his wingtip. From seven thousand feet the Caribbean beaches looked lush and benign, the coastline scalloped by surf. Hard against the waterline he could make out the feathery crests of palms, the huts of an occasional village. He rolled the PBY toward level flight. On the Atlantic seaboard he could see rollers shouldering from the east. The coastline was deeply etched, the shoreline rocky and windswept. Quite a contrast, he thought; almost like two different islands, the one tropical and serene, the other barren and rock-strewn.

It felt good to be at the controls again, even if only in the right-hand seat. The scuttlebutt was accurate: the Catalina was a little heavy on the controls, and with the fuselage stripped of insulation the engine noise was louder than anticipated. But all in all, it was a fine seabird, born to the sky. It was thoughtful of the pilot to give him the stick. Like the rest of the crew, the lieutenant was just a kid. They were all kids, but if the storm clouds drifted east they would sprout to manhood in a hurry.

Working the rudder pedal with the exuberance of an ensign, he angled the nose turret toward the lee of the island and checked his map. Martinique. Fifty miles long by thirty wide, a spine of lush green mountains anchored in the north by the majestic Mt. Pelée, and tapering in the center to the Plain of Lamentin. To the south lay brushwood flatlands and windswept foothills. All in all, a topography typical of the inner volcanic arc of the Lesser

Antilles. He accepted binoculars from the young lieutenant in the pilot's seat and banked for a better look at the main harbor. The capital city of Forte de France lay basking in the sun on the central Caribbean coastline. The bay that shared its name lay open to the sea like the claw of a crab. Its harbor was an impressive mooring, thirteen square miles of deep clear channel so configured that the entire United States fleet could drop anchor in its sheltered waters. Beyond the inner harbor snaked coves and inlets with sufficient depth for ships of all sizes. Scattered around the bay, Dante could make out dozens of merchant vessels. Near the tip of the claw some auxiliary craft were patrolling the approaches. At the lower mandible, hard against the stonework of Fort St. Louis, three warships lay menacingly at their moorings, their coloration the distinctive grey of the French navy, light with dark trim.

The pilot had been briefed to respect the three-mile limit. Somewhere down there the French were manning coastal batteries. While it was unlikely they would fire on an American military plane, the gunners were reported to be fidgety of late.

Shouting over the drone of the Pratt & Whitneys, Dante addressed the young lieutenant in the left-hand seat. "I make it two cruisers and a carrier, Mr. Whitely."

"That would be right, Captain. The cruisers are the EMILE BERTIN AND JEANNE D' ARC. The carrier is the BEARN. It's the only carrier the Frenchies have."

"Too bad it's hung up out here where it can't do them any good."

Lt. Kevin Whitely sat slumped in the pilot's seat with his hands folded behind his head, his stockinged feet tracing the throw of the rudder pedals. At his midsection the pilot's yoke was pitching and yawing in reaction to the Captain's manipulation of the controls. A pair of cowboy boots was stashed behind his bucket seat, a deflated yellow life vest draped loosely over his flying shirt. Dante had noticed the gaudy orange piping on the boots. The lieutenant was single, he supposed, with a string of bobbysoxers painted brightly on his own personal fuselage.

"The British would love to get their hands on those warships, Captain."

Dante tapped a fuel gauge. "So would the Germans."

"How's she handling, sir?"

"Like a pelican in a tailwind."

Pleased that this salty-looking sea dog was enjoying the ride, Whitely hooked his earphones over the yoke. "We don't get many flag officers up front, sir. You're my first."

"I appreciate the confidence, Lieutenant. It's been a while since I've taken the controls."

"Anybody weaned on open cockpits could fly this goony bird blindfolded, sir.

A hand materialized over Dante's shoulder, strong slender fingers clutching a mug of steaming hot coffee. He gripped the porcelain handle and sipped the unsweetened black brew. "Thanks, mister."

The flight engineer touched a finger to his brow and nodded brusquely to the pilot. Before he evaporated back into the cabin, Dante noticed he had cotton stuffed in his ears to muffle the noise of the engines.

Whitely twisted a radio dial. "Think the French will try to liberate those warships, Captain?"

Dante winced at the coffee. "De Gaulle could certainly use them in Africa. The officials on Martinique are in a pickle, though. The French High Commissioner is a fellow named Robert. Admiral Georges Robert. He takes his orders from the puppet French government at Vichy. From Marshall Petain. Petain's in his eighties now. He was a hero in the 1917 War, but these days he's in the grip of the Nazis."

"So what's all the fuss about out here, sir?"

"The British are fearful the Germans will try to confiscate those warships, so they're determined to bottle them up. The Germans, on the other hand, are not inclined to let them fall into British hands. You can bet those French skippers down there would like to make a run for it."

"Word is that you're somewhat of an expert on the French, Captain.

"Logged some time as an attaché at our embassy in Paris. Had a front-row seat at the disintegration of the French government. When the Germans were crossing the Seine, I retreated with the truncated French Cabinet to Vichy."

"Where's that, sir?"

"A small town about 400 kilometers south of Paris. It's where the French set up their new government. Rather than see the entire country overrun by Nazis, Marshall Petain signed an armistice with the Germans. It gives the French administrative control of the southern third of the country while the northern sectors are occupied by the Krauts. Puts a lot of pressure on outposts like Martinique, though. Any false moves out here and the screws are tightened at home."

"When did you leave France, Captain?"

"Last July. Arrived in North Africa just in time to watch the British clobber the main body of the French fleet at a place called Mers el Kébir. Steamed in and blasted them to hell, they did. Churchill was afraid the Germans would muscle the French warships away, so he gave the French a choice. Turn the ships over to England or see them sunk. The French commander refused to do either. In the shelling that followed, more than a thousand French sailors were killed. They're still in a boil over that."

"Can't blame 'em, sir. Helluva way to treat an ally."

Dante pumped a finger toward the island. "So you can see why they're a little nervous about those warships down there."

With Martinique receding beyond his wingtip, Dante took a final look at the harbor. He counted twenty-eight merchant ships. At the piers near one of the harborside forts the French men-of-war looked sleek and deadly, their dazzle-striped hulls dramatic but ineffective camouflage against the azure depths.

He took in the surrounding islands. Twenty-five miles off his nose turret lay Dominica, dressed in a sea haze and looking as lush and peaceful as Central Park. Twenty miles beyond his tail section he could see St. Lucia with its capital port of Castries and its salty crust of beach. Both islands were British, the latter housing an American air base with barely enough aircraft to threaten Staten Island. Geologic burps, all of them, Dante thought. A hell of a place to fight a war.

He scanned the sea around him. The shoals in this Windward chain reflected the pearly opalescence of their coral underpinnings. Gardens beneath the sea, Dante mused. A rock-hard harvest of flame and flamboyance to tempt the eye and gut the keel. He wondered how many vessels had left their bones on those reefs. Easing the Catalina toward the darker cobalt of the Martinique Passage, he set a heading for St. Thomas.

Satisfied that the four-striper could handle the controls, Lt. Whitely eased out of the pilot's seat and slipped nimbly back to the shadows of the navigator's compartment. Alone in the cockpit with the drone of the power plants and the rhythmic vibrations of engines in sync, Dante tried to relax. Beyond the cabin Perspex the sun sparkled warmly on a dead calm sea. A mile beneath his wingtip he could make out the thin white wake of a merchant ship. Far to the west long shafts of rain were arching from some thin high cirrus. He set the controls to autopilot and eased his frame against the padded bucket seat. After the frenetic retreat from Paris, the hedgehopping across France, the leap to North Africa and a stint in the South Pacific, he was heading home. It felt more a retreat than a homecoming, a bittersweet return to the islands where he had launched his career and raised a family.

The flight over open water offered little sense of motion. The Catalina seemed to hover in place, the only sign of progress its shadow scurrying crab-like over the glassine surface. Mesmerized by the dazzling play of sunlight and the monotonous drone of engines, Dante could feel his control slipping. To this point he had managed to fight it off, but as he succumbed to the cadence of the engines the memory grabbed him from behind like a mugger in an alley. Before he could break its grip he was deep beneath the surface, in the cabin of the sunken hull, the water engulfing him green and opaque, the taste of fear like vomit in his throat. It was always the same, Caroline's long silky hair fanning the filtered sunlight, the debris from the galley blocking the ladder to the hatch, her arms outstretched as though beckoning him enter. And her smile, that tranquil, eternal smile that spoke forgiveness even in the terminal clutch of Fate. It was always the same, his brain half hoping his lungs would burst, his hands reaching out for her hands, the stubborn indifference of her lifeless fingers.

The memory resisted dismissal so he fought it off. He switched to manual flight controls and coaxed the Catalina back on course. Nudging the throttles, he gained a few hundred feet of altitude. He would deal with the nightmare on his own terms; in his own time. When he reached St. Thomas he would put it to rest. For Caroline's sake. For Casey's. For his own.

Suddenly he was gripped by an enormous thirst. He would mortgage his soul for an ounce of scotch. The liquor was in his kit, disguised as cough medicine in a dark brown bottle. He swiped his palms against the crease of his trousers and retrieved the coffee from beneath his seat. When the pilot returned to the flight deck, the memory scampered for cover. As the lieutenant folded his lank anatomy into the left-hand seat, Dante fingered the trim wheel.

"First trip to the Virgin Islands, Lieutenant?"

"Aye, sir. We were en route last night when we got diverted to Barbados to pick you up. You know St. Thomas, Captain?"

"Served there in the 20's. After we bought the Virgins from the Danes. Our Navy governed St. Thomas for years, you know. I've got a daughter at Charlotte Amalie. Grandson, too."

Whitely was tempted to ask why an officer of Captain O'Shea's experience would be transferred to a backwater billet like the Caribbean. With the bulk of the fleet massing in the Pacific, you'd think he'd be stationed at Pearl or Manila. Sensing the Captain's romance with the flying boat, he decided to forestall any further questioning.

An hour out of St. Thomas, off the southern reaches of the Anegada Passage, a cigar-shaped shadow caught the corner of Dante's eye. For a second he thought he could make out the feather of a wake, the telltale track of a periscope. He banked for a better look, but the shadow ghosted quickly into the depths leaving only a slight percolation on the surface.

"Did you see that, lieutenant," he asked, pointing beyond the starboard wingtip.

"See what, sir?"

"1 thought I saw a periscope out there, the cavitation from a submarine's propellers."

"Could be one of our own boats, Captain. We've got a handful of subs at the Marine base on St. Thomas. Could also be a trick of the eye, a coral reef or a school of fish. So far as we know, there haven't been any U-Boats reported this far south."

Dante eased the Catalina back on course. "Let's check it out when we land."

Nudging the throttles for a touch more speed, he urged the flying boat toward the tiny archipelago known as the American Virgin Islands.

***

Deep in the Anegada Passage, beneath layers of diminishing light, the submarine designated Unterseeboot-143 settled silently toward the ocean floor. As it reached equilibrium and skimmed the bottom, clouds of coral-flecked sand billowed darkly in its wake. More adapted to the cold grey Atlantic than this warm and fecund sea, the barnacle-encrusted hull hovered meters above the seabed like some prehistoric monster in search of prey. Behind the shark-like sweep of its prow, seaweed fanned like streamers from the railings of its slender deck.

Inside the welded steel carcass the air was stale and clammy, the recycled residue of grease and diesel fuel combined with the fetid exudation of human pores. Reeking of oilskins and soggy boot linings, of mustiness and mildew, of un-aired bedding and unlaundered clothing, the smells clung like barnacles to man and machine alike. The long cylindrical hull was hermetically sealed and chokingly claustrophobic. It contained no discreet compartments, no bulkhead divisions between quarters, just a single cave-like aisle with bays cleaving off to either side. The bays were crammed with turnwheels and pipes, levers and gauges, valves and flanges; the passageways cramped by bunks and machinery, the metal projecting hard unyielding surfaces.

With a crew of fifty-seven, the U-143 had departed its base on France's Brittany coast a full two-weeks before. In addition to machinery and armament, it was burdened with the necessities that humans must carry whenever they leave the sanctuary of the earth's surface for extended periods. From overhead pipes hung slabs of ham, clusters of sausages, wheels of cheese. Every spare bin and locker had been crammed with sacks of coffee, crates of apples, cartons of grapes, and loaves of bread. Though most of the spoilable foods had been eaten by now, a two-week supply remained, contributing their odors to the raw mélange of smells. And for all of this, one solitary toilet for nearly sixty adult males, and that unserviceable if they descended below eighty feet. A second toilet was stacked with provisions; it would not be available for another week or so. Having slipped into this West Indian sea at first light, the U-143 had yet to surface. As it nosed its way south of 18 degrees north, the latitude that bisects the United States Virgin Islands, its crew had yet to savor the scent of southern seas, the balmy breath of the tropics.

In the green-curtained cubicle that passed for his private quarters, Kapitanleutnant Dieter Hurst tilted his white-topped submariner's cap to the back of his head and poured ersatz coffee for the man seated opposite. The captain had long since shed his leather jacket and the sleeves of his shirt were rolled over pale white biceps. When Viktor Reinmann entered, the captain was cleaning a Walther pistol with an oily rag. To make room for his visitor, he secured the tip-up wash basin and folded the drop-leaf table that served as a desk.

"Four hours to sunset, Viktor. The moon rises late tonight. You should get some sleep. By midnight you will be ashore. You say you know that cove?"

Viktor Reinmann sipped the tepid brew and swallowed without tasting. He was training himself to ignore his taste buds, cry out as they might against the bilge that passed for coffee on this voyage. Unsavory as he found most coffee, at least this resembled coffee, not the brew of acorns that was replacing the real stuff in Paris.

"Yes, Herr Kaleun," Reinmann said, using the standard U-Boatwaffe abbreviation for his commander's full title. "I know that cove well."

Both men were young, the U-Boat commander twenty six, Viktor two year his junior. The captain passed him a loaf of soggy black bread. By now they were so hoary with mold the crew called them "white rabbits". Viktor tore the crust away and nibbled at the insides. For a minute they sat listening to the hum of the ventilator fans.

The U-Boat commander scratched the stubble of a beard. "Tomorrow is Sunday. A day of rest for civilized men. Perhaps we too can find a cove. The men could use some sun. Already they have stowed their heavy underwear. Tomorrow they break out their shorts and tropical shirts."

Viktor allowed a barely-detectable grin. Fight it as he would, anticipation as flooding in.

Sun.

Rest.

Solid earth.

After weeks at sea in this welded cocoon, to shave in hot water, to shower with abandon, to feel the sun on his back, the sand beneath his feet. It was difficult to believe this sea around them was actually the Caribbean. He had rechecked the charts. They were adrift above a submerged mountain range, a chain of peaks stretching from the tip of Florida to the Venezuelan coast. The peaks were higher than the mountains of his beloved Black Forest, the depths unfathomed. The Caribbean. A temperate sea beneath a sky of endless summer. A far cry from the iron-grey oceans to the north, the cold bleak skies of Odin. The past several weeks were beginning to take on the spectre of a nightmare: the squally cold Atlantic, the freezing spray on icy decks, the stench of burning tankers. It was a world removed from the exhilarating nights with the Lebensborn ladies, the languid mornings at sidewalk cafes in Paris, the bracing weekends on the Austrian slopes. And now he was back in this West Indian paradise, four full years in the returning. Palm trees and tropical flowers, fresh fruit and pristine beaches. To sleep on clean sheets. To waken to birdsong. To laze in the caress of the Trades.

And most tantalizing of all, to see Casey.

Would she forgive him?

She would be angry at first. That was understandable. He had been unable to write, even in the early days. Orders from the top. He could see why now. He had left abruptly those four years before. The cable from Berlin had commanded him to take the first boat to San Juan, the first flight to Miami, the first connection to Frankfurt. When he had called at her cottage on the morning of his departure she had been on the far side of the island tending to her studies. He had left a note promising he would return. He was thoroughly convinced that he would. But the stupid British had declared war. The arrogant British, coming to the defense of the ignorant Poles. What folly. What misplaced loyalty to an ill-conceived treaty. But they were paying now. The Luftwaffe may have failed to bring them to their knees in the skies over England, but they were dying in the African desert, on the Greek islands, in the bloodstained Atlantic.

Yes, Casey would be angry, but she would forgive him. They had shared some magical nights; her first as a woman, she had assured him. In the very cove he would enter this night. On the very beach. He was glad he had chosen that particular beach to be put ashore. It was fitting. It would lend a measure of continuity. Symbols were important.

Casey would forgive him.

Women never forgot the first time.

THAT SAME AFTERNOON

FORTE DE FRANCE, MARTINIQUE

Feeling a trifle self-conscious in a suit of tropical whites and a pith helmet, Christopher Delon strode the Rue de Liberté toward his apartment above the quay. Heat hung over the island like a blanket,and the humidity was as high as the temperature. He had forgone an offer by Madame Molay to avail himself of her driver, using as his excuse the slightly-exaggerated fact that the distance was only a few hundred meters downhill and that, despite the heat, he needed the exercise. In actuality, escaping the Madame was reward enough to compensate for the midday cauldron. Besides, the sun would do him good. Cooped up in a classroom all day, he was getting a touch pasty.

The streets of Forte de France were near deserted, the noonday lull after the morning market. Despite the purgatorial heat, Delon was growing fond of the island's scents: the perfumed Trades, the creole spices, the aromatic essences baked into the pavement by centuries of sun-drenched afternoons. The salt air was an invigorating tonic. And despite the cataclysms in Europe, there was comfort in the sight of the French tricolor snapping smartly from flagstaffs over every public building.

He crossed the street and entered the Savanne, the park that bordered the quay. The natives called it the green lung of Forte de France, a haven from the heat and bustle of the commercial district. Choosing a spot beneath the sheltering leaves of a mature mahogany, he sat on a crude wooden bench. The shade was a few degrees cooler and the breeze off the bay chilled the perspiration beneath his shirt. The Savanne was lush in the extreme, replete with a variety of well-manicured trees, giant royal palms, and fan-shaped palmettos. A scattering of Martiniquais were strolling the lanes or lounging on benches beneath the windblown palms. Beside a sandbagged gun emplacement, a child was playing with a large red ball. An old man sat dozing in the sun on a bench nearby, probably the grandfather. Dozens of women wearing wide-brimmed hats and light green smocks were working the greensward, dragging long-handled rakes over freshly-cut grass. As they stacked the grass onto dome-shaped piles, it was pitched by workmen onto flatbed trucks.

Delon looked beyond the quay to the grey stone walls of Fort

St-Louis. Pock-marked and dinghy with centuries of grime, the walls jutted ominously into the bay from a spit of coral rock. The artillery facing the harbor was of another era, more suited to warding off the broadsides of Barbary corsairs than the cannon-spiked dreadnoughts of a modern navy. In the market at the edge of the park he could see dozens of sea turtles laying belly up in the sun. The turtles were balanced on their shells, their lusterless eyes grey and opaque, strands of netting clinging to their mouths where they had failed to escape the seine.

Jacques had been blind.

Jacques had not escaped the seine.

Christopher felt a pang of depression. Perhaps he should have remained in France. He might have repaired the damage. At the very least he could have retreated to Paris. The City of Lights was large enough to absorb his secret. But Paris was a German city now, a rookery of vice. A village in Brittany would have been better; a village near the coast.

Would it have mattered?

How far could he run?

He had run as far as possible and still he had settled on French soil. Four thousand miles and still the curse pursued him. He forced it from his mind, squelched it before it blossomed into remorse. Fighting a nagging feeling of lassitude, he rose from the bench and resumed his walk. He left the Savanne and crossed the Rue Blenac. In the sultry heat the lines of his suit had rumpled and a patch of damp had formed between his shoulder blades. A hot draught of wind swept down from the hills, bringing beads of moisture to his upper lip. Through the soles of his shoes he could feel the heat in the cobbled pavement. He cut through the dark veins of alleyways that paralleled the waterfront. The upper levels of the roughhewn dwellings were given over to cold water flats, the lower to the rear of tradesmen's shops. Dodging puddles of rainwater from a mid-morning shower, he was beset by the smells of cooking: vegetables frying in oil, the piquance of spiced poultry. He emerged at the quay and caught a glimpse of himself in a shop window.

"Well made", Madame Molay had said. "You are well-made, Delon. Even under that ridiculous helmet and in that ill-fitting suit you are a sight to behold. It must be a curse," she said, fingering a lapel of his jacket. "Women must be drawn to you like shavings to a magnet, irresistibly and in droves."

The madam fit the mold. If the mademoiselles were cheeky, the matrons were bolder yet. They tried to mother him. Suckle him.

A gift, she had called it. "You have a God-given gift, Delon. You are one of God's masterpieces. Adonis in the flesh."

God-given, indeed, Christopher thought. Would that the Lord had bestowed his grace in something other than physical form... the gift of discretion, perhaps.

Since arriving on Martinique the month before, he had spent his time establishing his classes at Government House. He felt competent teaching English to the children of diplomats. Even at the the church school in Dijon, English had been his long suit. It was troubling, though, to see the island's schoolgirls dressed in white tunics and marching arms outstretched to Schubert's March Militaire. It reminded him of some pagan ritual. Vichy rules, the headmaster had explained. Nazi rules, he meant, but he lacked the courage to admit it. Yet, the teaching might be the tonic he needed. It might help him to feel useful. Despite his lack of credentials, he had been readily taken in. Readily, indeed, since the screener-of-record had been Madame Molay herself, a svelte matron in her late forties with a septuagenarian for a husband and an appetite for young Legionnaires. Claiming to be a "professeur" spit out of the cauldron of North Africa, Christopher had but to flash his smile and the position was his. At the first signs of danger he should have retreated; the first flutter of lashes, the brush of fingertips against the clipped black hair, the coy flush of vulnerability. But retreat was impossible here. He had retreated from Sedan. From Dunkirk. From Dakar. There was nowhere left to go.

Be careful, Delon, he told himself. Martinique is a small island. There is little room to maneuver. Tonight at the High Commissioner's reception he would remain politely remote, especially from the sloe-eyed Madame Molay.

When he reached his hotel he was perspiring freely. He was pleased with his new quarters, satisfied he had made the right decision in changing from accommodations near Government House. The Hotel de la Paix had seen better days, but it retained a seedy elegance. He had been lucky to get the room. Most hotels in Forte de France were bulging with European refugees seeking ships to Mexico or the United States. What he liked best about this new location was the view, two stories above street level with a balcony overlooking the harbor. The unobstructed view of the sea was a bonus, particularly on hot nights and cool mornings. The room was more than adequate, and the steep flights of steps could be considered a self-imposed penance.

There was a door ajar in the apartment next to his. As he approached to within a few steps, a breeze from the harbor nudged it outward. He turned to edge past and noticed that the shutters to the balcony were open. Beyond the shutters he could see ships in the harbor, a cutter plying between large merchantmen, and some gulls balancing overhead. He caught sight of a woman's underthings on the bed, a silk chemise, a lounging robe, a filmy peignoir. Before he could turn away, the figure of a woman materialized in the steamy surface of a mirror. But for lace-fringed panties and a fluffy pink towel piled ornately on her head, the woman was naked. Her face was smeared with a pasty white cream and her body graced with a suntan free of strap marks or other impedimenta. The body was young, no more than twenty, he assumed. So compelling was the gaze behind the mask that it engaged his attention for what seemed like minutes. So assured was her presence that she made no attempt to cover herself. In the instant that it all transpired, Christopher caught a hint of amusement in the bold dark eyes, the trace of a smile on the moist full lips.

He felt the color rise instantly to his cheeks, a flush so prominent that his face went hotter than the kiss of the sun, hotter than the airless climb up the long narrow stairway.

With a nod of embarrassment, he pushed his way past her doorway and fumbled with the key to his apartment. Safe in the sanctuary of his quarters, he drew a deep and welcome breath.

Is there no end to it?, he thought. Must I be tested at every turn?

ONE HOUR LATER

THE ISLAND OF ST. THOMAS
U.S. VIRGIN ISLANDS

Three hundred miles to the north Captain Dante O'Shea strode the flagstone pathway to his daughter's cottage. A dilapidated lorry was parked in the driveway, a ladder and some lengths of pipe in a cluttered truckbed. The vintage Chevrolet he had left with Casey was nowhere to be seen.

He rang the doorbell and removed his cap. He had telephoned from the airbase, but there was no answer. Casey was not expecting him; he had opted for surprise. It had been fourteen months since he had managed a brief stopover in the islands after a trip to Washington. He wondered how she would react, how tall little Sean would be.

A man opened the door, an islander clutching a sturdy wooden toolbox in an outsized fist.

Dante peered over his shoulder. "My daughter...she lives here...."

"Nobody be here," the man said. "I be fixin' d'plumbin'. Big storm last week. Miss O'Shea be stayin'in town."

"Do you know where?"

"She be at d'Trade Wind."

Dante was pleased and disappointed. He had hoped for a quiet reunion, with just the three of them. But at least she was in Charlotte Amalie. He'd been billeted at the Trade Winds himself. The Navy had booked half the rooms pending completion of the sub base.

"I be finish for t'day," the man said. "I be leavin' now."

"Is the plumbing usable?"

"Not d'kitchen, only da bat'room."

"I'll lock up," Dante said.

The workman looked past him to the grey Navy sedan parked on the roadway. He took in Dante's uniform, the four gold stripes on the pressed white sleeves, the scrambled eggs on the white peaked cap. He hefted the toolbox to a shoulder. "D'lock, mistuh... Just turn d'knob."

"I know, Dante said. Thanks."

When the plumber reached the truck, Dante closed the door and gathered himself. The living room was dark. Casey had drawn the drapes. As he made his way down the hallway, each step involved a decision. Memories were breathing at him from the very walls. The kitchen was brighter, with sunlight streaming through a half-open shutter. He walked to the table and pulled back a chair. As the room came together, the past seemed to wash around him. Casey had left things virtually untouched. The ice bucket was still on its stand in the corner near the window. Though he couldn't see it, he could envision the inscription on the bottom: ANNAPOLIS, JUNE 7, 1914. Caroline had purchased it the day after their wedding.

Wherever we're stationed, hon, at least the wine will be right.

There was the small brass bird cage that had never held a bird, a Tuscan vase from a villa outside Florence. For a numbing moment, he expected to hear Caroline's voice in the next room. The realization that he would never see her again left a cold empty void in the pit of his stomach.

He drew back the curtain. The view was as magnificent as ever, the swayback palm in the foreground, the sea dotted by small humpbacked out-islands. In the fourteen months since he had sat at this table, little had changed on this peaceful hillside. But beyond the horizon the world had erupted in flames. The mind reeled at the speed of it. Since last he had climbed the steps to the cottage the Germans had invaded Russia, the British and Germans had firebombed each other's cities, and the carnage was spilling into Africa. In the north Atlantic the British were fighting a blockade of their island, U-Boats were ravaging convoys like piranha, and the sea lanes were running red with blood. Closer to home, President Roosevelt had won an unprecedented third term, the U.S. Navy was regrouping its fleet in the Atlantic, and Nazi saboteurs had been uncovered in Cuba and Venezuela. Warclouds were boiling on the western horizon, too. The Japanese were chewing at the crust of China; and now that Holland and France were neutralized, the Sons of Nippon were eyeing the Dutch East Indies and Indochina. How long could America stay out of it, Dante wondered? Would Casey and Sean be sucked into the vortex of a world gone mad?

He left the kitchen and walked the hallway to the rear of the house. Apparently Casey was still using her old room. There was an infant's crib in one corner and a scattering of toys on the bedding. On the rug beside the bed lay the pee-wee football he had sent for Sean's third birthday.

He proceeded up the corridor to the master bedroom. It looked the same as he remembered. Beyond the window in the cozy garden a hummingbird hovered at a flower, its head a coral green, its wings a gossamer blur. At the sight of the canopied bed a greyness overcame his spirit. Caroline had found the antique four-poster on their honeymoon in Paris. They had spent a month's pay to have it shipped by steamer. Unsuitable as it might be for the islands, Caroline had insisted they bring it to St. Thomas.

It makes me feel special, hon. Someday we'll be stationed in the south of France and it will fit right in. If not, we'll enjoy it when we retire.

Suddenly he was glad that Casey wasn't there, that he was alone with these relics of the past. He wanted to absorb them, to stockpile them for the years ahead. He sat on the bed and ran a hand over the coverlet. He looked at the dresser. Casey had resurrected a photo they had taken on their honeymoon. Caroline looked elegant in a silk print dress belted at the waist. She had purchased the ensemble in Italy with a flowered hat that looked plucked from a painting by Renoir. The memory hit him like a wrecking ball. He felt an overpowering sense of loss, as though life and love had ebbed away on the same tide. He went to the dresser and lifted the photo. He brushed a finger over Caroline's hair. He could almost smell her skin, perfumed and fresh, like gardenias after a rainshower.

It had been his fault. Everyone had assured it him it had not, but it had. He had insisted on diving off the reef. Caroline had preferred the beach. The SEAWIND had seen better days, a thirty-foot cabin cruiser with a clunker for an engine and a terminal case of dry rot. He should have checked it out before renting. They were not going far, only a mile or so offshore, and the weather was fine. But he should have checked it out. Afterwards, it was assumed there had been a gas leak. The tanks were old, the fittings corroded. He discovered only afterwards that the owner had installed a makeshift pump in the bilge. A spark had ignited the fumes. The explosion had taken the bottom out, and Caroline had been cut off from the ladder, trapped in the galley. The reef he was diving was just a few hundred feet to seaward. He heard the blast from thirty feet beneath the surface, a pounding in his eardrums, as though a mine had exploded. By the time he surfaced, the SEAWIND was down at the stern and sliding beneath the waves. Swimming as fast as he could, his blood surging to the hammering of his heart, he felt like he was mired in molasses. By the time he dragged her to the surface a trawler was circling the debris.

They tried to revive her on the trawler's deck. They worked on her for more than an hour. Twice they tried to drag him away, but he wouldn't let her go. When they finally convinced him she was gone, he retched, grew furious, disconsolate, morose. Were it not for his daughter, he would have plunged back into the sea. Were it not for Casey, he would have preferred to end it then and there, to follow her to oblivion, to hell, to wherever. It hurt. It hurt so badly that he was beyond pain, beyond grief. They had never finished their love story; they had never even said goodbye.

Still in shock, he had returned to the cottage. He had been at sea for months and had only returned the night before. Casey was spending the night with a friend. Caroline had insisted that they spend a quiet weekend before their daughter returned. He thought the request strange, out of character, but Caroline had insisted.

With his clothes still wet, his body numb, his brain detached, he sent a car for Casey. While he waited at the cottage, the torment was as palpable as if he had lost a limb. He anguished over how to tell her. How did one tell a daughter that her mother was gone? That her father was responsible for her death?

And then she arrived.

And then he saw her, swollen with child.

And then grief turned to shock. And shock to anger.

He pressed the honeymoon photo to his brow.

"I'm sorry, hon. I'm so terribly, terribly sorry..." He was weeping now, the tears coming freely, unabashedly. The sobs were deep and painful. He sat on the bed and let it happen, waited for it to pass. Wade through it, he told himself. For sanity's sake. For Casey's. For Sean.

He kissed the woman in the photo then walked to the bathroom. In the scalloped basin, he splashed handfuls of water over his face and doused his eyes. When he stood to face the mirror he searched the eyes for a hint of the ambitious young midshipman, the lover of sport, of the sea, of a girl named Caroline. In the weathered face he found an absentee father, a delinquent grandfather, a widower and a washout. He rubbed his face with a towel and left the house abruptly. He would visit the cemetery tomorrow, bring flowers in the ice bucket. Caroline would like that. The pain was part of the healing. He realized that. He realized, too, that in some ways he welcomed it, that he needed it to prod him on. There was a reason he had not been trapped on that boat, a reason yet to be revealed. He wanted to believe that. He clung to it, depended on it.

Tonight he would see Casey. He felt a desperate longing for his daughter. He prayed it was not too late, prayed they could put it back together. She was a good kid. They had loved each other deeply. Trusted one another. They could draw on that.

THAT SAME NIGHT

THE NORTH AFRICAN COAST
TANGIER, NEUTRAL SPANISH MOROCCO

Three-thousand miles to the east, the Italian submarine SQUALO lay silent in its mooring in the moonless Mediterranean light.

On his bunk near the forward torpedo room, Ensign Aldo Arazi could feel the officer's dirk in the waistband of his shorts pressing firmly against his hip. There was little he could do with the dagger, but its sharply-honed blade just inches from his fingertips gave him a semblance of control. It went hard against his nature to remain so passive.

His shipmates were lying as still as he was, all bare-chested, some wearing shoes, all in the black cotton undershorts favored by submarine crews. Though there were six of them within touching distance, Aldo could not detect a breath escaping any of them. Like him, they were waiting. Feigning sleep and waiting.

The air in the submarine was heavy, the oppressive offering of the parched North African mainland. The harbor was sheltered from the wind by Tangier Point, and though the hatches lay open to the night, every breath had to be coaxed to the lungs as through sandpaper.

Minutes were dragging like hours. Two weeks they had been holed up in this pestiferous harbor, and though their repairs had been completed for two full days, still they waited. Perhaps the Captain was being overcautious. Soon the moon would be up. What was Valerio waiting for, Aldo wondered? Had the plan leaked? Tangier was crawling with spies.

They had been reminded that British Corvettes were patrolling the approaches to the harbor. Tangier was close to British waters. Situated on the Moroccan coast, it lay less than forty miles from the embattled British fortress of Gibraltar. Ashore, British agents were keeping a not-so-surreptitious watch on their submarine. With the exception of parts smuggled in by frogmen, they were aware of every move the Italians made.

Aldo was hoping that Valerio had calculated well. Dining at the yacht club with his Spanish hosts might relax their vigilance. In the tedium of another long night, the Corvettes might let their guard down a bit.

Might.

A tenuous proposition for so deadly an action.

At the thought of the patrolling warships, Aldo ran a finger over the blade of the dirk. For an instant he experienced the rancid taste of fear. The SQUALO would have to clear the harbor on the surface. If they timed it wrong or were unlucky, they would be an easy target for the waiting corvettes. If the British were alerted or got wind of the plan, this could be the final night of his life. At eighteen. And still a virgin.

Or was he? The signorina in Livorno had been free with her hands, her lips, but she had permitted limited access beyond the garter line. Still, he had been satisfied beyond his wildest expectations. So was he a virgin or no? There was no one on board he trusted enough to ask.

He felt a nudge from a seaman padding barefoot down the aisle.

At last. Some relief from the heat.

So as not to arouse suspicion, Valerio had insisted that they hold to routine. Normally at this hour a crewman or two would be smoking on deck, a luxury not permitted at sea. So as not to alert the sentries ashore, members of the crew were going topside in seemingly random fashion. The Spaniards guarding the quay invariably dozed through the late watches. It was not their war. Spain was neutral. To satisfy their role as non-belligerents, they had removed the SQUALO's charts and the breech block of her deck gun.

Aldo slipped quietly from his bunk. Barefoot and in his shorts, he climbed the ladder to the foredeck. The harbor was dark, the piers on the waterfront deserted. Beyond the walls of the palace the town lay Moorish and somnolent above chalky white cliffs. Half moons of light glowed in the towers of the Casbah and the sky was awash with stars. He sat with his back against the cannon mount and touched a match to a cigarette. A breath of wind rippled the oily black surface. As the breeze brushed his nostrils he caught the scent of the Mediterranean. It was a scent from home. From his youth. The Ligurian, they called it in Torino. He permitted himself a small reminiscence: his family's apartment on the banks of the Po, the giraffes in the zoo on the opposite bank, the aroma of warm *zuppa di panna*, bowls of fresh flowers on his mother's piano. Then slowly the breeze faded and the breath of the Sahara seeped from the headlands. He scanned the long dark pier. A single red bulb glowed dimly above a guardhouse. When the heat from the cigarette reached his fingertips, he flipped it into the bay.

Did Valerio know what he was doing? Could they run the gauntlet and survive? Valerio was an Alpha wolf, a leader. The crew had confidence in him. But this was his first cruise as Captain. They had, after all, run afoul of the British in the Gibraltar Straits. They were lucky the damage had been slight, that they could repair to a neutral port. What if the SQUALO had been damaged on the open sea? Would they have made it then?

A fist poked up through the hatch. His smoking time had expired.

He stood and stretched, trying to act casual on the chance the sentries were watching. He was gripping the hatch cover when he heard voices on the pier. He recognized Valerio's cultured Milanese dialect. For a moment there was silence. Then a splash. And then another. Then footsteps. Running.

Aldo searched the darkness. He felt the chilling sweat of anticipation.

Valerio was sprinting up the pier.

It was on! They were going!

A sentry in the conning tower thumped twice with his rifle butt on the deck plates. Seamen emerged rapidly from the hatches, three forward, three aft, a handful more on the bridge. Aldo checked the guardhouse. He scanned the approaches from the harborside gates. The captain was scrambling up the ladder to the con. "Forget the guards," he heard Valerio whisper. "I have seen to them. Cast off! *Fretta! Fretta!*"

Someone had already singled up the lines. Fore and aft men were tugging at the ropes, lowering them over the side as quietly as possible. Water roiled at the stern, and under the quiet hum of electric motors the submarine eased smoothly from the dock. From the bridge Aldo could hear the Captain's whispered commands; from the maze below, the click of switches, the hiss of valves. Once past the inner harbor, the boat shuddered slightly as the diesels clutched in. Aldo felt the vibrations in the soles of his feet, the forward surge as the SQUALO picked up speed.

He took up his position at the forward deck gun and looked warily out to sea. His shipmates stood expectantly at their posts, some shirtless, most still in their underwear, all staring anxiously toward the batteries on the shore. As the SQUALO nosed the swells, the breeze felt bracing against his face. Suddenly the night seemed kinetic, as though the air was charged with electricity. Aldo placed a hand over his ribcage. His heart was beating an accelerated tattoo against his chest. From the chain around his neck, he clutched the holy medal his mother had given to him at the train station. It was an image of St. Christopher, patron saint of travelers.

With the moon below the horizon, the harbor was mercifully dark. The lights of Tangiers were receding steadily beyond the stern. Aldo looked apprehensively toward the bridge. The Captain had reversed his cap and was scanning the shoreline with binoculars. Would the alarm come? Had they gotten enough of a jump? Not a word had been spoken since Valerio had regained the con. So far everything had gone as planned. Once past Tangier Point they would broach the current. If they had fooled the British as well as they had deceived their Spanish hosts, they would have a fighting chance. If they could clear the headland before the Corvettes detected their screws, they could head for deeper water. In the narrow channel a dive would be dangerous. The British would track them like a ferret after a mole. Better they should slip the pickets on the surface and run for open sea.

Within minutes the SQUALO found its stride. Aldo could see the surge of the bow wave, hear the hiss of seawater against the distended hull. His mouth was dry, his cheekbones aching from the press of binoculars. He checked his wristwatch. At any moment the moon would rise and they would be silhouetted against the skyline. Despite the fear, he felt proud. Proud to be running free again. Proud to be part of a fighting ship again. Proud to be an officer in the Royal Italian Navy.

Another sweep of his binoculars. They were passing the headland. As coastline merged with sea-line, every shadow took on the shape of a mast. If one looked too hard, the eyes played tricks. He sharpened focus and the shadows remained shadows.

"*Rapida! Rapida*!"

The signal to dive came as a balm to his spirit. Though action had tightened his nerves, his legs were as weak as linguini.

"We're going to make it" he whispered to himself. "By the blood of Christ, we're going to make it!"

As they slipped past the Strait of Gibraltar, Aldo heard the flip of the intercom. Captain Valerio's voice rang metallically through the SQUALO's cramped compartments. From his position in the forward torpedo room, Aldo strained to listen over the hum of the electric motors.

"Congratulations, signori. You have eluded the British and participated in an heroic escape. It is a tale with which you can regale your grandchildren. And your mistresses."

There was a pause while cheering rose from throughout the boat.

"Now that we are on our way again," the Captain continued, "I can announce our destination. We are told by our German allies that the design of Italian submarines is inefficient, that we would be far too vulnerable in Atlantic waters. So we are on our way to a place where our configuration will maximize our potential..."

The boat was silent now, with only the drone of the battery-driven power plants.

"It is virgin territory, gentlemen. A submariner's dream. Once we have replenished our stores at Bordeaux, our destination will be...the Caribbean!"

A shout went up from the crew.

"Paradiso!"

"Tropicale!"

One of the enlisted men slapped Aldo on the back. Despite the breach of protocol, the young Ensign grinned.

He settled onto his bunk and re-fingered the holy medal. They were escaping the cold Atlantic. They were heading for happy hunting grounds. He pressed the medal to his lips.

"Dio grazie," he whispered. "A toast to our designers. To our wonderful, inefficient Italian designers."

THAT SAME NIGHT

CHARLOTTE AMALIE, ST. THOMAS

Dante was beginning to wish he had worn civilian clothes, but what mufti he owned he had left in Paris. The Trade Winds bar was crammed with uniforms, only a few above the rank of lieutenant. In his freshly-pressed tans, the four gold bars on his shoulder boards stood out like neon. They were gathering deferential nods from foreign servicemen and hesitant half-salutes from baby-faced Marines and enlisted seamen. He was flanked by civilians on either side, so at least he wasn't dampening the party atmosphere.

The Trade Winds Hotel was built on a bluff overlooking the scimitar-shaped harbor. Since his last visit, an open-air bar had been tacked on adjacent to the swimming pool. The bar was ringed by bamboo stools and capped by a tightly-thatched roof to protect against rainshowers. The terraced grounds, somewhat rundown since he had last seen them, offered a panoramic view of the southern end of the island. From where he sat, Dante could see the overgrown village of Charlotte Amalie. The town had expanded since he had first seen it as a young ensign in 1927. Now it stretched along the bay until it occupied all but the horns of the crescent. It had always been a busy port, Dante knew, even back when the Danes had ruled the island. The painter Camille Pisarro had lived here as a young man. His family had owned a trading company on Dronningens Gade. Dante imagined the quayside shops looked much the same now as when Pissaro had sketched them. Even then it was a commercially active port, but now, with the increased military presence, the harbor was netted and boomed and naval exercises were being conducted in the waters surrounding the island. A submarine base was being constructed somewhere west of town, and farther out the Marines were paving a runway for their patrol squadrons.

Dante sampled his drink, island rum young and fruity and salted by the fire of the sun. Though it was just after sundown, the noise level in the bar was high. There seemed to be an urgency in the chatter as though the revelers were cramming as much as possible into every waning moment. Many of the seamen were billeted on foreign ships, merchantmen bound for the north Atlantic where German wolf packs lurked just beneath the surface. Each had his own particular method of allaying fear. For some it was drink, for others conversation, for many a brothel; for a few it was the comfort of a good pipe, for many it was thoughts of home, and for some, prayer.

For Dante there was the anticipation of seeing Casey. She had been out when he had returned from her cottage, so he had slipped a note under the door of her room. It had been fourteen months since he had seen his daughter. Sean would be nearing his third birthday. Dante wondered if his grandson would remember him. They had a lot of catching up to do, he and Casey. A few ghosts to bury, not to mention a hatchet or two.

The mellow tones of a island combo drifted from a bandstand near the pool area. As couples began making their way to the dance floor, Dante ordered a second drink. He reminded himself he was on an empty stomach and that immature rum hit a notch harder than watered scotch. He was fishing for a cigarette when he felt the press of flesh against the center of his back. Arms circled his neck and a familiar accent drifted over the scent of unfamiliar perfume.

"Capitan O'Shea! Dante, *mon ami*! You are back! It's so happy to see you!"

He swiveled to face the ruby lips and mascaraed eyes of a woman who conjured the best and worst of what had happened to him in these islands.

"Contessa! How marvelous you look! As stunning as ever!"

"Dante! *Cara mio*! When did you arrive? How long will you

stay? You must take dinner with me. And your daughter, she stays with us too. She must join us for a grand celebration."

Dante felt a sudden glow of affection for this shrewd hotelier. Before the accident she had been companion and confidant to Caroline; and afterwards, a comfort to Casey. Apparently this island was more home to him than he had let himself admit. The Contessa reminded him of an eccentric aunt, dependable, affable, yet charmingly lascivious. When he offered his barstool, she placed both hands on his shoulders and pressed him down.

"I have work, darling. How do you say, no rest for the wary."

Dante laughed. "It's weary, Contessa, but I guess it could go either way. I flew in only hours ago. I haven't seen my daughter yet. How's she doing?"

"She's a fine young signorina. You will be proud of her."

"And the baby?" he asked. He has grown, no doubt."

"An *enfant terrible'*," she exclaimed, mixing her colloquialisms as was her wont. "A joy to all. But you will see for yourself. Come, let me introduce you."

She tapped the shoulder of a man on an adjacent stool. As he swiveled to face them, Dante read him as British: ruddy complexion, regimental moustache, eyes awash with an aura of gin.

"Capitan O'Shea, be pleased to meet my friend Geoffrey Blake."

The Britisher's appraisal was thorough but friendly. He thrust a hand and his grip was firm. "A pleasure, Captain. Geoffrey Cavendish Blake, to be precise."

"Dante Patrick O'Shea. Nice to meet you, Mr. Blake."

The Contessa signaled the bartender to refill their glasses. "Duty calls, gentlemen. The drinks are on the house. To celebrate the Capitan's return."

Dante caught the eye contact between the Englishman and their hostess. He suppressed a smile. Still at it, he thought, God bless her inconstant soul. The Britisher managed a discreet nod.

"Are you passing through, Mr. Blake?"

"It's Geoffrey, Captain."

Dante looked him over. He was wearing white cord trousers and a rainbow-striped shirt. Despite the heat, an expensive silk scarf was knotted inside the collar. His ankles were bare above strapped leather sandals, and with his yachting cap cocked at a rakish angle, Dante thought he looked a perfect example of British phlegm. As smooth as a gravy sandwich.

Blake downed a healthy measure of gin. "To answer your question, Captain, yes, in a sense, I'm passing through. I have business on Tortola, complicated by this nonsense with the Nazis. Have you known the Contessa long?"

"Ten, twelve years. She and my wife were friends.

"Were?"

Dante stirred his drink. "I'm a widower."

Blake raised his glass and offered a nod. After a pause, he said, "What say we touch up when you get settled in, Captain? I'd enjoy talking to the American Navy. Bit of a navy man myself. Some trawlers of mine have been pressed into His Majesty's service. Got a schooner moored quayside in town. The DEVON STAR. If you're free for a spot of brunch tomorrow, I'd be more than pleased to have you. Come aboard and have a wet."

"That's generous of you, Geoffrey. You can bring me up to date on the picture out here. Fill me in on how the British see things."

"Delighted, old boy. Shall we say around eleven? I'm a week behind on my sleep. And I intend to put a serious dent in my gin locker tonight."

"Eleven it is."

"By the way, Captain. As a widower and an officer, you'll find the pickings slim out here. The white hats are telling the women that bars on the shoulders mean the wearer has gonorrhea." Dante laughed, the Englishman guffawed, and they downed their drinks in unison.

There was a discernible drop in the noise level as one by one the men around the bar began turning from their conversations. At first Dante thought they were looking at him, but it soon became apparent that the object of their attention was above and beyond his right shoulder. He swiveled on the barstool.

It took an instant to register...long tanned legs, well-formed hips in a fitted white dress making their way down the steps from the lobby.... Dante was taking in the nicely pinched waist when his eyes shot up to the auburn hair.

"My God," he said aloud. "It's Casey..."

"Very dishy," the Englishman said. "You know her, Captain?"

"I…uh…it's…she……she's my daughter...."

Casey spotted him as he pushed to his feet. He tossed her a wave and she waved back. Weaving through gaps in the crowd, they came together in the center of the dance floor. She flung herself into his arms and their embrace brought a barrage of hoots and cheers from the onlookers.

"Nice going, skipper!"

"The brass gets the class!"

"Semper Fi, Captain!"

Dante blushed clear to his earlobes. When Casey kissed him hard on the cheek, a patter of applause broke out.

With his daughter on his arm, he maneuvered his way back to the barstools. All eyes were on the lady in white. Dante swept the room with a tolerant smile and the oglers returned to their drinks.

"Well," he said, an arm around her waist. "That was quite an entrance, Case. You always stop the show like that?"

Casey blotted lipstick from his cheek with a lace-fringed handkerchief. "I think it's your stripes, daddy. They probably think I'm some floozy you shipped in from the States."

From behind Dante's shoulder, the Englishman cleared his throat.

Dante tore his eyes from his daughter. "Forgive me, Geoffrey. A little family reunion here. Geoffrey Blake, my daughter Casey O'Shea."

The Britisher raised his glass. "Ruffles and flourishes, Miss O'Shea. Only the islands could nurture a flower of such beauty."

Casey proffered a hand. In a gesture of detached sophistication, Blake brushed her fingers lightly past his lips.

"Ah yes," she said. "The gallant Commodore Blake. The Yorkshireman who sails over from Tortola. The Countess has mentioned you, Mister Blake."

"My reputation precedes me, does it?" He patted her hand

between calloused fingers. "Believe not a word of it, lassie. It's sauce for the goose. Look, I really must be off. I have some Homeric drinking to do. I've invited your father to brunch in the morning. If you're free, my barge awaits." He shook Dante's hand and bowed curtly to Casey. Then he turned and maneuvered unsteadily through the crowd.

Casey took his place on the barstool. The bartender had already placed a Planter's Punch on a coaster.

"So!" Dante said, looking hard into his daughter's eyes. "How are things, Case? I'm years behind the curve. How's Sean? What's with the cottage? How's the teaching going?"

"You look marvelous, daddy. Where did you get that tan? And you've slimmed down so much."

"Polynesian sun and very little booze. I've been moving so fast I've outrun some meals."

"It suits you," she said, pressing his hand in hers, "Sean is fine. He's at the room with Rina. When I got your note I screeched so loud I frightened him. I promised he could stay awake until you came by. He's so excited, I had to leave the light on ....."

Dante brushed a hair from her cheek. "We'll go as soon as you finish your drink."

When Dante followed his daughter into her bedroom, his grandson was sitting propped against a pillow. No sooner had the door closed than the youngster slid to the floor and ran barefoot to his mother, his eyes never leaving the tall suntanned stranger in the pressed uniform.

"Sean," Casey said, hugging her son to her cheek, "this is your grandfather."

Dante took in the threadbare pajamas, the tousled mop of thick rusty hair, the shy hesitation in the great blue eyes. From behind his back Dante produced a model airplane. They had stopped by his room to retrieve it. When he held it out, the eyes lit up like landing lights.

"Airplane! Airplane!"

"A Dauntless, "Casey said. "A torpedo bomber."

Dante placed the model in his outstretched hands. Then

scooping the three-year-old into his arms, he lifted him, airplane and all, toward the ceiling.

"He's a husky little tyke, Case. As solid as a torpedo."

Sean giggled as Dante tickled his ribs.

"Where'd you get the airplane?" Casey asked. "It's exquisite."

"A Marine pilot at the base. He was reluctant to part with it until I explained the circumstances."

"Morrrre!" Sean giggled, and Dante hoisted until his hair literally brushed the ceiling.

"He's beautiful, Case. Just like his mother."

He sat his grandson on the bed and the youngster slipped instantly to the floor. Without missing a beat, he began rolling the airplane across the carpet.

"To bed now, honey," Casey said. "It's late. You can sleep with your Dauntless. Tomorrow you can visit with your grandfather."

"I'll take him fishing," Dante said. "We've got some catching up to do."

Dante watched as Casey tucked the youngster between the sheets, the model airplane firmly in his grasp.

"Nite, nite, honey," Casey said, kissing his forehead.

For an instant, Dante felt a catch in his throat. Suddenly Caroline was in the room and Casey was the toddler, an arm around her ever-present Teddy, her mother bending over to adjust the bedclothes.

Casey turned the light down and Dante followed her silently into the sitting room.

"He's a bonny lad, Case. You must be very proud."

"I love him beyond words, daddy. I'm eternally grateful for him.

They exchanged glances. Dante clutched her lightly by the shoulders. Relieved that she had put it out front, he kissed her firmly on the forehead. It was time for straight talk.

"You did the right thing, Case. I didn't think so at the time, but I was wrong."

Tears welled in Casey's eyes. Dante took her gently in his arms and stroked her hair. It was like a stone dissolving in his stomach.

She sobbed softly. "Oh, daddy. I'm so glad you're back. I've missed you terribly."

"I've had a lot of time to think, honey. I've seen some terrible things these past few months. Devastation. Death. And worse. Life is too short for grudges. For insensitivity. We have to squeeze out all the love we can. I love you, Casey."

"And I love you, daddy. Oh dear, I've got makeup on your uniform."

"Good. It'll enhance my credentials at the bar."

Casey managed laughter through the tears. "How long do you have?"

Dante handed her his handkerchief. "A few days here, then on to San Juan for orders. For sure I'll be stationed somewhere in the area. They wouldn't ship me here just to bounce me back to the Pacific."

"Oh, I hope it's St. Thomas," Casey said, dabbing the handkerchief against her cheeks. "There's a sub base west of town, and the Marines are building an airfield."

"I'm a flyboy, Case. It'll more likely be one of the larger air stations. Probably San Juan. That's Tenth Naval District headquarters now. They've renamed this area the Caribbean Coastal Command."

Casey repaired her makeup in a mirror. "Can I join you for a nightcap?"

"Of course. You've already boosted my stock immeasurably on this island."

Casey tapped lightly on the door to an adjoining bedroom. It was opened by a short, dark woman with island features and long ebon hair she had apparently been brushing.

"Daddy, meet Rina. She helps out at the school."

The woman extended a hand. "A pleasure, sir."

Dante clasped the fine-boned fingers. "Nice to meet you, Rina."

"I'll be back within the hour," Casey said. Sean's had a long active day. He's a tired puppy. He's probably asleep already."

"Enjoy your evening," Rina said. "I'll leave my door open. Sean will be fine."

"Thanks, Rina."

"Goodnight, Captain O'Shea."

The bar was crowded, crammed with uniforms and locals in everything from soup-to-fish finery to clamdiggers. A table came available near the dance floor and Dante outmaneuvered a Dutch seaman who hesitated a second too long after glancing at his stripes. On a terrace that served as bandstand, a sergeant from the Marine contingent had joined the local jazz combo. With minimum accompaniment and a golden-toned trumpet, he was managing a fairly competent rendition of Bunny Berigan's "I Can't Get Started".

Dante had just ordered drinks when a young Navy lieutenant in summer tans edged hesitantly through the crowd and came to a halt a respectful step or two from his table.

"Evenin', Captain. I see you're billeted here too."

Dante saw the lieutenant's eyes dart fleetingly toward his daughter. When she glanced his way, he wedged his cap under an armpit.

"Right, lieutenant. Seems the Navy has commandeered the place. Lt. Whitely, my daughter Casey O'Shea."

When Casey smiled at him, Dante was amused to see the broad-shouldered bomber pilot shift awkwardly on his feet like a timid schoolboy.

"A pleasure, ma'am. The captain bragged about you the whole flight in. Justifiably, I might add."

Letting the exaggeration pass, Dante motioned the lieutenant to a seat. "Join us, Whitely. We're rounding off the evening."

"Thank you, sir.

Casey fished a cigarette from her purse. As deftly as a magician, Whitely came up with a shiny new Zippo. As Dante raised and eyebrow, Casey smiled coyly through the flame. He had never seen his daughter smoke.

She exhaled fluidly and gave him a playful wink. "What do you fly, lieutenant?"

Whitely edged his cap toward a corner of the table. It brushed her arm, so he snatched it up and cupped it over a knee. "Patrol bomber, ma'am. PBY."

"A Catalina."

"Right. I forgot. You're Navy."

Dante watched his daughter closely. He was impressed with her poise, a far cry from the self-conscious teenager he remembered in her first party dress.

The waiter brought drinks and Whitely ordered a beer.

"The Captain tells me you teach school on the island, ma'am."

"Yes. Kind of an advanced kindergarten for the native children.

Dante pushed from his chair and stood to survey the room. "Lieutenant, did you spot a telephone on your way in?"

"Through the lobby and left at the desk, Captain."

"Carry on, you two. I'll be back in a minute."

The trumpeter was warming to the task. Backed by the combo, he was venturing a danceable interpretation of "Stardust".

"Care to risk it, Miss O'Shea?"

"Call me Casey," she said. "I'd love to."

If there was one place beside the controls of a Catalina flying boat that Kevin Whitely felt secure, it was on a dance floor. Since he had been tall enough to fill the bill, he had served as manikin in motion for three teenaged aunts, two sisters, and a brace of female cousins. Yet, when he came together with the Captain's daughter to the simplest of beats, his legs went to rubber and his feet to lead. She was taller than most women he had danced with, at least five-ten, yet she moved with a grace that had him shuffling as in sand.

Casey seemed not to notice. "Your first night in the islands, Lieutenant?"

"Please. It's Kevin. Yes. We were only at Trinidad long enough to refuel and pick up your father. When we left Lakehurst the day before yesterday it was snowing.

"Snow! I love snow, she said. I've only seen it up close once, on a trip to Chicago to visit my grandparents."

"Your father mentioned you were born here."

"In a cottage on that hillside." She pointed to the darkness beyond the pool. "I was a bit of a surprise. I suppose my parents had it worked out that I would arrive at the naval hospital at San Juan. But one minute my mother was picking flowers in the garden and the next I was bawling like a banshee."

Whitely was finding his feet. His tempo smoothed and he ventured a double shuffle or two. "So you did your schooling here."

"My mother was a teacher. I had a live-in tutor."

"Your father must rate some salty billets."

"Somehow he manages the sun. We've been stationed in Hawaii, Florida, California. My mother always brought me back here when daddy got sea duty, though. She was Danish. She was born here. She loved these islands."

"Dante said he had a grandson."

"I have a son, Casey said. "His father was...well, we're separated."

"I'm sorry. I didn't mean to pry."

When they returned to the table, Dante was sorting through his wallet. As they sipped their drinks, Dante noticed his daughter's eyes were misting. Like her mother, he thought. Two's the limit. After three she'll either stifle a yawn or get gushy and coy depending on the company.

She stifled a yawn. "Think I'll turn in, daddy. It's been a big day. I shouldn't keep Rina waiting."

"I'll walk you back," Dante said.

As Casey pushed to her feet, the young lieutenant rose smartly from his chair.

Casey took his hand. "Thanks for the dance, Kevin. Sorry I'm such a wet blanket, but I'm really bushed."

"Thank you, Miss...eh...Casey. I enjoyed the company."

He released her hand reluctantly. Dante noticed the softening in her eyes. They were tending toward gushy.

Whitely stiffened a bit. "Goodnight, Captain. Thanks for the hospitality. Oh, by the way, I checked at the sub base. None of our subs were in the Anegada Passage this afternoon."

Back at the bar, this time for a solo nightcap, Dante ordered Dewar's on ice. Island drinks were fine, but nothing pushed his buttons like scotch and rocks. The musicians were packing their instruments and the crowd was thinning as rapidly as it had formed. Twenty minutes later, Dante was halfway through a follow-on scotch when a woman crossed the pool area and took a seat one barstool removed from his. She was curves from shoulders to ankles, and poured like candle wax into a silky green dress. She ordered a daiquiri, and while she waited for her drink, Dante felt her glance shift gradually in his direction.

"Well, son of a sea dog," he heard her say. "If it isn't O'Shea!"

Dante turned to face her. She looked vaguely familiar, but he couldn't come up with a name. He was on the verge of a demur when she said, "Nottingham, you old goat. Rita Nottingham."

"0f course," Dante said, making the connection. "Jeff's wife. How is the old four-stacker? Haven't seen you two since Pearl. Must be eight years at least."

He managed a smile, but he was somewhat taken back. A decade before, Rita Nottingham had been the belle of the fleet, a knockout in the style of another Rita, namely Hayworth. While she was still attractive, the years had taken their toll. So, he could see, had the booze. Rita Nottingham had always been notorious for her hollow leg. Judging by her sallow complexion and the pouches under her eyes, it hadn't been as hollow as everyone had supposed.

"Jeff's back at Pearl," she said, drawing a cigarette from her purse.

Dante offered a candle in a red string jar. She leaned over and sucked the tobacco alive.

"He's on TDY. Be back in a few weeks. We heard you got a fourth stripe, Dante. Belated congratulations. Let me buy you a drink."

She slipped fluidly onto the barstool next to his.

"I'm at saturation, Rita. But let me get you one." He motioned to the bartender. She was obviously drunk. Drunk and in heat. He never did like Jeff Nottingham. Starched as a collar and a class-A prick.

"I heard about Caroline, Dante. I'm sorry as hell. I only met her once, but she seemed a helluva lady."

"She was that," Dante said. "She was definitely that."

"Look," she said. "Let's take a swim." The amenities behind, she was reverting to form. In her heyday, the pilots had dubbed her Lollipop. Because her husband was a sucker, one version went. Other versions weren't so kind. Dante figured her at two drinks below par. He'd been hitting it pretty heavily himself since Caroline's passing, but she could still probably spot him a chaser or two.

"Not here," Rita said. "I hate pools. I prefer the sea. It's a fabulous night. I have a car. We can drive to Megan's Bay."

She touched a hand to his forearm. Dante caught the scent of perfume, subtle yet spicy. She swiveled on the stool and his knee brushed her thigh, the flesh as soft as camembert. It occurred to him that he hadn't been with a woman since Paris. Thirty months on the run, in official meetings, scampering through France on the roads to Vichy, the all-male encampment in Morocco, a backwater billet in the Philippines. Her perfume was heady, the night seductive. Beyond the palms the moon was laying a golden streak across a dead calm sea. He was aware of the electricity in her touch, the swell of hips beneath the clinging dress. Something tugged him in the opposite direction. Was it conscience? Cuckolding a fellow officer? He doubted it. With the tables turned, Nottingham would be halfway to the car by now. Was it Casey and Sean? The island? The memories lurking in the shadows beyond the torchlight? Whatever it was, it took the edge off long enough for Nottingham, as inebriated as she was, to regroup and regain her composure.

"Ah, it's a lousy idea anyway, Dante. Sand in the crotch and all that. Besides, I'm stoned to the gills."

"I'm bushed myself, Rita. Just got in this afternoon. He held up his drink. Gonna polish this off and hit the sack."

She drained the daiquiri in one long swallow. "Ever the loner, eh Dante. Have another. Even a Captain can't fly on one wing."

As she staggered past the pool, Dante took a long stiff pull at his scotch. With the whiskey fuming in his brain and the ghost of her thigh haunting his kneecap, he watched her climb the steps to the lobby, the silk shifting provocatively over her hips, the calves stretching taut in her suntanned legs. He downed the drink and almost set out after her.

No, he said to himself. Not here.

"Bartender! Another scotch!"

***

On the far side of the island the sea was slag black. The moon had not yet risen and the approaches to Magens Bay were swathed in darkness.

Near the mouth of the bay a towering sentinel of rock jutted sharply from the sea, a craggy outcropping inhabited by land crabs and seabirds. Beyond the rock the bay was as flat and hammered as a fjord. Suddenly the surface rippled, then eddied, then erupted into a shower of spray as a steel-nosed prow punched stoutly toward the sky. Shedding seawater as it emerged, the U-143 rose balefully into the night. Like some undernourished Leviathan it sniffed the air then flattened against the surface with a hushed and precipitate splash.

With shock waves chasing from the hull and the vents still shedding sea water, shadowy figures appeared on the bridge. Hatches opened fore and aft and additional figures materialized on deck. As crewmen dispersed quietly along the dark and slender hull, they fell silently in behind an anti-aircraft weapon near the bridge and a 40mm cannon on the foredeck. From the high gun platform aft of the conning tower, a seaman whispered up to the bridge. "Manned for surface attack, Kapitan."

High on the tower, Captain Dieter Hurst swept rubber-coated binoculars through the arc of the cove. Behind him, lookouts scanned the approaches for any sign of a ship.

Viktor Reinmann emerged through the hatch wearing white yachting trousers rolled to the knees and a faded denim shirt. His legs were pasty, his ankles and forearms bone white.

Aware that sound travels inordinate distances over water, the U-Boat's captain kept his voice low. "You look anything but an islander, Viktor. Catch the sun for a few days. Tomorrow you will be *tartar*, by next week *braten*."

A seabag was handed up through the hatch.

"Bury the raft well," the captain reminded. "Deep in the treeline. What if the hut is gone? Occupied by natives?"

Viktor dropped the seabag to a petty officer on the deck. "It's been standing for decades, Dieter. If it's occupied, there are others. Relax, Herr Kaleun. I'm at home here."

The captain touched a finger to his cap. "One week, Viktor. At this very spot. At the stroke of midnight. It's an excellent rendezvous point, sheltered from the island and in a good deep channel."

From the ladder on the weather deck, Viktor Reinmann tossed him a short smart salute. "One week, Dieter. Good hunting."

He descended the ladder and stepped into the raft. With the sea slapping gently against the hull, he pressed a finger to the cool dark superstructure. He touched the finger to his lips. Cramped and inhospitable though it was, the U-Boat was an extension of Germany, a vestige of the Fatherland. One never knew when one might return.

A crewman shoved him off, sluing the dinghy into the current. It rotated slowly then nosed itself toward the shore. Viktor fingered the paddle and centered himself on the thwart. A breeze drifted from the island bearing the scent of vegetation. In anticipation of a late-rising moon, the sea shone like lavender ink. Viktor looked back at the U-Boat. Its silhouette was barely discernible in the darkness, a dusky shadow on a sable sea. Urging the raft around the pyramid of rock, he paddled silently toward the cove. At every stroke the paddle sent greenish-yellow swirls eddying slowly to the rear. As the night thickened around him, the air took on a steamy quality. The blackness clotted around him. A night bird squawked from a bouldered shelf. On the humpbacked island dead ahead a few faint lights glimmered high on a ridge. Beyond the peaks lay the village of Charlotte Amalie.

And Casey.

He glanced back. The submarine had disappeared, swallowed by night.

He was alone.

Far up the coastline be could see a cluster of lanterns, the distant glimmer of a bonfire. A beach party, perhaps, or some late-night revelers in a fishing village. On the eastern end of the island be could make out the long silent sweep of a lighthouse: a thread of white, a blue-white flash, a thread of white again. He centered the dinghy on the cove ahead. Though it was dark, he could envisage the crescent-shaped inlet, a lush wall of sea grape framing a rind of beach. Beyond that a double-rutted lane that wound into the hills. He made his approach on feathered oars. A hundred yards from the beach, assuming nothing had changed in four years, the lane would give way to a steep winding footpath.

With the paddle feeling weightless at his fingertips, the dinghy slid smoothly over the swells. He was experiencing the elation that accompanies danger, but still he could not bring himself to think of the island as alien, its inhabitants as adversaries. He had spent carefree days on those sun-warmed slopes. Memorable nights. Would the beach be patrolled? Probably not. St. Thomas was an American island. America was not at war. Besides, it would take hundreds of men to patrol the numerous coves and inlets. Natives, that's the worst he might encounter. Natives taking a late-night swim, or lovers seeking ecstasy under the stars.

His thoughts turned to Casey. He remembered a night on this very strip of beach. The water had been warm, her body drawn to his, their swimsuits on a towel on the sand.

"You're the first, Viktor," she had assured him.

They had been teenagers. With her body fused to his and her flesh as yielding as papaya, he had never felt more fulfilled, more content. A far cry from the crisp, cold nights of the Tyrol, the dirndl-skirted flanks of the frauleins.

Was she still in the cottage on the hillside? He tried to remember her face. The best he could recall was a magnificent sweep of auburn, smiling green eyes, the hint of a dimple at the corner of a cheek. Was she seeing someone? Was she married? At twenty-one, four years is a lifetime.

He forced his attention to the shadowy loom of the island.

Though it was nearing midnight, his shirt was damp with sweat, a trickle of perspiration creasing his brow. He raised the paddle and dragged a finger through the water. As warm as bathwater.

The beach was warmer still, the sand leaching heat from the sundrenched days. He dragged the dinghy beyond the smooth pale trunks of the sea grape. There was the chirping of frogs, the chatter of insects. He had forgotten the frogs. He had forgotten the fragrances too, the delicate perfume of flowers, the rich damp scents of vegetation. The sensations brought a prickling to his skin. For a moment he forgot the war, pushed it to his subconscious as one would an unwanted memory. So harsh was the spectre of greased torpedoes and burning tankers that it seemed the stuff of nightmares. A fish leaped somewhere in the bay and jarred him back to the moment. With the raft buried deep in the brush, he pushed through a curtain of fern and began his ascent toward the hideaway in the hills.

ONE HOUR LATER

FORTE DE FRANCE

Martinique was blacked out. From a ship at sea or an aircraft overhead, not a flicker of light could be seen across the breadth of the island. Blackout regulations were strict. Streetlamps were extinguished and headlights on vehicles had been painted blue to mask their movements from above. A curfew had been in effect for months. Lookouts had been posted in the hills to make sure that no lights were visible in the coastal towns. Anyone on the streets after dark faced the prospect of arrest. Fearing an invasion might be imminent, schools had been closed until further notice, the pupils given an extended holiday.

On the shores of its sheltered harbor, the city of Forte de France lay silent and dark, its quayside deserted, its buildings shuttered, its streets and alleyways blue-shadowed in the spill of the moon. High above the town the walls of Fort Desaix traced a meandering path across the starlit hills. Deep within its ancient battlements lay the wealth of France.

All was darkness.

All was silence.

Suddenly, as though someone had raised the lid on a music box, the strains of a waltz drifted from the suburb known as Didier. From the palm-lined boulevard that ran past its gates, the High Commissioner's mansion looked dark and unoccupied. Inside, behind thick velvet drapes that served as blackout curtains, a lavish reception hall had been transformed into a miniature ballroom. The party was fast approaching its zenith. The affair was an unusual one, part Christmas gala, part military ball, part bracing oneself for the shortages that lay ahead. From this day forward food would be rationed on Martinique. Already supplies were being shipped in twice a month from New Orleans. By arrangement with neutral America, the Germans were allowing a supply ship to pass unmolested once every two weeks.

Be that as it may, tonight there was no shortage of elegance, no rationing of gaiety, no stifling of pomp. In the streets and alleyways beyond the blackout curtains the citizenry of Forte de France might be making due in their shuttered apartments and electricity-starved flats, but inside the High Commissioner's residence chandeliers blazed and the dance floor was a swarm of military dress uniforms, bureaucrats in white tie, and ladies in expensive finery.

Christopher Delon stood uncomfortably beneath the glare of a chandelier feeling trapped and conspicuous between the orchestral offerings of the military constabulary and the pirouettes of whirling dancers. Delon had eaten much too much, and the food had been far too rich for his taste. Marveling at this display of extravagance in the midst of so much deprivation, he sipped his champagne, the last, he had been assured, for the foreseeable future. As the dancers whirled by in a shuffle of shoe leather and the rustle of taffeta, he surveyed the hall. The mansion was decorated with Parisian flair and embellished with a mixture of French and island artwork. A marble staircase graced by an ornate balustrade swept to the upper chambers where the hallways were lined with portraits of long-deceased dignitaries.

As he had throughout the evening, Christopher was keeping a wary eye on Madam Molay. From across the room, he noticed, the madam was keeping both eyes on him. Talking thirteen to the dozen, she was regaling an aristocratic-looking woman sporting pince-nez and a highly-perched chignon. Not infrequently she and Christopher exchanged long-distance glances, he hoping someone would monopolize her card; she, he feared, awaiting an opportunity to corner him. Pretending to stifle a yawn, he checked his wristwatch. Try as he might, he remained intolerant of these affairs. No matter how one tried to avoid it, one was beset by the banalities of the privileged, the fatuities of the urbane. Protocol demanded that he suffer through another half hour, but Saturn would be prominent tonight. He was anxious to return to the telescope he had borrowed from a junior administrator. He placed a half-empty glass of champagne on a sideboard and stifled a burp. If his consumption continued at its present rate, he would be intoxicated within the hour. Perhaps it was best that the wine cellars were nearing depletion. He had passed a scant four weeks in this outpost and already he was in search of a bracer before lunch. Another few months and he would be at it before breakfast.

The door to an anteroom opened and Delon caught sight of the lady in blue. She was trailed, as she had been throughout the affair, by a *coterie* of officers and members of the diplomatic corps. Since she had arrived, men had been milling about her like bees in a poppy field. She was the only woman in the building who had not fluttered an eyelash at him. Though she looked fifteen years his senior, she was by far the most attractive female he had seen on the island.

The waltz was nearing completion. As the dancers whirled past in a final whisper of silk and satin, Delon caught the eye of Madame Molay. Taking a bearing, he noticed that he had wandered near the vicinity of the powder rooms. To avoid an encounter should the Madame avail herself, he strolled to the rear of the hall and pushed past a heavy oak door. He found himself in one of the anterooms. The chamber was unoccupied, lit only by candles. Someone had stacked records on a phonograph and their taste had run to jazz. He was browsing through a bookcase when a figure slipped noiselessly into the room. There was a flicker of light before the door was pressed shut with a quiet hand. Fearing it might be the dauntless Madam Molay, Christopher took refuge in the shadows of an alcove. When the silence extended beyond that probability, he watched as the lady in blue picked a cigarette from her handbag and began scratching through her purse.

"Allow me," he said, picking a taper from the base of a candlabra.

She turned as if he had fired a shot past her ear.

"I'm sorry," he said, cupping a hand behind the flame. "I didn't mean to startle you."

She regained her composure rapidly. "I... I thought I was alone." She put the cigarette to her lips and touched it to the flame.

Christopher snuffed the taper between thumb and forefinger. "If you would rather I leave...."

She drew lightly on the cigarette. "No...please...I hope I didn't disturb you. I discovered these recordings on a shelf when I was here some years ago. Since then I have used this room as a sort of retreat. No one seems to venture past the door. I suppose the darkness drives them off."

"It's preferable to...to that....," Christopher said, gesturing toward the ballroom.

In the candle glow, Christopher caught the gleam of straight white teeth. The lady in blue had mastered a most beguiling smile.

"Decidedly," she said. She offered a hand. Her grasp was firm but tractable. "Nikole Rollet."

He flushed uneasily under her gaze. "Christopher Delon."

"I noticed you at dinner, Monsieur Delon. You looked...... distracted."

"I was thinking the same of you."

Her smile bore a hint of derision. "And you were right. But I'm a guest of the Admiral. As the occasion demands, I suffer through."

"Do you live in Forte de France?"

"In Ste-Anne."

If he had heard of it, it had escaped his memory. "Ste-Anne. It's......"

"The southern extremity," she offered. "Just north of Pointe Dunkerque."

At the sound of the word, Christopher's blood chilled. He had no idea such a place existed on Martinique. What a fateful coincidence. Perhaps he was cursed. The unthinkable had followed him even here. He had a vision of roads clogged with refugees, retreating columns of troops, carcasses in ditches, a surf littered with corpses....

And Jacques. Always Jacques.

"You look pale, monsieur. Are you well?" Her eyes were liquid in the candlelight.

"I'm...I'm...fine. The southern extremity, you say."

"I prefer it. It's the provincial in me."

"Then you were not born here."

"In Deauville," she said. "My husband was a painter. He liked working here."

"Does he still?"

"He's dead. The Germans. At Abbeville."

"I'm sorry...."

"We're all sorry," Madame Rollet countered, a hint of sadness in her voice. "And you, Monsieur? You don't seem the military type."

He found that he could not lie to her. "I'm a priest."

He was surprised that he had blurted it out. And to a perfect stranger.

Her eyebrows arched and she exhaled a plume of bluish-grey smoke. "The clergy is dressing better these days."

"I...I haven't told anyone," he said, somewhat relieved at having confided his secret. "I don't know why I'm telling you. I'm on a sabbatical of sorts. Working things out...."

The lie brought a tinge to his cheeks, but she seemed not to notice. She accepted the confidence as though they had been friends for years.

"Your secret is safe with me, Pere Christopher."

"And you?" he inquired. "What does one do at Ste-Anne?"

"I'm a doctor. I have a small clinic."

Christopher studied her with renewed interest. A confection of brains and beauty, he thought. A rare bird indeed. "I'm new to Martinique," he said, still abashed at how easily she had drawn him out. "I have never been to your corner of the island."

"You would find it relaxing. Like Villefranche, actually. You're young for a priest."

He managed a smile. "Twenty-eight. I've been meaning to tour the island. Would you...I mean, if I'm in the vicinity...it would be nice to...to talk...."

Again he was astonished at how readily he responded to this stranger. She was beautiful, yes. Indeed, she took beauty to a new level. But it was something beyond that. For reasons he could not yet fathom, he found he trusted her. She would not betray him. Perhaps it was the healer in her; perhaps that is what he sensed.

Nikole searched his eyes. He seemed astonishingly masculine for a priest. She wondered at this sabbatical business, but his apparent shyness and a lack of pretension allayed suspicion. "I'm free on Sundays," she said. "There are rooms at the clinic. Nothing stylish, of course, but serviceable. It would be nice to have some company."

The door pushed open and the strains of a gavotte drowned out the jazz. The man who entered wore the uniform of an artillery officer. Beneath a pencil-thin moustache, he sported a trim sable beard.

"So there you are!" he said, leaving the door ajar. "The room grows stale without you!"

Nikole Rollet drew heavily on her cigarette. "Captain Boucher. Monsieur Delon."

The officer responded with a casual nod.

A papier maché fop, thought Christopher. A cockatoo, prim and primped.

"Monsieur Delon has been telling me, Captain, that a rumor is circulating. The British are planning an occupation. They want the harbor. The ships. The gold."

Christopher glanced at her, puzzled at the fabrication. Her gaze held steady.

"We're well garrisoned," the cockatoo said in a small priggish voice. "They'll find us more prepared than in North Africa. But no talk of war tonight. You promised a dance, Madame. If the gentleman has no objections...."

Christopher nodded politely.

As she took her leave, Nikole Rollet snuffed her cigarette in an ashtray. "I look forward to your visit, Monsieur Delon."

The cockatoo threw him a papery smile.

Back at the party, Christopher waded self-consciously through a dance with Madame Molay. The band, more practised in bandshell waltzes than the music of the day, struggled through a labored rendition of "The Last Time I Saw Paris". Pressing against him provocatively, the Madame informed 'the professeur' that her husband would be off to Guiana for a fortnight. Feigning a touch of fever, the priest-in-hiding managed to slip away before she could pursue the topic further.

***

In a rear chamber of the building, Admiral Georges Achille Marie Joseph Robert, High Commissioner to Martinique, Guadeloupe, and French Guiana, was reading a freshly-decoded cable. The sender was identified as Marshall Philippe Petain, head of the Vichy government in France.

IF ATTACKED
DUMP GOLD INTO SEA

Admiral Robert fumed. "Idiots! Do they think it's stored in a teacup?" He touched the cable to the flame of a candle and dropped it into an ashtray.

Henri-Louis Sambre, the only other person in the room, watched the cable smolder then burst into flame. An aide to Admiral Robert, Sambre was stout and balding. He wore thick rimless glasses and an ill-fitting linen suit. Despite the breeze playing coolly through the shutters, perspiration lined the creases of his neck and stained the armpits of his jacket. With the muscles of his jaw tightening, he watched silently as the cable was reduced to ashes.

***

Christopher Delon crossed the Rue de Liberté and took up his stroll along the quay. The driver had dropped him at his apartment, but he felt the need to walk. So long as he remained in the vicinity of the harbor he need not fear. The guests at the party had been given stamped invitations excusing the breach of curfew.

The palms were yielding to an offshore breeze. He felt the clean salt air in his face. In the harbor he could see the outline of ships, ghostly in the spill of the moon. At the edge of the Savanne he passed a slit trench sandbagged and earmarked for a gun emplacement. Trenches were being dug all over the capital. The locals referred to them as Spitz trenches, a backhanded slap at the city's mayor.

Christopher sat on a bollard on the verge of the quay. The waters of the bay looked like black wine, the surface etched by cat's paws. Below him on the rocks he could hear the scuttling of crabs, while far up the beach the moon was painting itself on the walls of the harborside fortress. He was glad to be quit of the noise, the glitter.

Dunkirk.

She had said Dunkirk.

"We're transferring you to Sedan, Father Christopher. You'll find it quieter than Dijon. With less temptation."

"But your Eminence. She was helpless. I felt sorry for her. Her husband had been killed in an auto accident. She was so young......so alone......life was breathing heavily on her......"

The prelate adjusted his glasses. "I understand, Delon. So vulnerable......so starved for affection. You're not the first, my son. Many young priests out of seminary have succumbed to temptations of the flesh."

"But Sedan. Where is Sedan?"

"North of Paris," he said, with an acid little smirk. "Near the Belgian border. Out of harm's way. Don't blame yourself, my son. She seduced you."

Out of harm's way. Sedan. A fortress town in the heart of the Ardenne Forest where even a hot-blooded young cleric could avoid the song of sirens. A tight community. In such an outpost everyone knew everyone's business. And if Sedan was considered safe for a wayward priest in May of 1940, it was considered *safer still for the small garrison of French irregulars manning its ancient fortress. Sitting as it did on the flank of an impenetrable forest, it was unthinkable that an attack could emanate from the wasteland to the north. So unthinkable, that the fortress served as the eastern terminus of the Maginot Line, a meandering string of forts that stretched from Switzerland to the Belgian border to safeguard France's northern frontier from the barbaric Hun. With the largest land army in Europe in 1940, France seemed eminently safe behind its impregnable Maginot.*

Safe.

Impregnable.

Out of harm's way.

***

"You simply cannot begin your stay in Sedan with that awful food they serve at the rectory, Father. You're too young, too healthy for such tripe. You must take breakfast with me. I insist."

Christopher Delon shifted uneasily in his chair. His hostess, one Madame Picard, was the wife of one Colonel Picard, a recent transferee to North Africa. The madame had collared him at the rectory the day he'd arrived. Word travelled fast in Sedan. To some, the arrival of a new priest was as much an occasion as the visit of a foreign dignitary.

Breakfast.

Still chafing from his censure at Dijon, Christopher had accepted her invitation with a wary eye. No sooner had he arrived at Chateau Picard than he had begun to wonder whether champagne for breakfast was, as the madame insisted, a tradition of the region.

"Champagne," he protested. "Isn't it ...I mean...it's a bit early....

"It's wine, after all, Father," the Madam said, pouring the golden liquid into *a slender fluted glass. "You take wine with the Mass."*

"Yes, but...."

At that very instant the shells came crashing through the trees.

Though the carnage was a mile distant, the earth beneath Sedan trembled, sending priest and hostess and a liter of golden brew scrambling for the floorboards. Impenetrable though the Ardenne may have been for the mechanized units of 1914, the Panzers of 1940 traversed it swiftly and without warning. Within minutes the city was under siege, and yet another skirmish for Christopher Delon's chastity ended as the battle for France began. The Germans overran the city in hours. Thus did Hitler's Wehrmacht prove the Catholic Church and the French High Command wrong about the attributes of Sedan and its Ligne Maginot.

That very afternoon Christopher Delon set out for Dunkirk.

***

In his apartment overlooking the harbor at Forte de France, Christopher draped his borrowed evening clothes over a ladder-backed chair. He changed to a short-sleeved shirt and denim trousers, then sat on the embrasure of the window and surveyed the boundaries of his new domain: an iron-framed bed protected by mosquito netting, a well-worn love seat, a small writing table, an armoire, and a faded threadbare rug. There was a wash basin with a pitcher to match, a rack with wooden pegs for his clothes, and a single jaundiced print on the wall over a sideboard, some genus of sea anemone awash on a beach. For light a low-watt bulb hung from a chain, its pierced metallic shade casting dappled shadows on the paint-starved walls. French doors opened to a generous balcony with ornamental grillwork and a magnificent view of the bay. One end of the hall offered a shower and a toilet, the other an ornate tub astride iron claws.

Relieved to be free of the company of men and the vulpine Madame Molay, Christopher assembled a tripod and carried the telescope to the balcony. Though he had abjured all worldliness, the night was his chamber; the hunting ground of theologians, someone had written. It was a relief to be able to lock oneself behind a bolted door and revel in the silence of the galaxies. As always, he was enchanted by the starlit immensity of the tropical sky. Looking to the heavens he could hold discourse with the universe and ignore for a time the pulsing arteries of this war-torn globe. In the stars he could seek some insight into a God who could on the one hand assemble such an impressive array of galaxies and on the other permit the inhabitants of this minor planet to hack one other to pieces like so many sides of beef. Would Christ die for these? The paradox was beyond comprehension, where reason gave way to faith. If God was making this experiment to see if He should populate the universe, the stain on the Petrie dish must be discouraging at best.

The night was clear, with all the elemental powers at hand. The blackout helped. In the harbor all was darkness, and the island seemed as one with the sea. The stars were diamond bright and there was not a single light to taint the firmament save a slim young moon.

When he turned from the telescope she was standing on the adjoining balcony, his neighbor of the face cream and the unblemished torso. She was dressed as though she, too, had returned from a party; barelegged but in heels, an open necked blouse, a skirt slit to mid-thigh to accommodate, he supposed, the heat of the tropics. Beneath tidily clipped hair she wore large circular earrings, white, in contrast to her flawless tan. From her wrists hung matching bracelets, slender and pale in the chalky light of the moon. She was watching him, one hand clutching a bottle of rum, the other planted primly on a hip. A well-formed hip, Christopher noted. She studied him for a moment, a curious half-smile on her lips, then she tilted the bottle and drank deeply. Christopher watched the slide of her throat as the rum ran its course.

"What is it you see?" she asked, embracing the bottle as though it were an infant.

Flustered but not dumbstruck, as with the lady in blue, Christopher pointed to a section of sky. He was about to launch into the arcana of astronomy when she hiked her skirt and climbed unabashedly over the railing. The movement revealed a moonlit sliver of smooth white flesh.

"May I?" she asked, handing him the bottle.

He gestured to the eyepiece. "Yes...yes...but of course..."

She arched her back and placed an eye to the lens. "What is it you are looking for?" she asked, pointing a finger at the sky. "What am I seeing?"

She smelled of perfume and talc.

"...uh...Saturn," Christopher said, his eyes on her back. "It's thousands of miles...." He gestured with a hand then drew it back as it brushed her arm. "...tens of thousands...I mean... it's...it's beyond comprehension...." Feeling uncomfortable with a stilted explanation, he paused and waited for a comment.

"It looks so near," she said. She raised up and looked him in the eye. "You are making a joke on me, monsieur?"

"I assure you I am not," he said meekly."

She returned to the telescope.

He pointed out Orion's Belt, some other constellations.

"It's all so mysterious," she said. "So beautiful. What happens to them in the daytime?" She glanced up at him.

He realized she was serious. "They...they don't move. They remain fixed. We move. Where they are, there is no day. No night."

"How can that be?" she asked, reaching for the rum.

He handed her the bottle. She took a short breathless swig and handed it back.

"What we know as night is...it's...it's a cone of darkness," he explained. "It's merely the earth's shadow... the shadow the earth casts as it revolves around the sun."

"Out there," she said, pointing to the star-studded sky. "That's merely our shadow?"

"More or less," he said sheepishly.

She turned rain-colored eyes under long slender lashes. "For one so young, you are a learned man, monsieur."

As she bent back over the lens, he found himself examining her suntanned shoulders, the downy hair at the base of her neck, the smooth landscape of skin over flesh. There was a slight red weal on one of her shoulders. It looked suspiciously like a suck mark.

"May I ask your name, mademoiselle."

"Lillette," she said without looking up. "Lillette Bonnier. From Nice."

"And you have come to Martinique to...."

She glanced up at him. "To make my *nichet*. My nest egg."

He handed her the rum. For an instant, words escaped him.

She smiled and shrugged. "There are few white women in the islands, and the military are far from home. It's patriotic, no?" She swallowed from the bottle and handed it back. "And you, monsieur? What is your name?"

Christopher Delon."

"You are very handsome, Christopher Delon. Are you an entertainer? An actor, perhaps?" She raised a hand toward the contour of his cheek.

He flinched and took an involuntary step backward.

She giggled. "I won't harm you, Christopher Delon."

She traced a finger along the edge of his brow. He felt the heat in her veins. She had the face of a cherub and the body of a courtesan. Try as he might to avoid it, he was beset by a vision of her sprawled on the sheets as naked as God made her while a sweating *poilu* breathed gouts of passion in her ear. She turned to face him and the vision died aborning.

"And what of the earth," she asked. "Can we penetrate the shadows of the earth with this tube?"

He returned to the telescope and lowered the lens to sea level. When she bent to adjust the eyepiece, he studied the weal again. It was definitely a suck mark.

She scanned the harbor. Sighting on a ship, she reached out with her fingertips as if to touch it. Christopher thought she seemed guileless, as artless as a child. Her talcum smelled of lilac. A popular joke among the bureaucrats was that the *putains* on Martinique were from Guadeloupe and vice versa. Surely this fetching young beauty would never grace the chambers of a bordello. At best she would be a butterfly of the night, not a common whore.

The moon was bathing the rooftops in a soft white glow. As the echoes of a waltz drifted serenely from the High Commissioner's mansion, the night seemed to wash around him. He edged hesitantly toward his room.

"It's late, mademoiselle. I have an early appointment. If you like, I can place the telescope on your balcony."

"Tomorrow is Sunday," she said. "Do you find me a bore, monsieur?"

Her low-cut blouse revealed the well between her breasts. He felt the color rise warmly to his cheeks.

"Very well," she said, sipping from the bottle again. "We'll be friends. You'll be my friend Christopher, and I'll be your friend Lillette."

He fumbled with the telescope. "I'm...I'm somewhat weary, that's all."

He looked hard into her eyes and came up against a wall of indifference. "Bon nuit, friend Christopher," she said, a bit petulantly. "I shall retire with my rum."

As she stepped back over the railing, the bottle at her bosom, her legs bronzed by moonlight, he could not help but notice the skirt drawing tightly over her thighs. As he turned to look away, he caught a fleeting glimpse of silk, white fringed in pink.

Back in his room, he doused his face at the basin. He shed his clothes and sprawled on the bed. As he lay staring at the darkness, he could hear movement beyond the wall. He lay there for what seemed like hours, a ladder of moonlight on a shutter, the sea shimmering faintly on the ceiling. Gradually the sounds from her apartment ceased and the night grew quiet. Was she asleep, or was she too staring at the ceiling? Was she listening to the silence as he was, or was she deep in the slumber of the righteous? As he lay there in darkness, his thoughts fell on the universe, his suspended vows, her endless legs, the attack on Sedan, the High Commissioner's ball, a fleeting glimpse of pink.

THE FOLLOWING DAY

DEC. 7 1941

ST. THOMAS

U.S. VIRGIN ISLANDS

Oberleutnant Viktor Reinmann sat bolt upright in the hut. A thunderous roar seemed to come from nowhere. For an instant he thought he was back in the U-Boat, that they had struck a mine or were being depth-charged. It took a second to realize he was on the island. When the noise diminished, he recognized the receding drone of a patrol plane.

The Americans had a squadron on St. Thomas. He must be just below the flight path.

He lay back against the rotting floorboards. Light filtered dimly through a crack in the wall, etching a ribbon of sunlight against the weathered ceiling. He pushed to his knees and peered through the crack. The sun was a fried egg on the horizon, but already the shack was hot. He had slept fitfully, his inner ear mocking the motion of the sea. His mouth felt dry and there was a throbbing at his temples. He remained on his knees until the engines were a distant echo, until there was only the cry of a seabird. He had slept with his clothes on. Uncertain as to what he might encounter at first light, he had kept his Luger beside him in a pocket of his gripsack. He took a few tentative steps and the rigidity of earth had him swaying for balance. He propped a hand against a wall and steadied himself.

The hut was a ramshackle affair that looked as though it went back to the Danish occupation. It was enough to keep him out of the rain, but not much else. He and Casey had discovered it years before on a slope overlooking Magen's Bay. They decided it had been built by a fisherman as a retreat from the bustle of the seaport. Shrouded by foliage, it was virtually invisible from the beaches below. The roof seemed intact, but the floorboards had all but rotted away. What passed for a door was torn from its hinges, and the windows had been boarded over. In one corner there was an ancient pot stove; on the wall opposite a small green lizard clung tenaciously to the rotting window frame, its pop-eyes fixed unblinkingly on the intruder.

When finally he stepped into the sunlight, he winced. Dazzled by the lazulite splendor of the sea, he braced himself against the door frame and waited for his eyes to adjust. The hut was situated on a leeward slope and the jungle was a veritable hothouse. The hills were clad in a vapory mist and there was the sweet warm smell of vegetation. Even the breeze was hot. He relieved himself against a tree and wondered why, when given the choice, men, like dogs, will choose something upright.

To loosen his joints he fell into knee bends, slowly at first, then picking up speed as equilibrium returned. He worked up a thirst and returned to the hut for a long satisfying pull from his canteen. Its metallic taste reminded him of the U-Boat. Feeling steadier, and refreshed by the water, he walked outside and collected some brush. He opted against dry-shaving; he'd had enough of that at sea. Instead, he heated some water on the pot stove. At the first dry crackle of flames the lizard scuttled smartly through a crack in the wall. For the first time in weeks he shaved with his feet on solid ground, manipulating the cutthroat razor in a small metallic handmirror. That done, he stripped to his shorts and a pair of well-worn sneakers.

He decided to forego the rations he had brought from the U-Boat. Instead, he plucked a grapefruit from a tree and stripped it of its skin. For drink he could catch the rainwater that fell like clockwork every afternoon. His Bavarian skin turned crimson before it tanned, so the first order of business would be to take some sun. When he had gained some color, he could find a more permanent base of operations, perhaps in the seaman's quarter of Charlotte Amalie. From there he would look up the contact who would brief him on the activity in the islands.

In the interim, he would see Casey.

He found an outcropping with a view of the cove. In the soft morning mist the sea was a palette of light blues and greens, darker blues and greys. Far out to sea the pendant islands were purpling in the haze. He sprawled on the boulder and closed his eyes. The sun lay like a hot iron on his chest. He breathed in the murky scent of the jungle. A shadow brushed his face and he glanced upward to see a seagull gliding on a thermal, its neck craning seaward in search of a meal.

On the far side of the mountain another aircraft was preparing for takeoff. He could hear the run-up of the engines, the surge of power as it roared down the runway. As the plane cleared a nearby peak, it came suddenly into view...a Catalina flying boat. Viktor could make out the insignia on the fuselage, a blue star in a white field... United States Navy. Though he was barely a speck in the jungle, he slid from the boulder to the shade of a tree. When the aircraft banked seaward, he settled back on the boulder.

To reach Charlotte Amalie he would need transport. The roads were hilly, and few were paved. He would hike the hills, find a village, and steal a bicycle. Once near town he could stash the bike and manage a mile or so on foot.

He tried to envision the quay where he and Casey had met. The memory came easily; he had re-assembled it over and over again on the Atlantic crossing. She had been sixteen. It was the spring of 1938. He had been touring the islands, courtesy of the Kriegsmarine, he and a fellow cadet now somewhere on the northern seas. They had sailed the entire Leeward chain from Antigua to St. Thomas. When the leggy teenager with freckled cheeks and copper-colored hair came strolling down the embankment at Charlotte Amalie, their sloop was tied to the quay. Viktor was hosing the deck. He was deeply tanned, his skin conditioned by Alpine slopes, his body hard from weeks at sail and helm. The tan gave depth to his agate eyes, a gleam to his strong white teeth. He had called to her from the boat. His English was good even then.

"Your hair! It's beautiful!"

He saw the color rise to her cheeks. Their eyes met briefly, and she looked away. But he had staked his claim; he sensed it.

He jumped ashore. The quay was all but empty.

Her pace slowed, but she continued on.

“Don’t run,” he laughed. “I’ve been far too long on that rolling boat. My legs are like seaweed.”

To his delight, she stopped and turned to face him. He was taken by her abundant red hair, her sea green eyes.

“Are you Danish?” she asked.

“German. Would you like to see the boat? Come. I’m about to take breakfast. Have some coffee.”

“I don’t care for coffee, thank you.”

Viktor feigned a limp. “I don’t either. I drink tea. Wait. My leg....”

She hesitated, unable to squelch a grin.

He dropped to one knee, clutched painfully at an ankle.

Her grin grew to a smile. The smile broadened and she giggled.

With a gesture of supplication, he beckoned her aboard.

“I’m on my way to church,” she said.

He rolled to his back on the pavement. Squirming as in pain, he clutched the ankle again. Despite herself, she laughed. He groaned and she laughed again.

“Tea, he moaned. “A spot of tea. The doctor claims it helps the knee...”

As though weighing her alternatives, she looked up the quay. Then boldly, as though it was no decision at all, she strolled casually back and stepped blithely into the cockpit.

“Tea would be nice, thank you.”

He vaulted to his feet and leaped nimbly aboard. Catching Viktor’s glance, his sailing companion muttered something unintelligible then jumped ashore and strolled casually up the quay.

Viktor managed tea on a heating coil while Casey explored the sloop.

“So.” he said. “You live on St. Thomas?”

“I was born here. My mother...she teaches school on the island.”

“And your mother? She has red hair too?”

“Yes.... She’s English. Part English and part Danish.”

Viktor handed her a pitted porcelain cup. "Your father is in business here also?"

"He's out to sea. He's Navy."

She tasted the brew. It was strong. Try as she might to avoid it, she pulled a face.

He snatched the cup from her fingers and tilted it over the side. "The first pancake is never any good," he said. "I'll make another."

She laughed again, genuinely this time. She was easily amused. He liked that. "And you?" she asked. "Where are you from?"

"I was born in Freiburg," he said. "At the edge of the Black Forest. My parents own an apartment above a hofbrauhaus. I was raised on *wurst* and *spaetzle*. You know *spaetzle?*

"No."

"It's like noodles. My mother says it's where I get my blond hair. You're on your way to church, you say. The first sounds I remember were church bells. Our apartment was directly across from the cathedral."

"I love bells," she said. "The island rings with them on Sunday mornings. We should hear them any minute now."

***

On the boulder near the abandoned hut, Oberleutnant Viktor Reinmann rolled slowly to his chest and let the sun beat hotly on his back. The rays were strong, the sunshine penetrating the marrow of his bones. He must be careful not to overdo it. Either Casey was free or she was not, he thought. If she was free, there was no hurry. If not, it would not matter.

Another aircraft was revving on the runway.

From the opposite side of the mountain, he heard the peal of bells.

Appropriate, he thought. Another Sunday.

So hot was the hillside that he had trouble believing it was December.

The seventh of December.

December 7, 1941.

CHARLOTTE AMALIE, ST. THOMAS

Dante O'Shea sat nursing a hair of the dog in the cockpit of Geoffrey Blake's schooner, an island veteran that had seen better days. At his feet two dachshund puppies were rolling and tumbling and nipping at one another's ears. Dante had left his uniforms at the base laundry. He was wearing chinos and a tropical bush jacket he had picked up in North Africa. His host was seated on the stern sheets stirring a fruit drink laced heavily with gin. The Englishman was sporting white sailing ducks and a gaudy print shirt. On the foredeck laying face up on a hatch, the Contessa was absorbing her yearly ration of sun. Clad in a black bathing suit and dark sunglasses, she had combed her anthracite-slick hair beneath the folds of a turban and lotioned her skin to an oily sheen. From time to time she rolled to a hip to sip from a straw buried deep in a frothy pink drink.

Dante felt buoyed. He and Casey had come a long way the night before, and for the first time in months he had a renewed sense of family. Reconciled with his daughter and with the sea at his elbow, he felt as relaxed as he had in months.

The DEVON STAR was secured to a dock near the center of town. Ashore a scattering of locals and military were strolling the streets and doing the shops. Though the island was bathed in sunlight, a few miles to the east the sky was dark, the clouds low and heavy with the prospect of rain.

Geoffrey Blake tilted a well-worn yachting cap to the back of his head. "It wouldn't surprise me, Captain, if that submarine you think you saw out there yesterday was German. U-Boats have been spotted south of Bermuda and the Bahamas."

Dante sipped gingerly at his second drink of the morning.

Mindful that the day was young, he had insisted on three parts water, one part scotch, just enough to conjure the mists of the moors.

"I suppose it's only a matter of time before they work their way down here, Geoffrey. It's no big secret your Royal Navy is spread rather thin. If the Krauts can muster a few long-range subs, the tanker route through the Caribbean looks an irresistible target."

"Nice of you chaps to send us those destroyers," Blake said.

"If you're referring to the fifty tin cans Mr. Roosevelt swapped in exchange for some bases out here, there's more to that than meets the eye, Geoff. Couldn't be your Mr. Churchill leased us those bases hoping we'd get suckered into this thing, could it?"

Blake laughed. "He's cagy. Make no mistake. But I doubt the Germans would accommodate him. They've got their hands full with the Russkies right now."

Dante sipped at the scotch and wished he had forgone the water. "What of Nazi spies? One would think these islands would be infested with undercover agents. Venezuela and Argentina are seething with German sympathizers."

Blake scooped both dachshunds onto his lap. "They've been rounding up German aliens on Jamaica. Nailed a few on Aruba and Curacao, too."

"And what of you, Geoff? How do you tie into this thing?"

"Some of my trawlers have been commandeered for coastal patrol. From a distance they look innocent enough, but they're fitted out to take on a U-Boat. We're to hold this area safe from infiltration. Another debacle like Scapa Flow, or, heaven forbid, a German invasion of the home island, and the Royal Navy may have to take refuge down here."

"Much like the French warships at Martinique," Dante said. "I saw the best of them on our flight in yesterday. Speaking of the French Antilles, I understand His Majesty's government sent a contingent of diplomats to Martinique in the wake of France's surrender. Tried to talk the High Commissioner into letting the British take control of their islands out here."

"And rudely rebuffed we were, I must say."

"Hard to blame them, Geoff. After your Navy sank the bulk of their fleet in North Africa, it's a wonder they didn't greet you with a broadside."

"Off the subject, Captain, your daughter is delightful."

"Thanks. I'll have to get used to the looks she draws. She's only twenty, but she's matured a lifetime since I saw her last."

"Twenty. Scarcely out of nappies," Blake said, in his plummy British accent.

"Dante. Dante O'Shea. It's an intriguing name. Father Irish, I take it."

"And mother Italian."

And your wife was...?"

"Danish and English."

"Powerful combination, Captain. No wonder your daughter is such a stunner."

From the cabin below came the sweet big band harmonies of Glenn Miller's "Moonlight Serenade", above it an unintelligible jabber, half-singing, half-humming. Blake's mate, Sugar, was preparing omelettes in the galley. Suddenly the volume increased and the music was interrupted by a deep-throated commentator. Sugar's head popped up from the cabin. "Mistah Blake! D'radio...!"

Dante and Blake strained to listen.

"...we repeat, the Japanese have attacked Pearl Harbor in Hawaii from the air..."

The men stared blankly at one another. On the foredeck, the Contessa rose to a sitting position and removed her sunglasses. Dante had planned to spend the balance of the day with Casey. The following morning he was scheduled to fly to Havana to meet with the Commander of the Caribbean Coastal Frontier. Suddenly the holiday was over. Not a plan had been made in the entire military establishment that would not be changed in the next twenty-four hours.

For a few seconds the trio sat stunned at the news.

Blake broke the silence. "A sneak attack. And with their ambassador talking peace in Washington. Slanty-eyed sods..."

Dante pushed to his feet. He downed the balance of his drink and crouched at the hatch while the bulletin was repeated. Along the quay the news was spreading fast. A crowd had gathered near a shop which had turned up its radio. The few American military Dante could see were jogging toward the Marine base west of town.

Dante walked astern and shook the Englishman's hand. "Thanks for the hospitality, Geoff. And the scotch." He turned back to the foredeck. The Contessa was making her way down a ladder. Extending a hand, Dante helped her into the cockpit. She stretched to her toes and kissed his cheek.

"Adio, mon ami," she said, giving him her deep dark eyes. "*Bon chance.*"

Dante stepped ashore. Blake turned and tossed him a final salute, snapping his fingers to the peak of his cap as smartly as any sergeant major. "Cheeribye, Yank. You're in it now. You're in it up to your scuppers."

Dante tossed him a soft return, then turned and strode up the quay. Suddenly it began to rain, large pulpy drops that splattered the cobblestones and dotted the swells rolling steadily into the harbor. The wind gusted harshly, rocking the boats at their moorings and nudging the squall line ashore. Dante paused at a quayside shop beneath a dilapidated awning. The scudding rain drummed heavily on the canvas, its edges leaking as freely as a sieve. He looked back at the DEVON STAR, its Union Jack flapping in the breeze, Blake standing arms akimbo in the cockpit, the rain soaking his yachting cap, the flowery shirt pasted wetly to his chest.

It seems Mr. Churchill has gotten his wish, Dante thought. Perhaps it was inevitable after all.

FORTE DE FRANCE, MARTINIQUE

Christopher Delon awoke with an erection. Lying on his back in his harborside apartment, he was aware of the press of his member against the threadbare sheet. The dream was slow to fade. He was swimming underwater and he was naked. Sun was filtering from the surface and the sea felt warm against his thighs. Ahead he could see a woman's legs scissoring in shimmering sunlight. Except for panties, the woman, too, was naked. The panties were fringed in pink. She was a strong swimmer. No matter how forcefully he engaged the current, she managed to maintain her distance.

There was the rumble of a truck below his balcony. Lying damp and inert beneath the flimsy sheet, he stretched full length and in the flutter of an eyelid the swimmer evaporated. As he swam to the surface of consciousness, he tried to ignore the blatant pyramid formed by the bedclothes. Dawn was clawing at the shutters, scratching pale grey streaks on the ceiling and walls. Rapidly, as though melted by the sun, his erection faded. Had something in his consciousness killed it, or like a vampire, had it perished with the dawn?

He listened for a sound from beyond the wall. Silence. From deep in the harbor he heard the thrum of an inboard. It was Sunday. A garbage scow, perhaps, servicing one of the warships.

He sat on the bed and pulled on his trousers. With the telescope and tripod occupying the few square meters of open space, the room felt cramped. Sleepy-eyed and bare-chested, he shuffled to the double French doors and stepped barefoot onto the balcony. A blue dawn was coloring a calm sea. It was barely six a.m., but already the mist was burning from the hills. Heat was rising from the pavement below and the sea lay as flat as a lake. Ships were scattered about the harbor like flies on a mirror...men-of-war, tankers, merchantmen, trawlers. The high-masted warships lay serenely at anchor, their prows pointed seaward, their riding lights pale and ominous in the encroaching dawn. A camouflaged gunboat was edging slowly toward the breakwater at Fort St. Louis. Christopher could see a lookout poised in the bow.

On the terrace adjacent to his, a makeshift clothesline had been stretched between the railings. On it were pinned a blouse and a slip; between them, the pink-fringed panties.

Christopher shaved in a porcelain basin then showered at the end of the hall. Sunday. What was it, the seventh? Yes. The seventh of December. He laid out his white tropical suit and a pale blue shirt. Knotting a necktie beneath the soft yielding collar, he felt a sudden emptiness, a draining of the spirit. Now that he had foresworn his dog collar and frock, he had not said Mass for more than a year. Try as he would, he could not push the guilt of it from his mind. Was he afraid to risk it? Was it that he might find solace in the Sacrament? Or that he might not. He could manage the deed right here in his room. Alone. Somehow it seemed wrong. Belief should accompany ceremony.

He arranged the bedclothes and checked for stains on the bed sheets. There were none.

Chez Rosette was only a short uphill walk from his hotel. The food was a bit more expensive than in the cafes near the Savanne, but he favored it for its view. Like his apartment, the dining area was on an upper floor, and it featured a terrace overlooking the bay.

The walk to the restaurant took him past St-Louis Cathedral. There was a lull between Masses, so on an impulse he climbed the steps and pushed through a heavy wooden door. In the cool twilight of the interior there were the familiar smells of incense and tallow, the flicker of votives in red and amber glass. The nave was deep and spacious, the ceiling vaulted and laced by girders. Long wooden pews flanked the broad open aisles, and confessionals flanked the stony rear walls. An ornately carved pulpit stood just beyond the communion railing, a pipe organ to the left of the altar. On stained-glass windows were scenes of Joseph the Carpenter and an adolescent Jesus carrying wood. A statue of the Madonna stared down from an elevated marble pedestal.

He knelt in a pew and uttered a prayer. It did not come easily. Feeling trapped and hypocritical in the dark womb of the cathedral, he crossed himself then rose and descended to the freedom of the street. Night lingered in the alleyways. Near the quay, some vendors were preparing for the morning market. There were strollers in the Savanne and the village was coming to life.

At Chez Rosette, he climbed the long narrow stairway and paused at the top to let his eyes adjust. The interior was dark, but beyond the terrace the sea was sparkling in sunlight. Though the air was stirred by overhead fans, there was an odor of baked fish, of fried plantains. There was an early-morning stillness to the room, the kind one remembers of pre-dawn lobbies in Europe. An inner room featured a bar with rough-hewn stools and a thatched roof. There was seating on the terrace overhanging the street. Christopher preferred the terrace. It could be shaded by an awning and there was usually a breeze. The waitress recognized him and led him to a table overlooking the harbor. On the slightly stained tablecloth a single red hibiscus drooped forlornly from an empty Perrier bottle. The flower was small, its fragrance faint. Christopher passed it beneath his nose. After the waxy scents of the cathedral, it offered a welcome reprise. Sunlight shimmered on the bay. So hurtful was the glare that he turned to divert his eyes. He had misplaced his sunglasses; he would have to purchase another pair. On the promontory south of town the battlements of Fort St. Louis were aquiver with heat, while in the apartments along the quay people were preparing for the Sabbath behind partially-closed shutters.

Christopher turned his attention to the restaurant. The previous evening's s menu was chalked in yellow on a blackboard over the bar:

Couscous Maison
Tripes à la Provençale
Filet de Saumon Grill é
Fillet de Saumon Meunière

A native couple sat talking at a nearby table, she in a saffron dress, he in a striped seersucker suit. They were leaning across the table and smiling warmly at one another. When the woman spoke, the man seemed to listen intently. They gestured with animated hands, and both were laughing freely. Suddenly Christopher felt alone, as lonely as he had felt in his life. When the waitress arrived he ordered his usual, a sugar-dusted roll and *cafe au lait*. While waiting for the coffee, he smoked a cigarette.

A pair of gendarmes appeared at the top of the stairs, their tan shirts and tailored shorts crisp and freshly laundered, their *kepis* squared smartly over keen observant eyes. Christopher thought they looked immune to the heat, as though the uniforms granted special dispensation. Even the armpits of their tunics looked free of perspiration. They glanced over the room as though searching for someone in particular, nodded to the proprietor, who had materialized from a back room, then evaporated down the stairwell as quietly as they had arrived.

From the direction of the Savanne came the brassy peal of bells, the matin bells of the cathedral. The belfries of Martinique offered a sonorous chime, Christopher noted, not the sepulchral tolling of the cathedrals of France.

He was on his second coffee when his neighbor of the pink fringe appeared at the head of the stairwell. She was wearing a summery white skirt and a filmy mauve blouse. The skirt was knee length, the blouse as diaphanous as mist. To compliment the blouse she wore a floppy mauve hat. Without makeup she looked luminously youthful. As she stood there, pausing as he had to let her eyes adjust to the dimness, a shaft of light from the stairwell silhouetted her lean shapely figure. The effect was more provocative than if she had been naked.

She spotted him on the terrace and immediately strolled over.

"Bonjour, my friend Christopher," she said, removing her hat. "I see you favor this view also. It reminds me of Nice."·

Christopher stood and pulled out a chair. He could smell her hair, almond toasted by the sun. "Please," he said. "Join me."

She sat and rummaged through her purse. Extracting a small porcelain mirror, she pinched lightly at her cheeks. Christopher offered her a cigarette. She pressed it lightly between pouty lips. Fearful that his hands might tremble, Christopher lit the tobacco with fingers cupped tightly around a match. She ordered *cafe noir.* When it arrived, they exchanged trivialities. Try as he might to avoid it, Christopher was drawn to the swell of her breasts, the indent at the base of her throat. It was as though she generated a current of sexuality. She met his eyes and smiled coyly. Despite the heat, he felt a shiver course the length of his body. The waitress turned the handle of the awning until their table was in the shade.

The man in the seersucker suit got up to leave. Having seen to the check, he bent to kiss his companion's cheek. When he disappeared down the stairwell, the woman resumed her breakfast alone, the pulpy juice of orange-yellow mangoes.

"I have a car," Lillette said, as casually as though they had been discussing it for hours. "On loan from a friend. I have never seen the mountain Pelée. Would you drive with me?"

If she remembered his excuse of the night before, his early appointment, she was not so indelicate as to remind him.

The volcanic Pelée dominated the entire northern end of the island, looming large over the landscape near the town of St-Pierre. As she wheeled the ancient roadster through the rutted coastal roads, Christopher could feel the troubling proximity of her thigh. He studied his new-found neighbor as he would a star in the firmament. Gazelle-eyed, and with her hair blowing freely in the wind, she was intense and animated. Like a child on holiday, she pointed excitedly to every change of scenery with a flurry of exclamation that left little room for comment.

For one day, Christopher decided, he would forget his fall from grace. He was no longer a priest. He had foresworn his vows, if unofficially, and no one from his past knew where he was. He had left no letter, no word, no hint of where he had gone with the single exception of a note to his mother. He was alive, the note assured. He would explain his disappearance when events permitted. Whatever the outcome, he was resolved to fight his battle alone, out of reach of family, of clergy, or of papal influence. This was his retreat to the desert, his search for resolve, for his immortal soul. The battle for self was fought where one found it, he believed. In the hedgerows of France, or here, on this tranquil island beside this child of the night. As the roadster scaled the rocky heights, he spotted a warship patrolling off the coast. From this distance, it looked like a toy, like one of the miniatures sailed by children in the playgrounds of Paris.

"It's American," Christopher said, pointing beyond the windscreen.

Lillette allowed a fleeting glance, then returned her attention to the road.

"It's curious about the Americans," Christopher said. They're sympathetic to our plight, yet the islanders resent them. They're blamed for the food shortage, yet they're the only nation sending supplies. And now they have frozen French assets. They won't release any money to the Bank of Martinique until our glorious High Commissioner accedes to a list of demands."

Lillette returned an indifferent smile.

Politics, Christopher decided, was not her *metier.*

The road turned inland and the terrain changed abruptly. Within minutes they were entering the foothills. Ahead lay the rain forest, a lush green universe of trees and vegetation that clung to the flanks of the mountain.

"Look!," Lillette screeched. A *Pitt*!"

So heavily did she stomp the brake that the priest-in-exile jammed a wrist against the windscreen.

At the side of the road, a potbellied attendant in a battered straw hat and a two-day beard rose sluggishly from a dilapidated chair. He was chewing on a wedge of papaya. Behind him, shrouded by thick jungle foliage, stood the gates to a shambling arena. As

Lillette stepped smiling from the car, the eyes beneath the hat rolled lazily to the line of her leg. When Lillette smoothed her skirt, the man nodded deferentially to Christopher.

"You are much too early for the fight, monsieur. But if you would like to see...." his finger pointed beyond a rickety fence while his dark ferret eyes surveyed Lillette's anatomy as though she were a morsel for his prize mongoose.... "I would be happy to show you the *combatants*."

"Yes. Please." Lillette said, grasping Christopher's arm. He felt an urgency in the clutch of her fingers. Their host, he noticed, was more concerned with the breeze teasing playfully at her skirt.

The *Pitt* was a shabby affair, a dirt arena surrounded by tiered wooden slabs that served as benches. Beyond a barrier at the rear of the arena were the cages. In most of the cages were mongoose and snakes, fighting cocks from Cuba, cocks from Spain.

"The snakes have no ears," their guide explained, his eyes rolling hungrily between the venomous coils and the bodice of Lillette's blouse. "They can't hear. They react to"....he paused, raised a fist, then thumped the top of a cage.

The coils sprang to life, heads erect, tongues flicking, necks as rigid as lead pipes. As the snakes swayed warily in search of an intruder, Lillette shrieked. Christopher felt the bite of fingernails through the fabric of his jacket, the softness of a breast against an elbow.

The guide exposed a row of small carious teeth. "And over here," he said, pleased with Lillette's reaction, "the *adversaries.*"

A mongoose, sleek and sinuous, paced a low wire cage, its body flowing restlessly over the ribbed wooden slats, its jowls pulled back over needle-sharp teeth. Christopher thought it looked anxious to get on with the game.

The fighting cocks were varied and mean-looking. In a far corner, the guide dramatically stripped the covering from an oversized cage. "The current champion," he said, expanding his feral grin. "From Madrid."

The gesture elicited the desired reaction. Lillette sucked in a gasp of air and clutched Christopher's sleeve in a vise-like grip. Aroused, the cock began strutting his domain. With one eye missing and his head jerking haughtily with each arrogant stride, he strut his stage as proudly as any gladiator. The guide, Christopher noticed, was enjoying the play of breasts beneath his companion's gauzy blouse.

"Before the fight," the guide said, "his spurs will be tipped with steel."

As they moved from cage to cage, Christopher could feel the ghost of Lillette's bosom on his elbow. As she stared wide-eyed at each and every *coq-de-combat*, twice going back to the one-eyed champion, he wondered at her reaction to their macabre strut of death.

Later, in the village of St-Pierre, they viewed the heights of Pelée from an outdoor cafe. Far above the town the hills were hung with the thinnest of mists. After sharing an indifferent omelette and a *petit punch*, Lillette insisted they walk the streets. The air was hot and humid. There was a sheen of perspiration where her blouse met her neck. Anxious to keep the discussion impersonal, and haunted by her phantom touch, Christopher dredged up the few historical tidbits he remembered.

"Before Pelée erupted," he said, "Ste-Pierre was considered the Paris of the Antilles. The volcano, of course, was the creation of subterranean fire. From the eruption in 1902 that claimed 30,000 lives, a single man survived, a prisoner in a local jail."

Lillette listened attentively, staring wide-eyed at the lava-encrusted ruins as though transported by his words to the event itself. To Christopher she seemed guileless. Innocent. A far cry from the plumed predator that had alighted his balcony the night before. Part of her appeal, he decided, sprang from a coarse vitality. She was seldom at rest, from the batting of her llama lashes to the darting insistence of her lively fingers.

"How sad," she said, gazing at the truncated walls and charred volcanic sands, still black forty years after the catastrophe. "And the entire town was levelled?"

"When God eats," Christopher said, "He cleans the plate."

On the drive back to Forte de France, they heard the news of Pearl Harbor on the car radio.

"America will come into the war now," Christopher said, remembering the patrolling destroyer. "Perhaps now the tide will turn. Perhaps now France will be liberated."

"War is good for business," Lillette countered blandly.

Back in his room at the Hotel de la Paix, Christopher lay brooding on his bed. He pondered the destruction of St-Pierre, the combatants in the cages at the *Pitt*, the beguiling creature beyond the wall, the outbreak of war in the Pacific.

A door closed. He heard the click of heels in the corridor.

Darkness had fallen.

She was going out.

To return the car.

And the favor?

He stared blankly at the ceiling. He was in desperate need. Where to begin? He remembered the lady doctor. She seemed wise. Sympathetic. Ste-Anne was isolated, she had said. Restful.

Perhaps the answer lay in solitude. Far from the warriors and the weapons. Far from this solitary cell with the temptations beyond the wall. They had something in common, he and the lady doctor. Something he would have to face if he was to begin again. He was in need of a friend, someone who could share his secret, offer some advice, some intimacy, perhaps. Without understanding, without love, life was an uphill plod to the grave.

He suffered a spasm of derision. Of self-contempt. How could he be so selfish? So myopic? He was alive. In Paradise. He had the island, the sun, his health. What would others give for a day such as he had passed?

What of those who had nothing left to give?

He jammed a pillow beneath his head and closed his eyes.

In May of 1940, Dunkirk the beach was indistinguishable from Dunkirk the city. Smoke. That was the overriding impression. Smoke blotting the ruins, smoke blanketing the dunes, smoke obscuring the harbor and the ships. It was a blessing of sorts. With the pall of smoke from smoldering tank farms and burning ships, the bombers could not see their targets. The Luftwaffe was at the mercy of the winds. On the morning Christopher arrived there was very little wind, so the bombers were seeking other game.

Retreating with the refugees from Sedan, Christopher had spent long and arduous days on roads crammed with retiring troops and fleeing civilians. Most secondary roads were clogged, the routes strewn with abandoned vehicles, horse-drawn carts, broken troops, broken spirits and broken dreams. Some of the roadways were pitted by bullets from strafing dive bombers. Occasionally, one would come across a tank stripped of its treads. In the quiet intervals, people were drinking their best cognac so as not to leave it for the invaders. After strafings by German dive bombers, sleepless nights in hostile landscapes, pleas for food, for medicine, for roadside confessions and prayers for the dead, the young priest arrived at Dunkirk on the fourth day of the siege. The port was in chaos. Dunkirk had been an industrial shipping center. Situated on the Straits of Dover between French Calais and the Belgian frontier, it lay a mere thirty miles from the British coastline. In the few short days since the German invasion of the lowlands, its beaches had been transformed into a death trap by encircling German armies. When Christopher arrived from Sedan, Dunkirk was besieged from air and land. Almost 400,000 men, the entire British Expeditionary Force and the northern contingent of the French Army, were trapped on its beaches. And more men were arriving every day. French. British. Belgian. Dutch.

For days on end ships of every size and shape had been braving the harbor, running the gauntlet of German dive bombers and shuttling from England's Devon coast in an heroic attempt to evacuate the trapped and dispirited armies. While the French were manning the perimeters to fend off the German attackers, the British were shipping their forces back to England in every type of vessel available.

Christopher took refuge in the basement of the church of Ste-Martin. Though its windows were shattered and its doors unhinged, the church was miraculously unharmed. A priest no older than himself was saying Mass on the morning he arrived.

"Where can I be of help?" Christopher asked.

The local priest pointed to the beaches. "Out there."

Christopher departed that very night, feeling his way along the dunes south of the port, trusting in God to take him where he could do some good. Everywhere he looked there were men... hundreds and thousands of men...ragtag regiments of British, pockets of French, cadres of Dutch, hordes of Belgians. They were hunkered behind dunes, strung along moles, cowering in craters, slumped together in groups, gathering every inch of cover from the withering onslaught of German shellfire.

In the darkness before dawn he came upon the wounded, a group of new arrivals from Lille, where the fighting had been heavy. Beneath a grimy moon, shrunken and sallow in the charry sky, he slumped against a dune to catch his breath. From beyond the dune came the murmur of surf, the sucking draw of the sea. He had been there for a full two minutes before he realized there was someone beside him.

"Cigarette?" a voice asked. "Do you have a cigarette?"

Christopher dug the last of his Gauloise from a pocket of his tunic. Pinching it in the middle, he held the larger half out to the voice beside him.

The voice did not respond.

"Take it," Christopher said. "It's all I have."

"You must...you will have to help me," the voice said. The voice was husky. Frightened. "I can't see. My eyes...."

Christopher propped himself on an elbow. He strained to penetrate the darkness. A shadow shifted on the sand. The shadow had a face. It was the face of a boy. He could be no more than seventeen. His forehead was slimy with sweat, his hands twitching fitfully with the palsy of fear.

Christopher lit the cigarette with a wooden match. In the glow of the flame, the eyes did not flinch, the lashes did not blink. He inserted the cigarette between parched and swollen lips.

"What's your name," he asked.

"Jacques," the voice said. "My name is Jacques."

Propped against a pillow in his apartment on Martinique, Christopher could see the moon floating serenely over a dead calm sea. An alabaster moon, free of smoke or grime.

It was time to confront his phantoms.

He would visit the woman doctor.

It was as good a place to begin as any.

MID-ATLANTIC

In the minutes before sunset, the Italian submarine SQUALO was butting the swells in the frigid north Atlantic. With the sea dancing wildly around him, Ensign Aldo Arazi stood on the pitching, tossing bridge in rubber pants and an oiled-canvas coat with his safety belt clipped securely to the railing. He was in the final minutes of his watch, binoculars pressed firmly to his brow, his knees and elbows sore from chafing against the rigid steel coaming. He had drawn the troublesome sun sector. In the past half hour the cold pallid disc seemed frozen in space a few degrees above the horizon. Behind him on the bridge stood three other officers, one of them Commander Valerio Martucci, his cap tugged tightly over his brow, the collar of his oilskin raised casually against the cold as though strolling a wintry beach. Aldo noticed that, despite his reputation as a womanizer, the skipper was wearing the scarf his wife had given him as a birthday present.

They were six days out of Bordeaux. That very afternoon they had passed up a vulnerable merchant ship. Orders for the crossing prohibited them from firing on any vessel less than 10,000 tons. They were to save their torpedoes for the easier pickings in the Caribbean.

Scanning the sea, ever-changing in its constancy, Aldo sucked in lungfuls of cold bracing air. In the teeth of the wind, his eyes were being reduced to slits. Night was gathering swiftly. In their wake the sky was already dark; ahead, the fiery threads of dusk were beginning to streak the western horizon. At this time of night every shard of cloud conjured a wisp of smoke, every shred of spume the mast of a ship. He would barter his soul for a cigarette. Smoking was not permitted on watch; it was also forbidden to smoke when submerged. When his watch was over he would duck into a storage compartment and smoke four or five cigarettes in succession.

To get his mind off the cold, he tried to envision the Caribbean. Could it be as hospitable as they claimed? It was said that, even in winter, the breeze was as warm as a human breath. The hunting should be easier there. They had been told they could attack on the surface, that few if any of the merchant vessels were armed. The Captain had been serious about the unsuitability of Italian submarines for Atlantic waters. The Royal Submarine Command was catching a good deal of flack for the unwieldy design of its *sommergibili*, most of it from its German counterparts. Some of it was professional scorn, some of it no doubt justified. But while it was true that their oversized conning towers were easier to spot and that their bulkier hulls decreased the speed of the dive, Italian submarines had been designed to fight a defensive war, to submerge and await the approach of enemy shipping, not to pursue zigzagging convoys on the open seas. And while it was true that their fire control systems were primitive compared to those of their German counterparts, Italian crews were just as highly trained, and most had more experience. For the most part, Aldo was immune to criticism. He was proud of his fellow submariners. At the war's outset, Italy boasted the second largest underwater fleet in existence: 115 boats. Only the Russians had more.

When German seamen derided the inadequacy of Italian submarines, Aldo reminded them that the Calvi Class VENIERO was the first to negotiate the Straits of Gibraltar submerged. Despite underwater currents the Germans had termed unmanageable, the VENIERO's captain had braved the deadly whirlpools to slip into the Atlantic and attack enemy shipping. When the Germans sent U-Boats into the Mediterranean the following year, five were lost attempting the passage.

Aldo remembered the naval review honoring Adolph Hitler in the Gulf of Naples in 1938. He had been standing on the deck of a Coast Guard cutter when eighty Italian submarines surfaced simultaneously and fired welcoming salutes. That very night he had volunteered for undersea duty. Shortly thereafter he was sent to the submarine school at La Spezia.

With the SQUALO bucking the heavy seas, Aldo clutched the wind deflector and felt the sting of salt in his eyes. A maverick wave smashed heavily over the bow. The spray felt like crystals of ice against his cheeks. He thought of his shipmates inside the slender hull, most at their posts, some asleep in their bunks, others preparing for the next watch. As a crew they were young, like himself. Buoyed by their escape from Tangier's harbor, they seemed in good spirits and anxious to reach the waters of the western islands. Despite the lack of action on the long Atlantic crossing, there was little fear of tedium setting in. Realizing that monotony was the bane of all mariners, the flinty-eyed Valerio was keeping them on their toes with constant drills. The captain was a stickler for exercise. Only officers stood deck watches, and on the Atlantic crossing enlisted men were rarely permitted beyond their workstations. So when all other options were foreclosed, Valerio had the ratings jog in place. Observing his shipmates carefully, Aldo was beginning to appreciate the benefit of the captain's discipline. Of all the insidious problems that sprang from weeks at sea in a steel cocoon, constipation was one of the worst. With little or no exercise and a limited ration of water, one's bowels compacted for lack of liquids. One of the first things a submariner sought when he returned to base was an enema. An enema and fresh fruit. Cleanliness could be a problem too, but with the SQUALO heading for tropical waters the men would be allowed to shower on deck. And they had real coffee aboard, a brand called "Cheerio". And best of all, the battery room doubled as a wine cellar. There was nothing like the juice of the grape to conjure the vineyards of the Motherland. The men protected the *vino* more assiduously than the food, Aldo noticed, though some of the bottles had been smashed when they'd been surprised by a British patrol bomber off the Brittany coast. He checked his wristwatch. Ten minutes. When his relief arrived, he would take that first cigarette to the nub. He scanned the horizon again. A click of the voice tube brought the clipped Veronese dialect of the executive officer.

"Captain. We have just received word that the Japanese have attacked the American fleet at Pearl Harbor."

A shout rose up from below decks. Aldo turned to Valerio. With dark eyes blazing, the commander raised his cap and snapped it sharply against the railing. "That should keep the Yankees off our tails for awhile."

Aldo felt ambivalent. He liked Americans. His great aunt Carmella, now living in New York, had taught him English when he was a child. Was she the enemy now? Italy had no argument with the United States. How did these things get started anyway?

Night was all but upon them, the only remaining light a cold grey sliver on the western horizon. Aldo tightened the neck of his sou'wester. He blew lukewarm breath over freezing fingertips. At least the Caribbean would be warm. Like most of the crew, he was as yet unbloodied. He wondered what real combat would be like. Through the weight of the oilskins he felt the Beretta on his hip. Now that they were at sea, the pistol had replaced the dirk. He felt a trifle uncomfortable with the sleek automatic. It was a reminder that, should the unthinkable occur, should it become necessary to squelch panic, or, Mother of God to revert to the unthinkable, the means were at hand. Aldo had yet to see a corpse, and he would rather not think about it. Once in the Caribbean he would replace the Beretta with the dirk again. While not as effective, the dagger was far more fashionable. It reminded him of his days at the Royal Italian Naval Academy in Livorno, when *poniards* were worn suspended from a belt beneath high-waisted trousers. In the tailored jacket and white linen spats he felt dapper to a fault. He had enjoyed those days at the academy, especially when the townspeople invited the cadets to their homes with an eye to a match for their daughters. Of course, the signorinas were under maternal supervision. Still, the couples would take in the latest American movies or stroll the town making small inexpensive purchases while the chaperones remained discreetly to the rear. Caught in the memory of quieter days, his thoughts turned back to Torino, to the soft Piedmontese hills, the *ristorante* his father managed on the slopes overlooking the Po. He remembered his brother's wedding, when he had slipped away with the bride's sister for some petting in the woods. He was recalling his mother's *zuppa pomodoro*, could almost smell the crispy warm bread ripe for the dipping when the alert came sharply from the portside watch.

"Smoke on the horizon, Captain! Port beam!"

All binoculars swung instantly south.

"A destroyer, Valerio said calmly. It's steaming in our direction. *Immersioni! Immersioni!*"

With fear brushing the walls of his stomach, Aldo stuffed his binoculars into the folds of his jacket. Scrambling down the ladder to the control room, he felt the surge in his stomach. Crash dives always had the same effect. They had fifty seconds to make a 220-foot boat racing over the water at 15 knots vanish completely. A second or two could spell the difference between life and death. If he was cringing at the prospect of a distant ship on the horizon, how would he react when facing an enemy at the range of a deck cannon?

He arrived at his post below and made the sign of the cross with a thumbnail against his forehead. When the heart quailed, his father had counseled, trust in the soul. Gradually the fear was digested by the discipline of routine.

THE VILLAGE OF STE-ANNE

MARTINIQUE

"D'doctor be dere", the driver said. He pointed to a low stone fence backed by a compound of shrubs and trees.

Christopher Delon paid the agreed-upon fare and exited the taxi. He watched the rattling old Citroen trundle down the hillside and stop at the curbing beside an open-sided stand. The driver left the taxi and joined some men sitting on cane stools beneath a sign that read 'Jambon et Fromage'. After a thirty-mile fare from Forte de France and drawing on a tip that was far too generous, the driver was apparently through for the day. Christopher supposed he had decided on an early supper or a bracer or two before embarking on the return journey. The odds of finding a return fare from Ste-Anne at this time of evening were as remote as the village itself.

Nikole Rollet had not exaggerated when she'd described Ste-Anne as the southern extremity of the island. Despite the inflated fare, which the driver had doubled before they had left Forte de France, Christopher was relieved that he had not attempted the journey himself. He had been granted *carte blanche* on the use of Madame Molay's touring car, but once beyond the capital, road signs had been scarce and the drive through rugged hills over makeshift roads had taken him past remote plantations and dozens of unformed villages. The detours alone would have cost him an extra hour or two if he hadn't gotten lost completely. Besides, he did not want the Madam or anyone else, for that matter, privy to his destination. This weekend he had reserved for himself.

He brushed the dust from the small green gripsack he had purchased in Casablanca. After Dunkirk, he had arrived on the north African mainland with the clothes on his back. He had left for the Caribbean with not much more. It was amazing, he thought, how little a man could get by with if he had to. He surveyed his surroundings. The village was as compact as it was picturesque, a cluster of dwellings at the edge of the sea, a handful of modest storefronts framing a cobbled lane. At the top of the square rose the graceful spire of a church, tall and imposing against the clear blue sky. The church was Catholic. There were some things a man could not escape.

Doctor Rollet's cottage looked homey and inviting. He pushed through the gate and rang a small ships bell that hung beside the door. After a minute or so the door was opened by a pretty half-caste woman, her hair done up in a saffron turban, the slate-colored eyes in the rich brown face betraying a mingling of European and African blood.

"I'm here to see Madame Rollet," Christopher said, bowing slightly from the waist.

"D'Madame be making d'picture," the woman said, gesturing to the interior. "Enter, please. My name be Persia."

He followed her through a comfortably furnished sitting room to a bright and airy kitchen.

"Please", she said, taking his bag and depositing it in an alcove. With a nod and a smile she led him through a door that opened onto a garden. The lush quadrant of the garden ran hard up against the hillside, the rest sprawled colorfully toward the sea before falling off to a secluded sliver of beach. In the midst of the garden stood a flaming red hibiscus with large showy blossoms. The lawn was framed by bougainvillea, purple and red and a bright flaming scarlet. A variety of orchids grew on well-tended palms.

The woman led him to a gap in a hedge. A rocky incline pitched steeply to the strand below. She jabbed a finger toward a strip of powdery white sand at the base of a footworn path. In the shadows beneath a coconut palm, Christopher could see a solitary figure in a broad-brimmed hat seated upright before an easel.

"Thank you," he said.

The Creole withdrew with a nod and a smile.

The footpath cut a dizzying swath down a rocky incline. Christopher felt his way along the backs of roots, grasping at ferns to keep from stumbling. Halfway down the cliff he came across a stone shelf. There he stopped to study the woman on the folding stool. She was tall and straight of spine, with well-formed shoulders and a waspish waist. She would cut a handsome figure in any setting, Christopher thought, but in this tropical Eden she looked plucked from a painting by Monet. Despite a late-afternoon breeze, by the time he reached sea level he was breaking a sweat. As his shoes pressed the sand, the woman at the easel turned. In the reflected light of the cove, she looked younger than he remembered. She removed her hat and looked more youthful still, her cheeks lit by the lowering sun, her hair blowing freely in the wind.

"Monsieur Delon," she said, setting brush to palette. "Forgive me. Your message.... I thought you would arrive this evening. I would have received you at the house."

"Please," he said. "I'm the one who should apologize. When I telephoned, the connection was bad......."

"Never mind," she said. "You're here. Welcome to Ste-Anne. It's good of you to visit."

"It's a paradise," he said. "I caught a glimpse of the town. It's like a tropical Provence."

She rose from the stool. "It's eventide. You're seeing it at its quietest. The drive is long and hot. You must be thirsty."

"No. Please. Finish what you're doing. I'm fine. I drank a liter of water in the taxi."

He looked at the easel, a seascape replicating the cove and some hills beyond. "You're very good, Doctor Rollet."

"Merci, monsieur. Or should I call you 'Father'?"

"Christopher, if you please. I have yet to end my sabbatical. I was not just being polite. You have real talent."

"I paint to relax," she said. "I see what I like to see, and I remake what I don't. Come. You can freshen up while I change into something more suitable. I thought you might prefer dining at the house. Our choice of restaurants is limited. It must be some time since you've had a home-cooked meal."

"An eternity," he smiled. "In truth, an eternity."

They dined by candlelight on a patio overlooking the sea. Rarely had he eaten such food. Not only was his hostess a physician and an artist, but she could conjure a meal as well.

Christopher had changed into his white linen suit. It had rumpled a bit in his gripsack, but the candlelight masked the flaws. Nikole had chosen a simple white dress with a necklace of jade. The dress made her hair look darker; the jade added depth to her eyes.

"Delicious," he said, sampling a dish he could recognize only as fish. "Utterly delicious. You cook as artfully as you paint."

Her color deepened. "It's traditional island fare. Local recipes handed down by mothers and grandmothers. Persia is tutoring me. I really can't take the credit. She scours the markets and concocts the menus. I see only to the sauces." She raised her glass. "You were kind to bring the wine, monsieur. Good wine is a rarity these days."

"A contact at the Admiralty," he lied. The wine had been a gift from his neighbor, the gamine of the adjoining balcony. She had an endless supply. He did not question her source.

Nikole sipped her drink. Pausing to savor the bouquet, she asked, "Are you free to discuss your 'sabbatical', Pere Christopher, or is it of a more personal nature?"

He raised his glass. "It's far too heavy a subject after so buoyant a meal. Perhaps when I understand it better myself."

The guest room was on the second floor. Sated after the meal and light-headed after the wine and brandy, he sprawled on the bed and surrendered to the night sounds. The shutters were open in a dormer opposite. Through it he could see clouds burnished by moonlight, a pewter sea beneath a canopy of stars. The wind sighed in the angled spaces beneath the roof. He was not anxious to sleep. Sleep brought dreams, and the dreams had been bad of late. He recognized the trilling of the *cabrit-bois*, the ubiquitous island crickets. They reminded him of sleighbells, the distant tinkling of a horse-drawn sled. His students claimed the crickets fell silent at precisely four-thirty in the morning; that for early risers too poor to purchase an alarm clock, the cessation of their song signaled the onset of a new day.

The food and the brandy had more than relaxed him. He felt detatched, composed, unwound enough to let his thoughts just ramble. He played back the events of a pleasant evening. Nikole Rollet was a charming hostess. A fascinating woman. She did not look at him as though he were a commodity. They had talked of France, of art, of the islands and the war. He had come to Ste-Anne to relax, to gather himself. So far it seemed to be working. Perhaps this was the tonic he needed.

As he surrendered himself to the tranquility of the hour, he lost track of time. He was suspended between consciousness and sleep when he heard voices beneath his window. At first he thought it might be a lover's quarrel. The tone was excited, desperate, the voices hushed. Then he remembered where he was. A deep baritone in a local dialect mingled with the lyrical French of his hostess. Though he could not make out the words, he felt like an intruder, an eavesdropper. When the knock came to his door he was sitting on the edge of the bed.

"Monsieur Delon! It's Nikole! We need your help!"

In seconds he was into his trousers and buttoning his shirt.

When he descended the stairs, Nikole was pacing the kitchen, her blouse stuffed into a broad peasant skirt, her feet shod only in sandals. Her hair looked damp and windblown; a film of perspiration lined the hollows of her neck.

"There's been an accident. A man is dying. He needs a priest..."

"...the church," Christopher stammered. "...the local cleric..."

"We cannot. The man is...", she hesitated, searching for the words, "...it would bring trouble to the village. He has fallen from the rocks in the darkness. He was there for some time before they came for me. I've done what I can, but we dare not move him. He may be dead even now. He is Catholic. He needs the sacrament...."

"...but I have...I am...."

"You're a priest," she said. "Please. We must hurry. He's dying."

The words rang down through the years. *Tu es sacerdos in aeternum.* "You are a priest forever."

There are vestiges of one's calling one is loathe to surrender, like a slide rule after graduating from the drawing board. Christopher ran his fingers along the lining of his gripsack. Finding what he sought, he stuffed a small metal vial into a pocket of his trousers. "Take me...," he said.

As they passed through the kitchen, he snatched a bottle of wine from the rack...

"Bread...?" he asked.

Nikole fetched the remnants of a loaf from the cupboard. He followed her to the garden. As she scurried down the slope to a remote section of beach, he had trouble keeping pace.

The man was barely conscious. He had not fallen far, but his temple had been pierced by a spur of coral. A bandage encircled his forehead, a makeshift wrapping that looked torn from someone's shirt. The sand beneath the bandage was stained pink. Christopher fell to his knees and removed a wad of cotton from the small metal vial. He anointed the wounded man's forehead.

He turned to Nikole. "Will he...?"

She shrugged. "He has lost much blood. His back may be broken...."

He could not complete the viaticum without a confession. He decided to administer a final communion. Searching his memory for an offertory prayer, he consecrated the bread as he spoke...

"...on the night He was betrayed, Jesus took bread, broke it, blessed it and gave it to his apostles saying: 'Take, eat, all of you. This is my body which will be given you for the remission of sins...."

Holding the dying man's head in his arm, he placed a morsel of bread on the lolling tongue.

Barely conscious, his eyes turning slowly in their sockets, the man managed a swallow.

Nikole knelt behind them, her head bowed, her hands steepled in prayer.

The wayward priest intoned solemnly over the wine, his voice calm and soothing in the darkness..."this is my blood..." He poured some wine to the man's lips. "...whoever drinks of it shall not die but shall have life everlasting..."

He had barely finished when the head jerked in spasm and the patient drew a final breath.

As Nikole examined the body, Christopher sat exhausted on a boulder. For a quavering instant the sky seemed tainted by smoke, the sea stained darkly by oil.

***

"Where are you from, Jacques?"

The sightless eyes held the middle distance; the lips, swollen by burns, drew lightly on the cigarette. "La Rochelle," he said, his voice weak and toneless. "We were stationed at Lille."

There was no dawn, just a thinning of darkness as fog pressed the dunes beneath columns of greasy black smoke. Off Dunkirk's beaches the sea lay calm, the Channel swelling between spring tides. When a breeze stirred the mist, the sun emerged a misshapen disc over the besieged Flanders coastline. Sea and sun were trapped like the evacuees between the hammer and anvil of two German armies.

As the mist lightened, Christopher could see the rest of them. On this single dune there were a hundred wounded, perhaps a hundred and twenty.

He slumped in the sand and thought back to his journey from Sedan. He had been sent here. He was convinced of it. From the clutches of Madame Picard and her champagne breakfast to this tragic, tormented beach. The message was clear. There was work for him here. God's work. The Lord had set him among the stricken.

The boy called Jacques drew heavily on his cigarette. He coughed, then gathered his breath. "...a doctor had been in charge," he said. He coughed again, his body trembling violently against the dune. "...he was killed...yesterday. We're awaiting orders...."

Before he could check himself, Christopher heard himself saying, "I will help you, Jacques. I'm a priest."

The youngster reached out a hand.

Christopher clutched thoughtlessly at the grimy fingers.

"He's a priest," the boy muttered weakly to the man beside him. "He can help us."

The word spread rapidly along the dune. As heads turned toward him, bloodied and bandaged, Christopher felt eyes shift hopefully in his direction.

"Get us off this beach, Father," a voice pleaded from the edge of darkness."

"It's a terrible place to die..." another said.

"Christ himself would not be sacrificed in this fiendish inferno..."

Christopher stood upright on the dune. "Have faith," he said, surprised at the conviction in his voice. "I will help you. All of you...."

Surveying the rubble on the strand, he took a bearing on a burned-out ambulance. Assuring the wounded he would return, he trudged up the beach amid pockets of disillusioned men and discarded equipment. Twice he was ordered back at gunpoint by British officers. Far up the beach he could hear the crump of bombs, the detonations muffled by sand. High above the clouds, as they had been day after day, the German bombers were being attacked by the fighter squadrons of the Royal Air Force. When the wind was right, the clatter of gunfire was punctuated by the desperate gunning of engines.

Christopher paused to catch his breath. The predominant emotion along the beach was fear, fear of the enemy, fear of being stranded, fear of dying helplessly in this God-forsaken hellhole. Farther up the coast men crammed the waterline, trying to escape the inferno in one of the smaller boats. A number of ships were ablaze offshore, some in the main channel, some in the inner harbor, some drifting aimlessly at sea. The rise and fall of the tide was sixteen feet; the waterline might shift a hundred yards in a single hour. Where one might be high and dry one minute, one could be neck-high in surf a short while later. Thankfully, the tidal terrace was sandy. Ignorant as he was of such matters, even Christopher could see that a rocky shoreline would produce a far more deadly result.

The British were loading from the moles nearest the port.

Deep-keeled vessels like corvettes and makeshift transports were steaming heedlessly up to pier heads where planks were put down so men could scramble aboard. Fishing craft, trawlers, yachts, tugs, launches and even some ferry boats were venturing perilously close to the shoreline. At the tideline thousands of men were forming queues. When a boat arrived, there was a danger it might be capsized. The surf was littered with debris, the wreckage of battered hulls, discarded equipment, watersoaked uniforms, and bloated corpses.

Christopher approached a bomb-splintered pier where men were being loaded onto a corvette. At the foot of the pier he encountered a chaplain, a Scotsman.

"I have wounded of my own," the chaplain said. "The French are loading somewhere south of here."

Christopher worked his way down the strand. A quarter mile south of where his wounded lay, he found a French lieutenant directing a shuttle of private yachts and fishing craft to ships lying farther offshore. So steep was the shelving that even with the tide at flood, the smaller ships could not approach the beach.

Christopher pressed his case. "Lieutenant, in God's mercy, you must help me. I have wounded. A hundred at least. They are just beyond those dunes."

The lieutenant looked exhausted. Hollow-eyed, with a shaggy beard and grimy uniform, he was in no mood to argue. "The wounded must wait. Fighting men first, that's the order. We need men who can return to fight once they get to England."

"...but, Lieutenant. One trip. I beg you. I'm in charge of these men," Christopher lied. "They need immediate attention. Many will die unless we get them to hospital. Surely the men who are fit can survive a little longer...."

The lieutenant took in the spectre of the young priest...his filthy collar, his grubby tunic, his face reflecting a long and arduous journey.

"Bring them down, Father. But hurry. The wind is rising. It's now or never. It's no easy chore loading small boats in rough surf."

His heart soaring, Christopher sprinted back to the men on the dune. A thin drizzle lay lightly on the air, like the gossamer rain of a Highland morning. He organized the wounded: those who could walk to carry those who could not, the sighted to help the sightless, the stronger urging the weak. Using rifles as crutches and hobbling and limping, they made a shabby-looking caravan straggling over the dunes toward the rising surf. When they reached the tideline, some shallow-draft vessels were shuttling to a trawler a few hundred yards offshore.

The lieutenant called anxiously. "Father. These men are too sick. Too weak. They'll never make it. Send them back. Send them back...."

Christopher waved him off. "They will. They will make it. I take responsibility. They will make it...."

Christopher's wounded fought their way through the surf. Wading chest deep in water, they formed a quavering human jetty. Arms linked, torsos battered by swells, they handed the stretcher-ridden and hobbled inch by tedious inch, foot by agonizing foot, hand over trembling hand, to the men in the boats.

Christopher stood in the center of the chain. As each man passed, he heard an utter of thanks.

"Bless you, Father..."

"Thanks, Padre..."

...you saved us, Father..."

Jacques was near the end of the chain, his hands on the shoulders of the man in front, his eyes staring blankly at an unseeable sky. With the surf swelling heavily against his chest, the sergeant guiding him said, "It's your priest, Jacques. He's pulled it off, he has...."

The youngster squeezed Christopher's arm.

"Bon chance, Jacques," the priest said.

There were tears in the sightless eyes. "You're coming with us, Father?"

"I have work here, Jacques. God be with you."

With the boats bobbing steadily out to sea, Christopher stood waist-deep in surf. Drenched and exhausted, he was comforted to know that his wounded were being lowered through hatches, positioned on decks, free at least of the blood-stained beach. Feeling satisfaction such as he had never known, he watched as the last of his stricken charges was hoisted on board a trawler. As the trawler inched its way toward the harbor, the smaller boats made for another part of the beach.

He did not see the Stukas, he heard them. Screaming out of the smoke, they came diving toward the water. When the shooting began, Christopher stood frozen in horror. The trawler with his wounded was picking up speed. The skipper could not hear the Stukas over the sound of his engines. Christopher watched petrified as a bomber came scudding in low, strafing and roaring. The bomb that tumbled from its fuselage seemed a living thing.

"Nooo!....God!...nooo!...." Christopher howled, the wind tearing the words from his lips.

As he watched in horror the trawler erupted in flame, debris splintering into fragments in a ghastly eruption of flesh and wood that scattered like kindling over the oil-slick waves. There was not a single scream, not a solitary human utterance, just a dull concussive blast, a maddening silence, and a tail of sound that was the Stuka's receding engines.

In seconds the trawler was gone.

Pulverized.

Evaporated.

Christopher stood frozen in disbelief.

The sea was strewn with pockets of debris...the effluvia inert, silent, obscene.

Sagging to his knees in the surf, he felt stunned to his very soul. He stretched his arms to the sky. "No!" he shouted. "No! . . .no! . . .no! . . .no! . . ."

Thrashing furiously, he ripped the Roman collar from his neck.

With tears stinging his eyes and despair clawing his chest, he flung the collar out to sea.

He stumbled to his feet and began wading through the surf. Strong arms restrained him.

"Easy, Father," the lieutenant said behind him. "They're beyond help now."

"They're...I've got to...I promised....I assured them..."

The lieutenant wrestled him to the beach.

Collapsing at the tideline, Christopher pounded his fists into the sand. In rage and despair he groaned through bitter tears...

"...they had faith in me...they...had...faith.....faith...."

Then suddenly the anger drained, the strength, the despair. He pressed his face to the sand and something crumbled inside, something not of the flesh, not even of the spirit. Something more painful still.

"Faith in me...."

"Thank you, Father."

The voice jolted him back.

He felt Nikole Rollet's hand on his shoulder, the breeze off Ste-Anne's bay ruffling his hair. "I'm sorry to have presumed on you like that, friend Christopher. There was no time. He was fortunate you were visiting. Perhaps it was God's will."

"Perhaps," he said, replacing the cap on the vial of oil. He looked down at the dead man. Nikole had pressed his eyelids shut. He lay as if asleep, his face reflecting the pallid moon, his arms folded loosely over his chest. Christopher thought of Jacques. How closely related is passion to death.

He looked at Nikole. Her face was anointed with sweat. "You must tell me what has happened here tonight," he said. "Why the secrecy? Why not the local priest?"

"I'll tell you," she said. "I'll tell you everything if you'll hear my confession." For a brief moment he lost patience with her. "The purpose of confession is not to reveal secrets. It's to cleanse the soul."

She looked forlornly out to sea. "I know, Father. I've felt the need to confess for months now. Years. I'm in need of support. Will you help me?"

He looked at her face. Pale in the moonlight, a flowerlike fragility had overtaken her. She too had been shaken by the death on the beach. Had she known the man? Perhaps he was asking too much. She was a doctor, but she was a woman first. Perhaps she felt responsible for this particular death. Perhaps beneath that controlled exterior lurked a lonely, frightened child.

Realizing it was an exchange of vulnerability, he said, "Very well. We will help one another."

She sat beside him on the boulder. Though it was dark in the shadows, a mild radiance stained the pallor of her cheek.

"Bless me father for I have sinned..."

As she labored through her confession, something loosened inside him. It was as though the shackles had been sprung from his soul. For the first time in months he was a priest again, a vessel of Christ. Not only had he performed the sacred ritual for the dying, he had the power to comfort the living, to absorb the transgressions of his sister and to pass them to the Almighty.

For a few brief moments he was filled with an obscure happiness. The bay at Ste-Anne lay serene and quiet beneath the stars; the woman beside him had affirmed her trust in his worth. But gradually the cool benediction of night was tempered by doubt. The more he listened to her words, the more he realized a new set of decisions was at hand. She confessed to deficiencies that were well within the ordinary. But as she approached the story of the man who had died, he felt a sudden unease. The more she talked the more he realized he was more than priest to her now, more than confessor. As her tale unfolded he was becoming her confidant, her co-conspirator.

When she finished, he gave her absolution and doled out a small penance.

He looked at her inquiringly, but she made no comment.

The balance of the night he slept lightly. At one level he felt a priest again, at another, a Frenchman. With both, he realized, had come new responsibility.

CHARLOTTE AMALIE, ST. THOMAS

Casey O'Shea swam effortlessly to the edge of the Trade Winds pool. She put a foot to a ladder and hoisted herself to the decking. She was toweling down beside a beach chair when Kevin Whitely came striding across the lawn wearing pressed Navy tans and dark aviator sunglasses.

"Looks inviting," he said, gesturing to the pool.

Casey removed her bathing cap and shook her hair down. Feels terrific, Kevin. Why not suit up and try it?

"Wish I had time. I'm due at the base in ten minutes."

A Marine corporal materialized on the steps to the lobby. "We're all set, Lieutenant. Everyone's aboard and we're ready to shove."

Whitely acknowledged with a thumb's up. "Assuming I'm still on the island tonight, Miss O'Shea, would you join me for some seafood?"

"I'd enjoy that, Lieutenant."

"Eight sound okay?"

"Perfect."

He jogged up the steps and disappeared into the hotel.

In the lobby near the reception desk, Casey noticed the bulletin tacked on the board reserved for messages.

SNEAK ATTACK ON PEARL HARBOR

She walked the hallway to her ground floor apartment wondering how the war would affect the Caribbean. Where would they send her father? Would the Japanese bomb the American mainland? Would the United States declare war on Italy and Germany? They were, after all, Japan's allies. Thinking Sean might be napping, she opened the door and entered her room quietly. A man was seated on the bed. At first she assumed it was a friend of Rina's. When Viktor Reinmann turned to face her she felt as though the air had been sucked from the room. She went lightheaded, then faint, then her knees began to buckle.

She clutched the door facing. "What...how...when did you?...."

With a smile akin to a smirk, Viktor pushed slowly to his feet.

Instinctively, she rushed to the adjoining room. Her thoughts a blur, she scooped her son from the bed. He had been playing with his model airplane. Sliding open the glass door, she deposited him on the patio.

"Play here, honey. Mommy will be back in a minute...."

When she returned to the room, Reinmann was standing at the foot of the bed. For what seemed like an eternity, they stood staring at one another.

PART TWO

JANUARY, 1942

SAN JUAN, PUERTO RICO

"Two destroyers, Dante. Two ancient four-stackers. They constitute ninety-five per cent of our Caribbean fleet. And both of them are patrolling off Forte de France. That's how much steam is on this Martinique situation." Rear Admiral J. H. Hoover paused to test the steaming black coffee that had been placed on his desk by an immaculately turned-out steward.

Dante O'Shea sampled the time-honored Navy brew. The Admiral must be harboring a private stock, he thought. The coffee in his blue and gold porcelain cup was to regular Navy issue as Comte de Champagne was to torpedo juice. While the Admiral unfolded his charts, Dante let his gaze wander to the expanse beyond the window. A gunboat was checking the boom in San Juan's harbor. He had already been briefed on the Navy's appallingly weak forces in the Caribbean, but it came as a shock to hear it from the horse's mouth. A few short weeks after the Japanese attack on Pearl Harbor the head of the Tenth Naval District had under his command two outdated destroyers, two Eagle boats, one seaplane tender, three obsolete submarines, and an assortment of converted yachts. That and a few patrol planes to cover hundreds of thousands of square miles of sea lanes.

"Churchill is raising hell about the oil shortage," the Admiral continued. "He and President Roosevelt have been exchanging correspondence on the situation down here, and both are dismayed at our lack of anti-submarine forces. In the past few weeks German U-Boats have begun sinking tankers off America's east coast. It's only a matter of time before they move their act to these waters."

Dante knew that if Admiral Doenitz turned his wolf packs loose in the Caribbean, the wall-length map behind the Admiral's desk would be pock-marked with the graves of sunken ships. The gauntlet, which would have to be run by unarmed tankers funneling up from South America through the Caribbean and into the Atlantic, would be formidable. The Admiral had been promised some additional support, but to date few of the available ships could outrun a U-Boat on the surface, and most patrol planes were being flown by Army pilots with no experience in tracking submarines.

"So where do I come in?" Dante asked.

The Admiral turned to his map. "Martinique is the lynchpin of our Caribbean strategy, Captain. The Bay of Forte de France is one of the most coveted harbors in the Northern Hemisphere. Those French warships have been bottled up down here for a full eighteen months. More than once we've been tipped they were getting up steam. We can't afford to have them on the loose. And the Germans don't want them joining our side."

"Can we demobilize them?"

"It's a volatile situation. Our relations with Vichy are shaky as it is. Washington wants the ships neutralized, but they want it done voluntarily. The French are in no hurry to comply. I've issued orders to sink the carrier BEARN and the destroyers EMILE BERTIN and JEANNE d' ARC should they try to run our blockade. If the authorities on Martinique continue to resist our demands, we'll have to go in and take the island. It's not only the warships and the harbor that are at stake. There's French gold on Martinique. We don't want that falling into the wrong hands. And the Germans are afraid it might be used to finance the Resistance."

Despite his even tone, Dante could see the Admiral was worked up. As he talked, he jabbed a pencil into his desk blotter... eraser ...point...eraser...point.... Catching Dante's eye, he dropped the pencil and sipped at his coffee.

"How does this tie in with my assignment, Admiral?"

The Admiral rose from his chair and walked to the window. Beyond his shoulder Dante could see a flying boat circling for a landing above the mouth of the harbor.

"This mission is strictly in the weeds, Dante. And strictly

volunteer. You'll be entering Martinique illegally. If caught, you could be interned as a spy. Technically, you could be shot."

Dante remained silent. Drawing an assignment in this backwater was due in part to his drinking; he had reconciled himself to that. In the wake of Caroline's death he'd been hitting it fairly heavily. He had tapered off of late, but he was still not the officer he had been, even he wouldn't deny that. With a war on, they wouldn't retire him, but they might wonder at his ability to handle a war-zone command. The Admiral was giving him a chance. If he proved he could handle this assignment, the next step might be the Pacific.

The Admiral turned to face him. "Any reservations, Captain?"

"None, Admiral."

"Part of your mission is to help devise a plan for the invasion of Martinique. You've been picked because you're fluent in French and you're familiar with the islands. Short of a native, you'll melt into the background as well as anyone."

"We've got a Naval Observer on Martinique, Admiral. Why do you need an undercover man?"

"Reconnaissance is only part of the assignment, Dante. You're packing too much horsepower for a mere scouting expedition. We're in touch with an agent of sorts on Martinique. He's not our man. No one on our side has ever met him, nor do we know who he is. Calls himself "Skipjack". Contacted us through a defector some months back. He's sent along some pretty useful information. Always accurate. Always timely."

"And I'm to look him up."

"He claims to have some hot new intelligence. Insists it's too sensitive for the usual channels, so he wants to discuss it face to face. One of his quirks is that he refuses to work with the British. Defectors are given strict instructions to bypass British Intelligence and channel information only to the Americans."

"Probably had a relative at Mers el Kébir."

"The French have good reason to mistrust the British, Dante. Within a day or two of France's surrender, British missions all over the world were trying to take what they termed "administrative control" of French possessions. When they arrived on Martinique, old Admiral Robert told them in no uncertain terms that the French were not yet ready to hand their Empire to the Brits. He's a tough old bird, is Admiral Robert. And none too accommodating of late. It galls him that he was steaming foreign seas when the Germans clamped handcuffs on his beloved France."

"And we have no idea who this "Skipjack" is, or what he does?"

"None."

"What if he's a plant?"

"It's possible. That's another aspect of your assignment. That, and to find out what's so hot that it can't be passed through regular channels."

"There's that much steam on it?"

The Admiral turned to the map. "We're losing a ship a day out here, Dante. And it's just the beginning. The Germans are sending more U-Boats across. Yesterday, British intelligence notified us that four or five Italian subs are making the crossing too. Roosevelt wants this U-Boat slaughter stopped. This SKIPJACK character has reported U-Boat skippers being entertained on Martinique."

"Are they refueling German subs?"

"We can't be sure. This far from home, a U-Boat is limited to about two weeks on station. If they start getting supplied locally, the Caribbean will run red with blood. So far we're operating mostly in the dark. Perhaps you can dig something up that will help us get a handle on things."

"When do I leave?"

"As I said, this is strictly volunteer. Martinique's a cauldron right now. Frenchmen are conspiring against Frenchmen, the natives are restless, and the gentry are ambivalent. If this Skipjack's information is as hot as we've been led to believe, the lid could be ready to come off down there."

"So where do I hang my hat?"

"You'll be operating out of St. Lucia. It's only twenty miles south of Martinique. We've leased an air base there, one of the tradeoffs for our sending destroyers to the British. Officially, we've got you down for physical rehab. Ulcer, or somesuch. You'll be assigned to liaison between air bases. Give you an excuse for moving around as you please. Good luck, Dante. And remember. I know you like the French. While technically they're not the enemy, realistically they're under the heel of the Krauts. You'll be as much in jeopardy down there as if you were in occupied territory."

Dante glanced at the Admiral's map, at the vast sweep of blue that represented the Caribbean basin. Totaling over a million square miles, the huge inland sea was ringed by the Greater Antilles in the north, the Lesser Antilles in the east, the coasts of Venezuela, Colombia and Panama on the south, and Central America and the Yucatan peninsula in the west. With names like St. Thomas, St. Lucia, and St. Martin, the dots on the map seemed the essence of tranquility. But those who knew better would tell you that barely a generation had passed without some outbreak of persecution, insurrection, or war. From the conquest of the Arawaks by the Caribs to skirmishes by British, French, Dutch, Spanish, Danish and Americans, the area had a history as bloody as any on earth.

"Still hard to believe there's a war on out here, Admiral."

"Tell it to those seamen clinging to debris on those oil-soaked rafts out there, Dante. Torpedoes don't discriminate. Two days ago a pregnant woman gave birth in a life boat."

BELLEFONTAINE, MARTINIQUE

Oberleutnant zur See Viktor Reinmann leaned comfortably back in his chair and let the smoke from his panatela curl lazily toward the ceiling. The island dish called *blaff,* a fish delicacy which had been cooked and served by the elderly Martiniquais now pouring cognac, sat lightly on his stomach.

The residence of Henri-Louis Sambre was built on the heights above Bellefontaine, a small fishing village a few miles north of Forte de France. Formerly a plantation home, the compound was set among stately palms and gardens of flamboyant flowers. The villa itself was elegant, long and low with broad picture windows and a wide, open verandah. To seaward it looked over a carpet of lush green lawn. Behind a pool in the rear, foothills thick with vegetation climbed steeply toward the truncated plateaus known as *Pitons du Carbet.*

Reinmann was wearing a dark civilian suit, a gift from a collaborator on Guadeloupe. The collaborator, who despised Jews and had rapidly embraced the Nazi cause, had seen to the tailoring himself. The result was a slim-waisted garment in the style worn by the island's diplomats. A gray silk necktie had been supplied by his host along with a tailored white shirt. Despite the comfort of civilian clothes, he was finding that he missed his uniform, his badge of authority.

Viktor was listening to the Frenchman, but his eyes were on the girl. She was a girl, after all, not a woman, no matter what the Frenchman said. Nineteen? He didn't believe it. She looked no older than his sister Elsbeth had at sixteen: silky blonde hair cut short in the Parisian manner, skin the texture of an immature peach. Her mouth was a pout of innocence. When occasionally she glanced at him, it was coyly, with fawn's eyes. A gamine playing a game.

It had been almost eight weeks since Viktor had shocked Casey with his unexpected visit. Eight weeks, and he could still not bank the fires she had stoked. In the end she had turned him away in anger, but an anger tinged with grief. Had it not been for the Americans entering the war, he might have remained on the island and repaired the damage. But with the attack on Pearl Harbor, the Americans would be stepping up their surveillance. Rather than risk a return visit, he had turned to the business at hand. Her father was an American naval officer, after all, and while he doubted she would turn him in, he could not under any circumstances take the risk. He had rendezvoused with the U-Boat as planned and had set out as scheduled to see to Admiral Doenitz's plan.

His trek through the lower Antilles had been productive. His transport had ranged from fishing packets to yachts to submarines. The U-Boat that had picked him up at St. Martin torpedoed a tanker off Monserrat. He had steered clear of the British-controlled islands, concentrating instead on the French and Dutch where the security was less intense. The Americans, he had learned, were as unprepared to deal with the newer U-Boats as the British had been. For the foreseeable future submarines could roam the Caribbean with impunity, striking from the surface with little fear of retaliation. If the rest of his assignment went as smoothly as the surveillance, he would be back on German soil in weeks.

Still, the encounter with Casey had left a void, a void akin to hunger. Thoughts of her haunted his nights, bedeviled his days. Up to now he had dampened his lusts with action, but now the heady bouquet of perfume and the proximity of this woman-child were combining to rekindle a flame. She was breaking his concentration; he was ignoring his French host. They still had some feeling out to do. To put the girl beyond his vision, he edged around in his chair.

"...so you see, monsieur," the Frenchman continued, beads of sweat on his upper lip, "this outpost is undergoing the severest of hardships."

Viktor swirled the cognac slowly. He wondered how this

Gaullist bureaucrat would endure real privation, a tour in the Atlantic on a boat crammed to the hatches with greased torpedoes and overripe bodies. He drew on the cigar: Cuban tobacco. He fingered his glass: cognac, some of the last to be shipped from the banks of the Charente. And fresh fruit, the Creole even now retrieving a dessert cup from beside his napkin.

"Yes," he said, inhaling the fragrance of the brandy. "Things are tightening, even in Paris."

The girl spoke up. "I have never been to Paris...."

With a low-watt smile, Henri-Louis Sambre reached out and patted her hand. "Indeed, my sweet. In due time you can regale Monsieur Suisse on where you have and have not been. For now, though, you will excuse us, please. A matter of business."

The girl slipped Viktor a demure glance. Taking her wine, she rose from her chair and sauntered toward the sitting room. Viktor watched her leave. His gaze ran over the swell of her hip. She was as supple as a jaguar, with smooth shapely calves and the buttocks of a dancer. What had the Frenchman called her? Lillette? Yes, Lillette Bonnier.

And he was Monsieur Suisse. A pitifully transparent pseudonym. Swiss businessman? Even if the girl was naive she would not be taken in by so obvious a charade. No matter, he thought. The girl was the Frenchman's problem. Despite his arrogance, Sambre's neck was out as far as any. He might be a collaborator, but he didn't seem a fool. Though his bearing was officious and his manner gruff, he was not devoid of courage. And for the moment, at least, he was managing the game, so the erstwhile Monsieur Suisse would play by his rules.

The Frenchman pushed wearily from his chair. "Shall we repair to the lawn, monsieur? It will be cooling down by now."

On a patio overlooking the sea, the Frenchman gestured toward a cluster of umbrellas. Evening was drawing in, and the sea was in transition. The air was damp and briny, a breeze stirring the wavetops in the bay.

The Creole wheeled out a trolley laden with spirits. When he had freshened their drinks, he set them on the armrests of their chairs. Before leaving, he bowed stiffly to host and guest alike. Viktor watched him depart. He walked with the swagger of someone who had spent years in the lurching instability of a small boat. His skin harbored a depth of color that spoke of outside living. A seaman, no doubt. The sun had etched its signature on his face, making his age difficult to determine. The Frenchman called him Honore.

"So, Monsieur Suisse," the Frenchman said, you must tell me of your journey. One does not move readily between the islands these days."

"As readily as need be, Viktor said, resuming his *affair petite* with the cognac. Of course it helps when one can move beneath the surface."

Sambre forced a brusque laugh, a strained guffaw that Viktor found particularly unpleasant, especially as it was delivered between ill-fitting dentures. How could this lecher gain access to a beauty such as Lillette Bonnier, Viktor wondered. He was so besotted with vanity that he dyed his hair. His eyes were piggish in a pink face and there was a whiskey bloom on his nose and cheeks. Was she indentured to him? Did he hold her family hostage? Despite his wealth-fortified arrogance, Viktor had pegged him as a bottom feeder, a barnacle on the hull of life.

"An *Unterseeboote* must be a wonderful convenience," the Frenchman said, pleased with his German. "Did you enter our harbor submerged? What of the American destroyers?"

"We laid off until it was dark," Viktor said. "When they reached the limits of their picket, we slipped quietly between them. We did not attempt the harbor. I was put ashore a few miles north of the nets. At Point des Negres."

"I see. Are you authorized to brief me on the details of the plan?"

"How much have you been told?"

"An emissary arrived a week ago. From Pierre Laval. I know of the concern for the gold. I assured him I could get it out to sea. The rest, I was told, would be revealed to me by one Monsieur Suisse.

I must confess that when I received your message last night, I was surprised. I did not expect you so soon."

"You have told no one I was coming?"

"Absolutely not. So far your presence is known only to the girl. The servants will say nothing. And the girl has been warned."

"And if she disobeys."

Something malign colored the Frenchman's gaze, a narrowing of the pupils that bespoke a streak of cruelty. "She will not disobey, monsieur. I assure you."

"Good. So you know nothing of my mission."

"Only that it concerns the gold. I'm to rely on you for details. Be assured I am prepared to extend my full cooperation."

"I've been told there are some three-hundred tons of bullion."

"Three hundred and fifty," Sambre corrected.

To mask his surprise, Viktor let his gaze wander out to sea. The number came as a shock. It was unlike the *Abwehr* to be so far afield. A differential of fifty tons! Someone in the Vichy Government had not been totally honest with the occupation authorities. Three hundred and fifty. He returned to his host.

"To move that much gold across the Atlantic unobserved will require a type of transport not yet available," Viktor said. "Within weeks, days perhaps, the first of our undersea tankers will be departing Kiel. Stripped and gutted, a vessel of that size could handle the gold in a single crossing."

The Frenchman settled back in his chair. "An undersea tanker?"

"Admiral Doenitz calls them *milch cows.* Their primary purpose will be to serve as supply ships for fleet submarines."

The Frenchman held up his glass. The Creole crossed the lawn and poured a refill. Sambre waited until his manservant left.

"There's talk of an invasion," Sambre said. "Rumors, mostly. Admiral Robert has balked at the American demand that we demobilize our warships. It's unlikely they'll risk the casualties, but nothing is certain. The sooner we evacuate the gold the better. Support is building in some quarters for shipping the gold to De Gaulle and his outlaws in North Africa."

"How long will it take to move it from the fort?"

"Two days. Three perhaps, depending on when the order is given. There are almost 9,000 containers. Crates and sacks of thirty-five kilos each."

"And the embarkation point?"

"We cannot risk the main harbor. Even your *milch cow* might have trouble evading the picket ships near the harbor."

Viktor turned his gaze out to the sea. Somewhere in the gathering dusk lurked the American destroyers. There were two of them, his Intelligence had reported, steaming continuously between Martinique and Guadeloupe.

"If not the harbor, then what?" Viktor asked.

A cove," the Frenchman replied. "On the southern end of the island. A pier is under construction. Only a handful know the location, and only Admiral Robert and myself know the purpose. The operation has been given top secret status."

"It's a small island. Can such an undertaking be kept secret?"

"Senegalese troops have been shipped in for the construction. No islander or otherwise permanently-based personnel have been, or need be, informed. Besides, many such projects are underway. Safeguards against an incursion. Already we've received coded cables from Marshall Petain ordering us to dump the gold in the sea should an invasion seem imminent. I have persuaded Admiral Robert to leave the disposition of the gold to me. Should the Americans decide to move against us, his plate will be more than full with fighting off the invasion."

Viktor nodded. The Frenchman was not as oafish as he looked.

"When the *milch cow* draws near," Viktor said, "we can set a date. Pierre Laval will see to it that an appropriate cable is sent over Petain's signature. After that, it is up to us."

The Frenchman drained the last of his cognac. "I trust my cooperation will not go unnoticed when the Reich is victorious."

"I've been authorized to give you Admiral Doenitz' personal guarantee on that," Viktor lied. "You can rely on the gratitude of the German people."

"Three hundred and fifty tons," the Frenchman repeated. "Give or take a ton or two."

For a long moment, as though he were shopping a bazaar of ideas, the Frenchman held his gaze. Viktor thought he perceived a flicker of interrogation in the predatory eyes, a suggestive shift in posture. No doubt Sambre had also picked up on the discrepancy in the figures.

"So," the Frenchman said, as though stepping back from the edge of decision, "enough business. In the days to come, you will be a frequent visitor to our island. A man should have something to look forward to in these uncertain times. Unfortunately, I have an appointment that will tie me up for the evening. Accept these humble walls and all they contain in the spirit of, shall we say, comradeship. I think you'll find most of what a man of your vigor would require." When he stood to take his leave, he bowed and clicked his heels.

Viktor pushed to his feet. With a smile that cost him an effort, he grasped the Frenchman's hand. He had a handshake like fresh bait. Turncoats are vile creatures, Viktor thought. What rejection or debasement could one suffer at the hands of one's government to permit a treason of this magnitude. Had he been banished to Martinique for some political slight? Was his wife the mistress of a powerful minister of state? Or was it pure and simple greed?

As the Frenchman's car was drawing from the forecourt, the girl appeared at the doorway to the cottage, a snifter in one hand, the other shading her eyes from a lowering sun. She had changed from her dinner dress to a simple white shift. Transparent in the slanting rays, it revealed a figure neither shapeless nor immature. Only her high-pointed breasts interrupted the flow of the garment.

"Mr. Suisse?" she called. "Honore is driving M. Sambre to his appointment. Will you have another cognac?"

Viktor glanced out to sea again. Out there beneath the wind-stirred surface hundreds of sweating bodies were laboring in the cramped and inhospitable confines of U-Boats. To the northeast, far beyond this lush green crescent of islands, scores of seamen were clapping ice-coated binoculars to frozen brows in the teeth of Atlantic gales, men who would neither see nor touch a woman of even moderate endowment for weeks, perhaps months, to come.

Viktor turned to the girl. She stood leaning against the door, the sun burnishing her golden tan, a hand balanced lightly against a ripening hip.

"Yes," he said. "A cognac would be nice."

The following morning the sea was lacquered with a golden sheen, but Bellefontaine lay deep in shadow. The sun had not yet cleared the peaks, and the waters beneath the villa shone like liquefied sky. On the lawn below the cottage, Lillette Bonnier sat sipping coffee from a glass. Still tingling from a shower and with her hair hanging limply in thick damp strands, she applied a coating of cream to her nose and cheekbones. Her feet were bare, and she was wearing a short summer wrapper that left her legs and thighs exposed. She had stopped wearing underwear because it was too hot and all but impossible to buy.

Watching the shadow of the mountain draw nearer the shore, she felt a prickling chill of unease. It felt strange to be alone in this place. Honore had come for the German in the hour before dawn. That he was German, she had little doubt. His French was not quite up to the mark, and when she inquired about his home in Switzerland, he had awkwardly dodged the questions. Besides, she had listened from the kitchen when he and Sambre had discussed his arrival. A Swiss businessman was unlikely to arrive by U-Boat in the middle of the night. At least he had been a considerate lover, far more sensitive than some of the Frenchmen she had entertained of late. But afterwards she had detected a feeling of agitation, as though he was not entirely at peace with himself.

A hundred yards offshore she could see a fishing boat, one of the planked dugouts the natives called *gommiers*. Honore had told her they were carved from gum trees. The hull was painted blue, the interior red. Near the bow she could make out the figures of three fishermen, two bent over a seine, the third beating the surface with a long flexible pole. The seine was being fanned into the shallows; the beating was to panic the fish into the net.

A tenuous living, she thought, to beat the sea and trust to nature. How had they come here, these Martiniquais? Why did they stay? It was a paradise, of sorts, but it could grow tiresome. One perfect day after another, with no change of season, no change of temperature, no change of wardrobe. They had never seen a locomotive, those fishermen, or a snow-capped mountain. They had never felt the hint of autumn or the kiss of spring; they had seen no other skies, known no other horizons but the all-encircling sea. A city absorbs the essence of its inhabitants, leaves something for those who follow, but these unformed villages swept clean by the Trades retained nothing of those who built them, at least nothing she could discern.

And what of herself? What was she doing here? She had come for the promise of adventure, a fast fortune. And now she was like the fishermen, a prisoner in paradise, a slave on a sun-washed island. Her dream was to shop the boulevards of Paris, to ski the Tyrol, to stroll the piazzas of Rome. The dream had once seemed attainable. But now, within months of her nineteenth birthday, she was in danger of being dashed on the rocks of her own ambition. Sambre was not going to give her up. She could see that now. He was not going to honor their pact. She was a prisoner and he was going to keep her caged, squeeze the juice until she was as dry as a fig, keep her embayed in this palm-lined stockade until she had entertained, as he liked to put it, every military and diplomatic lecher that could advance his goals. And then he would discard her, pawn her off on some minor official. By the time she returned to France, if there was a France, she would be shopworn and frayed and lacking the fire to live her dream. She had to escape. His tastes were becoming more bizarre by the day.

She did not regret her profession; it was what she had chosen. Her mother's small hotel in Nice had been a haven for prostitutes. They were the closest thing she had to sisters, to aunts, to cousins. She had disposed of her virginity at thirteen. At first it seemed an easy life, entertaining the tourists who came to the Cote d'Azur to gamble and take the sun; rich Germans, prominent Italians, lusty Scandinavians. But there was a limit, even to that.

"Find a benefactor, her mother had told her. Find a *patron* and your journey will be shorter, the trip easier. Find a *protecteur* while you are still young, while the sap of life flows freely, while you are bright of eye and firm of body, a morsel the rogues find impossible to resist."

She had met Sambre at a party at Cap Ferrat. Almost instantly she was convinced she had found the benefactor her mother had so ardently desired. While he was no physiological paragon, he was not abhorrent either. He took care to bathe, and he was not cruel. She had learned to look past the unattractive aspects of men, to concentrate on the task at hand rather than their physical insufficiencies. Flabby. Bony. Of unpleasant countenance. Foul of breath or armpit. Those were as excrement to a nurse. One became anesthetized.

The party at Cap Ferrat had taken place a month before the Germans invaded France. Sambre had been introduced to her as a prominent politician. She learned later that he had selected her the moment she appeared at the poolside affair. Dazzled by the flow of champagne and the glittering array of guests, the teenager from Nice had turned all heads in a simple schoolgirl's jumper and calf-high stockings. After brief introductions, she had been ushered by their host to a room overlooking the sea. Before the cork had shed the moisture from the magnum, she had brought him to climax in a series of shuddering toe-stretching spasms. He had graced her with an inordinately generous fee, more than she had managed in any three encounters combined. And when he offered her a year in the western islands, she had accepted before discussing it with her mother. He knew, after all, many high officials, men of means both military and civilian. Under his tutelage she could amass a fortune and return to France before her twentieth birthday.

France carved out its armistice with Germany the week after her arrival on Martinique. At first, the island was all that Sambre had promised. Lush. Sunny. Benign. She was young. Ripe. Ambitious. Sambre introduced her as his stepson's daughter, a ploy which deceived none but the eminently gullible, but which satisfied the protocols of the gentry, especially since he put her up in an apartment in town and kept her at arm's length from Admiral

Robert and his immediate staff. The Admiral was no prude, but he brooked no lechery from his subordinates.

She rapidly became a pearl in the oyster that was the French Antilles. Sambre arranged liaisons with a handful of highly-placed officials. His jewel was not to be valued lightly. The price was steep, negotiated by her *patron*, who was less interested in the money, he claimed, than the leverage his little pearl could gain him among his peers. In her second month on the island she celebrated her eighteenth birthday. Her suitors were men in their fifth and sixth decades.

It wasn't long before Sambre revealed a side she had not seen before. After an encounter with a particularly lecherous major-general, her benefactor had insisted on a full accounting. When she returned from the tryst, he was waiting at her apartment.

Claiming he could use the information to his political advantage, he insisted she review in the minutest detail the events of the evening, even down to the color of the general's drawers. At first, Lillette found the exercise amusing. The fact that the storytelling aroused him she chalked up the proximity of the event and her talent as a yarn-spinner. The questioning was repeated after her next encounter. It soon became a ritualistic aspect of their relationship. It was not without its merits. Aroused by her narratives, the details of which she began to embellish as a sort of game to see how fast she could bring him to conclusion, she would lace her tales with lascivious asides. It became a diversion of sorts, to see how rapidly she could close the curtain on their little charade and free herself of his presence.

As the months wore on, her clientele began to decline in quality. Whereas in the beginning she had bedded only high-ranking officers and a handful of senior bureaucrats, of late he had been selling her to enlisted men, one a particularly nasty supply sergeant who had bruised her with his roughneck tactics and taken her like a farm animal.

When she complained of the sergeant's brutality, Sambre had merely sloughed her off. His obsession seemed to grow. Of late he had intimated things, things that did not bode well for her future.

There were men in the ranks. Coarse men. Men of no refinement and less compassion. Though low on the totem, they had access to critical equipment, useful hardware. Should the worst occur, Sambre might find their gratitude worth trading on. The more Lillette protested, the more her patron ignored her pleas. But his indifference was wearing thin. She was finding it anything but assuring. She was what she was, but she would not be treated as chattel. Who would be next? Young boys? The scum in the prisons? The goats on the hillside?

A month after the liaison with the sergeant, she had mentioned that she was ready to return to France. She had saved a tidy sum and she felt her contract fulfilled. Sambre had chided her severely.

"Return to France? I will not hear of it. You are using me, as I am using you. Our bargain is not yet complete."

He was not yet through with her, he said. He had taken her papers. If she threatened to leave he would have her arrested and given to the lepers on Guiana. In the blinking of an eye she uncovered his ultimate betrayal.

It was time to break away.

But how?

To where?

With the Germans in control of Europe, and with Sambre's influence in the corridors at Vichy, flight to France was unlikely. North Africa? America?

"The world is at war," Sambre reminded her. "You cannot move about as on holiday. There's money to be made in these islands. There are influential men on Guadeloupe. In French Guiana."

She had an abiding picture of her mother taking tea on a balcony overlooking the Mediterranean, the ever-present poodle on her lap, her *robe-de-chambre* drawn tightly at the waist, a cigarette holder at her lips. Sitting as she was on this lawn overlooking the sea, it occurred to her she must look the mirror image of her mother. She had enough of this island, this paradise. She missed the *Cote d'Azur.* Like a flower cut for a vase, one gave the illusion of life, but severed from one's roots, death was only a matter of time.

The sun was inching up the hillside, the shadows shrinking

from the beach. She pushed from the chair and made her way across the lawn. She was trapped. It had not occurred to her how shackled she was until the German had left that morning. He had been free to leave, but she would remain indefinitely.

She must find a way. Quickly.

On the walk to the cottage, she came to a decision. She would find her papers. Find someone to help her to escape. Someone she could trust.

She returned to the bedroom she had shared with the German. The sheets were rumpled, the pillows stacked haphazardly against the headboard. There was an ashtray stuffed with cigarette butts. He was a heavy smoker. He'd be back, he had said; not immediately, perhaps in a week or so. She wasn't certain if he had sounded pleased or not.

She sat on the bedsheet.

Whatever his peculiarities, Sambre was a meticulous man; he betrayed a clerical bent, and he kept his papers in order. She had seen him, on the occasions when she had spent the night, sorting through notebooks and poking through files. Sometimes, after the lovemaking, when she retired to her bedroom, he would shuffle his papers and wield his pen beneath a shaded lamp. Most of the papers he kept in his desk. But one book, a ledger of sorts, he returned to a closet of the bedroom. She had watched in the mirror as he stretched to his full height and stashed the ledger behind a travelling case on the uppermost shelf.

She lifted a chair from the dressing table and carried it to the closet.

She paused to listen.

The hillside was quiet, with only the wind worrying the leaves.

Balancing on the chair, she reached behind the luggage. She felt the binding. The ledger was heavy. She pulled it from the shelf and took it to her bedroom. Sitting where the German had lain only hours before, she thumbed the pages. There were scrawled notations, dated transactions as in a diary, but no papers belonging to one Lillette Bonnier. Disappointed, she was about to return it to the closet when another thought occurred. She might never find her papers; he might pass them on to someone else, sell them. Failing that, perhaps she could find something just as potent. He was a scheming man. He lived dangerously. She had overheard conversations. The talk was not all friendly to France. Some of it bordered on treason.

The notations in the ledger were profuse. They included names, dates, summaries of discussions. Perhaps her benefactor had something to hide. Men who have nothing to hide do not stash ledgers behind valises in closets. Whatever it was, she would find it. Armed with an indiscretion, political or diplomatic, perhaps she could blackmail him, gain some leverage. It was a dangerous game, but it was all she had.

The groan of an engine drifted from the road below. A vehicle was feeling its way up the hillside. She went to the window. Rising dust behind the low stone wall announced Honore's return from the city.

She replaced the ledger. Taking care to smooth the indentations in the carpet, she returned the chair to the dresser. When she scurried to the kitchen she felt considerably lighter in spirit. Though she had found nothing blatantly incriminating, she'd had little time to peruse his notations. There would be other opportunities. Too many, unfortunately. But at least she had made a beginning.

At least now she had hope.

FEBRUARY, 1942

THE WATERS OFF MARTINIQUE

Somewhere ahead lay the island.

Captain Dante O'Shea tightened his grip on the paddle. His arms were beginning to ache and a cramp had taken residence in his lumbar region. In the darkness that precedes the dawn, the night was as black as any he could remember. Clouds stretched from horizon to horizon, masking the stars and snuffing out the moon. The sky seemed so low he could feel the weight of it. Dipping the paddle, he resumed his snail-like progress toward the southern tip of Martinique. The oar stirred dim eddies of light in the sea. No matter how forcefully he broached the current, it seemed to anchor him to the spot. He was wearing fishermen's clothes and carrying false identity papers. In his briefing on St. Lucia he'd been told that, despite the blackout precautions, the lighthouse at Îlet à Cabrit had remained operational. If he hadn't seen its beam brushing the base of the clouds, he would have begun to doubt he was anywhere within sight of land. He should be under the lee of the coastline by now, but there was no discernible change in the swells, not a whisper of surf. Where there were supposed to be peaks, there was a sooty grey ceiling. Where he had anticipated a sniff of vegetation, there was the warm strong scent of the sea. The breeze shifted fractionally and he sensed the imminence of rain.

Propelling the small rubber dinghy through the darkness, he pondered the speeds at which wars were fought. Eight hours earlier he had been winging the sickle-shaped arc of the Antilles in a Navy flying boat. A few hours later he had begun the high-speed run in the British torpedo launch across St. Lucia Channel. And now the snail-like approach in the two-man raft where progress was measured by the phosphorescent swirls in the wake of his paddle.

The night was mild, the tradewinds catching their breath after a long landless journey from Africa. After the stale, brackish atmosphere of the PBY, he found the sea air bracing. The raft rose and fell on the long gentle swells and suddenly it began to rain, a tropical downpour that soaked his clothes and sizzled like bacon in a skillet. It stopped as suddenly as it had begun, and when the wind veered slightly to the east, he was beset by the odor of fish. As the breeze freshened stoutly he felt a change in the sea again, a shift from free-rolling swells to the choppier surge of a bay.

He checked his wristwatch. He should be within minutes of the shoreline. Another hundred yards and he would try the flashlight. He had done some homework on this island called Martinique. Set deep in the necklace of the Lesser Antilles, it was washed by the same gentle winds that had guided the intrepid Columbus five hundred years before, winds that swept the southern seas to bathe this tropical basin in a year-round silken caress. When the island was discovered by Columbus on his fourth and final voyage, it was occupied by the Carib Indians, a warlike tribe who had migrated from South America and conquered the peaceful Arawaks. In the turbulent eddies of Caribbean history, the French were the first Europeans to settle the island. There followed a large-scale importation of African slaves, when tobacco and sugar became the dominant crops. After repeated attacks and intermittent occupation by the Dutch and British in the nineteenth century, the island was permanently restored to France. Slavery was abolished in the 1840's and sugar replaced by rum and bananas. As to topography, Dante recalled, the island was about 400 square miles in area. In the north, where the mountains were flanked by lush green rain forests, there dwelt the volcanic Pelée. In the south, somewhere beyond the darkness ahead, the terrain was dominated by scrub woodlands and green-mantled hills. The rainy season fell somewhere between July and November, so at least he would escape that. On the Atlantic side the beaches were beset by rugged headlands and offshore coral reefs. Thankfully, he was approaching on the tranquil Caribbean side.

Suddenly, as though he had willed it, there was a shape in the darkness; a shadow within a shadow. Through a veil of mist he saw the outline of peaks, a silhouette of foothills. The mist thinned further and he caught the shape of trees, some hardwoods, mostly fern-like palms. As the land took on a harder outline, he raised the paddle and heard the plash of surf. Balancing the paddle across his thighs, he checked his Bulova. Nine minutes to four. With the raft yielding slowly to the current, he pumped the flashlight six times. The reply came a few degrees to the south...three blinks...pause... three blinks....pause....

He was closer than he thought. To his left stretched a tongue of land; to his right, a cove. As the swells subsided he managed the last hundred yards in smooth silent strokes, his fingers never far from the service .45 in his waistband.

He was wading to the beach when a man about his own height emerged from the shadows. Together and without a word they dragged the dinghy to the treeline. Still silent, they set about deflating the raft. When the task was complete the man dragged the dinghy to a pit that had been dug in the sand. Dante watched silently as the raft was covered over with a crude looking spade.

"No one will find it here," the man said. His English was virtually without accent.

From the shadows, another voice. "Hurry. It will soon be light."

It was a woman's voice. Dante turned to face her, but she had melted against the treeline. When she reappeared, he caught a glimpse of a slender silhouette.

With the woman leading the way and the man bringing up the rear, they made their way up the palm-lined beach. The air was heavy, the footing firm. He noticed they were avoiding the softer sand. In minutes they had clambered up an incline and gained the solidity of a road.

The woman stopped. Dante sensed the man move up behind him. He felt the press of something firm against his vertebrae.

"Now, monsieur, I will relieve you of your weapon. You have a message for us, please?"

Dante felt his ribcage contract as the muzzle sought the vicinity of his kidney.

He handed over the .45.

"The message, please."

"*Il n'y a plus de Pyrénées.* 'The Pyrenees have ceased to exist'."

The man slipped the .45 into his belt. "We cannot be too cautious, monsieur."

From the darkness of the treeline, the woman spoke barely above a whisper. "If we're detected, you're a seaman returning to visit. We've been lovers since before the war. I live in the village of Ste-Anne. My name is Nikole." Her English was spiced with the piquance of France.

Dante caught another glimpse of profile, the contour of a cheek. The rest was shadows.

"The French understand lovers," the man said amicably, and they resumed walking again.

With trees pressing the roadway and branches masking the heights, the island felt as black as the sea. Though of medium height, the woman walked with long fluid strides. They crested a hillock and the road fell away in a gradual descent. More than once Dante took a bad step on the pock-marked asphalt. Through an opening in the treeline, he caught a glimpse of the sea. The wind was tugging the palms and the moon floated free of the clouds.

They left the pavement and entered a meadow of sorts. Wading through waist-high scrubland, Dante stumbled over something in the grass. He felt it yield, then rise against his kneecap. Reflexively, he clutched the waistband where the pistol had been. A mound of flesh rose slowly toward his chin. He caught a barnyard smell and felt a soft wet muzzle poke firmly against his chest. There was a low bovine moan, and he found himself staring into the moist dark eye of a cow. The woman chuckled, a low feminine sound that gave dimension to the figure in the darkness.

They climbed a leg-wearying hill. When they reached a plateau, he could see they were circumventing a village. Below, he could make out the silhouette of buildings, modest wooden structures, none higher than the local coconut palms. They joined a footpath and climbed another hill, this one shorter than the last. When at least they pushed through a screen of vegetation, he realized they had entered a garden. The grass was clipped beneath his feet, the scent of bougainvillea heavy on the air. Looking over the heights to the sea, he could make out the outline of a cove, the same, he assumed, where the dinghy lay buried.

The garden gave way to a patio, the patio to the rear of a cottage. Without recourse to a key, the woman opened a door and Dante followed her through a hallway. It was windowless and dark. A match was struck and a candle flickered on a sideboard. They were in a kitchen, the windows lined with drapes, the air heavy with the scent of spices. The man closed the door behind them and the woman touched the match to a stove. Dante waited as she filled a kettle with water. In the glow from the burner he caught a glimpse of her face. It was devoid of makeup, but there was a flush to the cheeks, a luster to the eyes. Though not a beauty in the classic sense, she had a gypsy darkness, features that would qualify as striking. She caught his eye and looked away, busying herself with a tea service on the sideboard.

He turned his attention to the gunman. He was dressed casually, in a blue batiste shirt and grey trousers. A bulge was noticeable beneath the shirt where he had wedged the .45. He did not wear it comfortably. He was young, Dante noticed, and handsome, in a rugged sort of way. He wondered if he and the woman were lovers.

The woman lit an oil lamp on the table. Dante noticed her hands. The skin was smooth, the fingers slender, the nails unvarnished but carefully trimmed. Not the fingers of a peasant. The match had been split down the center. Matches were scarce in the islands, he knew, even among the more affluent residents. Many households were keeping a permanent fire.

The woman scooped tea from a container. She wore dark shapeless jeans and a loose-fitting shirt. Her shoes were canvas and stained with dew, her hair swept under a fisherman's cap. Aware that he was watching her, she turned to face him.

"Welcome, monsieur." The hint of a smile broke the corners

of her mouth, but her eyes remained noncommittal. "My name is Nikole. Nikole Rollet. You know me as SKIPJACK."

Despite the wavering lamplight, Dante was certain they had registered his surprise. He had assumed that SKIPJACK was the man; that the woman had been brought for the returning lover story.

The man removed his hat and extended a hand. "And I am Christopher," he said. "Christopher Delon. We can dispense with pseudonyms, monsieur. Once we greeted you on the beach, we committed ourselves. Martinique is a small island. There are few white civilians and fewer white women. We're putting our trust in you."

"I appreciate the confidence," Dante said. "Unfortunately, I cannot reciprocate in kind. But I can assure you I'm a friend of France. Call me Paul."

The woman spooned something into the kettle. She gave him an inquiring glance. "You're the first in some time to cross the Straits in this direction, Paul."

"These are peculiar times," he said. "We're all heading in directions we would not have thought likely."

"*Avez-vous faim?*" she asked, in her liquid accent.

"*J'ai faim. J'ai soif.*" Dante replied without hesitation. "*Quell est la specialit é de la maison*?"

A smile broke the corner of her lips. Removing her hat, she shook down her hair. It was short, falling just below her ears. The bangs that framed her forehead were black and shiny. When the lamplight fell on her profile, he could see that she wore no makeup and had no need of it. With the ice seemingly broken, he anticipated a slackening of features, but her gaze remained analytical, like that of an entomologist studying an insect. In the glow of the lamp she was trying to classify him. Friend or foe? Ally or spy? Was it caution or curiosity, he wondered? Or both?

She placed a cup at his elbow. He watched as she moved away. Despite the drape of her clothes, they revealed the contours of a good figure.

"May I ask why I've been summoned?" he said.

The woman took a seat across the table. The man drew up a chair beside her.

The woman spoke first. "You know of the gold, monsieur?"

"I'm aware of it, yes."

"We have reason to believe the Germans will attempt to steal it."

Dante looked hard into her eyes. "Steal it? If our intelligence is right, it would take a full-scale invasion to get that gold off this island."

"Perhaps. Nonetheless, we have certain information which leads us to believe a plot is underway."

Dante sampled the tea. It was strong and spicy; the flavor eluded him. "One obvious question."

"Monsieur?"

"If you're aware of a plot to steal the gold, why not go to the authorities?"

The man answered. "To begin with, we do not have all the details. Moreover, we have reason to believe that someone very close to the High Commissioner is involved. If we play our hand too soon, we could alert the conspirators. And since we cannot yet prove what we suspect, we might endanger the lives of people who have placed their trust in us. Patience, monsieur. You're in good hands."

"You have come to Martinique only to see us?" the woman asked.

"I have other business," Dante said. "It will involve a tour of the island. Can you manage that?"

"It can be arranged," the woman said. She walked to the window and tugged at a curtain. "Ste-Anne is a small village. A stranger would stand out like the statue in the square. A small Army contingent is stationed near the coast road. I have given my housekeeper the day off, but occasionally a patient will arrive unannounced. So for today, you must remain upstairs. Tonight you will be taken to Forte de France. There we can discuss what you have come to see. You can stay at Monsieur Delon's apartment. He will fill you in on what we know. When you have the facts, you can decide for yourself."

Nodding toward her companion, she left the room.

Businesslike, Dante thought. She had dealt in the bazaar before.

The Frenchman slid a basket of fruit across the table. “Some bread with your tea?” he asked. “An omelette, perhaps?” His English was as good as Dante’s French.

“Bread will be fine. What patients was she referring to?”

“Nikole Rollet is a doctor,” the Frenchman said. “A medical doctor. You look tired, monsieur. The crossing was wearying, no? Nikole has prepared a room.”

Dante stirred his tea. “I’m too pumped up to sleep. Tell me about the island. How’s the war affecting the locals?”

“I’m new to Martinique,” the Frenchman said. “I have only arrived a few weeks ago.”

“From where?”

“From France, by way of Morocco.”

They had travelled similar paths. Dante was tempted to feel him out, but this was no time to exchange travel tales.

“Is the sentiment pro-Vichy here?”

“Vichy rules are...,” the Frenchman hesitated, “...tolerated.”

Dante had heard of the Vichy rules. In France, Jews of all occupations were losing their positions. In some cities, they were being deported en masse. There were inquiries into the backgrounds of Freemasons and suspected communist sympathizers. Some officials were being dismissed because of their sympathy for DeGaulle. There was more, much more, he knew, but he was not familiar with the details.

The Frenchman continued. “Our High Commissioner is loyal to Vichy. As for the military, they are loyal to France. Some see France’s future with De Gaulle, while others place their trust in the old guard.”

“And the Martiniquais?”

“There are factions, of course. The ruling families follow the High Commissioner’s lead. Many of the locals have volunteered for the military. The islanders will fight at France’s side, whoever the enemy.”

“What of everyday living?”

"Food is rationed. Fortunately, the drinking water comes from springs. The diet of the islanders is based on fish; flour and salted fish. Codfish, mostly. For cooking, they use wood charcoal; for light there are kerosene lamps. Petrol is in short supply. Reserves are so meagre that businessmen are running their vehicles on a mixture of low-grade gasoline and alcohol made from sugar cane. They are in desperate need of medical supplies. Dr. Rollet is short of ether and catgut for operations."

"And morale?"

"There has been some slackening. It's forbidden to listen to the BBC, but antennas are raised by ropes after dark. Those who have it, listen on short wave."

"Has there been talk of invasion?"

"It's on everyone's lips. If it comes, they expect it to fall on the Atlantic side. Of course, they anticipate it will be the Americans.

"And what of the woman," Dante asked, nodding at the door.

"Madame Rollet is a patriot. She would give her life for France."

"You said 'madame'. Is she married?"

"Widowed. Her husband was killed by the Boche. She despises the Germans and mistrusts the British. I should warn you, monsieur, she has no particular love for Americans, either."

"And you, Christopher Delon. Where do you fit into this?"

"I'm a Frenchman. A friend of Madam Rollet's. Beyond that... well, perhaps we can compare biographies when we have more time."

Dante sampled the bread. It had a banana flavor. "This SKIPJACK business. What is it?"

"A resistance, of sorts. Some of the military prefer to fight with De Gaulle rather than sit here and rot."

"So you smuggle them to St. Lucia."

"That's Nikole's operation. She has the trust of the natives. She has contacts in the hierarchy at Forte de France and friends among the local militia. She is above suspicion."

"So far."

The Frenchman broke off a morsel of bread and lowered his eyes. "So far," he repeated.

Dante was taken to a second floor bedroom immediately beneath the eaves. It had a view of the sea and a narrow but comfortable bed. There was a wash basin in one corner and a water pitcher on the dresser. A closet had been converted into a small but functional toilet and a shower had been rigged over a drain in the floorboards. The cottage sat perched on a hill; the sounds from the village were swept by the wind. Knowing he should get some rest but unaccustomed to sleeping in daylight, he dozed fitfully throughout the afternoon, rising to consciousness at the tap of a shutter or the waspy buzz of a *velo* on the hillside below. When the knock came to his door shortly after sunset, he was shaved and waiting.

The woman was in the kitchen. She had changed to a skirt and blouse. In the low-heeled shoes she was taller than he had judged in darkness. She looked rested, more at ease. She was attractive in an earthy European way. She could be more than attractive, he thought, if she'd risk a smile. She was playing a dangerous game, he realized. Perhaps there was little to smile about. She had prepared some food in a basket. From beneath a towel poked the neck of a wine bottle.

She handed him the basket. "Forte de France is thirty kilometers to the north," she said, "but you'll be going the long way. The inland roads are tedious. Most are unpaved."

A man pushed through the doorway from the garden, a dark-skinned Creole wearing a floppy straw hat. Dante put him in his twenties.

"This is Lucien LeClerc," the woman said, her tone softening, her eyes betraying the first faint hint of mollification. "I trust him with my life. Lucien, this is your passenger, Monsieur Paul."

The Creole was a great crane of a man, lofty and gaunt and bent at the waist. He had a reedy neck and stilt-like legs. His eyes were friendly and his handshake firm. With a timid nod he smiled readily, ivory teeth in an ebon face.

Dante warmed to him immediately. "Nice to meet you, Lucien."

"Good," the woman said, getting back to business. "You are prepared, monsieur?"

"All set," Dante said.

The Creole tipped his hat and ducked silently through the door.

"Christopher Delon is at the truck," the woman said. "It's a bakery truck. Lucien delivers twice a week. A special bread baked here in Ste-Anne. He's known along the route. Remember, if you're questioned, you have a rendezvous with your lover in Forte de France. I'll meet you at Christopher's apartment on Saturday morning and we can arrange a tour of the island. This tour," she asked, meeting his eyes. "Is it a reconnaissance of sorts?"

Ignoring the question, Dante took her hand. *"Merci, Nikole. Je suis enchanté d'avoid fait votre connaissance."*

"Bon voyage, Paul."

Her eyes softened a bit, and for the first time she smiled. She even smiled in French. It was not unpleasant.

EASTERN CARIBBEAN

"... torpedoed! ...."

"...we're torpedoed and abandoning ship..."

......torpedoed......

.........abandoning ship......

Second Officer Julian Brodsky pressed the embers of a cigarette against the tip of a fresh Lucky Strike. He could not shake the finality of it. Leaning against the railing clad only in shorts, he was haunted by the desperation in the static-charged voice that had echoed through the ACADIA's radio receiver only hours before.

...torpedoed!...abandoning ship....

Earlier in the night they had seen a roseate glow on the horizon. Soon afterwards the ACADIA's radio operator had picked up an SSS...the signal for attack by submarine. Somewhere out there men were adrift in the darkness, some in lifeboats, others clinging to debris, others weighing the agony of burns against the numbing alternative of the sea. Some would be killed outright, some would die slowly, others would suffer dismemberment, their bodies prodded and ripped by opportunistic sharks.

Brodsky propped a foot on the railing and peered anxiously toward the horizon. The night was hot, the moon playing tag with some thin high cirrus. In the flickering wavelets the eyes played tricks. At times he thought he could envision the malevolent eye of a telescope. Beneath his feet the ACADIA was grinding along at an agonizingly slow speed of eight knots, a snail's pace, it's 2500 horsepower engine whirring like a sewing machine, it's 7,000 ton bulk barely laying a wake. The freighter was a pineapple clipper, so called because before the war it carried sugar and pineapples from the islands to the mainland. Now it was en route from Baltimore to

Barbados with aircraft and vehicle parts. Before leaving Baltimore, two volunteers from the Navy Reserve had shipped aboard to man a five-inch gun that had been mounted on the poop deck. Zigzagging through the Caribbean night, the ACADIA's captain was being careful to maintain the course laid down by the Navy. Not to do so could cost him his license; and far more permanent, his life.

In the past two hours Brodsky had seen the executive officer make three hurried trips between the radio shack and the bridge. When he dropped by the shack, 'Sparks' had confirmed what every man aboard had feared. They were receiving reports of submarines sighted, of distress calls from torpedoed ships.

Brodsky flipped the cigarette over the railing and watched as it was swept astern. Something was churning in the bow wake... the splintered remains of a wooden table...a life preserver...some unrecognizable bits of flotsam. He was trying to catalog the debris when he spotted what looked like lanterns bobbing gently in the darkness. The moon slipped free of a cloud and the lanterns resolved into lifeboats. A single boat at first, and then another. And then a raft, with figures huddled grimly against the mast.

Brodsky called hoarsely to the bridge. "Lifeboats! Starboard bow!"

After what seemed like hours, he felt the deck plates shudder as the engines slowed. With the word spreading rapidly throughout the ship, crewmen began scrambling to the railings. As the ACADIA hove to, there was shouting from the lifeboats.

"Keep moving...."

"Don't stop! We were sunk only two hours ago......"

"You're a sitting duck! The sub is still out there...."

Brodsky scaled the ladder to the bridge. In the pilot house, the captain and first mate were weighing the risk. Brodsky scurried back to the railing. The ACADIA began picking up speed. Apparently the captain had decided to radio their position and have the survivors rescued in daylight. He checked the sea around them. The bobbing lights were re-absorbed by darkness. To the south Brodsky spotted another light, blinking well off the starboard bow.

A cloud chewed a piece of the moon and the sea grew dark again. Suddenly the new light flared, then dimmed, then disappeared. It was difficult to determine the distance.

And then he saw it. The phosphorescent wake that haunted his dreams, the deadly spear of bubbles that traced a path to eternity. Stunned and speechless, and realizing it was far too late for words, he stretched a finger toward the frothy wake and formed the unspeakable with his lips.

"......Tor......pe......do......!!"

He was sprinting toward the lifeboats when the ACADIA exploded beneath his feet. Engulfed by light and a bone-rattling concussion that shattered his eardrums and jarred his teeth, he felt himself lifted from the deck and flung weightlessly into the void. Flames leaped past him as in a nightmare and the earth seemed to slip its axis. He felt a looseness in his bowels and a white hot pain in his legs. Grasping at air, he felt the impact of water, warm at first, and then as cold as slush. With the sea closing darkly around him, he felt a blockage in his throat, a pressure in his lungs.

Too deep.

He was going too deep.

Despite his panic, his limbs were shackled by the sea, his joints welded tightly by fear. A shiver of pain ran through his entire being. He would never make it. He was drowning. With his arms straining futilely against descent, he struggled to reverse direction. Slowly, with the desperation of an insect mired in varnish, he clawed his way toward the surface. The ACADIA was going down; he was fighting the sinking ship's suction. An eternity later he felt the slightest measure of success...a steady easing upward... upward... ever so slowly upward. With his senses reeling and every synapse screaming for relief, he was seconds from gasping a final breath when he broke the surface. Sucking madly at first, then gagging on oil, he inhaled the restorative sweetness of air.

The sea was aflame, greasy black smoke roiling inches above the surface. He lashed out desperately while struggling to maintain some buoyancy. Flailing his arms to keep the oil at bay, he felt a stitching pain in his legs. He rolled to his back and attempted to float. On the swells around him men were groaning and choking. To escape the inferno he splashed......then ducked......then rose and splashed again. When he surfaced for breath he vomited up water. It was clotted with oil.

At the crest of a swell he searched for his ship.

He looked left. Nothing.

Right. Nothing.

Nothing.

But for the flaming sea, all horizons were empty. The ACADIA was gone. He thought of the men who had not escaped. Trapped in the freighter, they would remain forever entombed beneath the trackless sea. Lightheaded and nauseous, he looked for something to cling to. He was exhausted, making no headway. His breath was coming painfully. Every hair had been singed from his body, and his throat was constricted by burns. Gradually he began to sink. He sucked in draughts of air. Realizing he was losing consciousness, he tried to kick out.

......left leg...

......right...

......right leg...

......right......

He clutched at his leg...tried to draw it to him...

There was a burning sensation where his knee had been... below that... nothing...

......nothing....

His leg......it was gone. He felt a mind-stabbing instant of clarity. It was rational enough to persuade him he was dying, cruel enough to snuff out hope. Traumatized by fear, his mind began to twist in anguish at the futility of his struggle. In a final spasm of lucidity, it permitted an inane, ridiculous thought:

...all the king's horses, and all the king's men...

Numb with terror and dazed by shock, he took a final futile swipe at the sea.

As the cadaver that had been Second Officer Julian Brodsky turned slowly with the current, Ensign Aldo Arazi played the beam of his flashlight over the debris-strewn waters. Standing on the SQUALO's foredeck, he wished despite the heat that he had worn his watch cap. He would pull it firmly over his ears. Were if not for the men around him, he would plug a finger into each aural canal to block out the hellish screams of the drowning.

The tower of flame that had erupted when the torpedo had struck had illumed the night for miles around. With the freighter in its death throes, the SQUALO was cruising nakedly on the surface, gun crews at the ready, the men on the bridge watching silently as the stricken ship turned turtle and slipped beneath the waves. With the sea going dark again, all that was left was the cries of the drowning and the thrum of the SQUALO's diesels.

The ACADIA had steamed helplessly into the trap. Captain Valerio had been right. All they had to do was remain in the vicinity of the lifeboats and sooner or later a ship would stop to render assistance. The rescuer would be an easy target. Not very sporting, Valerio admitted, but war was war; they must take their advantage where they found it. Still, Aldo thought, it would be months before he could purge the screams of the drowning. They would forever haunt his dreams. One of the victims he would remember until his dying day. Naked and blackened by oil, his flesh hanging loosely from a blistered torso, Aldo had looked on helplessly as his face had boiled away. There was a curse in the dead seaman's eyes, as though someone would pay for this affront to the brotherhood. The entire affair was a tragedy, Aldo thought. There were no victors, only victims. They were all praying to the same God, were they not? For victory? For mercy? For survival? What did it mean, he wondered? To what end were they slaughtering their fellow mariners?

Despite the kill, there was no jubilation among the SQUALO's crew. The ACADIA was their third hapless victim of the week. Fish in a barrel, Valerio had called it. Little glory could accrue to that. While the score was mounting, the thrill was draining from the hunt.

Aldo forced his attention to the task at hand. Valerio was intent on finding the freighter's skipper. He could not save the crew;

the SQUALO would be at sea for weeks. It would be physically impossible to accommodate survivors. Though he would prefer to tow them to a neutral island, the risk to his boat precluded that. He had little choice but to leave them adrift. But Captains were worth saving. They knew the codes, the recognition signals.

As the SQUALO slipped silently through the debris, its spotlights playing on the life vests of its victims, Valerio called through a bullhorn to each and every raft and lifeboat, to every piece of floating debris that might have men aboard. "Your officers! Have them identify themselves! If you identify your captain, we will leave you food and water. He will be put ashore at a neutral port. We want only to check our charts."

For the most part, he was met with silence. Those who could raise their heads just stared at him with lusterless eyes, their faces singed by flame, their flesh charred, their hair spiked or plastered by scummy black oil. There was a reply from one of the rafts, from an elderly seaman with a blackened face and a gash oozing blood on his cheek. Pushing shakily to his feet on the bobbing, drifting platform, he thrust a scorched right arm at a stiff right angle to the crook of the other.

"Fuck you, you wop cocksucker!"

From the SQUALO there was silence.

Unable to find the captain of the stricken freighter, the Italian skipper ordered his helmsman to make for open water, to clear the debris and set a course for the Grenadines. The night was young. There would be other stragglers. The Caribbean was rich with targets.

As one by one the crew descended the hatches, Aldo turned back to retrieve his St. Christopher medal. He had hooked a finger through the chain in the heat of battle and it had fallen between the slats in the deck. He could see it glinting beyond the base of the gun mount. He was reaching for the chain when the sea went bright with light. Thinking Valerio had rekindled the spotlight, he turned to see the bridge empty, a powerful beam descending from the base of a cloud. As though attracted by the submarine's hull, the beam came speeding toward him. It scurried across the oil-slick surface and locked onto the SQUALO's foredeck. Suddenly another sound was mixed with the throb of the diesels...muffled at first, then loud and growing louder.

In the SQUALO's belly the klaxon bonged harshly.

Aldo pivoted quickly and took a running step toward the supply hatch. He slipped and cracked a knee against the decking. A pain knifed sharply through his kneecap. With the knee shooting daggers to his groin, he stumbled awkwardly toward the railing. The boat lurched forward and his leg went as limp as a rag.

The SQUALO was gathering speed.

Aldo crawled painfully toward the deck gun. He was scrambling to gather some purchase when the forward hatch clamped down. He saw the wheel spin tightly as the dogs were drawn. Glancing anxiously over a shoulder, he saw that the after hatch was secured as well. With a rush of fear he felt the bow nose downward.

The SQUALO was beginning its dive.

They had forgotten him.

They had not seen him.

He had been hidden by the gun mount. With everyone scrambling for their posts, someone had blown the head count. He felt his bowels shrivel.

He was trapped!

Stranded on deck!

A nightmare beyond a nightmare!

The new sound powered closer now, a high-pitched drone at the base of a cloud. An aircraft! They were under attack by an aircraft! Aldo could see the shape of it now, the gull-like wings beyond the cone of light, a spotlight swelling ominously from the darkness. He felt a clutch of panic, a weakness in his entire being. With pain lancing his leg and his brain scrambling desperately for control, he scuttled like a crab toward the ladder to the bridge. As the boat tilted steadily beneath him, its bow plates angled steeply on dive, he shinnied painfully up the ladder. The sea came churning over the cannon mount; the angle of decent was immutable. Trapped in the cone of light, he clung to the railing of the gun platform and pounded against the skin of the tower.

“Valerio!...per favore! Dio mio!...per favore!....

One thousand feet above the SQUALO, Whitely had the Catalina angled precisely down the beam. This one he was going to get. This killer he was going to obliterate. Slowed almost to a halt as it melted beneath the surface, a submarine was at its most vulnerable during a dive. With the sea roiling greenish-white in the beam of the spotlight, he’d never find a better target.

The bombardier’s voice crackled calmly in his earphones. “Steady, skipper. He’s seconds away. He’ll never make it.”

Second Pilot Jeff Pritchard was on the edge of his seat; the entire crew was frozen in place, holding their collective breaths. Only bombardier Larry Killigan seemed relatively at ease. With the Catalina sliding steadily downhill and his finger poised on the bomb-release button, he crouched in the nose turret and watched the heaving green incandescence.

“MSteady, skip...steady.... Come to papa, you murdering bastard....”

At 600 feet Killigan muttered, “Climb, skipper! Climb!”

On the flight deck, Whitely eased the Catalina skyward so the bombardier could release the depth charges by airman’s eye.

“Now!” Killigan shouted, his voice ringing sharply in their earphones. “Now!”

He squeezed the pickle and two Mark 37 depth bombs slid instantly from their racks. In a lazy tumbling descent, the tail-finned projectiles plummeted straight toward the bow of the submerging submarine. The 650-pounders were loaded with enough explosive to split the SQUALO’S carcass in half. When Killigan shouted “bombs away!, Whitely shoved the throttles to the wall and gunned the Catalina toward the moon.

On the SQUALO’s partially-submerged gun deck, Ensign Aldo Arazi, late of Torino, lover of poetry, questionable virgin, and in the winter of his eighteenth year, stood huddled against the skin of the conning tower. With spray drenching his face and fear fogging his senses, he raised his eyes toward a pair of torpedo-shaped projectiles wobbling crazily through the gossamer beams of light. For a moment the plane seemed to thunder above him, then the light disappeared and the sky went as black as death. In an instant of agonizing anticipation, Aldo squeezed the ladder and waited; awaited the unthinkable...the unfathomable...the unimaginable.

ST. JOHN'S

U.S. VIRGIN ISLANDS

The sloop was the only vessel in the shallow basin of the cove. So clear was the water beneath its hull that it hovered over its shadow as if suspended in air. On the sunbaked decking of the cockpit, Casey O'Shea wedged a bottle of wine into a cooler of ice. From the ladder to the galley, Lt. Kevin Whitely handed up a pair of sandwiches, roast beef smothered with onions and wrapped in wax paper. He had coaxed the sandwiches from a cook at St. Thomas' Marine Base.

That should do for lunch," Casey said. We'll save the lobster for later.

"I'm starved," Whitely said. Climbing through the transom, he stretched to full height on the polished teak deck.

He had rented the 40-footer for the weekend. As it drifted over the diamond-clear waters, its bow gently nosing the breeze, he surveyed the beach, a crescent of sand backed by lithe swaying palms.

Whitely was wearing Navy-issue bathing trunks, regulation blue. He had a lean athletic build and broad sinewy shoulders. Though his face was tanned, his chest and legs were as white as the underbelly of a tortoise. On the sail over from St. Thomas, Casey had warned him against too much sun. The sky was blue and cloudless. Deep in the cove, it was almost too hot to breathe. Even the gulls seemed to cry out against the heat. Whitely had purchased a broad-brimmed hat from a native lad in St. Thomas. It was frazzled at the edges and the straw was a brittle banana yellow. Though the boy had protested it was new, there was a suspiciously dark stain where the brow touched the forehead.

Casey looked stunning in a one-piece bathing suit. The color, Whitely noticed, matched the pale blue vein at the base of her throat. She had long auburn hair as thick as sargasso, skin so fair it would never tan. Whitely had spent the sail over oblivious to the heat. Mesmerized instead by her flawless figure, he could not believe his sudden good fortune. Here he was on this idyllic island, about to spend a day and perhaps a night with a woman the likes of whom his flying brethren the world over could only fantasize. He felt the heat in his groin and had an urge to skip the picnic, forget the island, and take her below where she could cut whatever deal she would in any one-sided bargain for his soul.

He slipped the dingy over the side and steadied it with his foot. Casey lowered the cooler and he untied the painter and cast off. The cove was pure crystal, sapphire shoals washing a bottom ridged with sand. As they paddled ashore, a school of silversides took refuge in the shadow of the dinghy. When they reached the shallows, Whitely did the unloading and Casey dragged the dinghy onto the beach.

They chose some high ground in the shadow of a palm. Casey unfurled a blanket and they anchored it with the cooler then smoothed it with their knees.

"Perfect," Whitely said, scanning the horizon.

He turned to face her. She was smiling, the breeze stirring her hair, her eyes absorbing the turquoise of the cove. This was their third date, if one could call drinks and dinner in the confines of the Trade Winds a date. But this was the first time they would be alone, removed from the byways of Charlotte Amalie and the all-seeing eyes of a tight island community.

"I'll scrounge some driftwood," Whitely said, feeling the need to cool down a bit. "A souvenir for your patio."

As he wandered down the beach, Casey propped an elbow on the blanket. She searched the horizon. Beyond the reef a sailboat was bending to the wind. In the distance lay St. Thomas, a vaporish green promontory that seemed afloat on the sea. She had vowed to let nothing intrude on this outing, to keep the present in focus and to enjoy the day. Viktor Reinmann was out there somewhere. Sooner or later she would have to cope with that. So shocked had she been at his sudden appearance on the day after Pearl Harbor, so much turmoil had there been in the wake of the war news and the subsequent scrambling of personnel and priorities, that she had blocked his return from consciousness, stowed it in a small dark place until she could deal with it. Eventually she would have to deal with it. Viktor was the enemy now. Could that have been six whole weeks ago? Had she put it off that long? She had not even confided in Rina. Apparently she had buried it deeper than she thought. Perhaps she should bury it forever.

She had been stunned to find Viktor in her room that December afternoon. Flustered and confused, she had hustled her son to the patio without realizing the youngster was barefoot. When she returned, Viktor was standing near the bed opening a carton of her cigarettes. He looked older, leaner, less boyish. His features were harder, his hair shorter.

"What the hell are you doing here?" she asked, her cheeks flushed with anger. I mean...when...where did you......?"

He just stared at her. She had come from the pool. She was still in her bathing suit, the lining damp against her skin.

"You're beautiful;" he said. "More beautiful than ever."

She snatched a robe from the dresser and draped it over her shoulders.

"The boy?" he asked. "He's your son?"

She reacted angrily. "Do you think you can drop in after three years and...and act like it's only yesterday? Why are you here? When?...how long have you been here...? Do you know there's a war on...?"

He shrugged. "It doesn't concern us."

"Haven't you heard?" she asked. "We're enemies now. Your Japanese allies have attacked Pearl Harbor."

His eyes narrowed a bit, but he betrayed no surprise. He reached out as if to touch her.

She pulled away and shuddered as though he had slapped her. She wanted to strike him. Instead, she found herself sobbing. "Jesus Christ...three years...three goddamn years......"

There was a rapping at the door.

Viktor strolled casually to the French doors. Casey dabbed gently at her eyes. When she opened the door, her father was standing in the hallway. He was wearing his uniform, his cap tilted back, the tans smartly pressed.

"Uh...it's..I'm...I'm with a friend, daddy. Could you give me a minute...?"

"Sure, Case."

He looked past her. Dante had never seen Viktor Reinmann; had never heard his name. Casey assumed that if he saw the man at all, he would think it was someone from the island. An old boyfriend, perhaps. Or one of Rina's friends.

"I'll wait in the lobby, Case."

"Okay, daddy. I'll be out in a minute."

She closed the door.

Viktor walked up behind her. "Your father. He's still Navy."

She slipped a cigarette from a package and fumbled with a match. She tossed both match and cigarette into an ashtray.

He placed his hands on her shoulders and spun her around.

She knocked his arms away. "I'm engaged," she lied. "You can't just turn up and expect...." Her shoulders sagged; she began weeping again. "My father's waiting. I have to go..."

Sean had been playing on the patio. Suddenly he ran to the sliding glass door, tears welling in his eyes. "Mommy. Mommy......"

Casey went out to comfort him. There was a trickle of blood on a heel. She tamped it with a finger. "It's all right, honey. Mommy will make it better."

Viktor followed her onto the patio. "I'll be back," he said. He looked at Sean as though assessing his features, gauging his age. When he turned to Casey again, his eyes had softened a bit. For an instant, she caught a glimpse of the boy she had remembered, the man-child of a distant summer night. It seemed another lifetime.

"It's good to see you, *liebling*," he said. He patted Sean's head then pushed on through the shrubbery.

***

On the beach at St. John's, the breeze was flapping a corner of the blanket. Casey rose to a sitting position and shielded her eyes from the sun. Kevin was strolling the water's edge, the hat cocked back on his head, his skin as pale as sand.

No, her father had never met Viktor Reinmann. When Viktor had quit the island in 1938, she was not yet certain she was pregnant. When finally she confided her condition to her mother, her father was serving at sea. Her mother was dismayed, but she took it calmly, as she did most everything that smacked of crisis. For that, Casey loved her all the more. But she was worried about her father.

"Your father will understand," Caroline had said. "He's a bit on the gruff side at times, but he loves you, honey. He'll understand."

Casey suggested a letter, but Caroline advised against it.

"It's too important for a letter, honey. It's better we await his next shore leave."

"You tell him, mamma. I don't think I could face him."

When Dante returned on leave, Casey was seven months pregnant. Caroline had sent her to Rina's for the weekend, ostensibly so that husband and wife could share a quiet homecoming. Sometime during the weekend, when it felt right and Dante had regained his land legs, Caroline would break the news. That would give him a day or so to adjust, to cool down.

Apparently she had never found the right moment.

That Saturday evening, a driver arrived at Rina's cottage. His orders were to bring Casey home. The car was official Navy, the driver strangely mute when she tried to engage him in conversation. Assuming her mother had broken the news and that her father was ready to discuss her pregnancy, she stepped from the car large with child. Thinking her mother had greased the ways, she could see the consternation in her father's face, the surprise. Dante looked haggard. Defeated. Ignoring her obviously delicate condition, he led her to a chair on the verandah.

He was all but unable to speak. "Case....". He hesitated. Cleared his throat, raked trembling fingers through his unkempt hair. She had never seen him so distraught. So deflated. She had not expected so harsh a reaction.

"Case. It's your mother.... We were... we rented a boat......I was diving off a reef.... There was a...a fire... An explosion... Your mom, Case...she...I.... I saw the smoke...I tried to get back... It blew.... It went down...." He choked back a sob. "...it went down....I tried...I tried to get her out...I... she's...gone, Case.... Your mother...she's gone..."

He broke down. Casey had never seen him cry. He turned away, as though in shame, but the tears were there. She could see his heaving chest. She stood there at a loss. Devastated. She and Caroline had been as close as mother and daughter could be. Caroline had passed her pregnancy making clothes for the baby. She had never once admonished the teenager for the pregnancy, never once suggested terminating or putting the baby up for adoption. What had happened, had happened, her mother had said. It was God's will. Perhaps the father would return, perhaps he would not. God had seen fit to place this gift in their hands and they would deal with it. If Casey decided she could not accept the child, they would find someone who could. Just now the priority was a healthy pregnancy, a healthy infant. When the time came she would make Dante understand. She would blunt the edge of reaction and bring father and daughter together. It was not the end of their world. They would become stronger for it, a more loving family.

Her father fought to regain his composure. Casey looked hard into his haggard face. He was stricken beyond recall, desolate with grief, his cheeks as bloodless as the knuckles on his fists. He ignored her condition entirely, as though her swollen abdomen was part of a conspiracy to complicate an already impossible situation, as though the shock of losing Caroline had rendered him blind to all but his immediate grief, as if his deformed daughter was some bizarre trick sent to distract him from the larger tragedy.

"It...it's best you stay with Rina for now," he said. "I've got to... to make arrangements..."

It was not until he was putting her in the car that he mentioned her condition. "My God, Case...when?...I mean....I didn't know... why didn't someone tell me...? I didn't know..."

They broke down in each other's arms, her father supporting her as though she were friable, she sobbing uncontrollably, feeling that at any second she might go lightheaded and faint.

"Mamma was going to tell you, daddy.... She was going to tell you this weekend..."

"It's okay, honey...it's....okay. We'll work it out. We'll work it out..."

She watched as he walked dazedly to the house, his shoulders sagging, his pace unsteady on the flagstone walk, like a blind drunkard feeling his way.

In the next few days they went through the motions as in a nightmare, a hasty funeral attended by friends, a burial in her mother's family plot. There was only passing mention of Casey's pregnancy. Caroline's sister lived on the island. She was a spinster. It seemed to Casey that her father was turning her over to her aunt, that somehow he was linking her pregnancy to Caroline's death, that he had decided to distance himself from her condition until he was ready to cope with it.

The Navy had granted him leave, but he refused it. He was anxious to quit the island and return to sea, to deal with his grief out of sight of land, of family. On his last night ashore, he sat with Casey on the verandah of their cottage. Singularly remote, he told her he was leaving.

"Your aunt will look after you, Case, until...until you're... all right. Afterwards you can stay at the cottage, or, maybe return to Chicago to stay with your grandmother."

Only once did he ask about the baby's father.

Casey lied. "A seaman, daddy...."

"American?"

"He said he was...Norwegian." She could not bring herself to say German. Her father had been soured on Germans since the 1918 War, had never forgiven them for the uncles he had lost on the Marne. And now, with the Nazis in Europe....

"He gave me a false name, she said. "He left before I knew I was pregnant. I probably won't see him again."

"Do you want to see him, Case?"

"I...I don't know, daddy. I don't know...."

Sean was born while Dante was in France. He phoned her periodically to see how mother and son were doing. The connection was always bad. They chatted awkwardly, he promising to take leave as soon as possible, she talking hesitantly about the baby.

His grandson was three months old when Dante flew in for a weekend. Casey had returned to the cottage and was teaching part-time at a nearby schoolhouse. Though he fawned over the baby, the cottage seemed to depress him, the island to suffocate him with memories. Casey noticed that he was drinking, something he had rarely done before. She noticed, too, his uneasiness with any intimacy, his mood swings, his inability to sleep. He left promising more frequent visits, but Casey could see he was relieved to go.

The night before Pearl Harbor, the night of their reunion at the Trade Winds bar, they had reached a turning point in their relationship. After three indifferent years Dante seemed a new man, a father again. And more than that...a grandfather. And that wasn't all that had changed that night. In the midst of her joy over her reunion with her father, she had met Kevin Whitely. She was feeling something with Kevin, something she thought she might never feel again. And it felt wonderful. Truly wonderful.

***

Whitely returned from his beachcombing and lay beside her on the blanket. She felt his fingers brushing her hair; the heat of his calf pressed her calf. She rolled to her stomach and thought of Sean. God's will. God's gift. He was a precious little boy. A spirited little towhead with his grandmother's even temperament and his grandfather's stubborn grit. He had Caroline's sunny disposition and her patient observation. And he had Dante's curiosity. His confidence. His need to plumb the unknown.

What of Viktor Reinmann? How much of his father was there

in Sean? Of that she could not be sure. They had known each other for only a few short weeks. Golden hair. Pale blue eyes. Sometimes when Sean lay asleep with a lock of hair curled over his forehead, she caught a glimpse of the Viktor she had lain with, much like this, on another beach, in another life. Had she loved Viktor Reinmann? Had she ever truly loved him? For two full years she had kept the fantasy alive, remembering their nights at Magen's Bay, his ready laughter, his tenderness when sensitivity overcame his rough exterior. Love him? Until she had seen him standing there in her room at the Trade Winds, she had not been sure. But whatever he had been before, whatever they had shared, he seemed hardened now, with cold blank eyes and a stone-like insolence. Whatever he had experienced in the intervening years had numbed him, calloused him. It was as though the tenderness had been distilled away, leaving only the dregs of arrogance. Of brutishness.

Love him?

Once, perhaps.

"O.K. pigeon, let's go for a swim. This sun is...h-o-t!"

Whitely scooped her up as though she were feathers. He carried her to the waterline and waded to his chest. When he laid her into the sea, he placed her gently, with an easy hand. Revived by his touch, she shook away the past. The sea was body temperature, the shallows effusing the scent of brine. While she was buoyed by his hand, balanced on his palm, he leaned over and kissed her lips. She returned the kiss with fervor. Then without a word he spun her to her belly and launched her into a long shallow dive. As they skimmed the floury ridges, her fingers tightened firmly onto his.

THAT SAME NIGHT

THE VENEZUELAN COAST

Silhouetted against a late-rising moon, a solitary seabird beat a northerly path across the oil-slick waters of Lake Maracaibo. Beneath the seabird's wingtips a forest of derricks protruded like miniature Eiffel Towers from the shallow bed of the lake, a lake so vast it assumed the proportions of an inland sea. The fields of Maracaibo were a major source of petroleum for the British war effort: for the Spitfires of the Royal Air Force, for Field Marshall Montgomery's "desert rats" in North Africa, for the embattled warships of the Royal Navy.

Winging high above the lighthouse at San Carlos, the seabird entered the Gulf of Venezuela, the body of water between the Maracaibo oilfields and the offshore refineries at Aruba and Curacao. As it soared above the shallows, its fisherman's eye took in a sizeable fleet of ships that lay at anchor off the entrance to the harbor. The ships were shallow-draft vessels called "lake tankers". Day after day the tankers transported thousands of barrels of crude oil from the lake to the refineries offshore, their flat shallow bottoms permitting passage over the sand bar at the harbor's entrance. Week in and week out, the sixty-three tankers shuttled the 160 miles between Maracaibo and the island refineries in a steady ocean-going caravan, their decks manned by Dutch and Chinese workers who labored by day under the hot Venezuelan sun and by night under the sultry lash of the Trades.

Wearying of its flight, the seabird turned eastward where, with some vigilance and a fisherman's luck, it might extract a heedless crab from the shoals. A mile offshore it overflew another flotilla, this one much smaller, with vessels never before seen in these latitudes, vessels long of line and low of silhouette trailing slim phosphorescent wakes. Running without lights and with engines slowed to deaden the sound, this peculiar armada edged toward the unsuspecting tankers like barracuda stalking mackerel.

As the tankers awaited the tide at the mouth of the harbor, hundreds of Chinese seamen lay sleeping on the moon-silvered decks. Despite the moon the night was dark, the ships drifting like shadows on a tranquil sea. Suddenly the silence was shattered by a thunderous explosion and the sky went ablaze with flame. Secondary detonations boomed in the night as pillars of fire erupted first from one tanker and then another. As the seabird fled the area, the sea was furrowed by the deadly wakes of torpedoes, and out of the darkness snaked the long lazy arcs of tracers.

The fleet was bracketed by U-Boats, a miniature wolf pack. Though the tankers rode high in the water, enough Venezuelan crude remained in their holds to touch off a dramatic display of fireworks. From orange tongues of flame, smoke billowed skyward in greasy black clouds. With tracers stitching the darkness, the barking of deck guns mingled with the screams of the dying. As one by one the deadly eels impacted their targets, men began leaping from decks to the oil-slick surface only to thrash for survival in a sea of flame.

A hundred and fifty miles to the north, Viktor Reinmann stood on the bridge of Unterseeboot-156 as it neared the island of Aruba. As an envoy of Admiral Doenitz, Reinmann was the guest of Korvettenkapitän Werner Hartenstein, one of Germany's most decorated U-Boat commanders. Accorded a position of honor on this strategically important assault, Viktor watched as below him on the foredeck the gun crew began manning the deck cannon. Already the men on the gun platforms were readying their anti-aircraft weapons, and beside him on the bridge lookouts were sweeping binoculars to all points of the horizon.

Having completed the crossing from Lorient only a few days before, the U-156 was spearheading OPERATION NEULAND, the assault that would bring the war to Caribbean waters, to the vulnerable shipping lanes between the Atlantic approaches and the Panama Canal. NEULAND was a follow-on to Admiral Doenitz's PAUKENSCHLAG, the roll of the drums, the successful attack on Allied shipping along America's east coast.

Hartenstein was a fearless commander. A decorated veteran, he had been sent to this submariner's paradise as a reward for his work in the Atlantic. Already other members of his group were attacking the lake tankers off Maracaibo. As his U-Boat knifed steadily toward Aruba, he took up a position beside his guest.

"The San Nicholas Refinery is one of the world's largest, Herr Reinmann. It produces millions of barrels of oil a year. It's a major source of aviation gasoline. If we knock it out, we will hit the British where it hurts, in the skies over England."

Viktor adjusted his binoculars. The tank farm lay dead ahead, silhouetted against the low-hanging moon like a village on a snow plain. A rich jungle smell came out on the wind. So flat was the island that the refinery seemed to be growing out of the sea.

"What of defenses, Captain? Surely such a prize is well protected."

Hartenstein propped an elbow on the wind deflector. "Our Intelligence informs us that the island is guarded by a single Dutch motor whaleboat. That, and a few small coastal guns. American troops were put ashore a few days ago, but they're still constructing their barracks. We'll be in and out before they know what hit them. Our target is the main storage tanks. You see those slightly to the left of the docks?"

Viktor swung his binoculars toward a cluster of tanks etched darkly against the sky.

"They're old tanks," Hartenstein said. "Decoys. They've not been used for years. The real tanks are over there, camouflaged under painted netting." He whispered into the voice tube. "Starboard, ten degrees."

Low in the water, its conning tower naked against the sky, the U-156 slipped steadily into range. From where Viktor stood between the bridge shield and the periscope standard, very little could be heard: the sputtering exhaust of the diesels, the hiss of water against the hull, the occasional click of a valve belowdecks. Through his glasses, he could see the lettering on the cylindrical tanks. He could not believe the inefficiency of this enemy they were fighting. The Dutch had resisted bravely when the Wehrmacht had blitzkrieged the Low Countries. Now they were leaving one of the world's largest refineries as naked and unprotected as a peacetime border crossing. Hitler had been right. Germany could not lose this war. With foes like these, the Reich would survive a thousand years.

The U-Boat crept closer.

Viktor focused on the refinery. With his binoculars gathering light from the moon, he could see a road to the rear of the tanks. There were people on the road. Civilians. Four or five, as best he could make out. On their way to work, perhaps; or finished for the night and going home. He lowered his binoculars and watched as the gunnery officer swung the deck cannon toward the camouflaged tanks.

It's like a dream, Viktor thought. Surrealistic. A peaceful night, a calm sea, the island slumbering under a tropical moon. With the U-Boat inching slowly toward the coastline and the tank farm pregnant and vulnerable in the indigo darkness, it reminded him of a party he had been to as a small boy, when he and his companions had cut silhouettes from tarpaper and peppered them with pellet guns.

Hartenstein whispered a command.

The gunnery officer raised a hand.

As the hand descended, Viktor swung the binoculars toward the island. A flash caught the corner of his eye. Immediately the boat lurched and rocked as though hammered by a massive blow. The jolt rocked the bridge and Viktor heard shrapnel whistling past his ear. Assuming they had been hit, he ducked behind the protective coaming as did the Captain beside him. When they rose again, the sea around them was hissing with steam as shards of metal rained down upon the swells. Viktor could see fumes smoldering from the barrel of the deck gun. The muzzle was shattered and the gunnery officer lay sprawled on deck, his trousers shredded, a bone protruding visibly from the flesh of a mangled leg. Two other crewmen clung dazedly to the safety railings, both seriously wounded, both twitching painfully as they tried to regain their feet.

"*Verdammt*! Hartenstein swore. "Come about. All ahead full."

Braced against the coaming, Viktor heard the gunnery officer call weakly toward the bridge.

"The bung! Herr Kapitan. We forgot to remove the bung!"

As the U-Boat veered sharply from the island, crewmen scrambled forward to assist the wounded. Viktor remembered the people behind the tanks, the civilians. Had the gunnery officer hesitated until they had cleared the area? Had that broken his concentration? Was he the victim of his own compassion? Viktor focused his binoculars on the cannon. The weapon was fractured near the tip, the barrel smoldering from the heat of the blast.

On the island, lights began blinking on in the vicinity of the refinery. A siren sounded, and the beam of a searchlight slid silently over the waters. Whoever was manning the light must have misjudged the sound, for the beam turned inland, in the direction of the town. Hartenstein paced the bridge as the wounded were lowered through a hatch. With only a pharmacist on board to tend their wounds, Viktor wondered at their fate.

As the U-156 fled westward toward the open sea, Hartenstein shook a fist at the island. "The next time you won't be so lucky," Viktor heard him say. "The next time we will have your tanks."

They resurfaced later that morning. Hartenstein ordered an inventory of hacksaw blades on board. Crewman located fourteen blades. As Viktor watched, the gun crew worked in shifts, sharpening the blades and sawing the cannon's tempered steel. The following night, with the truncated deck gun once more serviceable, the U-156 attacked a solitary tanker and shelled it to the bottom. That same night Hartenstein set a course for France, for their home port of Lorient. The U-156 was due for refit. Off Grenada, Viktor was transferred to another U-Boat, this one en route to the waters off Jamaica.

The night of the Maracaibo/Aruba raids had been a stellar night for the Kriegsmarine. In one swift thrust, the oil supply to England had been cut and Doenitz's grey wolves had tasted fresh blood. Before the sun could chase the darkness, a goodly percentage of the tanker fleet had settled beneath the waves and scores of seamen had been killed or wounded. Not a drop of crude would leave Maracaibo for seven days. To sweeten the victory, the surviving Chinese crewmen refused to put to sea. The Dutch had threatened to jail them, but just as they were beginning to reconsider, a Norwegian tanker was torpedoed off the coast of Curacao and the Chinese chose internment over death.

Two nights later, the boat to which Viktor had been transferred torpedoed a merchant ship at the entrance to Port of Spain, Trinidad. The cargo was bauxite. Without bauxite, there could be no aluminum. Without aluminum, there could be no aircraft. Without aircraft, there would be no England.

Viktor's new host was younger than Hartenstein, but what he lacked in experience, he made up for in enthusiasm.

"In the Caribbean, Herr Reinmann, we are reaping a golden harvest. There is little to stop us. We don't even bother to submerge. Our crews are tanned, and morale is high. With the Americans retreating in the Pacific, the British backed against the sea in North Africa, and all of Europe under the Wehrmacht's fist, victory is just a matter of time. Last year, when our submarines ruled the Atlantic, the U-Boatwaffe called it *die Gluckliche Zeit*, "The Happy Time" This year, with victories off the American coast and in these southern waters, they're calling 'The Second Happy Time'. On this boat," he said, breaking into a broad smile, "we call it the 'Paradise War.'"

FORTE DE FRANCE, MARTINIQUE

Dressed in seaman's attire and sporting a three-day beard, Dante O'Shea sat in a harborside bar in Forte de France sipping *mabi,* an island beer made from molasses. Between swigs of beer he was polishing his somewhat rusty French on the man who sat across from him, the man who called himself Christopher Delon. The Frenchman was drinking white rum and tonic. He was wearing blue linen slacks and a white polo shirt. He was nicely tanned, and Dante noticed he had a muscular physique for someone with such delicate hands. Despite his detached exterior, Dante thought the Frenchman looked uneasy in his role as undercover agent.

"You wanted a close-up look at the harbor," Delon said, gesturing toward the pier not twenty yards from where they sat. "It would be difficult to get closer than this."

The harbor at Forte de France was teeming with ships. Dante counted almost forty vessels at anchor, all captive to the American destroyers patrolling beyond the three-mile limit, Security seemed tight. A number of powerboats trailing thin white wakes could be seen crisscrossing between warships. Deep in the anchorage Dante could distinguish the supercruiser EMILE BERTIN. Another cruiser, the JEANNE D'ARC, was tied to a pier beside Fort St. Louis. He recognized the ships from photos he'd been shown in San Juan.

He glanced around the cafe. It was the type of establishment where young rum was consumed: round marble-topped tables, a zinc-topped bar, the smell of salt fish clinging to the air. The music from a radio behind the bar sounded Arabic. In a corner near the door three Martiniquais were tossing dice onto the slats of a barrelhead. Their Creole dialect was alien to Dante's ear.

He knew that few, if any, of the Frenchmen on the island could understand it either. It was an amalgam of French and African grammar developed on slave plantations. While the dialect drew on European expression, it retained the rhythms of its African antecedents. The men tossing the dice were being urged on by a cocoa-skinned lady with ruby lipstick and astonishingly white teeth. At each toss of the dice she drew heavily on a thin dark cigar. While she waited for the dice to fall, she exhaled fluidly through her nostrils and lips. Between drags on the cigar she sipped coffee, hot and sweet, Dante assumed, from a small porcelain cup.

The bar was open to the street. A *velo* clattered along the quay bearing the hunched physique of a military dispatcher in a colonial casque and shorts. From where he sat, Dante could see the walls of Fort St. Louis, the bastion that commanded the harbor. Scarred and bitten by sea winds, the walls stood thick and bronzed in the afternoon sun. Despite lengthening shadows, he could see gun emplacements above the barred portals. At this angle he could make out two anti-aircraft weapons and some heavier artillery, probably 155mm cannon. A soldier was jogging the battlements. He was wearing khaki shorts and combat boots and working over what looked to be an improvised obstacle course.

Suddenly it began to rain, a pelting tropical downpour that swept the bay with the speed of a sandstorm. The sea went strangely opaque and the rain darkened the waterfront in a steamy downpour that obscured the hills beyond. An elderly woman hobbled in off the street wearing a bright red turban and earrings that dangled from distended lobes. She was a dark-skinned Creole of enormous bulk. Shaking raindrops from her shoulders, she considered her options and took a seat at an adjacent table. As she settled onto a chair, she propped a wooden crutch between thickset legs. In her free hand she held an assortment of flowers, a hand-picked bouquet, perhaps, for a friend at a hospital. She pressed the flowers against a rain-slick thigh and sorted through the stems. The rain beating heavily against the windows sounded like sleet. Outside, the streets were steamy with mist, the warm rain dancing on the pavement. But the bar remained pleasantly cool. In minutes the rain tapered, then ceased, and it was sunny again. Dante watched the woman push slowly to her feet and shuffle to the door. As she waddled toward the embankment, he was reminded of an ancient tortoise, weary and torpid, dragging its way to the sea.

Christopher Delon broke a five minute silence. "There's something you should know, monsieur. It has no bearing on your mission here, but if we are to work together I think it best to clear the air. I'm a priest."

Dante studied the youngster with renewed interest. "Well you certainly had me fooled, Delon. I thought the priests in these islands wore shaggy beards and long black robes."

The Frenchman managed a sheepish grin. "Perhaps that will come with time. For now, that part of my past is known only to Madame Rollet. I trust you will keep my secret. By the way, the view from my apartment is better than this. And there are no gendarmes."

"I've seen all I can see from here," Dante said, sharing his host's discomfort. "Let's have a look at that telescope of yours."

They downed their drinks and departed by an exit that opened onto a sidestreet. Walking in silence, they wound through a maze of cobbled lanes. After the rainshower, steam rose in waves from the sunbaked pavestones. A confection of odors issued from storefronts, and above the alleyways sounds of life drifted from shuttered windows.

At Christopher's hotel they encountered an attractive young woman descending the staircase. As they passed on a landing, the woman and the priest exchanged a cursory nod. Though not a word was exchanged, Dante felt some unspoken communication had passed between them. As he entered the Frenchman's room, he wondered if he was underestimating his host.

Through the priest's borrowed telescope he surveyed the ships in the bay as well as the gun emplacements on Fort St. Louis. Afterwards, Christopher poured wine from a bottle and they sat on the terrace overlooking the sea.

"And what of the gold," Dante asked.

"The gold. Yes. It's a complex story, monsieur."

"I've got all night, Christopher. All week, if you like."

Delon pointed to the wrought iron railing that bordered his terrace. "It began beyond that barrier. The girl you saw on the stair. Her name is Lillette. Lillette Bonnier. She is...how shall I say...a lady of some... dexterity. We have become...," he blushed as though he had swallowed a beetroot..."friends..."

Dante was amused at his reticence, his apparent unease. The girl was pretty, in a flashy sort of way. She would not be mistaken for a socialite, but nor was she a product of the alleys. He wondered just how friendly she and the priest had become.

"Lillette has a benefactor on the island," Christopher continued. "One Monsieur Sambre. Sambre is an aide to Admiral Robert. Though she came to Martinique at Sambre's behest, the relationship has...to use her term... 'soured'. She is desperate to escape his clutches."

Dante tasted the wine, a French white from Vouvray. He and Caroline had spent a night at Vouvray, in a chateau on the banks of the Loire. Caroline had purchased some vintage from a local winery, and they had used it to grease the ways. At the thought of those happier days, a shadow passed over his mood. He waited it out, then turned his attention to the priest.

"Sambre is pro-Vichy," Christopher went on. "Pro-German. He is also a supporter of Pierre Laval."

The French turncoat Laval. Dante knew him well. He was one of Hitler's puppets, an early admirer of the Nazis. The last Dante had heard, Laval was vying with the aging Marshall Petain for leadership of the Vichy Government.

"According to Lillette," Christopher continued, "Sambre entertains military personnel at his Bellefontaine villa. His most recent visitor, masquerading as a Swiss businessman, was a mysterious young German. Lillette believes him to be a seaman. Off a submarine, perhaps."

Dante feigned surprise. "U-Boats put in here?"

"At least one. There's a wounded naval officer at the military hospital. He was put ashore by a submarine a few weeks ago. Admiral Robert was hesitant to accept him, but he had no choice.

The man lost a leg in a shipboard accident and would have died had he not been granted haven. Rumor has it he's the son of a German admiral."

Dante was aware of the story. The French High Commissioner had reported the incident to the U.S. Naval Observer on Martinique. He was pleased to see that the Frenchman's intelligence was accurate.

"And now to the gold," Christopher said. "In trying to secure some leverage over her benefactor, Lillette Bonnier has found occasion to sort through Sambre's papers. He keeps a ledger. According to Lillette, he is meticulous about his records. He expects the Germans will win the war, and he wants proof of his collaboration."

"Proof?"

"On the chance that his contacts may not survive, he keeps dates, the essence of conversations, a list of amenities he provides such as medical supplies, wine, women, access to his villa by the sea. He's very organized, very safe."

"And what of the gold? Does his ledger mention the gold?"

"Not exactly. He's too clever for that. But time and again he makes mention of a plan which will make him wealthy. "Project Milk Cow" he calls it.

"Milk Cow?"

"Yes. While besotted with drink one night, he told Lillette that the German masquerading as the Swiss is his link with fortune; important to his future. When the Allies sue for peace, he expects to be a wealthy man. Very wealthy, indeed."

"But no mention of the gold."

"Patience, monsieur. I am coming to that. As I have said, Lillette and I have grown close. She has come to confide in me."

"Does she know you're a priest?"

"No. She suspects I'm having an affair with Madame Rollet."

Dante suppressed a smile. He had harbored a similar suspicion. Christopher offered him a Gaulois Bleue. He accepted, and lit it with his last match. One puff and he was back in France, at the Hotel Raphael, on a balcony overlooking the Avenue Kleber.

Caroline was emerging from the shower, hair dripping wet, her firm slender body neatly packaged in a white monogrammed robe. Sensing his preoccupation, the priest-in-hiding waited him out. Dante was finding this young cleric easy to be with, like a younger brother or a classmate at the Academy.

Please," Dante said. "Carry on."

"Doctor Rollet and I have examined and re-examined Lillette's story," the priest said. "We were as skeptical as you must be, Paul. You need no proof beyond my being here that we think her theory has substance."

Dante held up both palms. "I believe you, Christopher. And I admire your courage. But I need facts."

The priest sipped his wine. "As a member of the medical profession, Nikole is not without connections. She is well received at the highest echelons of government, and she is trusted by the ruling families. We, too, wondered what some Vichy-loving aide to Admiral Robert could offer a member of the Third Reich besides sexual diversion that would prompt his return to the island. We too pondered what could make Sambre a rich man."

Dante looked out over the harbor. The light was fading rapidly, the ships melting like shadows against the green-mantled hills. A match flared and the priest touched the flame to a thin black cigar. It was a split match, Dante noticed, like the matches in Nikole's kitchen. Christopher exhaled and extinguished the flame.

"Nikole has learned from a highly-placed official, one who has courted her with indifferent success, that should the Americans attempt an invasion, the High Commissioner has been ordered to dump the gold."

"Dump it? Hundreds of tons? Dump it where?"

"Into the sea. For obvious reasons, Nikole was reluctant to press for details. We do know, however, that Sambre has access to the code room. He is no doubt in contact with his friends at Vichy. This German seaman could be a courier of sorts. As Nikole and I attempted to piece Lillette's story together, we came to the same conclusion. The gold. It must be the gold."

"But how?" Dante asked. "It would take a small army to move that much gold down that mountain."

"The how we do not know, monsieur. That's why Nikole has sent for you."

Dante drained his glass. "As a theory, it's a bit strained. Possible, but strained. They couldn't take it out from here." He pointed to the harbor. "We have destroyers patrolling twenty-four hours a day. Easier to sneak the sunrise past a rooster."

"It's a large island, monsieur. There are many inlets and coves, as you yourself have found."

The priest offered more wine. Dante held out his glass.

"Anything else?" Dante asked.

"The native who drove us here. Lucien LeClerc. He's devoted to Dr. Rollet. He has worked at her clinic for years. She delivered his three children. He has a cousin at Fort Desaix. The gold could not be moved without his knowledge. So if we're right, we'll have some time."

"Time? Time for what?" Dante asked. "What do you expect from me?"

"We decided to let the Americans work it out. It's your ships that are patrolling the harbor, your diplomats bargaining with Admiral Robert, your war in these waters against the Germans."

Dante was beginning to enjoy this erstwhile cleric. Behind the dark fathomless eyes lurked a sense of irony, if not humor. "Still, I'll need some evidence. All you have so far is theory."

"I've told you what we know, monsieur. Perhaps you can devise a plan."

They sat in silence for a moment.

"If our theory is correct," the priest continued, "Sambre would know the details, of course."

Dante sipped his wine. "So it's back to Lillette.

The priest-in-hiding shrugged his shoulders.

Dante returned to the telescope. Deep in the bay the lanterns of ships were winking on the quickening tide. He swung the barrel toward the hills above the town. Focusing on the bastion of Fort Desaix, he turned the lens on a guard patrolling the ramparts.

An emaciated goat grazed placidly among the rocks below. Three hundred and fifty tons. He had trouble imagining that much gold. He wondered how many boxcars it would fill.

"How did they get the gold up there?, he asked.

"A tunnel", the priest replied. "Lucien's cousin said it runs from the piers at Fort St. Louis under the Savanne and up to Fort Desaix on the mountain."

The light was fading now, the shadows lengthening over the rooftops and alleyways. In these low equatorial latitudes the dusk seemed to rise out of the sea. The coastline darkened first, and then the foothills, and finally the peaks. Soon, with the sun sinking swiftly beyond the hills, the lamps on the hillsides would be indistinguishable from the stars.

Dante swung the telescope out to sea. He scanned the mouth of the harbor. The horizon was scarlet and purple. In the distance he thought he detected a wisp of smoke. One of the four-stackers patrolling offshore? It was growing far too dark to tell.

BELLEFONTAINE, MARTINIQUE

Viktor Reinmann lay fathoms below dreams. In the instant before awareness he experienced the displacement that comes to travelers on the move. He swam to the surface of consciousness. Was he at sea?

No. It was too quiet. Too still.

The fog of sleep lifted like a shroud. The ceiling was high, the room dark, the mattress soft. He raised his head from the pillow. Wakefulness flooded in. Beyond the shutters he heard the clatter of palms.

Sambre's cottage.

Martinique.

At sea he slept lightly, like a hobo in a boxcar, dozing fitfully to the cradling rhythms of the ship. Never quite settled on the clammy thin mattress, he seemed always aware of the throb of engines, of the undertones of a vessel rigged for war. Here on the island the silence was narcotic, the stillness absolute, the slumber steeped in dreams. He recalled slipping ashore during the night. The U-Boat had dropped him at Pointe de Nègres, a fishing village north of the capital. A crewman had rafted him ashore. He'd waited until the crewman had paddled back to the submarine before dialing the Frenchman's number from a dockside cafe. Sambre had sent the Creole to pick him up.

He sat on the edge of the bed. A pounding at his temples reminded him of the cognac. The Creole had deposited it on the dresser, compliments of M. Sambre. The glass was on a nightstand beside an ashtray crammed with butts. That would explain the rawness in his throat. He sat on the edge of the bed and fingered the sole remaining survivor in a pack of Camels. He'd discovered the unexpected luxury in a drawer of the bedside table before falling asleep. He touched a match to the tobacco and inhaled deeply. The aroma was delicious, the draw smooth. It reminded him of the girl. On his first night at the villa they had shared a carton of American cigarettes. They were given to her, she claimed, by a French officer. In this very bed, he supposed.

When he was a teenager, his father had told him the engine that drove the world lay between the legs of its women.

Clad in the heart-studded shorts his sister Elsbeth had sent in retaliation for the Parisian silk stockings, he pushed unsteadily to his feet. There was a cramp in his calf. His back felt stiff and his mouth was as dry as cinders. He must have put away more of the cognac than he thought. Digging through his toilet kit, he came up with a pair of briefs and a bladeless razor. On his previous stay, Sambre had fitted him out with slacks and a sport shirt. He found them laundered in an *armoire* near the bed. The place was beginning to feel like home. He wondered if the Creole had returned.

"Hallooo. Is anyone here?"

Silence.

From the angle of the shadows he guessed it was well short of noon. Sour-mouthed and lightheaded, he raked grease-stained fingers through short-cropped hair. He walked barefoot and unsteadily to the sitting room, an airy chamber off the sprawling veranda. The glare from the windows made him wince. Though the villa was in shadow, the sea sparkled brightly with sunshine. He shaded his eyes and proceeded to the small but comfortable kitchen. The cognac stood on the wooden table, the bottle half empty, the cork in a saucer nearby. On a plate lay a half-eaten pickle and an empty teacup. He remembered constructing a sandwich from some cheese and sausage he had found in an ice chest.

In a femininely-appointed bathroom he filled the basin and began to shave. The water was tepid, the soap lightly scented, but it offered a suitable lather. He smoked as he shaved. Facing himself in the mirror, it occurred to him that he had met the enemy. Though the opposition had been weak, he was, it could be argued, a combatant. Now that he had encountered Germany's adversaries he was more convinced than ever that the war would be a short one. He had posited every conceivable outcome. Whatever else transpired, the Russians would collapse, the British would sue for peace, and Germany's victory would be assured. The Americans would defend themselves in the Pacific, but they would never send their sons to die for the French or the British. Hitler would inevitably carve out his Fortress Europa and Viktor Reinmann would return to Germany.

To what?

He thought of Hartenstein. The U-156 would be steaming the Atlantic toward a triumphant reception at Lorient. Resplendent in a leather bridge coat and white scarf, Hartenstein would approach the Brittany coastline with a score of white pennants streaming from his periscope, one for each and every ship he had sent to the bottom while on patrol. Admiral Doenitz would be tracking their arrival from the war room of his harborside villa at Kernével. By the time they docked, the Admiral would be waiting at the bombproof pens, Iron Crosses at the ready, a handshake and a smile for all. Crewmen who rated leave would travel the luxury train know as *BdU Zug* to points in Germany. Others would go to special camps at French resorts known as "U-Boat pastures". There they would spend their hazardous duty pay on accommodating Breton mademoiselles and spread the wealth among their newfound Vichy "allies". Outstanding crews like that of the U-156 would no doubt be flown to Berlin for parades...children and *hausfraus* cheering their victories and tossing handpicked bouquets of flowers into open cars. Valedictions to valor. Decorations for death. Medals would be handed out like favors at a party and Hartenstein would be declared a hero, as were all U-Boat captains.

And what of himself, Viktor wondered.

He would be awarded a Knight's Cross. Only months before, that had seemed enough. But now? After all the celebrations and back-slapping, then what? A return to some Black Forest *rathskeller*? A career as a hotel clerk? He could remain in the *U-Boatwaffe*, but of what use would the submarine service be after the fighting stopped? Was he really cut out to spend his life in a steel cocoon with men who rarely shaved and seldom bathed? He wanted more than that. Many would make their fortunes from this war. Empires would be forged. Dynasties. Would he truly be content with a sinecure in some steamy outpost? "Don't be one of the crowd," his father had told him. "Be one of a kind. Life is short. The candle flickers, then sputters, then dies. The darkness is forever."

He thought of the gold sitting high on the mountain. It would go to bankers. To generals. To gentry.

And what of him?

What would fuel his future?

He had an image of his father lying hollow-eyed in the spartan bedroom of their Freiberg apartment, a crucifix over the headboard, his lungs perforated by emphysema, his breath the tortured wheezing that presages the death rattle. And his mother, as frail as the flowers she snipped from the garden, her own heart laden with a faulty valve, climbing the steps to her husband's death bed and dreading the spectre beyond the door. Were it not for the monthly stipend forwarded from Viktor's paycheck, his father might be facing his last earthly hours in a ward of a veteran's hospital.

Is that to be your fate, Viktor, he asked himself? That, or worse? He would not permit it. When fate summons, even monarchs must obey, the adage went. But sometimes, as with his mumps, as with his meeting with the Admiral in Paris, one must work around one's fate. Not that fate had always been unkind to the Reinmanns. A decade before, when Viktor was still a tow-headed adolescent stretching toward manhood in the heart of the Black Forest, it seemed the future held nothing but promise. In that fateful year of 1932 Viktor's father, Gustav, had been a prosperous industrialist who, back before the Great War, had wooed and won the daughter of a Prussian General. After Versailles and the treaty which had imposed harsh reparations on Germany after its 1918 defeat, inflation had run rampant in Viktor's homeland. In the 1920's a pint of milk had reached the prohibitive cost of a quarter-of-a-million Deutschmarks. Throughout Germany morale was low, unemployment high, prospects for improvement zero.

And then, after years of seething unrest engendered by a failed economy and crushed national pride, a savior had appeared on the streets of Berlin, a failed Austrian painter who had tasted defeat in the trenches of Flanders yet bore in his oratory the power to unite a nation. After condemning Germany's oppressors and offering the promise of a revitalized economy, this vagrant from the alleyways of Vienna had risen to the rank of Reichschancellor. Almost immediately, a new energy was felt in the streets, a breath of restoration, the prospect of a return to self-respect.

In the spring of 1932, Viktor Reinmann was celebrating his fourteenth birthday. Oblivious to the calamities that had befallen his parents, the teenager knew little of politics and less of war. To the youngest Reinmann the highlight of the year was a birthday cake shaped like a sailboat with a candle for a mast and gifts wrapped in ribboned white paper. A small but authentic sailboat had been secreted in the garden, a present from his father. Heedless of the lesions on his father's lungs, or the defect in his mother's heart, the youthful Reinmann had frolicked with his friends at a party in the Freiberg garden. That night he had tied his sister Elsbeth's braids to the bedpost in return for the frog she had hidden in his lunch pail.

Other than a reduction in the number of days that meat was served at the dinner table, a teenager in the cathedral city of Freiberg Im Breisgau was not concerned with the devastated economy or the failure of his father's machine tool business. He was too young to be burdened with the news that the factory was becoming outdated, too sheltered to be told the plant was about to be purchased by a Jewish industrialist for pfennings on the mark. Nor was he aware of the stomp of jackboots on the streets of Berlin.

He did remember a night in 1933, however, when news came over the wireless that someone named Adolf Hitler had been named Chancellor of the Reich. He remembered the commentator describing the parades in the streets, the rivers of torches streaming the boulevards, the clamor of marching bands, the choruses of voices..."*Deutschland uber alles...Sieg Heil, Heil Hitler!*"

Viktor was allowed to stay awake past midnight to watch the crowds that gathered on Freiberg's cobbled lanes, to hear the people singing, the rejoicing in the torchlit square. He remembered the oom-pah! of the local bands, the flagstaffs on the buildings, the blood red banners with the black swastika against a white field.

By the time he graduated from high school the factories were humming again, milk was affordable, and swastikas were snapping on flagpoles from Hamburg to Munich. But by then the ailing Gustav was laboring for breath, a teenaged Elsbeth was undergoing preliminary vows at a Tyrolean nunnery, and Christiana Reinmann was struggling to salvage the small *gasthaus* her husband had purchased with the proceeds from the sale of his factory.

And always there were the radio reports from Berlin. Tens of thousands lining the Wilhelmstrasse to greet the new Reichschancellor.

"*...Heil Hitler!....Seig Heil! .. Heil!...Heil!...Heil!. . .*"

Caught in the shifting tides of history, weaned in the excitement of the hour, Viktor joined the Hitler Youth. It was as natural as matriculation, as popular as a berth in the Olympics. At age eighteen he passed to the ranks of the S.A., where for two years he absorbed the Nazi doctrine. Then came a mandatory six-month stint in one of the work battalions building roads and draining marshes to prepare him physically for the crowning duty of a German citizen, service with the armed forces. Determined to make his father proud, he volunteered for the Kriegsmarine, the German Navy. After a stint as a naval cadet and midshipman, he was promoted to Leutnant zur See and posted to the base at Wilhelmshaven. Then once again Fate intervened. At the North Sea port he was put under the command of Kapitan zur See Karl Doenitz. The name Reinmann had rung a bell with the up-and-coming Kriegsmarine commander. Doenitz had served with Viktor's father in The Great War. He remembered the elder Reinmann with affection. Impressed by Viktor's vigor and his keen eye for detail, Doenitz enrolled the ambitious youngster in the secret submarine school at Kiel. Shortly thereafter, looking ahead to the inevitable and planning for all contingencies, Doenitz sought out someone to scout the Caribbean, someone young and eager, someone who would cast not the faintest hint of suspicion should he be found exploring the remote beaches of distant seas. On a hunch he sent for Viktor and one of Viktor's highly-touted shipmates. In 1938 no one would suspect a pair of aspiring "naturalists" on a summer outing to be familiarizing themselves with the barren atolls and remote archipelagos of the Caribbean basin.

On Martinique, Viktor drew the razor over his chin and snapped the lather into the basin. He showered beneath an outdoor tank. The pipe hissed and gurgled with an airlock, then water dribbled stubbornly before spewing from the perforated plate. He felt his hangover drain away with the warm prickly water. After drying himself with a fluffy white towel, he let the breeze play bracingly against his skin. A few miles to the south, obscured by coastal highlands, lay the port of Fort de France. High above the city, on a plateau overlooking the sea, sprawled the bastion of Fort Desaix. In clammy stone dungeons beneath its antiquated walls lay tons of gold. The wealth of France. Three-hundred-and-fifty tons, if the Frenchman was correct. Enough to cram the belly of the largest *milch cow*. Enough to satisy the appetites of the greediest Caliph.

Glancing beyond the window, he remembered his sister Elsbeth's shiny golden braids. He wondered what her head must look like now, shorn beneath the white-fringed habit and never to be stroked by another human hand short of the embalming table. He had trouble picturing his free-spirited sister threading beads between her tanned slender fingers and muttering "Aves" in the candlelit corridors of a Schwenningen convent. So once again Fate has intervened, Viktor thought. Only this time, it is on the credit side. But for the outbreak of war, he might be rinsing mugs in a *bierkeller* in Munich.

Should he risk it? Should he go for the gold? Money deadened the moral sensibilities, he had learned. Who had said it? Probably some jaded aristocrat. The idea had been germinating for some time. Held against the blade of resolution, he had shied from a decision far too long. The temptation hit him hardest at night. Like all roots, he supposed it thrived best in darkness. Whenever he approached the brink of determination, he felt a nagging patriotism, the dregs of conscience. But what would Germany need after the war if not new blood, a stable gentry?

If he did succumb to temptation, what of the Frenchman? Would he go along? Sambre knew the island. He could enlist support. Would he take the risk? The question answered itself. He was a wart on the flank of humanity, the very cellar of morality. He would jump at the chance.

Who would miss a ton or so? German Intelligence had estimated three hundred tons. A fifty-ton shortfall. A single ton could go astray anywhere. When the gold arrived in Germany, who would dispute the figure? There could be no official verification. The French would be told that the gold had been dumped at sea. It was their own plan; ordered by Marshall Petain himself. As for the Abwehr, if the actual figures came to light, the discrepancy could lie anywhere. A ton could have been stolen during the loading in France, the unloading at Martinique. It could have been siphoned off at Fort Desaix.

Tonight at dinner he would feel the Frenchman out. Sambre was a traitor; that had already been established. Compared to treason, larceny was a paltry offence. The Frenchman was ambitious, with an appetite for expensive wine and attractive women. His cooperation was all but assured.

And if they agreed? If they were successful?

Frenchmen were dying the world over. One bureacrat more or less would make very little difference.

He would put it to Sambre tonight. With the main course.

And for dessert? Sambre said he was bringing the girl. He had no delusions that he was the first to penetrate that young and beautiful creature. She was a courtesan experienced in sex but innocent of love.

Viktor toweled vigorously.

Fate. For good or ill, let the wheel turn. He was the last of his line. It fell on him to restore the family honor. His sister was desiccating in a nunnery; his cousin, the only other male offspring bearing the Reinmann name, lay a frozen carcass on the Russian *steppes*. Even his own manhood had been tainted, and by all things mumps. Yet even in this, Fate had left him an opening. He was not without an heir. Before he was stricken he had planted the seed that had grown into a son. He had read it in Casey's eyes, in the boy's features. The lad was the right age. There was no mistaking the Reinmann brow, the cut of chin, the glint of eye. Casey had said she was engaged. Engaged, not married. With a baby. His baby. She would not admit it, but he was certain of it. Was he to abandon the final link in the Reinmann chain to some lizard-infested island? To be raised by Americans or Englishmen? From the bottom drawer of his memory he recalled his father saying, "…fear only feeble old age and death in bed…"

The *milch cow* was scheduled to leave Germany in a day or two. The crossing would take two weeks.

He had much to do.

FORTE DE FRANCE, MARTINIQUE

Dante was sitting on Christoper Delon's balcony. He had showered and shaved and was watching the ships in the harbor. The seaman's clothes he had worn since paddling ashore were stashed in his rucksack. In the style of the island's businessmen he had changed to a plain white shirt and dark suit. Christopher was down the hall showering. They had spent the night in the priest's small apartment, Christopher on the metal-framed bed, his guest on the floor on a folded blanket.

There was a tapping at the door. Wondering if the priest had locked himself out, Dante crossed the room and opened the latch to find Nikole Rollet standing in the corridor. As he ushered her into the room, he discovered yet another facet of this woman called SKIPJACK. There was the woman of the cove, mute, expressionless, with masked features and a lurking intensity. There was the woman of the cottage, relaxed, domesticated, hospitable yet aloof. And there was the woman who greeted him now, elegant, poised, and captiously feminine. She looked chic in a white cotton dress belted at the waist and unbuttoned at the throat. She wore a summery white hat and high-heeled shoes. Her legs were bare and strikingly attractive. As she crossed the room, Dante could see that he had underestimated her figure. She was taller than he remembered, with fluid hips and a nicely-pinched waist. Her makeup was laid on with an artist's touch, subtle yet effective. With her eyes enhanced and her hair meticulously shaped, she looked as elegant as any Parisian model.

"*Bonjour*, Paul, she said, extending a hand. "It's a good day for your tour, no?"

"Decidedly," he said, taking her hand.

Her smile reached warmly to her eyes. Dante found himself wondering which was the real Nikole Rollet, the unadorned country doctor or the chic sophisticate confronting him now.

"Christopher is not familiar with the northern coastline," she said. "So I will be your guide. As a physician, I've been issued a sticker for my windshield. It permits me to ignore the restricted zones and curfews."

"I'm in your hands, Nikole."

The priest returned in a robe and sandals, his hair still damp from the shower. He took Nikole's hand. "I expected you later, "he said, looking restless and uneasy in the cluttered room.

"It's a long drive," Nikole said. "I thought we would get an early start." She turned to Dante. "Are you ready, monsieur?"

Dante slung his jacket over a shoulder.

Christopher saw them to the stairwell. After kissing Nikole's cheek, he placed a hand on Dante's arm. "I trust we'll meet again, Paul. Good hunting."

Nikole took the wheel. She made straight for the coast road south of town. Her Renault was comfortable and roomy. On the outskirts of the city, they rolled down the windows and opened the vents. Dante tossed his jacket onto the back seat and slipped on a pair of sunglasses. Nikole removed her hat.

"Feels awkward being a passenger," Dante said. He offered her a cigarette, one of the local variety.

Nikole declined. "Are you a military man, Paul?"

"After a fashion."

"And this tour you requested. It has something to do with the military?

He preferred not to lie to her, but for her own sake, the less she knew the better.

"Look" doctor. "It's best we come to an understanding, or this will be awkward for both of us. I'm here because you... SKIPJACK... sent for someone. I'm here to explore your theory about the gold. If it seems plausible, I'll try to help decide what can be done about it. I'm here, I assure you, in the best interest of Martinique and of France."

"And America, of course..."

"America has no designs on this island. It's to America's benefit, and yours, that the Germans don't compromise Martinique. If, as you suspect, they were to take the gold from that fort, it would be to France's detriment as well as your own."

"So what is it you wish to see?'

"My assignment is to learn as much as possible about the present state of affairs on Martinique. That's about all I can reveal. Any assistance you can provide in that regard will be appreciated. You'll understand why I can't tell you more."

What he did not tell her was that he had committed to memory a contingency plan for the invasion of the island, a plan the Navy called OPERATION BUNGALOW.

"Very well," she said, fishing sunglasses from a drawstring bag. "As I believe you Americans say, you scratch our neck and we'll scratch yours."

He laughed. "It's back, doctor. Not neck."

They cleared the capitol and entered a stretch of rugged coastline.

Dante studied his map. Five miles south of the city, he took a bearing. "Point du Sables is nearby, is it not?"

"Just beyond those hills," Nikole said. "There's a new road. It's paved, but it's being used by the military."

They approached a dilapidated shack, someone's abandoned dream for a roadside cafe. Dante pointed to a stand of trees. "Pull over, please."

She eased the Renault to the shoulder.

"You wait," he said. "I'll make better time alone. If anyone asks, I went to relieve myself."

He slipped binoculars from his rucksack and stuffed them into his shirt. When he stepped out onto the verge, he listened for oncoming vehicles. Nothing. Just the twitter of birds. Seeing Nikole open the pages of a magazine, he pushed through the brush at the side of the shack. He had been briefed on Point du Sable. The

Army had taken aerial photographs. If his memory was accurate, what he was looking for was just beyond the ridge. The climb took only minutes. The hillside was blanketed with trees, but they were well scattered and the going was easy. From the crest of a ridge he played his binoculars over the surrounding terrain. He found what he sought on a plateau overlooking the sea. What he saw disgusted him. The plateau resembled a junkyard. His intelligence had been correct. This was where the Buffaloes had been put ashore. With war seemingly inevitable, the French had purchased more than a hundred American aircraft, Brewster Buffaloes and Curtis H75's. When the Germans swept through the lowlands, the planes had been in mid-Atlantic aboard the aircraft carrier BEARN. With access to French ports questionable, the skipper had turned about and brought the planes to Martinique. There was no airfield on the island, so when the Americans had warned the High Commissioner to neutralize the aircraft, old Admiral Robert had put them ashore. They were probably no threat, but there was always the chance that an airstrip could be hacked out of a cane field. If an invasion became necessary, a few operational aircraft could wreak havoc on the landing force. Dante could see there was no fear of that now. The planes lay strewn about the landscape like so many invalids, fuselages stripped, propellers skewed, landing gear collapsed. Someone had taken an axe to some of the tail assemblies and a few of the wings had been set afire.

When he returned to the car, Nikole Rollet was thumbing through the magazine.

"You have found what you came to see?" she asked.

"Yes."

"What's next?"

"Lamentin," he said.

The Plain of Lamentin. The central plain between the mountains of the north and the hill country to the south. As they drove, Dante concentrated on the terrain, fitting the topography beyond the windscreen to the military estimates supplied by Intelligence. Though the Atlantic coast had been suggested for landings, two areas in the Lamentin area were being considered as drop zones for paratroopers.

Watching his hostess maneuver the Renault along the sunbaked roads, her hair feathering softly in the wind, Dante recalled what he had been told about the island's defenses. Operation Bungalow called for air and sea support for invading troops as well as the destruction of any naval vessels attempting to leave the harbor. Military Intelligence had estimated that there were some 6,000 Army personnel on Martinique including the Colonial Police, the Gendarmerie, and reserves. Most of the artillery was located near Forte de France at one of the big three forts, St-Louis, Desaix and Tartenson. Infantry were scattered at encampments around the island, with additional concentrations in the hills. Observation posts had been established at the major coastal towns, including one in Nikole's own village of Ste-Anne. Intelligence surmised that the French Navy, which virtually ruled the island, did not have a great deal of confidence in the Colonial Army. As Nikole would know better than he, more than sixty French military had escaped to St. Lucia and Dominica in recent months. Though most of the officer corps remained loyal to Vichy, large numbers of colonial troops were said to be disaffected of late. Rumor had it that while ousted native politicians would favor American intervention, the bulk of the black population could be counted apathetic. White civilians were reported divided in sentiment. A French army officer had conceded that an American invasion could take Martinique, but only at a cost of 18,000 casualties.

From Lamentin they headed east across the pinched green waist of the island. In the broad central highlands the road meandered through mile after mile of sugar cane fields. The cane was the height of two men. The wind riffling the tips had it swaying against the sky like giant corn stalks. At the base of the stalks, men were swinging machetes, their torsos glistening with sweat, their blades flashing fire in the sun. Behind them women were gathering the cane and binding it into bundles.

Nikole slowed the car. "Persia's family used to work the fields," she said. "In her grandmother's day the workers cut the stalks to the beat of a drummer. She said they chanted as they worked."

"Persia?"

"Oh, I'm sorry. You haven't met Persia. She's my assistant at the clinic. A registered nurse. One of the few on the island."

"Is she the woman who stopped by when I was supposed to be resting?"

"Yes."

"I did see her. From my window. Is she Martiniquais? She looks white."

"She's Creole," Nikole said. "It covers a wide range. From milk with a drop of ink, to ink with a drop of milk. She's often mistaken for a *Beke*. They're the white Creoles born on the island, descendants from the first colonists."

"Where did she study.?"

"In France. Her mother worked for one of the Ten Families. You're familiar with the Ten Families?"

"I know they exist," Dante said.

"They own the island. Their ancestors emigrated from France centuries ago. They're extremely wealthy. They control the plantations, the real estate, the mercantile houses. Before the war, they would quit their villas in the hills each year to vacation in the chateaus of France. Some took their servants with them. As a favorite of one of the elders, Persia was taken abroad with her mother. In Dijon, she was permitted to share a tutor. When she came of age, she was given the opportunity to attend classes."

"And she chose medicine."

"It was chosen for her. She preferred art, but her benefactor was on the practical side."

"And you? Where did you study, doctor?"

"Paris."

"And you chose to practice on Martinique?"

"Not immediately. I was married to a French army officer. In my mother's footsteps, so to speak. My father was also a military man. He was killed at Verdun in 1917. He was twenty-two."

"And your husband?"

"Dunkirk. Two years ago."

"I'm sorry," Dante said.

She managed a dispirited grin. "It seems the women in my family have a weakness for uniforms."

At mid-morning they reached the broad central spine of the island. The air was cool, the breeze refreshing, the sea stretching to infinity on all horizons. From the commanding height, Dante had an overview of the entire Caribbean coastline. The great semi-circular basin of the Bay of Forte de France was dotted with ships. He estimated it would take thirty to forty minutes to traverse the main harbor by motor launch. A magnificent mooring, he conceded. No wonder the French were determined to defend it. As they made their descent on the Atlantic side, they passed a plantation that swept to the sea. The trees were stormy green, the air dry and rare, like good wine.

"Bananas," Nikole said. "The green gold of the islands. It's one gold or another, it seems. We're tireless in our pursuit of it."

They descended to sea level at the village of Le Robert. Though there was entirely no connection, it reminded Dante of the aged French Admiral who now controlled the island. How would he react should he find an American Naval officer poking surreptitiously around his command?

They picked up the coastal highroad and headed north, paralleling the dusky mountains that ran to the sea, pausing from time to time while Dante assessed the terrain, the suitability of the Atlantic beaches. Trinite. Ste-Marie. Marigot. Le Lorraine. Basse Pointe. Macouba. One by one they traversed the coastal towns as the sun soared high overhead and baked the roads to a fine grey dust.

By noon they had reached the northernmost tip of the island. For lunch they stopped at a village called Grande-Rivière. Over salad and a lemon-colored omelette, Dante noted the coastline. The ocean was foam-flecked and chopped by the wind, with a constant sea breeze too rough for a landing and too distant for an airborne assault. There was a useful harbor, though. In the channel a patrol boat raised swells that sent shivers through the rigging of the fishing boats. For an *aperitif* they had rum, the dusky Martinique variety, a match, Nikole claimed, for the finest brandies in France. To his delight, the rum made her giddy and she laughed readily at his jokes.

After lunch, with the village re-awakening from the torpor of noon, they strolled an outdoor market. The shoppers were a virtual mosaic: Africans, Latins, East Indians, a scattering of European and native-born whites, the faces ranging from tan to black to cocoa to bronze. With their shopping bags swelling and their purses thinning, the women were bargaining under umbrella-shaded stands laden with exotic fruits and vegetables. At a pier near the beach, fishermen in broad straw hats were marketing their wares, the catch ranging from broad-winged rays to strings of rainbow-colored fish to giant lobsters. Dante studied the Martiniquais women. They were uniquely attractive, he thought, with smooth burnished skin, long slender legs, firm shapely buttocks and well-formed hips. Their stride was slow and upright, a throwback to not-so-distant-times when their forebears walked days on end over hilly terrain balancing hundred pound loads on their heads. They had almond-shaped eyes, high smooth cheekbones, and full fleshy lips, most painted a bright ruby red. With small upturned noses and long slender necks they were, all in all, an elegant breed, like carvings of the finest mahogany. Without exception they seemed high-spirited, and they giggled a lot, the humor as much a part of their nature as the sea itself.

Dante watched as his escort strolled the marketplace, fingering a plantain here, squeezing a mango there. In the midday heat she had adopted the long easy gait of the island women, her skirt swaying nicely, chatting first with one and then another as she moved from vendor to vendor with the ease of a marchioness. When they returned to the Renault, he made a point to walk to the driver's side.

You navigate, I'll fly, he said.

Nikole shot him a look of placid severity. "Truthfully, Paul. I'm not drunk."

"Of course not," he said. "But you've been driving all morning. I'd enjoy it, really."

"As you wish." she said, stripping away her hat.

They headed south along the sea road. As he tested the Renault's reflexes, Nikole sat facing him, her back against the passenger door. Her skirt had ridden above her knees, revealing well-formed thighs.

"The conversation has been been a bit one-sided," she said, with just the hint of a yawn. "You know a lot about me, monsieur, but I know virtually nothing about you."

"Trust me," he smiled, "yours is the far more interesting story."

As the sun edged slowly to the west, they headed inland again, slicing off a tip of the coastline. Ahead and above loomed Pelée, placid and serene under a sweatband of cloud. When they entered the interior, the terrain changed dramatically. Within minutes they went from scrubby foothills to thick primeval forest. In the close-cropped darkness the trees soared majestically like the columns of ancient cathedrals. Shafts of sunlight pierced the cool green twilight and the shadows were choked by tropical verdure. On mossy wooden bridges they crossed gorges swollen by rain.

"So how did you get into the Resistence business," Dante asked.

"Probably the way you got into the spy business." She smiled at his with a spark in her eyes.

"Touché," he smiled. "Seriously, though. If you're caught ferrying these patriots, or whatever you choose to call them, it will go hard on you, Nikole. Doctor or no doctor."

"And you, Paul? If you're discovered? Would it not go hard on you?"

"It's my job. I volunteered."

"As I suspected," she said, her cheeks flushed from wine. "Military."

They emerged from the forest and drove south along the coast again, staying as near to the beaches as the roads would permit. Twice they stopped to honk off recalcitrant goats. As they wound down the coastline, the afternoon sun beat relentlessly against the windshield. The tires sucked like masking tape, and Dante felt his foot welded firmly to the clutch pedal.

North of Forte de France they turned inland again, skirting the capital and negotiating a dizzying maze of switchbacks. On the outskirts of Rivière-Salée, Dante noticed his hostess was becoming drowsy. Out of the corner of an eye he saw her yawn behind her hand.

"The booze, I hope."

She flushed again. "Forgive me, Paul. I never could drink in the afternoon. The rum was stronger than I thought."

"You're a delightful drunk, Nikole."

She gave him an indecipherable smile.

It was well past dark when he finally switched off the ignition. They had driven the last few miles in a downpour. It stopped as suddenly as it had begun. When they slid from their seats they stretched and groaned. Her cottage was dark. At the door to the kitchen, Dante massaged an aching spine. "I don't know about you, doctor, but I could use a nightcap."

"There's whiskey on the sideboard," she said. On the screened-in porch she touched a match to an oil lamp. "Could you tolerate some music?"

"Love it."

"Shall we sit on the verandah? It's cooler out here."

"I'll stand, if you don't mind."

She had a light easy laugh, like the tinkle of bells. Dante chuckled, then they both laughed, the laughter born more of fatigue than of mirth.

He took a bottle and two glasses to the verandah. The sea was black, an endless void, the sky hung heavy with clouds. He selected a wicker rocker and stuffed a cushion behind his head. Another rainshower blew rapidly over the island. He could hear it hissing across the bay. It lasted only minutes, lashing the cottage in waves of relief then fading beyond peaks toward the waiting sea. Afterwards, the leaves on the hibiscus were slick, the drippings forming moon-blanched pools in the sodden flowerbeds.

When the first faint strains drifted from the phonograph, Dante called to her through the French doors, "'Tristan and Isolde.' The most beautiful love theme ever written."

She walked barefoot to the patio and took up a seat in an armchair opposite. Swinging her legs to the cushion, she tucked her skirt beneath her legs. In the glow of the lamp, there was a sheen to her skin. She tilted her head and closed her eyes.

"And written by a German," she said.

***

Dante climbed the steps to his bedroom trailing a weary contentment. The day had gone well. They had shed absolutely no light on the gold theory, but he had seen the island and he felt better about the prospects for an invasion. As he stretched between the sheets and rummaged among the events of the day, he realized that contentment was not the most of what he was feeling. For the first time in years, he was suffering the raw pulsing ache of desire.

BELLEFONTAINE, MARTINIQUE

The voices were distant. Genderless. "*...maladie de l'eau....*"

"*Faute limé lampe ou pou fai la-Viege passé dans caie-ou.*"

He was hot. So very hot. Fire burned deep in his chest and every movement sent shivering pain to his loins. He could not raise his arms, and his face felt like dried parchment.

It was dark. Not a sliver of light to break the blackness, not a hint of grey.

"...has he wakened yet?"

"...no. He has fever. He sleeps like d'dead..."

The fire burned hotter. He felt thirsty. He tried to speak, but could only manage a guttural groan.

Something was pressing his brow. It was wet. Cool. Liquid moistened his lips and he felt it trickle to his tongue, his throat.

Your eyes, he told himself. Open your eyes. It's dark. So strangely dark. He shivered. Perspiration chilled his kidneys, and beneath his back the sheet was drenched with sweat.

He experienced a small dense pellet of comprehension.

A sheet!

He was lying on a sheet.

He struggled to remember. The rolling sea, the swells rising steadily to his chin. He had been adrift. It was dark. His strength had drained and he was exhausted; his lifejacket was losing buoyancy....

The SQUALO. The sunken freighter. He remembered the roar of the engines as the aircraft drew nearer, the bombs tumbling toward him through the halo of cloud, the concussion...the darkness. He had drifted for hours, clinging to debris like a cricket on a leaf. Then something... someone...had tugged at his shoulders. His legs....

A sheet.

A bed.

He was ashore.

Alive.

He had not drowned.

Aldo, you have not drowned!

Something cool was pressed to his forehead. He tried to raise his head, but he lacked the strength. He worked his eyelids and strained to shed the cobweb veil of drowsiness. It persisted. He felt a clutch of panic. For an instant he was on the spine of the current...rising... falling...rising... falling... He swallowed painfully and tasted the sea. Desperately, he tried to open his eyes.

Blackness.

Was he dying? There was no sense of space, of time. As in a nightmare, he felt perception slipping away. He tried to check it, tried desperately to speak. The liquid was pressed to his lips again. This time it trickled more freely. He gagged and choked; the spittle tasted of brine, the exertion sapped his strength.

And then the fire diminished, and with merciful swiftness he succumbed to the numbing narcotic of sleep.

"Monsieur? Can you hear me, monsieur? Take dis. Dis be good for you.

The shuddering resumed, flashes of heat followed by shivering cold. His throat felt as dry as a cloth.

Something was pressing his lips. Something moist. Gently his lips were parted and he felt the liquid penetrate his throat. He suffered paroxysms of coughing. His face felt parched, as though the sun had blotted the moisture from his skin.

"*Bien, monsieur. Très bien.* You is better now. D'fever. It be broken."

It was a woman's voice, husky but friendly, the accent clotted by an unfamiliar tongue.

Aldo clutched the sheet. He felt cooler now. A breeze was stirring his hair. He pursed his lips. They were swollen and chapped.

"Très bien, monsieur."

He swallowed the liquid. It was bitter but warm.

Dazed with weariness, he felt his eyelids growing heavy.

This time he did not try to open them.

Consciousness returned slowly. Though his brain favored sleep, he fought to overcome it.

A breeze.

The rustle of palm fronds.

The caw of a gull.

Rolling to one side, he found that his joints were stiff, his back wracked by pain. The fire was gone, but his throat was parched, his cheekbones sore. Groping for awareness, he opened his eyes. Darkness. Not the inky blackness of before, but darkness nonetheless, as though a gauze had been pressed against his pupils.

He raised a hand and touched a finger to an eyelid. With the tips of his fingers, he raised the lid of his right eye. Nothing. The left eye. Nothing: darkness, thick and opaque.

He pressed a palm against a cheek. It was warm. Sun warm.

Sunlight! There was sunlight and he could not see!

His heart went as cold as stone. His spirit seemed to collapse from within.

"*Dio mio*, I'm blind."

He called out. "Is...is there someone here?"

Silence. A silence so profound he heard the blood pulsing steadily past his eardrums.

He pushed to a sitting position and felt his stomach heave. Tentatively, he swung a foot to the floor and clutched the sheet. His legs felt wooden. Brittle.

He ran a hand over his body. He was naked.

"Bonjour, signor."

The voice cut like a bullet through the silence. He recoiled against the pillow. Reflexively, he clutched at the sheet and tugged it to his waist.

He felt fingers press gently against his shoulder. They were cool. Insistent. "You must rest, signor. You are not yet strong." The fingers pressed him slowly against the pillow. He felt a tingling in his scalp.

"Who?...where...where am I? Who are you? I cannot see. Am I blind...?"

"Please, signor. You must not get excited. You have fever. You will be fine."

The phrases were Italian; the accent French. He caught the scent of perfume, spicy and sweet. It was not the woman of his dream. The voice was soft-toned and pleasant.

"*Per favore, signorina.* Where am I? My eyes. Am I blind?"

"You are on Martinique, signor. Your eyes will be fine. The doctor assures it is only temporary. A week or so. A month, perhaps."

He felt a shiver of relief. Could it be true? Could it be temporary? "You are not humoring me? I will see again?"

"Yes. You will see again."

Her perfume was heady, her touch as light as foam. He felt giddy with the promise of restored vision. "And you, signorina? You are...?"

The fingers were deft. They bore the fragrance of aromatic oil, the scent of lavender. He felt a fluttering in his stomach, like the beating of a bat's wing.

"You must eat, signor. To regain your strength."

"You speak Italian."

"A little," she said. "I'm French. From a village near Monaco."

"Monaco!". He uttered it like a prayer. It had the ring of things familiar; a refreshing hint of home. He was buoyed by her touch, the proximity of her scent. He was alive. He would see again. He was in the hands of an angel.

"I'm from Torino," he said. "I've been to Ventimiglia. We...we are practically neighbors...."

"You are Aldo," she said. "The men who delivered you left your name. You have been here for days. Three days to be exact."

"Aldo Arazi," he said. "Ensign. Italian Navy." The exchange

came as a relief to him, as though he were once more in familiar territory, on solid ground."

"You are very handsome, Aldo Arazi. Such thick black hair. Such smooth skin. But you must eat. You have the pallor of a mushroom."

She had abandoned her idiomatic Italian. She had reverted to French.

"Have you been here long?" he asked. "With me, I mean?"

"I'm merely looking in," she said. "The woman caring for you is shopping in the village. Her name is Cyrilla."

"And your name?" he asked.

A cloth was pressed to his forehead. It was damp. Damp and cool.

"Lillette," she said. "Lillette Bonnier."

When she left, he lay there staring at the ceiling, seeing nothing. He heard rain splattering on the roof. It sent a fresh wet smell through the slats of the shutters. Gradually he relaxed, his body responding to the unshackling of his nerves. He was not blind. He had hope.

Martinique.

Where was Martinique?

He remembered the SQUALO. Three days, she had said. The SQUALO could remain on station for only a few more days before returning for resupply. If he was reported missing at sea, the Navy would wait ninety days before notifying his family.

Monaco. She lived near Monaco. It was near Ventimiglia. He remembered Ventimiglia. He was a lad of seven when he had driven with his father to the coastal town south of Torino. It was the first and only trip he had ever taken alone with his father. Guissepi Arazi had served as *maitre d'* at a luxurious restaurant in the hills embracing Torino. Once a year the owner would give him the keys to the villa's courtesy car and he would drive to the resort town to discuss the quality of the fish with the supplier. It was a mere formality and of no real consequence to the enterprise, but it gave the Signore an inflated sense of importance and a well-deserved day at the beach.

So excited was Aldo at the prospect of accompanying his father without the burden of his brothers that he had slept not a wink on the eve of the journey. It was a trip he would never forget. The road through the Maritime Alps kept folding back on itself. Twice his father was forced to pull the small fragile Fiat tight against the shoulder of the mountain to let lumber trucks crawling up from the coast swing their heavy loads around hairpin turns. He first glimpsed the Mediterranean from the heights above Ventimiglia, a wincing blue so bright and sparkling that it made his eyes ache. When they descended amid the sandy beaches and pastel umbrellas, he thought he had never seen so magnificent a place.

They had sat at a sidewalk cafe and watched the bathers. His father had bought him a sausage and a wedge of cheese. They shared some beer from a frosty mug, and later, the elder Arazi bought his son an ice. On the drive back into the mountains, weary from sun and excitement, the youthful Aldo had dozed contentedly on the cushions of the rear seat. When jolted awake on the dizzying lacets, he would regain his niche against the seat and listen to his father hum an aria from the pen of Giuseppe Verdi.

In the bedroom on Martinique, he felt an exhilarating breath of resurgence. "You're alive," he said quietly. "You are not blind, Aldo. You're alive."

MARCH 1942

BELLEFONTAINE, MARTINIQUE

"Then we're agreed," Viktor Reinmann said.

Henri-Louis Sambre studied the ash of his cigar. "Agreed. We'll consider our slice a commission. For our labors on behalf of the Reich."

So they could speak without being overheard, they were dining on the patio of Sambre's villa. Viktor leaned back and drew lightly on a freshly-lit panatella. He looked out over the cliffs. The sea was in harmony with the sky, the turquoise shoals mimicking high puffy clouds. For the first time in weeks he felt at ease with himself, in touch with his inclinations. The deal had been cut. When the order came to dump the gold, he and the Frenchman would siphon off a portion for themselves. Sambre had needed little prodding. As a matter of fact, Viktor was beginning to wonder if the Janus-faced Frenchman hadn't helped to plant the seed. He had sensed a subtle probing when they had first discussed the gold more than two weeks before. Once he had made his decision, he had put it to the Frenchman squarely, over drinks on this very same patio.

"You're aware, of course, that there is a discrepancy in the numbers," Viktor had said.

"I've known for some time," Sambre replied. "I have seen the cables from Vichy. They refer to three hundred tons of bullion. A clerical error, I assume, though one can't be sure. It occurred to me that an unscrupulous party might make something of that."

Viktor looked him squarely in the eyes. "Could they?"

The Frenchman returned his gaze. "Possibly. If they were careful."

"Might I conclude that you have given it some thought?"

The Frenchman held his brandy to the sun. "In the hands of

the wrong person, some of the bullion might...shall we say... go astray. Of course, that person would have to possess the means...."

"The means?" Viktor asked.

"Well...first to secure the gold. And then to secrete it."

"And if those means were available?"

"These could be dangerous opinions, monsieur."

"I'm the one asking the questions," Viktor said. "We're talking hypothetically, are we not?"

"It's an interesting exercise in speculation," Sambre said. "Perhaps we should sleep on it."

And they did. Viktor left the following morning to scout some atolls west of Guadeloupe. When he returned, he and the Frenchman had talked at dinner.

"About the gold," Sambre said. Your theoretical questions. I think with the proper planning, a portion of it could easily go adrift...."

Viktor sipped lightly at his wine. "Indeed. And by what means? How many people would it involve?"

"Two. Perhaps three. Are you serious about this, monsieur?"

"Dead serious," Viktor said. He reached out and tapped the Frenchman's glass with his own. At that juncture the girl had entered, so the subject was changed and a decision deferred to a later time.

That same night Viktor had left for a tour of the Venezuelan coastline. His transport had been a German surface marauder disguised as a Scandinavian freighter. Throughout the voyage he had ruminated on the gold. In the quieter moments, he thought of little else. The more he luxuriated in this tropical paradise, the more he saw how the Frenchman lived......servants to fetch his tea, servants to tend his laundry, to shop, to cook, to garden...the less he was inclined to settle for less. Germany would not miss the gold. Indeed, Admiral Doenitz had ordered the gold scuttled if the hijack plan should fail. There was enough bullion to start a revolution. They would be siphoning off a pittance. A single ton. A third of one percent. In the conquered territories, Viktor knew, corruption ran rampant: confiscated apartments, expensive mistresses, underhanded bribes, plundered art treasures. From the highest officials to the lowest footsoldier, everyone was dipping into the pot.

So now the deed was done. They had agreed. He and the Frenchman had cut the deal.

On the patio overlooking the sea, Viktor drew heavily on his cigarette. "When can you be ready on your end?"

"I'm all but ready now," Sambre replied. "A pier has been built; a plan is in place for the disposition of the gold should the Americans threaten invasion. And what of your *milch cow?*

"It's scheduled to leave within the week. Allow two weeks for the crossing. Timing is important. To optimize our chances, we'll need a diversion."

The Frenchman raised an eyebrow. "What sort of diversion?"

Viktor looked to the horizon. A cloud drifted over the sun, darkening the shoals at the base of the cliff. "I have an idea," he said, "but I'll have to check with someone first. If it's plausible, we may well earn our share of the gold. Do you have some people you can trust?"

"For what I have in mind, we should need only one. I have just the man. Come. You can judge for yourself."

Viktor followed him to the guest house beyond the pool. The cottage was larger than it looked from the main house, with a long looping driveway and a forecourt of its own. Once inside the door, the place smelled like a dispensary. There was the odor of harsh soap, a hint of disinfectant, of rubbing alcohol. Sambre led him to a rear bedroom. A man was propped against a pillow, a bandage encircling his forehead, various and sundry medical supplies on a table at his elbow. The man was turning the pages of a magazine; American, Viktor noticed.

Sambre gestured to the bed. "Monsieur Suisse, may I present Signor Arazi."

Viktor took in the soft dark eyes, the freshly trimmed beard, the coal black hair. He repeated the name. "Arazi. Italian, I assume."

The man placed the magazine on the blanket. He pushed

himself upright and squared his shoulders. “Ensign Aldo Arazi. Royal Italian Navy.”

Viktor clicked his heels and affected a formal bow. “Viktor Reinmann. Oberleutnant zur See, Kriegsmarine.”

The Italian took in his yachtman’s trousers, his open collared shirt.

“M. Sambre will vouch for my credentials,” Viktor said. “How did you come to these islands, signor?”

The Italian poured water from a half-empty pitcher. As he hoisted the glass, a hint of exhaustion clawed at the corner of his soft dark eyes. “By submarine. I was injured. We were attacked by a patrol plane. One depth bomb missed, the other failed to explode. My captain fished me from the sea.”

“A submarine, “Viktor turned to Sambre. “Is he aware of....?”

“Not yet,” the Frenchman said. “You’re his superior, are you not? He will do what you say.”

“Is he fit?”

“He’s walking better each day. His improvement has been remarkable. When he arrived, he was temporarily blinded, his eyes damaged by concussion. Now he reads. In addition to a few cracked ribs, he was suffering from dehydration and ulcerated sores from the sea water. As you can see, he has healed nicely.”

Viktor addressed himself to the Italian. “We’re not interlopers on this island, you and I. It’s important that you remember that, signor Arazi. We’re guests of the Vichy government. I’m on a mission. A mission under the auspices of the highest echelons of the German Navy. I may need your help. As your superior, I can command you, but I prefer that you volunteer.”

He could read the uncertainty in the Italian’s eyes. Was he subordinate to this German? Should he ask for credentials? Was he still a combatant? What were the protocols?

“Our host will fill you in on the details,” Viktor said. “There’s little danger, but secrecy is paramount.”

There was an awkward pause while the Italian sorted through his options.

"I'm an officer in the Italian Navy," he said finally. "If what you ask is in the interest of my country, you will have my support."

"Good," Viktor said. "We can discuss the details later. Meanwhile, exercise as much as you can. Are you up to that?"

"Yesterday I walked five kilometers. Tomorrow I try jogging."

As he turned to leave, Viktor noticed the cigarette lighter on the bedstand. It was an American Zippo, the same, he was sure, the girl Lillette had used to light their Camels a fortnight before. Outside, he turned to Sambre. "Why is he here? Why is he not in hospital?"

"He's an embarrassment to the High Commissioner. The Americans were angry enough when a German submariner was put ashore. If they find an Italian has been taken in also, they will accuse Martinique of harboring Axis combatants. To avoid another diplomatic flurry, I suggested the Italian be brought here. The Commissioner readily agreed."

"And afterwards?"

The Frenchman shrugged. "His wounds were serious. He could just as easily have succumbed. Any of a number of tragedies could befall him. Life is a terminal condition, is it not?"

Viktor eyed the Frenchman with new respect. He was more cold-blooded than he looked. He would have to play mongoose to this snake; not let his guard down for a second.

That afternoon Viktor strolled the beach alone, his mind cleansed of all but the present by a benign sea breeze. At the water's edge the sand was damp, the foliage lush, the shadows cool. Where the jungle crept down to the sea the mangrove roots grew thick and slimy. He kicked off his shoes and walked barefoot, savoring the soft granular sensation of powdered seashells. He waded out among the sea grape and machineel. Sitting astride a deadfall, he stripped to the waist and breathed in the hot murky scents of the island. The sea looked vast and alien. Some cauliflower clouds drifted high above the treeline. From somewhere in the brush came the scurrying of a small animal. He soaked his feet in the turquoise shallows and let the sun soothe the muscles of his back.

It was coming together. All of it. A door had opened. He had but to enter.

He could do it.

He would do it.

But there was one final detail, one critically important matter that would complete the picture. He would see to it tomorrow.

STE-ANNE, MARTINIQUE

Dante raised the paddle and let the dinghy drift. The sky over the island was clear and luminous, with moonlight washing the sheltered cove. This time the approach to the beach was easier; the patrol launch had dropped him closer to shore. The sea was calm, the breeze subdued. It was comforting to know there were friends beyond the darkness. With the dinghy rising on the heavy swells, he managed the beach with ease.

As on his first visit, there were two of them. But this time the woman was accompanied by the Creole. Lucien LeClerc; Lucien the breadman.

Lucien buried the dingy quickly. It was not until they reached the treeline that anyone spoke.

"Welcome, Paul."

Her voice came from deep in the shadows. He found himself moved by the sound of it. In the weeks since his last visit he had ruminated a good deal on that voice. He knew far too little about the woman behind it. The sketch he had patched together from their tour of the island was the stuff of dossiers. He was curious about the person, the woman beyond the masks. Physician. Artist. Widow. Resistance Leader. There was much he wished to learn about Nikole Rollet. And if his previous visit was any indication, the assignment should be far from unpleasant.

She moved from the shadows and he could see her face. In the soft white light of the moon her skin had an alabaster sheen. And this time the face was smiling, this time the expression was one of welcome, not of dubiosity.

He joined her at the treeline. "*Bon soir,* Nikole," he whispered. "It's good to be back."

"*Bon soir,* Paul. Christopher Delon is at the house. We will keep to the roads tonight. It will go easier on the cattle." He caught the softness in her eyes, the playful smirk at the corner of her lips.

Remembering his encounter with the cow, Dante chuckled.

On the trek through the foothills, he walked beside her. Though there was little conversation, something seemed to pass between them, an understanding of sorts......a cordiality......perhaps something beyond that. When they reached her garden, the Creole evaporated. Dante was about to enter when Nikole detained him at the door.

"We have a visitor, Paul. The girl."

"Sambre's girl?"

"Lillette Bonnier. She came with Christopher Delon."

"Does she know about me?"

"Only that you may help her escape the island. She'll trade on that. We've assured her that she's in no danger here. She has confidence in Christopher. Now that she knows he was...is...a priest, she trusts him even more."

Dante remembered the girl on the staircase at Christopher's hotel, slender, coltish, clipped blonde hair. When they entered the kitchen she was sitting at the table, a glass of wine in one hand, a cigarette in a seashell at her elbow. With fatigue dragging heavily at her features, she looked older than he remembered, less brash. Her cheeks were drawn and pale, with smudges of flushed high color; her hair looked bleached by the sun. Clad in a simple blue dress and leather sandals, she looked a world removed from the *cocotte* he had seen at Christopher's hotel.

Christopher Delon made the introductions. "Mademoiselle Lillette," the priest said, a bit formally for the occasion, "may I present Monsieur Paul."

Dante thought the priest seemed solicitous, more like a brother than a neighbor with common interests. Dante was wearing a sleeveless sweatshirt and khaki shorts. With a two-day beard and his hair still damp from the sea, he felt he looked grimy and hard. Lillette remained seated. She held out a hand and Dante gripped the fingers. They were supple but strong. No tea and scones for this youngster, Dante thought. More like *brioche* and *espresso*.

Lillette must return tonight," Christopher said. "It's best we begin."

Dante took a seat at the table. Nikole fetched rum from the sideboard. From a chest in the pantry she brought out wedges of lime and some ice. When she came to Lillette, the youngster held a hand over her glass.

Christopher came straight to the point. "Tell Monsieur Paul what you told me, Lillette. About Sambre and the gold."

Apparently the priest had done a persuasive selling job. The girl launched into her narrative as though they had been meeting for years.

She spoke in French. Dante recognized the clipped twangy dialect of Provence.

"They intend to take the gold, monsieur. Sambre and the German."

Dante replied in English. As good as his French was, he wanted no misunderstandings. "How can you be certain, Lillette?"

Her English was halting, with traces of pidgin. "I have hear them......overhear them."

"When?" Dante asked. "When did you hear them?"

"Three days ago. At Bellefontaine."

"Sambre's villa," the priest explained.

Dante nodded. "When do they plan to take the gold?"

"I'm...I'm no sure. I only hear it will be soon."

"When they talk of the gold, what gold is it?"

"In Desaix." She pointed toward the ceiling, as though they were at the foot of the fortress. "It makes Sambre rich. He has told me."

"You were alone when you heard this?"

"Oui...yes. There is another...person.... An Italian."

"An Italian?" Dante looked at Nikole. She raised an eyebrow. Christopher remained expressionless.

"This Italian," Dante asked. "Who is he? Is he Government?"

"He is Navy. From a submarine. He is wounded. He is...he is heal at Sambre's villa."

"Does he talk to the German?"

"At times..."

"Does he talk to you?"

"Yes. I am help him to...to nurse..."

She glanced at Christopher. The priest stared stoically into his rum.

"This plan to move the gold," Dante said. "Perhaps you can learn something of the timing."

"Perhaps," she said in a small toneless voice.

"It's important," Christopher said.

Lillette raised her eyes to meet his. "It is important that I leave this island, monsieur..."

There was a brief pause while the girl sipped her wine.

The priest shifted restlessly on his chair. "You have my word, Lillette." He remembered Jacques and the wounded of Dunkirk and suffered an uneasy moment. Who was he to assure her freedom? Was he being too free with his word again?

Dante resumed his questioning of the girl. "This German. What does he look like?"

The pale blue lids fluttered slightly. A pout formed on her full moist lips. "He is...young...," Lillette said. "...like Christopher Delon....hair the color like mine...eyes blue...big chest..." She held both hands out from her bosom.

Half the German Navy, Dante thought. "Do you know where he comes from? Where he goes when he leaves the villa?"

"To sea. He goes to sea. He brings no clothes. Sambre gives him clothes. He smells of...how do you say...*benzine*...from the boat...." Her eyes went to Christopher again.

The priest studied the gaslamp on the sideboard.

***

Later, when the priest and the girl had left, Nikole and Dante strolled the garden.

What do we do?" Nikole asked. "Should we alert the High Commissioner's office?"

"You say this Sambre is close to Admiral Robert. We have no details. If we alert the Admiral and he questions Sambre, we might tip our hand."

"Then we must wait?"

"Until we have proof. Something solid to go on."

"Lucien has a cousin at the fort," Nikole said. "If they attempt to move the gold, he's sure to hear of it."

"Good. That could buy us some time. This Italian intrigues me. Why would Sambre involve him? They must need him. But why?"

"It's why we sent for you, Paul."

BELLEFONTAINE, MARTINIQUE

Lillette Bonnier watched the taxi trundle through the arched stone gates. She heard the groan of the engine as the driver worked impatiently through the gears. As the engine noise faded, she dropped her carryall in one of the smaller bedrooms and touched up her makeup in a mirror. Sambre was on an inspection tour of Guiana with Admiral Robert. It was the first time he had left her alone on the island since the outbreak of hostilities. The manservant Honore had been given the weekend off. Only the Creole woman had been left to attend the villa. Before departing, Sambre had visited her at her apartment in Forte de France.

"But I will be in this stuffy hotel by myself for an entire week", she complained, hoping the petulance was not overdone.

Sambre seemed preoccupied, as though a matter of so little consequence was barely worth the effort to put it right. "It's a few short days," he said. "You can catch up on your reading."

"May I swim at Bellefontaine?" she asked with her most dispirited pout.

"Do that," he shot back, anxious to be on his way.

A swim was just what she intended. Since the Italian had regained consciousness, she had dropped by to see him from time to time, using as her excuse some domestic chore at the cottage. Now that his eyesight had improved, he was healing rapidly. He was burdened by a noticeable limp, but his mobility had improved to the point where he no longer hobbled like a one-legged spider. His hearing was still impaired; sometimes when she spoke to him he did not reply, but he was beginning to exercise. The last time she saw him he was doing pressups. And he was jogging longer and longer distances on the beach.

She kicked off her heels and peeled off her city clothes. There was something purgative about stripping down in this climate. Free of the binding skirt and clinging blouse, she felt like she had stepped into a cooling shower. Not bothering with underwear, she slipped into a flimsy sun dress and donned a floppy straw hat. Barefoot and bare-legged, she smeared coconut oil on her arms and legs and used the stopper of a perfume bottle to anoint her throat.

In the kitchen, she found a spoon. Taking a bottle of olive oil from her purse, she pulled a face, poured, and swallowed with a shiver and a grimace. There was bread in the cupboard. Breaking the heel from the loaf, she forced it down in large dry bites. The driver had deposited a case of wine in the foyer, compliments of an officer at Fort St-Louis. She stacked three of the bottles in an ice chest; a fourth she took with her to the garden.

The cottage where the Italian was recuperating was behind the pool area. Crossing the lawn she heard the gritty thud of a shovel striking sand. She rounded the cottage and saw him digging. In the heat of the afternoon? Had his illness affected his brain? Was he *pazzo*? He had his back to the villa, a foot jamming the shovel, an oversized straw hat tilted rakishly over his brow. He was tanning nicely, she noticed. A sheen of perspiration coated the muscles of his back and his shoulders looked like oiled wood.

"*Buon giorno,*" she said, strolling up behind.

Aldo glanced over a shoulder. *Bon jour,*" he grinned, the sweat dripping from his nose. He planted the shovel and doffed the hat with a small ceremonial bow.

"I like your hat," she laughed, mimicking his bow. "It's like mine, only bigger."

"The Creole woman calls it a *bakoua*. I found it in the cottage.

"You're feeling better," she said, gazing into his wine-dark eyes. "Are you building something?"

"My strength."

She saw a crate filled with sand, a tent-like tarpaulin near the treeline. A breeze was flapping the canvas, and beneath it she could see more crates.

"I thought you might like...." She held up a bottle of chianti.

He tossed the shovel against the crate. "*Signorina! Grazie mille!* The rum is up to here." He clutched his throat.

She tossed the bottle and he caught it with both hands. Taking her arm, he turned her toward the villa. As they passed the cottage, she caught a whiff of lye, the odor of harsh soap. The Creole woman was scrubbing something in the laundry.

They sat on a jalousied porch overlooking the sea, she in her sundress, he in his sandals and cutaways. The breeze was refreshing, the fronds on the palms clicking like wind chimes. They drank straight from the bottle, handing it back and forth between alternate swigs. Though he seemed not to notice, Lillette drank sparingly.

"Finish it," she said. "There's more inside."

So thirsty was he that he downed an entire bottle before the perspiration dried on his chest. Lillette produced a second bottle from the kitchen. When he tried to extract the cork with his teeth, he bit too hard and the cork disintegrated in his mouth. Lillette got the giggles. He spit the cork away and pushed the stub inward with a finger.

"The wine, it's wonderful," he said, stretching out in the chair. "Where did you find it?"

She noticed a jagged red scar at the base of his abdomen. "A friend."

He would soon be drunk, she knew. If not drunk, at least talkative. Sun and wine were an explosive combination. It was a game she had played before. They were in her territory now. If he knew anything of Sambre's project, she would charm it from him. If not today, then tonight; if not tonight, tomorrow. There was no rush. She would draw him to her like a flower to the sun. What he knew, she would know. When first they met, while he was drifting between consciousness and delirium, she had introduced herself as a friend of Sambre's family. He had bought the fiction as readily as a child. He seemed intelligent, but trusting; witty, but naive. Could this young Italian mariner be the key to her deliverance, a gift from the sea? She could only hope.

"It reminds me of my father," he said, gesturing toward the

cove. "He took me to the seaside as a boy. It was hot and blue like this. Hot and blue and wonderful."

"You were close to your father?"

He pondered a moment. "My family is close. My father. Mother. Sisters. Brothers. And you?"

"I was raised by my mother. I never knew my father."

He looked genuinely touched. "It must be sad," he said, "not to know your father. You have no grandfather? No uncles?"

"Only aunts," she lied. "Only women."

The wind was tapering to a breeze. It was growing extremely hot, even in the shade. Halfway through the second bottle Lillette could see the luster in his eyes.

"I'm...I'm lucky to be here," he said, The wine was in his head now. He was no doubt on an empty stomach. "I could be out there with the fishes...."

"What a nice idea," she said, teasingly. "Let's have a swim. In the sea. We'll take the wine."

"But I have no" ....he tugged at his truncated trousers.

"We'll swim off Sambre's boat. No one goes there."

He looked at her questioningly, his eyes misty with lust, his fingers drumming nervously on the neck of the bottle.

She managed her most fetching smile.

Ragged steps had been carved into the steep rocky slope. Far below, the cove was flanked by headlands. A pier had been erected near the base of the steps; it stretched a hundred yards offshore. Sambre's motor yacht was moored at the seaward end.

The RIVE GAUCHE was a pleasure craft, fifty feet long and as comfortable as a cottage. When they stepped aboard, Aldo went below to open the hatches. He had worked its decks before, once with Sambre for a run up the coast, once with the fisherman Honore to strip the aft deck for reasons yet to be explained. Lillette knew the RIVE GAUCHE also. On more than one occasion she had entertained a guest in a paneled suite.

Aldo placed the wine bottles in a net. "It won't chill them," he said, lowering them over the side. “But at least they won’t get warm.”

The anchorage lay in the lee of the mountain. The cove was oppressively hot, the sun blazing down from a brassy sky. Even the breeze seemed to hold its breath. The deck was sweltering, the cabins stuffy. Seated on a hatch above the galley, Aldo was dripping with perspiration. The sun sat on his back like a hot wash cloth.

Lillette was beginning to flush. “I’m going in,” she said.

She balanced on the transom and peeled the sun dress casually over her head. As the Italian looked on, she flung it behind her to the deck. In the second it took her to execute a graceful dive, Aldo noticed her flawless tan, her sun-bronzed back, the symmetry of firm white buttocks over well-formed hips. Taking his cue without hesitation, he unbuttoned his cutoffs and plunged headlong in his briefs. The water was tepid, near body temperature; there was a strong but pleasant taste of salt.

She was a good swimmer, far better than he. As he struggled to keep pace, she swam powerfully out to sea. Throwing her length into her stroke, she outpaced him easily. With her hair pasted tightly against her neck and her shoulders tanned and sleek, she reminded him of sea otters he had seen off the African coast. He tracked her doggedly, struggling to keep pace. Just as he was beginning to tire, she rolled to her back and began to float, paddling with her legs and treading water with her arms. When at last he drew beside her, he saw firm naked breasts pointed tautly at the sky. Twisting smoothly to his back, he was attempting to float when the panic gripped him. There was an instant of cold slimy fear when, without warning, the memory of the SQUALO flooded in...the swells washing the decks, the waves smashing the bridge, the sea tugging relentlessly at his limbs. He turned and began thrashing toward the yacht. Suddenly the sky and sea were as one, churning and spinning and dragging him down. He felt a tightening in his joints, a foundering in his limbs. Before he realized what was happening Lillette was beside him, a hand beneath his armpit, her legs kicking rhythmically beside his, the pressure of her fingers steadfast and reassuring. With surprising ease, she buoyed him with her body and soothed him with her voice.

"It's your wounds," she said, edging him slowly toward the yacht. "You're still weak.

He could feel the muscles quivering in his legs.

"Too much wine," she said. "Too much sun. Too much digging." As she spoke, she towed him steadily toward the pier, propelling him beside her while spouting miniature jets from a corner of her mouth. In the sanctuary of her grasp, he regained the fluidity of his joints. In seconds he stopped thrashing; in minutes he began swimming on his own. As they neared the ladder he experienced a moment's embarrassment; then drawing her to him, he locked an arm in her arm and they managed the final few yards together.

At the foot of the ladder the water was crystal clear, so perfectly translucent that he felt suspended in air. As his shivering eased, she pressed her body lightly against his. She was wearing nothing but the hair that fell between her shoulders. Her breasts were firm, her legs moving rhythmically against his, the heat of her breath a palliative on his cheek. He could smell the sea in her hair. Her calf brushed his calf; he felt the warmth of her inner thigh. It was pure heaven. Without warning, she kissed him, the taste of her at once salty and sweet. She feathered her tongue around his. He had never been kissed in such a wet sexual way. When he responded in kind, she drew her legs to the surface. In the gin clear waters she reached to his waist. In one easy motion she stripped away his briefs. He paused as though dumbstruck. He felt the tickling sensation in his testicles that preceded an erection. She felt him hardening against her leg. Before he could reply or react, she ducked beneath the surface and retrieved his briefs. Bursting to sunlight and spouting like a whale, she raised them over her head and flung them out to sea. Then naked and treading water they giggled, then laughed, she out of mirth, he out of relief and embarrassment.

They spent the afternoon on the yacht. He brought a mattress to the cockpit and rigged a canvas for shade. The swimming had sobered them both. Her inquiries into Sambre's project would await a more suitable time.

She was surprised to find that he was a virgin, her first, as far as she knew. He confessed it readily, as if out of gratitude, not so much for her rescue as for her tactful disregard of his plight.

"Of course, I have been with other women, he said, stretched naked on the mattress.. "But I have never...how should I say it... gone so far." He kissed her neck. "Now that I have tasted real wine......".

She found herself moved more to compassion than to lust. As a lover he was gentle, clumsy, apologetic. Responding to his ardor, she played the innocent. Yet she took him to erotic places. She felt him responding to her rhythm. So aroused was he, so hungry for her, that she was certain he never suspected.

Afterwards he dozed with his head on her abdomen. As she savored the breeze, she felt a strange satisfaction within. Was this how it was for other women? It was the first time she had shared her body, not sold it. The first time she had been accepted, not demanded. The first time she had felt clean, not soiled. She had never viewed sex as a bonding, but merely as a coupling, a collision of flesh, a game of tease and comply. In bed she was merely a stimulus and a receptacle. This was different, not like the love that hangs behind the bathroom door,that smells of douches and caustic powders. This was tender, unrushed. As she watched his steady rhythmic breathing, she realized he was a child. A muscular, attractive man-child. She brushed solicitous fingers through his thick dark hair. Did this warrior-child hold the key to her liberation? Tomorrow they would drink again. This time there would be no swimming. This time she would spend the wine to advantage.

ST. THOMAS, U.S. VIRGIN ISLANDS

A voice crackled thinly in Kevin Whitely's earphones. "There she be, skipper. Home sweet home."

As the flying boat emerged from a dank thin drizzle, Whitely banked toward the corona of light beyond his wingtip. "Roger, Alabama. Got it."

Savoring the familiar lift in his stomach, he eased back on the yoke and the Catalina settled slowly toward the island, its nose turret probing the cool night air, its fuselage arched and slender beneath a broad parasol wing. Below and to his left the lights of Charlotte Amalie formed a diamond-studded necklace at the throat of its bay. Whitely took a bearing on the crescent-shaped harbor and pressed his intercom.

"Buckle up, gentlemen."

His earphones sizzled with a short sibilant burst of atmospherics.

"I can spot the honky-tonk from here."

Whitely recognized the voice from the flight engineer's station. "Stow it, Joe Don Danny. Let's grease her in with some dignity."

The second pilot rapped a knuckle against a temperature gauge. "Number two's hottin' up, skipper."

"Got it, Jeff. We can glide in from here."

Behind them, Ensign Marshall Tobias extinguished the lamp over his navigator's table. "Hope they import some decent mechanics onto this banana farm."

"Forget it," the co-pilot cut in. "Just demon rum and virgin native girls. Whyn't they wear sarongs in these islands, skip?"

Whitely cut the power back and watched the air speed bleed away on his indicator.

"I swear," the navigator countered. "They do a lobotomy on you, Powers, they'll find a cauldron of seething vaginas.

"Whyn't we invade them Frog islands, Skip? That Martineek and Guadaloop? Give us a shot at them mad'moselles. You suppose they call 'em American ticklers over there?"

The co-pilot chuckled. "Ya can't trust the Frenchies, Toby. They fight with their feet and fuck with their faces."

Whitely banked the PBY toward the jaws of the harbor. "To work, gentlemen. Check the bay for freelancers."

He set the Catalina down gently, barely disturbing the glassine surface. When he opened the hatch, heavy viscous air welled warmly in around him. At the differential in temperature, the skin of the flying boat crackled and pinged.

He was toting his gear to the Quonset hut when he noticed a woman hurrying down the pier. She was accompanied by a Marine corporal wearing a cartridge belt and a holstered pistol. There was only one woman on the island with a figure like that. What would Casey O'Shea be doing at the airbase at this hour? Suddenly she broke from her escort and started toward him in a trot. He could see she was upset and on the verge of tears.

Her father, he thought. The Captain has bought it.

He handed the flight log to his co-pilot and strode out to meet her.

"Kevin," she cried. "For God's sake, you've got to help me. Sean's missing. He's disappeared..."

Her Marine escort jogged up behind. "She's cleared by the Exec, Lieutenant. She's all yours."

Whitely placed a hand on each of her shoulders. "Easy, Case. Missing? From where? When did you see him last?"

"This afternoon. At the Trade Winds. I went shopping and left him with Rina. He was playing on the terrace. One minute he was there, Rina said, and the next...he was...he was...gone...."

She was near to breaking down. Whitely took her hands and pressed them between his fingers.

"What time? How long has it been?"

"Hours. Since late this afternoon. We've searched all over.

When she first realized he was missing, Rina called the desk clerk. The Contessa rounded up the staff. They checked with everybody... the residents...the neighbors. Everybody's helping in the search. We've looked all over...the shrubs...the pool...the hillsides. Just before they called me, the Contessa notified the police. He's so small, Kevin...it's dark... he'll be frightened...he's so helpless...

"Easy, Case. We'll find him...."

"The base commander..." she said, her face drawn and pale, "...he knows my father. He's sending some men. They told me you were flying in. What can I do, Kevin? He's just a baby...so vulnerable.... What can I do...?"

"We'll find him, Casey. We'll scour the island. We'll check every house, turn over every stone, search every shack and vehicle. The entire airbase will help. I'll talk to the skipper at the sub base."

The tears were coming freely now. "My father, Kevin. I've got to get word to my father. He's on special assignment. St. Lucia. That's all they know."

Whitely turned her gently toward the hut. "I'll see what I can find out. Look. I know it's not easy, but you've got to pull yourself together. Let's take it from the top. You've got to tell me everything...everything and anything that might help...."

"Oh God," she said, choking back a sob. "I think I know, Kevin. I don't want to believe it, but I think I know...."

PART THREE

MAY 1942

FORTE DE FRANCE, MARTINIQUE

In the Admiralty Building at Forte de France, a stately residence ringed by royal palms and sandbagged gun emplacements, Henri-Louis Sambre sat in a hide-covered armchair watching the man behind the desk shuffle impatiently through a sheaf of papers. Despite his diminutive stature, Rear Admiral George Robert cut an imposing figure.

White-haired and thick of brow, with a trim white beard and moustache to match, the septuagenarian High Commissioner was as bright of eye and distinguished of demeanor as any in the colonies. Despite his seventy years, his temper was as fiery as ever and, to those who served him, every bit as unpredictable. In his beribboned white uniform with the gold braid trim, his very presence commanded respect.

The Admiral looked up from his papers. "The Americans continue to press us, Sambre. Not only do they insist our warships be immobilized, now they want control of radio communications, of immigration and travel. Last week they demanded we return the aircraft they sold us, the Buffaloes shipped in on the BEARN. The week before that they insisted we retain the gold in Fort Desaix." He slammed the file to the desk. "They're becoming as arrogant as the Nazis. I have pledged neutrality, but they no longer trust me."

Sambre leaned forward in his chair. "They're afraid our warships will make a run for it, Admiral. Now that Laval has been named Premier at Vichy, they're increasing their surveillance throughout the islands."

"I've agreed to immobilize the ships," the Admiral countered. "But useless or no, the warplanes belong to us. We paid for them."

"What of the gold?" Sambre asked. "Why do you suppose they want to keep it here? Do you think they might actually attempt an invasion?"

"Perhaps. If so, we'll defend the gold with our lives. It belongs to France."

The moment had come. Sambre produced a cable from an inner pocket. "A coded message, Admiral. The secret code, the one Petain did not turn over to the Germans. It arrived while you were in conference. I decoded it only minutes before you summoned me."

He handed the cable over the desk.

The Admiral propped reading glasses over his nose.

INTELLIGENCE ADVISES
INVASION IMMINENT
TAKE NECESSARY PRECAUTIONS
Laval

The admiral tossed the cable onto his blotter. "We're on alert. What more can we do?"

Sambre shrugged. The Admiral had ignored cables from Vichy before. But to ignore a message sent by the secret code could amount to treason. Besides, this was Pierre Laval he was dealing with, a Nazi sympathizer, not the patriarchal Petain.

The Admiral stared at the message. "Is the pier ready?"

Sambre nodded. "And the barge is in place."

"How long will it take to move the gold?"

"Working in darkness, two or three nights."

"Do it. Move the crates to the barge. But await my orders before proceeding with the final disposition."

"As you wish, Excellency."

The Admiral held up another sheath of paper. "Look at this. Now they insist we clear with them any movement of ships between islands."

"Will you comply, Admiral?"

"We are not lepers. "We will not carry bells."

STE-ANNE, MARTINIQUE

At first she thought she was dreaming. Then she heard it again.

Tap.. .tap. . .pause. . .tap. . .pause. . .tap. . .tap.

Nikole Rollet threw back the sheet and slipped naked from the mattress. She had never learned to tolerate bedclothes, not even in Paris, where in winter her flat grew as cold as the meat lockers at Les Halles. She slipped into a dressing gown and descended the steps barefoot. The clock in the sitting room read 3:22 a.m. Shafts of moonlight streaked the furniture and painted bizarre patterns against the whitewashed walls.

Could it be Lucien? It would require an emergency for him to waken her at this hour.

She slipped silently through the kitchen and into the walk-in pantry. From a small curtained window she could look unobserved into the garden.

"*Mon dieu*, she whispered to herself.

She returned to the kitchen and released the latch. Dante O'Shea slipped quietly into the room.

"Sorry about the hour," he said. "I received your message and decided not to wait. There was no time to send a reply."

His clothes bore the scent of the sea; his breathing was heavy from the climb up the hillside.

She locked the door behind him. "You have buried your raft?"

He smiled. "I'm getting good at it. I came over by seaplane. With the wind offshore, they taxied almost to the point."

"I'm happy to see you," she said. smoothing the robe around her neck. "Forgive my *deshabille.*"

"You look terrific."

She pointed to the table. "Please. Sit. Would you like some tea?"

"If I can spike it." From a rear pocket he produced a pint of scotch.

She filled a kettle with water and touched a match to a burner. The flame cast flickering shadows on the ceiling and walls. He watched as she prepared a tray. Though drowsy with sleep, she moved as gracefully as a cat. Devoid of makeup and with her hair disarranged by the pillow, she had an early-morning freshness, a womanish warmth.

"What's happening?" he asked. Is it the gold?"

She drew a pair of cups from a cupboard. "There are strange doings at Fort Desaix. When the gold was brought to the island, some of it was stored in sacks. Lucien's cousin tells us the sacks are being replaced by crates. The excuse is that the sacks are in danger of rotting. But it could be to facilitate their handling."

She placed the tray on the table beside a linen napkin. "The regular guards are gone." she continued, digging biscuits from a tin. "Some of the best marksmen on the island, have been relieved by troops newly arrived from Africa. And the officer in charge has been transferred to a camp in the mountains. An odd time for transfers when the island is on alert. Lucien's cousin has a friend in the motor pool. He says trucks are being rounded up. And buses."

"Any news from the priest?"

She sat and poured the tea. He uncapped the whiskey and held it over her cup. She nodded assent.

"Christopher contacted Lucien last night," she said. "The girl Lillette reports that Monsieur Sambre has been preoccupied of late. She has not seen or heard from him in days. The Italian is still at Sambre's villa. Lillette says he returns dirty and tired at night from digging. And the German is back."

"This German. Do we know anything more about him?"

"Only what Lillette revealed to us on your last visit."

"Has she mentioned a child?"

She looked at him inquiringly. "A child? No. Nothing about a child."

"I want to see this German," Dante said.

"Lillette says he comes and goes."

“I’d like to see him,” Dante repeated. “Could you have Christopher contact Lillette immediately? It’s very important.”

“This child,” Nikole asked, sampling the tea. “Whose child is it? Does it have something to do with the gold?”

“To the gold, no,” Dante replied. “To me, a great deal. He may be my grandson.”

PITONS DU CARBET, MARTINIQUE

Viktor Reinmann looked on impatiently as the Italian struggled with the heavy door. It was canted on its track and refused to budge. Beside him at the entrance to the barn stood Henri-Louis Sambre. The Frenchman was chewing an unlit cigar.

"Where exactly are we?" Viktor asked, hoping the Italian would manage on his own.

The Frenchman pointed to the surrounding hills. "A few miles inland from Bellefontaine. An abandoned sugar cane plantation."

Night was seeping into the valley and spreading a blanket of mist over the gray-green hills. As far as the eye could see they were surrounded by forest. What fields there were had been allowed to grow over, what cane survived was choked by weeds.

The Italian gave a powerful shove and the door slid back to reveal a truck. Like most of the military vehicles on the island it had an earth-colored chassis and a canvas-top.

"This warehouse is part of an old distillery," Sambre said. "Only lizards venture out here anymore. Lizards and land birds."

"And the truck?"

"It's listed as being in for repairs."

Viktor followed the Frenchman into the dusky interior where, in years gone by, oceans of rum had slumbered in charred wooden casks. The air reeked of rotted wood and sour earth. There was some rusted machinery against a cinderblock wall, some broken crates scattered randomly about the floor. Surprisingly, the panes in the windows were mostly intact. Twilight filtered weakly through the tainted glass.

The Italian vaulted onto the truck's tailgate.

"Open it," Sambre said.

Aldo peeled back the flap. Behind it were stacks of raw wooden crates, each about three feet square, each stenciled identically with the numeral 35.

"How many are there?" Viktor asked.

"Thirty," Sambre said. "Thirty five kilos each."

Viktor managed a fast calculation. More than a thousand kilos. With gold valued at thirty-five dollars an ounce, troy weight, it would come to more than a million dollars American, a veritable fortune in any currency.

"And inside?" Viktor asked.

"Sand," Sambre said. "Compliments of our Italian friend.

Viktor watched as Aldo Arazi hopped nimbly to the ground. Compared to the invalid he had witnessed just weeks before, his body bruised, his face disfigured by ulcerated scars, the Italian looked tanned and healthy, with good muscle tone and the beginnings of a spring to his step.

"Close it up," Sambre said.

Viktor motioned the Frenchman outside. While the Italian replaced the tarpaulin, they walked to the edge of the forest. In the murky green twilight, Sambre lit his cigar. Even from here Viktor could smell the warm green scent of the sea.

"And when the sand is discovered?" Viktor asked.

"It will shed more heat than light. This particular sand was brought as ballast from France. The *béké* who built my villa used it for mortar for the terrace. A touch of the motherland, so to speak. Tons of it was trucked to the site, some of it dumped behind the cottage, most of it into the sea. Thanks to our Italian friend, a good deal of it now resides in those crates."

"A nice touch," Viktor conceded.

"Insurance," the Frenchman said. "When your countrymen find the doctored crates, they'll be faced with a dilemma. Were the French siphoning off their own gold? Who dummied the crates? If anyone attempts to trace the sand, it had its origins on the Normandy coast. Was the hoax perpetrated before the gold left France? Who's to say? Even as we speak, that portion of the bullion that arrived in sacks is at this very moment being transferred to crates. A perfect opportunity for a less than honorable officer to skim some cream."

Viktor started back toward the shack. The Frenchman trudged beside him. "And my people, even the SS, can never inquire formally."

"Officially, the gold will be at the bottom of the sea."

As he circled the truck, Viktor paused at the crates. He envisioned a chateau on the Rhine, a comfortable drawing room, his son on his knee before a massive stone fireplace.

On the drive back to Bellefontaine, he sat beside the Frenchman on the rear seat. While he contemplated the details of the plan, he puffed one of Sambre's cigars. When they reached the seaside villa, the Italian deposited them at the entrance to the main house.

The three-year-old was at the kitchen table, a glass of milk untouched at his elbow, a half-eaten banana beside the glass.

"He no wanna eat," the woman said. She was the same ancient Creole who had nursed the Italian back to health, who ironed Viktor's shirts, saw to his laundry.

Viktor smiled at the boy. He took in the light blue eyes, the broad Reinmann chin. He ran a hand though the tousled hair. "You must eat, *liebchen.* You won't grow strong if you don't eat."

"I want my mommy," the boy said, his legs dangling from the chair.

"Your *muta* will join us soon, Viktor said. "You must eat, so you will be strong and healthy when she arrives."

The youngster sat sullenly on the edge of the chair, his eyes diverted from his captors, his lips on the verge of a quiver.

Viktor took the Frenchman aside. "I will take him with me," he said. "On the *milch cow.*"

The Frenchman poured a drink from the sideboard. "The boy is your business, monsieur.

"He's German," Viktor said. "Germany is the future."

MORNE BLANC, MARTINIOUE

Eyes were descending from the darkness. Dozens and dozens of eyes. Pale and unblinking. Winding down the mountain like the legions of the dead.

The potter hunched by the side of the road. An immense tropical moon, sallow and misshapen by the breath of the tropics, cast long ghostly shadows into every crevice and ravine, every hollow and glade. So profound was its impact on the wooded slopes that the shrill of insects was hushed, the call of the night birds subdued. From the roadside ditch where the potter crouched, the leaves of the papaya hung dark and silent like spectral bats against the cheddar moon.

Le Pays de Revenants, the Martiniquais called their island. The Land of Ghosts. On every road, trail, path, and bridge one comes upon shrines, icons, statuettes, crucifixes. In the forks of trees, on a niche in a wall, a thousand feet above sea level, in the depths of the forest. Almost every village has its spirits, it phantoms, its zombies. And here snaking down the mountain was the devil incarnate, a wriggling serpent with glowing eyes slithering slowly through the jungle toward the mangrove swamps below.

The potter was old, in his eighth decade. His eyes were weak and he was practically deaf. He had not ventured into the pit of the night in years. Never had he wandered so near the swamp in search of the loam to make his clay. If he survived this dragon, he would never do so again. As the monster slithered stealthily through the trees, the potterer scrambled up an incline toward his shanty in the hills.

***

Henri-Louis Sambre was at the wheel of the lead truck. Admiral Robert had commissioned him to take personal charge, to assure that every ounce of gold that cleared the fort was delivered safely to the barge. Behind him through the grimy wing mirror Sambre could see the ragged line of trucks and buses, headlamps on low beam, the upper halves of the lenses painted blue, the lower halves casting a serpentine glow through the dank foliage. On the fender of his truck sat a Senegalese soldier. He had memorized the route; it was all he knew of the island, all he would ever know.

Had there ever been such a caravan, Sambre wondered? Not in these islands. Not even on the Spanish Main had such a concentration of gold been hauled so nakedly through the tropical night. And this was only the beginning. Working only after dark, it would require two full nights to move the gold from the fort to the barge. Two nights and eighty men. And when it was complete, not a soul to tell of it.

The drivers of the other trucks were Senegalese colonials also. They had been diverted to the island while en route to Guiana. They had been told that the crates they were carting were loaded with munitions, that the exercise was part of the general alert, that if the Americans invaded, a counterattack would be mounted from the hills. It was more than they needed to know. In a few short days they would be history, shipped from the island to their original destination. Only a handful of those remaining on Martinique would know the real story: the Admiral, the officers on the tug and the barge, and Henri-Louis Sambre. The regulars at the fort would not be told that the gold had been moved until after the fact. By then it would be too late...too late to be certain, if not to speculate. For all they knew, the gold had been shipped back to France, to Africa, to a hiding place in the hills.

That was the plan. The official plan. Admiral Robert's plan.

But only he, Sambre, would know the real story. In a few short days the Italian would be disposed of and the German would be gone. One way or another his silence would be assured. Back in Berlin, Admiral Doenitz and the Abwehr would be celebrating their coup, but they would be doing so quietly. It was their own secret, the taking of the gold, a secret they intended to keep from the world.

The Germans were efficient, that he had to admit. A dummy cable had been sent to Admiral Robert over the signature of Pierre Laval. As the new head of the Vichy Government, his orders would not be questioned. A confirming cable had been dispatched, at Sambre's insistence, on the secret frequency supplied by Viktor Reinmann. Admiral Robert had taken the bait. He had little choice. The cables were authentic, all but the name of the sender.

It would go down in history as an unfortunate stroke of fate. A barge laden with gold headed for burial at sea mysteriously disappears with only two officers on board. How would Admiral Robert handle the dilemma? Would he suspect the officers towing the barge of making off with the gold? Would he conclude that the tug and the barge had been sunk? Waylaid? He would report back to Vichy on the same secret frequency. The Abwehr would acknowledge the tragedy over Pierre Laval's signature. Admiral Robert would order a search. The French, the Americans, the British...... they would scour the sea lanes, overfly every ship, every island in search of the missing gold, all the while suspecting one another. At war's end, it would matter not. By then there would be no need for high intrigue, for phony armistices. By then Germany would have taken control of the balance of France and Laval would be on the dungheap. By then the gold would belong to Germany anyway.

One more night and he would be at the wheel of the hindmost truck.

One more night and he would be on the verge of a fortune.

Showing nothing but its cat's eyes, the convoy crept silently through the jungle roads.

STE-ANNE, MARTINIQUE

In the bedroom beneath the eaves, Captain Dante O'Shea slipped a navy blue blazer over light tan trousers and a white cotton shirt. He had purchased the jacket on St. Lucia from an émigré of Bond Street. It was of tropical weight and, with the exception of a crease here and there, had survived the dinghy wedged into a compartment of a gripsack. Also in the gripsack was a bottle of Remy-Martin he had liberated from the officer's club at the air base, and beside it a carton of Lucky Strike cigarettes, courtesy of an accommodating supply officer.

A Sonata by Brahms and a banquet of dinner odors issued from below.

"Night, mam'"

"Goodnight, Persia."

Beneath his window a door pulled shut. Dante heard the tread of sandals on the cobblestone walk.

When he descended the staircase, Nikole Rollet was lighting candles in an alcove. The table was set for two, the crystal repeating the candle flames, a spray of flowers in a slender oblong vase. Nikole was wearing a tailored dress, white and luminous, the neckline embellished by a strand of cultured pearls. She had done something to her hair, but he could not decide what. The effect was to add a lacquer of sophistication, as though she were hosting a *soiree* on the Ile Ste-Louis instead of dinner for two in a small West Indian village.

"Compliments of the Allies," Dante said, placing the cognac on the sideboard. "Too bad we can't do the town."

"It's just as well," she replied, holding the bottle to the light. "We'd find no such *rareté* as this on the island." He placed the cigarettes beside the brandy. "What?" she smiled. "No silk stockings?"

He shrugged. "Just something for the pot. I'm beginning to feel like a freeloader."

"Your treat in Paris," she said.

"It's a date. And afterwards, popovers and champagne at the Ritz bar.

Dante poured the wine, a chablis. As they touched glasses, the crystal rang out a melodious note. After some fleshy iced-shrimp, they sat over a vegetable-laden soup.

"It's called *callaloo*," Nikole said. It's popular in all the islands."

He found it fragrant and spicy, with a rich exotic flavor. The soup was followed by a fish dish and a repertoire of vegetables, most of which he could not identify.

"So what is it you like about flying?" Nikole asked, as he freshened their wine.

"What makes you think I like flying?"

"When you took the wheel at Grande-Rivière you said, "I'll fly, you navigate."

Dante smiled. "You don't miss a thing, do you doctor? It's the freedom, I guess. If you're high enough, there's no such thing as cloudy. They say that happiness wears wings, sadness a leaden tail, or somesuch"

Nikole sipped her wine. "I'm afraid I'm not adventurous. I prefer my feet on the ground, hot to cold, south to north. I think I'd be terrified in an airplane."

"Or exhilarated," he said. "Frankly, I can't see you afraid of anything, Doctor Rollet. This little ferry service you've begun to St. Lucia is the very definition of courage. Afraid? I think not."

She held her glass to the candle. "Oh, but I am. I'm a bit of a coward, actually. I cringe at spiders, and I have a low threshold of pain. Were I an ice cube, I'd rather fall victim to what you Americans call a highball than a cup of scalding tea."

He laughed. "You wouldn't get much disagreement on that. Better yet, make that single malt scotch."

"The boy," she said, her mood sobering a bit. "The one at

Sambre's villa. You mentioned he might be your grandson. How extraordinary. What would a grandson of yours be doing on Martinique? Is that the real reason for your visits?"

"It's a long story," he said, his eyes darkening a bit. "Far fetched, actually. The odds are that it's not my grandson. But I'm learning to discount the odds in this war. I'd rather not go into it just yet. Security, and all that. I'd have to tell you where he comes from, that sort of thing. Later, perhaps."

"I understand. How many children do you have?"

"Just one. A daughter."

"And your wife? Does she approve of this work you do?"

"She died," he said. "It was some years back."

For dessert, she brought out a cake chewy with coconut. When they cleared the table, Brahms had given way to Edith Piaf, the wine to coffee with cognac. Dante lingered over his brandy, enjoying the music and studying his hostess in the wavering glow of a candle. She chatted easily about her life in the islands, and she was enjoying the cigarettes. When she finished the second, she lit a third. The recording ended and he played another, a danceable rendition of "Stardust".

On an impulse, he held out a hand. "I'm rusty as hell, I warn you, and I was never very smooth to begin with. But if you'd care to......"

She pushed from her chair and took his hand. "*Avec plaisir, monsieur...*"

He led her to the verandah. When they came together it was intimacy bordering on seduction. She was as soft to the touch as a cloud. Through the liquefaction of her blouse he could feel the resilience of her back, the smoothness of her skin. She moved against him lightly and turned a cheek to his chest.

"I've never danced with an American," she said.

"You drew two left feet."

She laughed. "You're very smooth, Paul. Quite good, actually."

He drew her lightly against him. Stirred by their movement,

the candles threw shimmering shadows against the stuccoed walls. From the garden came the scent of blossoms; beyond that the soft blue air of the hills. She hummed softly to the music. He could smell the perfume of her hair, feel the yield of her thighs. When the record ended, he searched through the stack and made a selection.

"To Paris," he said.

At the first familiar notes of 'La Vie en Rose', she said, "To Paris."

He played it again. And then again.

When they came together a third time, he kissed her lightly...a question. She responded willingly. When he kissed her again, he felt a slight electric charge up her spine. Her calf lingered against his. She placed a hand behind his neck and drew him closer. For time without measure they clung to the moment. From the very beginning they had seemed to understand one another without words. When finally the music ended, she led him silently up the stairs.

For a full half hour the darkness was heavy with their breathing. Afterwards, Nikole lay quietly beside him, her forehead damp with perspiration, a smear of lipstick on the pillow beside his ear. A fan sliced noiselessly against the ceiling. Dante watched its shadow sweep rhythmically across her face. As they lay in silence, her cheek against his shoulder, he realized that he was finding something with this woman, something he hadn't felt since Caroline's death, a kind of joy, somehow tempered yet unrestrained. He kissed her hair and tried to memorize her face.

"You're a giver," Nikole said, touching a finger to his cheek. "Somehow I knew you would be."

He kissed her forehead. "In this," he said, "the giving and taking are one."

He was hovering between sleep and consciousness when he heard a rapping from below.

Nikole sprang quickly from the bed. "Wait here, Paul. It could be a patient, an emergency."

She was into her robe and down the steps before he could locate his trousers. A door opened and he heard her talking in the kitchen. When finally she called to him, he was on the upper landing.

"Paul. It's Christopher. Christopher Delon."

The priest seemed overwrought. When Dante descended the stairs, he greeted the American with an embarrassed nod, his hat crushed shapelessly in his hands, his feet shifting awkwardly like a truant schoolboy. He was wearing a white linen suit and a black necktie. Dante thought he looked as though he had just stepped out of a christening.

"Forgive me," the priest said, coloring a shade. "I didn't mean to intrude...."

"It's nothing," Nikole said, tightening the sash of her robe. "Please. Sit. Are you in trouble?"

The priest took a seat at the table. "I borrowed a car and drove down myself. It took hours. Many of the roads are blockaded. I couldn't trust a telephone. Something's happening."

"The gold?"

"Possibly. Lucien came to my apartment. He brought his cousin from the fort. Trucks are streaming out of Desaix. They're keeping to the back roads. It could be troops; it could be anything. The fort has been secured. No one is allowed within the walls."

"We've got to be sure," Dante said.

Nikole lit some candles. From a cask with a spigot she drew a tot of rum. She handed it to the priest. "How? How can we be sure?"

Dante sorted through a myriad of possibilities. "We've got to see for ourselves."

Nikole extracted a map from a small writing desk. "But if the roads are blocked...."

"The trucks have to terminate somewhere," Dante said. "When they do, we've got to find them."

The priest knocked back the rum in a single swallow. "They're heading south, circumventing Forte de France. That's all Lucien knows for sure. The coast road is closed. I managed secondary roads. Twice I had to turn back. The highroad through Rivière-Salée is barricaded off."

"Then that must be the route," Dante said. "Where does it intersect the coast?"

Nikole traced a finger on the map. "Near Diamant."

Dante stuffed a package of cigarettes into a shirt pocket. "Let's go."

Christopher grasped his sleeve. "There's something else, Paul.·

"What?"

"The girl Lillette. She has been to Sambre's villa. You asked about a child. She has seen a child. A boy child. He was with the German."

Dante looked up sharply. Half hidden fears flashed just beneath the surface. "How old?" he asked. "How old is the boy?"

"Lillette's not sure. Three. Maybe four."

Nikole saw the indecision in Dante's face. "What will you do?"

It was a slender reed to lean on. It could be anyone's child, he thought. The odds were long that it was Sean.

"Let's find that convoy," he said. "Once that's resolved, I'll head for Bellefontaine."

"This boy?" Christopher asked. "Who is he?"

"God willing," Dante said, "we'll know by morning."

LE DIAMANT, MARTINIQUE

For the second night in succession the trucks of the convoy snaked the dark jungle roads. With dimmed headlights and with the lanterns on their tailgates winking like fireflies, the drivers were relying on the vehicle in front to negotiate the tortuous curves. As the last of the lorries crested the peaks above Diamant, Henri-Louis Sambre could see a glint of moonlight on the sea below. From his position at the rear of the convoy he calculated the lead truck would enter the coast road in approximately five to six minutes. Already the caravan was slowing as the less maneuverable buses began negotiating the hairpin turns.

The Italian should be a half-mile ahead, Sambre estimated, at a particularly nasty switchback. As one by one the fireflies flickered and died, he eased his vehicle gradually behind. Though he was the last of the convoy he checked his wing mirror: darkness, as black as the heart of a thief. They had entered the dense core of the jungle, where the canopy of trees snuffed out the light of the moon. He fingered the flashlight on the seat beside him. When the last of the fireflies dissolved beyond a turn, he eased to the shoulder and braked to a halt. With the truck idling coarsely in darkness, he flicked the flashlight toward a thicket of trees. For an instant he thought he had misjudged his mark. Damp with sweat and on the verge of a headache, he felt a disquieting flutter in the pit of his stomach. He played the flashlight over the thickets of trees. When the beam illuminated a roadside shrine, a white madonna on a wooden pedestal, he sighed in relief and swiped the sweat from his brow.

"Hurry," he whispered to himself, as though the darkness had ears.

As if by magic, the Italian materialized beside his door.

Wordlessly, Sambre scrambled from the cabin. In a moment of panic, he searched the darkness. Though they had rehearsed the switch in daylight, the night was as black as space: a dark void against the greater darkness. Nothing was as he remembered it. Disoriented by the press of vegetation, the eerie web of shadows, he clutched the Italian's shoulder.

"Where is it? I can't see a goddamn thing."

"In there," the Italian whispered. He pointed over a shoulder.

Sambre flicked the flashlight at a wall of ferns. Stumbling over a deadfall, he pushed clumsily through the brush. He could hear the Italian backing the truck laden with the gold around the curve. The doctored truck the Italian had secreted a few hours before was parked a few short yards from the road. So well had the Italian camouflaged it, that he stumbled awkwardly into the bumper, cracking a kneecap in the bargain. Muttering an oath, he slipped behind the steering wheel and fumbled with the starter. After some trouble with the gearshift, the truck lurched haltingly forward. As it nosed through the brush, there was another instant of disorientation. In another few yards he jolted roughly onto the road and, within minutes, caught sight of the lantern ahead. The caravan was slowing as the vanguard negotiated the intersection near Diamant.

Five miles to the east, near the village of Trois-Rivières, Dante O'Shea gave silent thanks for the bright full moon. Nursing a blacked-out Renault along pockmarked roads would be tough enough with total concentration. But his thoughts were elsewhere, at a villa in Bellefontaine.

On the seat beside him, Nikole Rollet touched a hand to his sleeve. "If we run into a patrol," she said, "let me do the talking. I have patients in these hills."

Behind them on the rear seat, Christopher Delon and Lucien LeClerc were pitching and swaying as the Renault responded to bumps in the pavement. The Creole had arrived at Nikole's cottage as they were preparing to leave. At Nikole's request he had made a hasty visit to his cousin of the motor pool. The cousin reported that many of the regulars at Fort Desaix had been removed from their posts, especially those in the vicinity of the gold. The reason given was a mobilization against a possible invasion, but the suddenness of the move had engendered speculation.

They reached an open stretch of high road and Dante breathed easier. His thoughts drew back to the boy, the boy Lillette had seen at Bellefontaine. When word of Sean's disappearance had arrived at St. Lucia, he had immediately hitched a ride to St. Thomas on an Army patrol plane. The pilot had radioed ahead, and Casey had met him at the airbase. She looked drained and exhausted. Through tears and sobs she related the story of her liaison with Viktor Reinmann, the details of which she had withheld before. She told him of the German who had visited the islands then disappeared as suddenly as he had arrived, of Caroline's decision to withhold the news of her pregnancy until Dante had returned on leave, of that fateful weekend when her mother was to soften Dante up before revealing his daughter's pregnancy. Prepared for just about anything, Dante was stung to learn the father was German. A German naval officer, no less.

"Yes," Casey sobbed. "He was the man you saw in my room at the Trade Winds the day after Pearl Harbor. I was shocked to see him again. I didn't know how to handle it, daddy, whether to tell you or not. German or no, he is Sean's father."

"It's okay, Case. It's okay. And you think he kidnapped Sean?"

"What else can I think? I'm even hoping it's so. At least then Sean would be alive. I mean, there's absolutely no sign of him. We've scoured the island. Oh, daddy, we've got to find him. I can't accept that Sean might be on his way to Germany. I can't accept that."

They were nearing the village of Diamant, feeling their way by the light of the moon. Dante was tempted to turn on the headlights, but he just couldn't risk it. If they ran into a patrol, they could be delayed indefinitely. On the seat beside him, Nikole Rollet was peering wide-eyed into the darkness ahead.

"Take the next right," she said. "It's a few hundred yards up that cutoff."

"Who's this Paquet?" Dante asked.

"A fisherman. I extracted his wife's appendix. He knows the coastline like no one else. If something's happening out there, he'll be aware of it."

The high road gave way to a narrow dirt lane. To maneuver the rutted slope, Dante dropped the Renault into low gear. The woods were thicker now. He illuminated the headlamps. It was unlikely they would encounter a patrol on this forested ridge.

The cottage was perched on a hill, with a splendid view of the sea. It was a wooden shanty with a roof of corrugated tin and windows draped with gauze. One of the windows was backlit by a lantern. As the Renault drew closer, a woman stepped from the doorway and crossed a low wooden porch. She raised a hand and shielded her eyes against the light. Dante killed the engine and Nikole slipped quickly out the passenger side.

"Madame Paquet," she said. "I'm Dr. Rollet."

There was recognition in the reply as well as welcome. "I hear d'motor," the woman said. "I tink someone be lost."

When she stepped from the porch Dante could see she was young, a tall dark beauty in a simple blue housedress. Like most of the Creole women on the island, she moved with a swaying grace.

"Is your husband here?" Nikole asked.

"He be asleep."

"Could you waken him, please..."

No sooner had she asked, than a wiry black man stepped warily onto the porch. He was slightly stooped and of middle height. Shirtless and barefoot, he was rubbing sleep from his eyes. As he stood there squinting at the glare of the headlights, he buttoned baggy trousers over a slender waist. Dante noticed his thick ropy arms, the washboard muscles in the area above the beltline.

"Monsieur Paquet. I'm Doctor Rollet. Do you remember me?"

He pressed a knuckle to an eye socket. "I remember..."

"I'm sorry to disturb you, M. Paquet. But we need your help. Could you spare us some time?"

"I have d'time...", he said sleepily.

Nikole motioned to the car. "These are friends, monsieur. We'd like to ask you some questions."

Shading his eyes, the fisherman bent to look.

Dante killed the headlights and stepped out on the driver's side. He extended a hand. The fisherman clutched it with strong calloused fingers.

"M. Paquet," Dante asked, "have you seen any activity along the beach? Any new buildings? Any men working?"

The fisherman stood scratching his head. "Dere be some. Dere be d'boat by Le Marin...d'house by Ste-Luce...d'pier near Diamant...." He gestured with a hand out to sea. D'...."

"Pier?" Dante broke in. "What kind of pier."

"Be long," Paquet said. He stretched his hands to the limit of his reach.

"Did you see any boats at the pier?" Nikole asked.

"No boat."

"This pier," Dante asked. "How long has it been there?"

"Two week. Three week."

Nikole drew a cigarette from a package of Camels. She offered one to the fisherman. He accepted and wedged it behind an ear.

"Would you take us to this pier," Nikole asked. "I'd be very grateful, Monsieur Paquet. It's a matter of some importance."

Flattered by the attention, the fisherman gestured to his wife. She disappeared into the hut and emerged with a palm-leaf hat and a sleeveless shirt. He slipped on the shirt and ducked nimbly into the rear seat beside the baker and the priest.

"How far?" Nikole asked.

"Two, maybe three mile."

"Alert us when we're about a mile away."

Standing as motionless as a quail in cover, Viktor Reinmann swept binoculars along the arc of the cove. From his vantage point in the tidal swampland, the cove looked deserted, the inlet just another palm-choked indent in the rugged shoreline. He sharpened focus and the barge came clearly into view.

The Frenchies were doing a workmanlike job. From where he stood the groan of their engines was barely detectable. They had resumed the loading after sundown. As the trucks arrived at the beach, they were dousing their headlamps. Working only by moonlight, men were shouldering crates along the length of the pier and stacking them onto the barge. Viktor noted they were taking no chances with the tow boat. It was a harbor tug, much like the type that escorted U-Boats through the Bay of Biscay to the submarine pens of Brittany. The tug lay dead in the water, its anchor chain gleaming in moonlight, the sea as slick a millpond where its propeller would be.

How had it gone with the truck, Viktor wondered? The Italian should be halfway to Bellefontaine by now.

He pushed through a veil of ferns and regained the shoreline. Hard against the beach there was not a light to be seen, not a breath, not a living sound save the chitter of insects. A mile offshore, where the moon was lamping the sea, the monolith that was Diamond Rock loomed like an island unto itself. He lowered himself between some boulders and extracted a signal lamp from a crevice in the rocks. He had stashed the lamp the week before on his initial inspection of the cove. It was a simple flashlight sheathed in a cylindrical tin sleeve. Pointed seaward, the shrouded beam sent a column of light toward the lookouts at Diamond Rock. He pressed the button....two... pause...two...pause...two.

In seconds there was a bluish double blink from a shelf on the Rock. The lookouts were on their toes. They would relay the signal to the far side of the Rock where the boarding team was waiting in a launch. The *milch cow* lay submerged thirty miles to the east, off one of the barren atolls Viktor had charted years before. Sambre had provided the launch that had transported the hijack team to the Rock. It was swift, maneuverable and high-powered. Once the barge cleared the cove, the hand-picked crew from the undersea tanker would overtake it in minutes.

When the Frenchmen were disposed of, the barge would be towed to the atoll and camouflaged until the transfer of gold was complete. If everything went as planned, the gold should reach the atoll a full two hours before first light.

Viktor had rendezvoused with the *milch cow* the night before. It had been his first look at one of the undersea tankers. To accommodate the gold, they had removed most of the bunks, one of the lavatories, all of the hammocks, and most of the lockers. Even a bank of batteries and part of the galley had been removed. Though it reduced the boat's underwater speed, every inch of space had been made available for their precious cargo. Instead of the normal complement of fifty three men, only twenty had been sent, most of those to help with the loading. Some of the twenty would return on other boats.

He wondered how the boy would react to the long undersea voyage, the failure of his mother to arrive on the island as promised. He would handle it well, Viktor told himself. After all, he was a Reinmann.

He pushed back some brushwood and glassed the cove again. It was nearing zero hour. Two French officers, Sambre had said. That's all that would stand between Germany and the gold. Since every effort was being made to conceal the hiding place of the French bullion, Sambre had convinced the High Commissioner the fewer who knew of the plan the better. The team from the *milch cow* would overpower the French officers before they knew what hit them. Then the barge and its tow-boat would disappear; sunk by a submarine, by American destroyers, a stray patrol plane. Who could prove what? No one would admit anything. Everyone would suspect everyone else. If the Americans invaded the island, so much the better. The Americans would be the most likely suspects. They had ships in the area. Patrol squadrons. A base on neighboring St. Lucia.

Viktor suffered a flicker of guilt. Though technically what he and Sambre were stealing was still French gold, the bullion was destined for Germany. He pushed the doubts from his mind. He had made his decision; he would live with it. The Reich would get its booty. More than it was counting on. He was chipping off a fragment for his future, for after all the ships had been sunk, all the battles won, all the enemies conquered.

For his life short of the grave.

For his son.

Above the cove, in the foothills overlooking Diamant, Dante O'Shea crawled the final ten yards on his stomach. When he reached the ridge, he gave thanks once again for the near full moon. At the edge of the treeline the shadows were as dark as pitch. They had left the Renault a half mile up the road. With the fisherman Paquet leading the way, they had trudged the beach to a point a few hundred yards below the cove. When they heard the whine of trucks, the growl of buses, they had left the beach and climbed a wooded slope. The slope led directly to a ridge. The ridge lay somewhere between the high road and the beach. From there, Dante and Nikole had proceeded alone. Behind them in the darkness, the priest was waiting in a stand of kapok trees with the baker and the fisherman.

Dante played binoculars over the moonlit cove. From the heights above the roadway the pier was difficult to see. Vehicles were streaming to the beach, that much was certain. He had watched a dozen blacked-out trucks followed by seven or eight buses turn onto a cleverly camouflaged cutoff.

Nikole inched up beside him. He felt her shoulder brush his arm. He handed her the binoculars.

"Take a look," he whispered.

Resting on her elbows, Nikole adjusted the focus. "Those crates, she said. It must surely be the gold. What else would they haul from the fort with so much secrecy? We've got to inform the High Commissioner."

"Agreed, Dante said. "But you should stay out of it. If some local bigwigs are involved, no need shining any light on you or your friend the priest. You two are in deep enough as it is."

They backed silently down the slope. Christopher was waiting at the treeline, leaning against a deadfall in his rumpled white suit, his necktie askew, his collar unbuttoned. On the ground beside him squatted the barefoot fisherman. He was smoking the cigarette he had stashed behind an ear. Lucien the baker was standing nearby, keeping an eye on the road below.

"Christopher, you come with us," Dante said. "We're going to alert the Admiral. We may need Lillette for proof. Lucien, you stay here with M. Paquet." He handed the Creole the binoculars. "They'll be hours emptying those trucks. If anything changes here, make your way to the nearest telephone and leave word at the American Consulate. Here's the number."

He extracted a scrap of paper from a wallet and handed it to the Creole.

"What of the fisherman?" Nikole asked.

"He'll have to stay with Lucien. He can't walk home, and we don't have time to drop him off."

BELLEFONTAINE

Aldo felt perspiration trickling to the small of his back. The night was hot and the crates were heavy, over ninety pounds apiece. There were thirty crates in all. He'd been told to load fifteen onto Sambre's yacht and leave the balance in the truck. The cove where the yacht was anchored was only accessible by foot. To reach the pier, he would have to haul the crates down the makeshift steps hacked out of the cliffside. The truck was on the crest of the lawn, high above the beach. He had wrestled only eight of the crates from the truckbed and already his legs felt rubbery.

It could be worse, he told himself. He could have to lug them up.

The Frenchman had given him a wristwatch. He checked the luminous dials. Eleven-fifteen. The Frenchman was scheduled to return by two a.m., the German an hour later.

"Have the launch loaded by 0300 hours," the German had ordered. "We'll clear the island in darkness."

From the tailboard of the truck, he hefted number nine. With a grunt and an oath, he eased it to the ground. He sat on the tailboard and lit a cigarette. From deep in the treeline came the croak of a frog. The sea shone like silver beneath a high-riding moon. Aldo felt ambivalent. He was going home. By U-Boat to Bordeaux, and from there to La Spezia. He had been on Martinique for nearly eight weeks. The good news was that he'd be back on Italian soil before he was officially listed as missing. His parents would be spared the agony of receiving the dreaded notice, the notice that presumed him dead. But he would miss the girl. She had left her mark.

He climbed aboard the truck. Crate number ten. He shoved it toward the tailgate. It felt like lead. What could be worth all this secrecy, this business with the truck? What could be on this island that was so valuable? Whatever it was, they had replaced it with sand. He was tempted to pry an edge, to look inside. Forget it, he told himself. It was none of his business. The less he knew, the better. But there was more to this switching of trucks on dark jungle roads than simple robbery, of that he was convinced. The Frenchman was a government official. He had friends in high places, yet he was conspiring with a German naval officer. France and Germany had signed an armistice. They were no longer enemies. So why the secrecy? Was anyone else involved? How high did this go? It was better not to think. Better to play the fool. The German had informed him they were stealing ammunition. Ammunition to restock U-Boats. Convincing enough for an ignorant Italian.

He hopped from the tailgate and muscled the crate to the ground. Concentrating as he was on the task at hand, the voice from the darkness startled him.

"Ah! There you are! I thought I heard something out here."

He turned to see the girl. She was standing with her back to the sea, the breeze stirring her hair, her shoulders bronzed by moonlight. He took in her fitted white shorts, the sheer peasant blouse.

"Lillette. *Bonsoir.* I didn't hear you coming."

"Wings of angels," she smiled. It was the smile of their nights together.

He sat on a crate and extended his arms. "*Angela mia.* You are an angel, indeed."

She sauntered blithely into his embrace. "I came to bring you this." She held out a bottle of wine. "And to bring chocolates for the boy. He seems so sad, so lonely. Who is he? Where is he from?"

"They tell me nothing," Aldo said. "Not even the old woman."

Lillette stroked his cheek. "It's the same for me. She won't let me near him. He speaks English, but like an American. I heard him asking for milk." She kissed his chin. "Why are you working so late? What's so important?"

He saw her eyeing the truck, the crates on the lawn. "Supplies for the yacht." He ran his fingers through her hair. Realizing he might not see her again, he felt an urge to take her to the cottage, to feel the heat of her passion one last time.

"I'm going away," he said. "Tonight. With the German. I...I will miss you..."

Her eyes softened. She seemed truly saddened.

He groped for words. "After the war.... Will you be returning to France? To Monaco?"

She raised her hands in a gesture of uncertainty. Her eyes grew the least bit moist. She wanted to tell him that she too expected to leave the island. If not tonight, then very soon. Christopher Delon had promised to smuggle her to St. Lucia. But the priest had warned her not to breath a word. To reveal her secret could jeopardize her freedom.

Aldo read the affection in her glance, the sadness in her eyes. He brushed a finger across her cheek.

She threw her arms around his neck and kissed his eyes, his brow, his lips.

The kisses were fervent, the embrace sincere.

FORTE DE FRANCE, MARTINIQUE

High up on Didier Hill, in a fashionable suburb of Forte de France, Dante O'Shea sat in a well-appointed drawing room feeling conspicuously out of place in his shaggy fisherman's clothes. To his left, in a starched white uniform despite the lateness of the hour, sat the official United States Naval Observer; like Dante, an Annapolis graduate, but with the rank of Commander. On his right, in a well-cut business suit that looked fresh from the tailor, sat the American Vice Consul who, despite his nervous drumming on an arm of an easy chair, was managing a flat-eyed stare. The three of them were seated across a low mahogany table from the man they had come to see, the High Commissioner of the French Antilles and Guiana, the commander of the military forces in the French Caribbean, Admiral Georges Robert. The Admiral was the only one of the four whose appearance conceded the hour. In an open-collared tunic with his hair slightly rumpled and his ankles bare beneath the cuffs of his trousers, he looked like a man who had been awakened shortly after he had retired.

Dante had telephoned the Consulate from the outskirts of the capital. Convinced that Nikole's involvement might put her in jeopardy, he had persuaded her to drop him at the Consul's residence. From there she and the priest continued on to Christopher's apartment, where he would meet them later.

Dante had been within yards of the Consul's doorstep when the Naval Observer drove into the forecourt. Spotting the small American flag on the fender, he introduced himself. After eyeing Dante's seedy clothes, the Naval Observer seemed relieved to find he was an Academy man.

"We've been briefed that an American agent might be

undercover on the island, Captain O'Shea, but neither the Consul nor myself have any knowledge of your mission."

"Naval Intelligence prefers it that way," Dante said. "Takes you off the hook if I screw up."

The Consul had received them in his study. After convincing himself that Dante was legitimate, his attitude changed from cool to lukewarm. Naval officer or no, French informers or not, he resented anyone snooping around his domain. As Dante briefed them on the activity at the cove, both men listened attentively. Then the Consul brought them up to date on the diplomatic climate.

"We've been dealing with Admiral Robert on a kind of 'gentlemen's agreement', Captain O'Shea. But earlier this month the State Department formally demanded complete neutrality on the part of the French Caribbean islands. The gloves are off. If Admiral Robert fails to accede to Washington's demands, our forces are prepared to invade Martinique and Guadeloupe. He has agreed to immobilize his warships, but he's still holding out on other demands."

"Martinique is an armed camp," the Naval Observer chimed in. "Beyond these walls all categories of military are being mobilized. Troops have been sent to cover probable landing sites, the forts are tightening security, and mines have been placed every half kilometer on the road between St. Pierre and Forte de France. Our air and surface patrols have been placed on alert. We're prepared to sink their warships if necessary. So the Admiral's a little testy right now. Tread lightly, Captain. He won't be happy to learn you've been working undercover on his island."

Testy, indeed. As Dante looked across the desk at the steely-eyed seadog, he looked anything but the affable old bachelor Nikole had described. He directed his first barrage at the Consul, reluctant, Dante thought, to acknowledge the ragged interloper sitting between his accredited counterparts.

"You would have me believe, messieurs, that this *agent provocateur* has information regarding French gold that my own officers do not possess?"

The Naval Observer shifted uncomfortably in his chair.

The Consul resumed his silent drumming. When he spoke, his tone was diplomatic but forceful. "Under the terms of our agreement, Admiral, you were to give twenty-four hours notice before moving the gold."

Beyond the dark blue lampshade, a concession to a possible invasion, Dante could see the roots at the Admiral's hairline redden. He stiffened in his chair.

"I agreed in general to give twenty-four hours notice. But I made it clear that in case of attack or threat of attack, no such notice would be given. The gold is the property of the Bank of France. As long as it's under my jurisdiction, I will do my utmost to protect it."

Dante broke his silence. "That being the case, Admiral, I respectfully suggest you reconsider the operation taking place at the cove near Diamant. I can give you no definitive proof, but I'm convinced the Germans are planning to take the gold. Though the evidence is circumstantial, I believe my sources to be accurate."

The Admiral looked at him as though he were a fly on the wall. He addressed his reply to the Consul. "You ask me to act without evidence. How can I be sure the Americans won't take the gold for themselves? We're well aware of your accelerated military activity in the area. My advisors are convinced an invasion is imminent."

The Consul took the cue. "I can assure you, Admiral. As of this moment, the United States has no intention of invading Martinique." The lie came off without a blink.

The Admiral eased back in his chair. He looked weary, his eyes shifting from one to the other of them. He steepled his fingers and pressed his thumbs against his forehead.

For a time, there was the Consul's muted drumming, the ticking of a clock, the Admiral's silent ruminating. More than anything, Dante feared an impasse. His thoughts were vacillating between the gold at the cove and the child Lillette had seen at Bellefontaine.

The Admiral rose. "I'll consult with my staff. If you like, I'll arrange some tea." He strode across the room and pushed through an ornate mahogany door.

Dante checked his wristwatch. Twelve fifteen.

The Consul leaned toward him as if to whisper, drawing in the Naval Observer as well. "I hope you're right about this, O'Shea. I expect the Admiral's confirming his orders. Just how would the Germans pull this off?"

"I'm not sure, Dante replied. Hijack the barge, I suppose. They could be anywhere out there. Can you alert our destroyers?"

"Not without the Admiral's permission. They'll think we're going for the gold ourselves. We'll have to be patient. See what he decides."

Dante pushed to his feet. "Gentlemen, I've done all I can to this point. The ball is in your court now. I'm just an irritant to the old man. There's someplace I've got to be, and fast." He gestured to the Navy man. "I'll need your car."

The Consul swiveled in his chair. "You can't leave now, O'Shea. You're the one who blew the whistle. The Admiral will want proof. Details. Names......"

"Precisely why I'm more of a detriment to you here. I can't give him names. That would jeopardize the very people who tipped us off. They're friends of ours. Friends of France. Tell him that." He held out his hand. "Your keys, Commander. Don't make me pull rank. What I have to do is important."

Reluctantly, the Naval Observer handed over his keys. "Second gear's a bit sluggish," he said. "Get a running start on the hills."

Dante tossed him a salute. "Thanks. I'll get back to you just as soon as possible."

The Consul stammered incredulously. "Dammit, O'Shea...the Admiral......he'll be furious. He'll..."

Dante turned back at the door. "You're the diplomat, sir. I'm sure you can handle it. Just don't let that gold leave the island."

LE DIAMANT, MARTINIQUE

At the cove near Diamant, Henri-Louis Sambre was beginning to feel uneasy. The loading was proceeding slower than expected. The Senegalese troops were either tiring or losing interest. The night was hot and they had stripped to the waist. As they shouldered the crates the length of the pier, he could see their blood red fezzes bobbing slowly in the moonlight. They reminded him of a colony of ants streaming implacably to the barge where they deposited their burdens before retracing their steps to the waiting trucks. In the interest of silence, the loading was being done by hand; no cranes, no forklifts, nothing mechanical. Nearly 9,000 crates were involved. Each crate was being carefully stacked to balance the barge and optimize space.

Sambre sat perspiring in the cabin of the truck. Despite the heat, the sweat soaking his shirt was the residue of nerves rather than temperature. This was the final string of vehicles. His would be the last to be unloaded. The dummied crates were in back. Would the Senegalese notice a difference in weight? In bulk? If they noticed, would they mention it? Why should they? They had no idea what the crates contained. Relax, he told himself. The transfer was proceeding without a hitch. Throughout the island there was a sense of minor chaos. Troops were being shuttled from one billet to another, lookouts were scanning the sea, and roads had been closed to all but essential traffic. The convoy's movements had been masked by the general mobilization. In all the distraction and confusion, no one would be concerned with a single truck.

He touched a match to a cigarette. It would soon be over. Around him the cove was awash with vehicles, the empties lumbering up the beach, the heavies cutting ruts in the sand. He was staking his career, his very life, on the next few hours. Could the German pull it off? Would the Admiral buy the sunken barge story? Waylaid by an Allied warship? Bombed by an American patrol plane? Low in the water, with its pyramid of crates, the barge could be mistaken for a submarine. Since the tow boat would also disappear, would the officers in charge be suspected of making off with the gold? Either way, he told himself, once they cleared the beach his hands would be clean.

A voice issued from beneath his window. "Monsieur Sambre?"

He looked down to see the shoulder loops of a colonel.

"A message from Admiral Robert. You're to stop the loading pending further orders."

Sambre paled. He felt a tightening in his abdomen. Had the officer slapped him in the face it would have come as no less a shock. "But why? We're on a critically tight schedule as it is...."

"Orders, monsieur. You're to report to the Admiral's residence. I have a car." He pointed up the rutted beach toward the coast road.

Sambre blew out the match. "Wait here, colonel. I'll give the order."

The colonel affected an indifferent bow.

Walking the length of the pier, Sambre felt his knees go to water. Did they have the Italian? Had he fallen prey to a patrol? Perhaps it was merely a delay. He sorted through his options, none pleasant, all the while aware of the colonel's eyes on his back.

The officer at the barge took the order to cease loading in stride. The military had been drilled to distraction of late. It would come as no surprise if they were to return the crates to the fort. As he retraced his steps on the pier, Sambre made his decision. When he reached the treeline, he ducked behind a column of trucks. A jeep was parked where the officers had left it. The driver was off somewhere, no doubt cadging a cigarette. Viktor Reinmann would be watching from the point. He would wonder at the halt in activity.

"Be patient, German," Sambre whispered to himself. "Don't do anything rash."

From his hideaway in the swampland, Viktor Reinmann heard a vehicle feeling its way up the strand. It was approaching his position from the direction of the cove. He fingered his pistol and insinuated himself into the roots of a mangrove thicket. The vehicle's progress was erratic; too steady for a straggler, too rapid for a patrol. The engine stopped and a door clicked shut. Viktor crouched deep in shadow. A figure was laboring ponderously up the strand. In the pallid moonlight Viktor recognized the balding pate, the corpulent waddle.

"What is it?" he whispered. "Why are you here?"

Sambre stopped dead in his tracks. He searched the darkness. "The Admiral," he said, keeping his voice low. "He has ordered the loading stopped."

"Why?"

The Frenchman scrambled awkwardly over some rocks. "I don't know," he said, breathing heavily. "I've been ordered back to the Admiralty."

Viktor stared at him in disbelief. "We can't stop now. My men are waiting. Everything is in readiness. In a few short hours the area will be swarming with ships. You must complete the loading tonight."

Sambre dusted his thigh. He had split a seam of his trousers. His face had the pallor of skimmed milk; his forehead was a sheen of sweat. "My hands are tied," he said, desperation in his tone. "The Admiral has ordered a halt..."

Straining to keep his voice beneath a shout, Viktor pressed a finger to Sambre's chest. "Go back and order the loading. Tell them it was a mistake."

The blood drained further from Sambre's face. His expression was one of peevish rancor. "Be reasonable, monsieur, I beg you. If the Admiral discovers the cable's a ruse, I'll be suspected. I must leave the island. You must take me with you."

Viktor clutched the Frenchman's lapel. "We didn't come all this way to fail at the final minute. Order the loading. Tow the barge with whatever gold is on board. I insist."

Viktor pulled a Luger from his belt. Sambre saw the barrel glinting dully in the moonlight.

"I...I can't countermand the order. The Admiral...he sent an officer to bring me back. By now they will be looking for me...."

Viktor gestured toward Diamond Rock. "My men are poised. We must take the barge tonight. The *milch cow* is waiting."

Sambre was perspiring freely now. He began to shiver. "It's a mistake. A bad mistake. We must call it off. When the gold reaches the fort, the doctored crates may be discovered. The dummy cable... only a few of us know the secret code. They could trace the truck back to me...."

Viktor jabbed the Luger into the Frenchman's midsection. He looked him hard in the eyes and squeezed the trigger. Sambre stared in disbelief. As the pain ripped through his entrails, his heart contracted and his breath caught as though he had swallowed his tongue. He uttered a grunt and clutched a hand to the hole in his stomach. Viktor fired again. The Frenchman slumped slowly to his knees, the pain swimming hotly in his eyes, his body twitching in spasm. The last thing he heard was the echo of the Luger's blast. His brain extinguished and the rest was silence. Viktor rolled him between some rocks and jammed him unceremoniously beneath the detritus of palm leaves and mangrove roots. Ignoring the stony gaze of the death stare, he thrust a foot against a shoulder and wedged him tightly below the waterline.

The reports from the Luger had been louder than anticipated. Someone at the cove might have heard the shots. Retrieving the signal lamp, Viktor aimed the cylinder at Diamant. In seconds the mission was aborted. When the acknowledgment was repeated a second time, he extinguished the lamp and flung the flashlight into the sea. Deciding against the battered Buick the Frenchman had provided for his drive out, he made his way to the abandoned jeep.

The keys were in the ignition.

FORTE DE FRANCE

Dante was striding down the hallway when the door to Christopher Delon's apartment opened. Nikole Rollet stepped out to meet him. She was followed by the priest.

"We saw you from the balcony," Nikole said. "Is the Admiral convinced?"

"We've done all we can. It's in the hands of the diplomats."

What now?" Christopher asked.

Dante tossed him the car keys. "Sambre's villa. You drive."

Nikole said, "I'll get my purse."

"You don't have to make this trip," Dante countered.

"I want to," she protested. "I want to very much."

They waited while Christopher locked the door to his apartment. "It's the middle of the night," the priest said. "There's a curfew. There will be patrols."

"We've got diplomatic plates," Dante said. "We'll take our chances."

BELLEFONTAINE

Viktor Reinmann checked his wristwatch.

Twelve-twenty-two.

Despite the blackout, he was making excellent time. Using the route he had driven earlier that night, he encountered only one other vehicle, an army personnel carrier. Recognizing the jeep as officer property, the driver had merely blinked his headlights and continued on.

Sambre's yacht should be ready by now, he thought. Working together, he and the Italian could load the crates in an hour. Time enough to slip the destroyer screen under the protective cloak of night. If all went as planned, they would reach his drop-off point before first light. He had chosen his hiding place carefully, one of the many pendant islands off the southern extremity of Martinique. Out of the shipping lanes, the nameless spur of lava and coral was surrounded by dozens of similar outcroppings, all protected by intimidating reefs visited only by seabirds and urchins. Even fishermen would steer clear of its razor-edged coral. The islet harbored a deep but accessible cave. He had found the cave by painstaking exploration of dozens of such coral reefs. He had risked life and limb finding a channel through the reef and probing its depths to make certain the bottom was suitable and the access obscured from sea or airborne eyes. There his gold would rest under protective fathoms until he returned for it after the war, invisible to passing ships yet under the very noses of its former guardians. He would need the Italian to help him lower the crates over the side. In the darkness, without coordinates, and after a series of random course alterations, no man, no matter how accomplished a mariner, could rediscover that particular sea cave.

Still, he could take no chances: the Italian would have to join the incompetent Sambre. Afterwards he, Viktor Reinmann, would be the only man alive who knew the resting place of the wayward treasure. When the crates were secure on the seabed, he would rendezvous with the *milch cow* and return to Germany with his son. The fiasco at Diamant had not been of his making. He would return to Germany without the bonus of the French bullion, but with his mission complete and his honor intact. Whatever had gone wrong at the cove would be laid at the Frenchman's door. Somehow Sambre had compromised the plan. It had been his responsibility to handle the Admiral. So he had died a few hours earlier than planned. So what? One way or another he had been destined to pay the price. Sooner or later Germany would get the gold anyway. It was but a temporary setback.

Had the Frenchman been lying? Had the Admiral's alleged change of mind been part of his plan all along? Perhaps it had never been his intention to dispatch the barge. Perhaps it was he, Viktor, who had been meant for the bullet. Once the Italian had switched the trucks, the Frenchman could call off the loading. Once the dummy cable had been sent from Vichy, Viktor had served his purpose. He regretted not having taken the time to search the Frenchman's corpse. Would he have found a weapon? It was academic now. Perhaps it was for the best, he thought. The more muddled the situation, the more difficult it would be to secure an accurate accounting. The pendulum may indeed have swung in favor of the Reinmanns.

From the bedroom in the cottage at Bellefontaine, Aldo Arazi heard the groan of an engine. It was somewhere near the base of the hill, a full two minutes from reaching the villa. Oblivious to the engine noise or to her partner's momentary distraction, Lillette Bonnier writhed fluidly beneath him. In the grip of passion, they resumed the rhythm of their lovemaking. Clinging to her with all the ardor he could muster, Aldo succumbed to the tempo of her quickening breath. As the flood of release overcame the rigor of anticipation, he drew her to him and smothered her with kisses.

"*Grazie, cara,*" he whispered. "*Multo, multo grazie.*"

She smiled, a tender wistful smile. *Merci, monsieur. Merci, merci_beaucou*p."

Aldo was stepping to the lawn when the jeep braked abruptly to a halt. He was expecting the Frenchman, but it was the German who leaped from the drivers's side. Aldo ran a finger over the buttons of his trousers, a reflex he immediately regretted. He and the German were approximately the same age. The German outranked him, but that was no reason for him to act like a schoolboy. He must change his attitude. His roots were as strong as that of any Aryan. He was beginning to dislike this German. Dislike him intensely. Although Lillette had never mentioned meeting him, he was beginning to believe there had been something between the German and the girl, something he would rather not think about.

"Where's Sambre?" Aldo asked.

"A change of plan," Viktor said. 'Where's the truck?"

"In back."

"Bring it around. Load the rest of the crates onto the yacht. *Schnell*!" We have little time."

Aldo responded with a hostile glare. "All of them?"

Viktor noted his perturbation. "I'll help you. The boy. Where's the boy?"

Aldo pointed to the house.

Viktor trotted across the lawn.

***

Christopher Delon nursed the Consulate's Buick around a hairpin turn. Ahead blinked the lights of a coastal village. "That's Bellefontaine," he said. "There's a junction ahead. From there we climb the hill. Sambre's villa is somewhere near the top."

Dante and Nikole were wedged beside him on the front seat. On the drive from Forte de France they had run across a dozen vehicles, all military. With the small official flag on their fender, they had proceeded unchallenged.

"Have you been here before?" Nikole asked.

"Not to the villa," Christopher replied. "Lillette pointed out this turnoff when we drove to Pelée."

"Will Lillette be here?" Dante asked.

The priest shrugged. "She hasn't been at her apartment for days. She could be anywhere."

The road wound steeply up a heavily-wooded hillside. As the coastline fell behind them, the shadows deepened and the vegetation drew closer to the road. With headlamps punching holes through the darkness, Christopher peered anxiously beyond the grimy windscreen.

"The villa overlooks the sea," the priest said. "Lillette has mentioned the view, the pathway leading down to the beach."

Dante checked his watch. "Kill the headlights. We'll proceed by moonlight. Whoever's up there, I'd rather they didn't see us coming."

Near the crest of the hill they were confronted with a decision. The road forked, the pavement continuing on into the interior, a narrow dirt lane angling back toward the cliffs.

The priest swung the Buick onto the minor road. "If the villa overlooks the sea, this has to be it," he said.

They wound through tree-shrouded lanes, proceeding slowly without lights, the drone of insects tremulant in the darkness. Gradually the terrain opened onto a broad sloping plateau. The night deepened to brighten the stars. Christopher braked as they approached an old stone arch. "That's it," he said. "Lillette has mentioned the arch. She calls it 'the gates of hell'."

The property was bounded by a low stone wall. In the distance they could see a cluster of lights, the silhouette of a low sprawling structure overlooking the sea.

"That's the villa," Christopher said. "The housekeeper's cottage is in the rear."

"Pull over," Dante said.

The priest cut the engine in the shadow of the wall. For a

moment, they sat in silence, with just the ping of the exhaust manifold.

Dante slipped quietly from the car. "Wait here. If I'm not back in fifteen minutes, meet me at the rear of the cottage." He pressed the door shut quietly. In seconds he was over the wall and into the fields beyond.

There was a jeep parked on the lawn of the forecourt. At the edge of the cliff he could see a troop carrier with a canvas top. Keeping to shadows he moved slowly, silently. He paused at a window and peered cautiously over the sill; a kitchen, some dishes on a sideboard, a table with a half-empty bottle of wine. Keeping his head below the window line, he duck-walked to a smaller window, this one in the rear. A bedroom. The bed was unmade, a blanket thrown back over the sheet, a single small indent on a naked pillow.

He felt the blood quicken rapidly in his veins.

He was about to proceed when he heard voices. Male voices. They were somewhere on the lawn near the cliff. Crouching in the shadows of the house, he strained to hear. The dialogue was hushed, monosyllabic. The men seemed to be dragging something from the truck. He could make out their silhouettes. The shorter one was hoisting something onto a shoulder, something bulky; the tall one flipped a cigarette onto the lawn. The men disappeared behind the truck and the hillside went silent again.

Dante sidled quietly to the rear. There was a swimming pool, its surface reflecting the high-riding moon. Keeping to shadows, he crossed the pool area and crouched beside a wall of the cottage. Light was filtering through a curtained window. The curtain was dark. Opaque. It prevented him from seeing inside. He worked his way rearward and found a door. He tested it. It opened to his touch. Slipping inside, he found himself in a laundry room. A second door led directly to the interior. That, too, was unlocked. He opened it quietly and entered a hallway.

He paused.

Listened.

Faint music, as from a radio.

At the end of the hallway a sliver of light defined the jamb of a door. He drew the military .45 from his waistband. With the weapon on safety and his breath on hold, he tiptoed quietly toward the door. He paused outside. The music was classical...symphonic. Slowly, ever so slowly, he turned the knob.

There was a dresser against a far wall, a mirror and some toiletries. Beside a conch shell ashtray, the radio. He eased the door open. A bed. Empty. On a nightstand a lampshade shrouding a low-watt bulb. Then a leg. Bare. Female. In a chair.

He stiffened and swung the door.

He saw the girl.

She stared at him with slack features, her expression fixed, the color drained ominously beneath her eyes. There was an unnatural sprawl of legs, a rag-doll slump of shoulders. He recognized the clipped blonde hair, the long slender neck. So serene did she look that it took him an instant to register the neat red hole in her neck. So surgical was the wound that it seemed to be dabbed on with greasepaint. There was very little blood, just a dark swollen orifice that must, he knew, terminate in a malevolent hole at the back of the neck. That, and the fish-belly pallor of death. For an instant his stomach heaved and he felt a clutch of pity. She was alone, staring sightlessly at the door. He walked to the chair and looked down at her face. She seemed relaxed. Composed. It was almost as though she might speak to him. He placed a hand on her cheek. It was cool. He searched for a pulse. Nothing. He glanced at his wristwatch. Nikole and Christopher would be waiting.

He made his way down the hallway. As he exited the laundry room, the doctor and the priest were traversing the lawn, masked from the villa by trees.

Dante stepped silently from the shadows. When they spotted him, he motioned with an arm.

““Inside,” he whispered. “The room with the light. It’s Lillette. She needs one of you in a hurry.”

A single crate remained on the pier. Aldo was breathing heavily. He looked at the German and noticed that he too was perspiring. It gave him a pinch of satisfaction to see that, given a little manual labor, even the master race was not immune to sweat. He lugged the last of the containers to the fantail and set it down with an audible grunt.

The German swiped his brow. "Our business here is finished," he said. "We can be off."

Aldo sat on the edge of a crate and lit a cigarette. He pointed to the cabin of the yacht. "And the boy? he asked, breathing heavily."

"The boy goes with us."

Dante was crouching almost directly beneath them, hip-deep in water on the ladder to the pier, his torso hidden by the curvature of the hull. He had heard them talking from the cliff, heard their grunting and swearing, the thump of heavy containers hitting the deck. Leaving his shoes on the beach, he had rolled his trousers to his calves and waded beneath the pier. Moving silently, he had inched forward when the noise above him resumed, pausing when it stopped. When he reached the deeper water, he pushed quietly between the crossbeams, the Browning automatic in the hand above his head, his free hand propelling him from piling to piling.

"We must reach our destination in darkness," he heard one of the men say. "By dawn the area will be swarming with ships."

There was no escaping the accent. It was German; Bavarian, to be exact.

"And then what?" the other asked.

Italian, Dante knew. Somewhere north of Rome.

"And then our task will be complete. We'll be home in a fortnight."

"And the girl?" Aldo asked.

"She'll be none the wiser," the German said.

With seawater lapping gently at his waist, Dante clung silently to the piling. There was a shuffle of shoes on deck as the voices moved steadily toward the bow. When the voices grew fainter, he climbed a support strut to the pier.

They were in the vicinity of the pilot house. Dante slipped silently aboard and crouched beside the railing. The moon was clear of the cliffs, glazing the cove and casting truncated shadows on the polished teak deck. He noticed the crates on the fantail, the telltale '35' stenciled in black. They were identical to the crates in the cove at Diamant.

He peered through a porthole: the aft lounge; a small cone of light from a bulkhead lamp. The woodwork was mahogany, the fixtures brass. Old world luxury, Dante noted. Antiquated but well-preserved. A light was switched on in the pilothouse. He saw its glow reflecting on the water. The bridge was above the main saloon. Dante climbed barefoot up the ladder. He was standing in the hatchway before they realized they were not alone.

"Keep your hands where I can see them," he said, leveling the .45 between them.

Both men froze. There was a startled pause. The Italian was bare-chested. Dante could a sheen of sweat on his broad, muscled shoulders. His light-haired companion was partially obscured by the corner of a map locker. The Italian stood staring at the pistol. He raised his hands above his head and looked quizzically at the German.

Viktor Reinmann reacted swiftly. Shoving the Italian forward, he lunged for the companionway. Dante tried to intercept him, but the Italian stumbled forward, blocking his way. Dante pushed him roughly aside, but he was a second too late. By the time he reached the hatchway, the German had descended the ladder.

Behind him, the Italian had regained his feet. Dante pivoted at the top of the landing and swung the pistol.

"Stay out of this," he warned. "This is not your fight. Unless I'm badly mistaken, it has nothing to do with you."

The Italian backed slowly toward the control panel. As Dante turned to face the companionway, the German reappeared with the boy. He was standing at the base of the ladder with the three-year-old cradled in one arm, a 9mm Luger in his free hand.

"Drop your weapon," the German said.

Dante held his ground. "You won't use that," he said. "And we both know why." He was trying to remain calm for the boy's sake. He could see confusion in his grandson's eyes, a hint of tears.

"It's all right, Seanny," Dante said. "Everything's all right. You're going home to mommy."

With a wave of the Luger, the German motioned him back. Dante retreated to the pilot house. With the boy in tow, the German followed cautiously.

"I warn you, Captain O'Shea. No stupid moves. You would not want the boy to see his grandfather come to grief."

The German turned slightly toward the maplight. Dante got a look at his face. Despite the fisherman's cap, there was no doubt at all that it was the man he had seen in Casey's room at the Trade Winds. The German sidled slowly toward the map table, the Luger pointed directly at Dante's midsection, the boy cradled snugly under his arm. Dante noticed he was holding the weapon where the boy could not see it.

"I'll use this rather than give him up," the German said.

Dante looked back to the bridge. The Italian stood frozen against the wheel, his eyes shifting uneasily between the Luger and the .45.

Dante wagged his pistol aft. "Keep the gold, Reinmann. I'm here for the boy." He glanced at the Italian, saw him look inquiringly at the German. "Give me the boy and I'll see you get the time you need." He was bluffing, but it was all he had.

The German's eyes narrowed. "And you expect me to believe that, Captain?"

"You have my word."

"Not good enough."

The cabin hatch was open to the deck. There were footfalls on the pier. All three men glanced down from the bridge. Viktor raised the Luger toward Dante's chest.

Nikole Rollett emerged from the darkness.

As she approached the gangway, Dante shouted, "Stay where you are. Don't come aboard." He turned to the German. "Leave the boy, Reinmann. Take me instead." He glanced over a shoulder. The Italian was backed against the chart table, a glimmer of confusion in his cold dark eyes.

Viktor Reinmann glanced quickly toward the gangway. Dante could read his thoughts. Who was this woman? Who else was out there? The American knew his name. Was his identity known to anyone else? Had Sambre set him up? Had the girl Lillette talked? There was no turning back. He was committed. One way or the other, he had to play the hand he was dealt.

"The boy," Dante repeated. "The boy for that." He pointed to the crates. "And for me. You have my word, Reinmann. No one else knows about your little game. Not that woman on the pier, not the French, not the Americans, not even your colleagues in Germany, I'll wager. It will be our little secret. The boy is worth it. He's worth it to me. To his mother. You'll have a night's head start. It's all you would have at any rate."

Viktor turned to face him. "Drop the gun," he ordered. He leveled the Luger at Dante's head.

"Grampa! Grampa!..."

Dante lowered the .45. "Let the boy go, Reinmann. You're running out of time. They know where I am. They'll be coming for me."

"The gun..." Viktor repeated.

Dante looked at his grandson. He was holding up bravely. Though confused and frightened, his chin held firm, his eyes remained dry. Dante searched the German's eyes. He had lost Sean's grandmother through a miscalculation; he could not risk another with the boy. With a flick of the wrist he tossed the .45 through the hatchway. It disappeared in darkness. An instant later they heard it splash.

He faced the German with open palms. "I don't want you, Reinmann. I want the boy. You're risking his life. You might not make it back."

The German glanced quickly at the Italian, at the woman on the pier. He lowered the boy to the deck and dropped to one knee.

Dante watched as he embraced his son. As he whispered in

the boy's ear, his cheek to the youngster's cheek, Dante picked up fragments of what he said:

"...would not hurt you, *mein sohn...*"

...a good boy....

"....meet again...."

...*auf Wiedersehen....*"

There was moisture in the boy's eyes, but he was not yet crying. He was trying to be brave. Dante felt a stab of pride. The German had noticed too. There was a nod of approval as he touseled the boy's hair. Then gently, he pushed him toward his grandfather. As the boy rushed quickly to Dante's arms, Viktor lowered the Luger.

The tears came readily now. When the youngster squeezed his grandfather's neck, his lips quivered and he sobbed and whimpered. Dante felt the heave of his chest. He smoothed his rumpled hair and kissed his forehead. Ignoring the German's Luger, he carried the boy to the hatchway. After hugging his grandson a final time, he hoisted him over the railing.

"You're mother's waiting, Sean. This lady will take you to her."

Nikole Rollet crossed the gangway. When the boy was safely in her arms, Viktor leveled the Luger at Dante's back.

"Take care of him," Dante said, relieved that his grandson was out of the equation. "Tell his mother I love her."

Nikole hugged the boy to her side. "Your mama has missed you," Dante heard her say. "We'll have you home in no time." She turned to the railing and searched Dante's eyes.

He tossed her a small salute. "Paris," he said.

She forced a smile. Her eyes glistening with unshed tears, she held out a hand. "The Ritz."

He reached down and squeezed her fingers. "My treat."

Viktor shouted down from the cabin. "Eight hours. No alarm for eight hours or..." he jerked the pistol toward Dante, "...or he's the first to go." He wagged the Luger at the Italian. "Underway! *Schnell!*" He turned the gun on Dante. "Don't make me shoot you, Captain."

The yacht was a veritable palace, steel-hulled and sleek with two powerful diesels and roomy staterooms below. Aldo opened the engines to full throttle. Water churned and fanned out behind the stern. As the yacht veered past the point and out to sea, it sliced a creamy bow wake from the smooth dark waters.

With the lights of Bellefontaine softening gradually through the haze, Dante took a position on a stool near the companionway. Viktor Reinmann stood behind him at the navigator's table. The Italian was at the controls fingering the throttles and taking his heading from a compass at his elbow. The seas were on the starboard bow, light with moderate swells.

Dante kept his eyes on the German. He was a cool customer, this Nazi who had charmed his daughter. He had never intended to harm the boy, Dante could see that. Holding the Luger where Sean couldn't see it, he had taken particular care not to frighten him. For that, Dante was grateful. Something as traumatizing as a pistol to the neck could mark a child for life.

"Tell me, Reinmann," Dante shouted over the drone of the diesels. "Why did you abandon my daughter? If you cared enough to come back, why no word from you in years?"

Viktor kept the Luger aimed at his midsection. "The war, Captain. Surely your American Navy keeps you busy. Besides, I had no idea your daughter was pregnant."

Dante remembered the girl in the cottage. The bullet hole in her neck. That had nothing to do with the war. Sean's father or no, this German was a killer.

"Then why take the boy?" Dante asked. "Casey bore him. She birthed him and nurtured him. You had nothing to do with that."

"He's my son, Captain. I want the best for him. Germany will win this war. And afterwards, he'll have...that...." He pointed to the crates on the afterdeck.

"Assuming you pull this off," Dante asked, "how do you propose to explain this to your people? How far can you get in this rig?"

"Far enough, Captain. Far enough."

"And what if you make it? Even if you kill me, you can't risk returning to Germany with those." He pointed to the crates again. "When the war's over, someone on the island might still be around to incriminate you."

Viktor smiled, but there was little or no mirth in it. "I'll make it, Captain. I'm not so stupid as to paint myself into a corner. I have left myself some options. One way or another, I'll make it."

Dante assumed he would. He could dump the crates off any of a hundred unmarked atolls and come back for them after the war. He might even desert. From here he could make it to South America. The coastline was vast. Perhaps he had friends waiting. No, he was not stupid; yes, he had options.

"And me? Dante asked. "Do you intend to drop me at the nearest yacht club? Or have you something more permanent in mind?"

Viktor remained silent.

"And what of him?" Dante pointed to the Italian.

Viktor turned to his charts.

Dante wondered about the Italian. From the conversation he'd overheard on the ladder, the Italian seemed uncertain, confused as to the turn of events, as though he was not privy to the German's plans. At the mention of the gold he'd looked genuinely surprised.

Dante noticed they were heading south. Every lamp had been extinguished including the running lights and the map light. The Italian was navigating by moonlight. The German crossed to the Italian and whispered something he could not make out. Almost immediately they turned seaward and began a series of long sweeping turns. As they circled beneath the moon-blanched sky, Dante could see they were keeping to within a short half-mile of the coast. Was the German aware of the picket ships? If he continued south, he'd have to cross the Bay of Forte de France. Surely he knew the mouth of the harbor was well patrolled. Even if the American Consul had failed to convince the High Commissioner that a plot was afoot, the French patrols would be on routine alert.

The German kept looking at his wristwatch. After ten minutes of circling, he ordered, "Cut the engines. We drift awhile."

The Italian looked puzzled. He was about to protest when the German wagged the pistol again. "Cut them! Now!"

The Italian returned a stare of black resentment.

These two are not allies, Dante decided.

Aldo eased the throttle back and the yacht drifted slugglishly on the swells, a dusting of blue smoke venting its exhaust ports.

As the German studied the maps, Dante turned his attention to the Italian. "You don't seem the killer type, young man. He murdered the girl, you know. The girl at the villa."

The Italian stared at him blankly, then turned his gaze to the German. His face was a mask of suppressed fury. "You killed her?"

Viktor eyed him coldly. "She could identify us."

Aldo reddened. The scent of her juices were still on him. His stomach hardened like a stone. "We were leaving the island. She knew nothing. I know nothing. Why would you kill her?"

Dante could see the flush of anger. The Italian's eyes went as hard as granite. His body tensed, and for a long uncertain moment Dante thought he would attack the German with his hands, Luger or no Luger.

Dante swiveled slowly on the stool. "He'll kill us too, you know. Once he stashes the gold."

By the look in the Italian's eye, Dante could see he was a pawn. A simple pack mule. The German had used him. He was expendable.

And Sambre?" the Italian asked. "Is Sambre dead too?"

He was a traitor," Viktor said. "He was executed."

Dante tossed a glance at the German. "So you pulled his ticket early. And that," he added, pointing to the crates on deck, "that's not treason?" He looked back to the Italian. The youngster seemed to be piecing it together. His thoughts were as transparent as the windscreen. He had obviously been close to the girl.

For a time they drifted in silence, with only the slap of the current against the hull. On the heaving black sea, a moon path rode the long silky swells. Suddenly from the north came distant thunder, a muffled explosion that rolled across the surface like a shock wave. Dante turned to see a fireball erupting on the distant horizon. It illuminated the sea and belched a column of oily black smoke, thick and coagulate against the blue-black sky.

"We go," the German said, wagging the gun at the Italian.

"A U-Boat...," Dante said, his eyes reflecting the distant tower of flame.

"A diversion," Viktor said. "While your picket ships head north in search of the attacker, we slip behind them and out the back door."

Dante pushed to his feet. He leaned against the control panel and studied the glow on the horizon. "Another civilian ship, you bastard? Like the passenger liner in Castries harbor?"

Viktor leveled the Luger at his midsection. "More likely one of your warships, Captain. One of your destroyers, I suspect."

They were pounding steadily toward the southern tip of the island, spray bursting from the bow, the sea ahead dusted by moonlight. The German had been right about the diversion. Whatever had been torpedoed, every vessel on call would be scrambling north in search of survivors. Against the glow on the horizon, the smoke was rising in greasy black clouds. As the eyes of every mariner turned seaward, the yacht was clinging stubbornly to the shoreline. When they reached the Bay of Forte de France they slipped unchallenged across the harbor. South of Diamond Rock they veered sharply out to sea again. As the yacht met the deep sea swells, the German was scanning the coastline. Far to the east, near the southern tip of the island, Dante could see the loom of a lighthouse. Îlet à Cabrit.

"That's Ste-Anne off the port bow," he said, addressing the German but loud enough for the Italian to hear. "That's where I met the girl. The girl with the bullet in her throat at the villa."

In the glow from the compass binnacle he saw the Italian's jaw tighten.

"You knew her?" the Italian asked.

"She was a friend," Dante said. "A friend of a friend."

The Italian kept his eyes on the darkness ahead. "Why was she there," he asked. "At Ste-Anne?"

Dante glanced at the German. He was glassing the horizon. "The woman at the pier. She's a doctor. Perhaps the girl was ill. Pregnant, perhaps."

Before Dante realized what was happening, the Italian released the wheel and lunged across the cabin. He leapt at the German and caught him off-guard, one hand chopping at the Luger, the other clutching at the German's throat. Despite the attempt at surprise, he failed to dislodge the Luger. Dante leaped from the stool, but the space was cluttered, confined. The German was twisting away. Before he could reach the pistol, the German was firing point blank. There was the thwack of a bullet striking bone. The blast slammed the Italian against the bulkhead. With the German twisting awkwardly toward him, Dante pivoted deftly to one side. Viktor regained his balance and leveled the Luger at Dante's chest.

Dante froze.

"You're making it difficult, Captain."

"You're a murdering scum, Reinmann. The boy will be better off without you."

Viktor backed cautiously to the center of the hatchway, the gun pointed directly at Dante's midsection, a smear of blood where the Italian had grazed his cheek. "One more step and he'll be without a grandfather also. Take the wheel, Captain."

Dante wondered why the German hadn't shot him. He probably needed him. For what? With the Italian wounded, to unload the gold, perhaps. To hesitate was to die, he decided. Once beyond the sight of land, beyond the reach of coastal patrols, the German's hand would be strengthened immeasurably.

The Italian lay bleeding from the thigh. He was pushing to his feet when the German leveled the Luger at his head. Dante gave the wheel a violent twist. The ship lurched just enough to upset the German's balance. In the instant it took him to adjust, Dante dove headlong at his midsection. He felt the point of his shoulder ram the German's ribcage, felt the yield of bone, a grunt of pain.

Viktor reeled heavily against the bulkhead and dropped awkwardly to his knees. Before he could regain his feet, Dante was ripping a fire bottle from its bracket. He slammed it against the German's arm. It struck him hard enough to jolt him against the controls. In the instant it took him to recover, Dante was at his neck, one hand on the Luger's barrel, the other clawing roughly at his throat. They fell heavily against the throttle, the pistol pointed skyward between them, their fingers in search of the trigger, their legs straining for purchase on the heaving deck. As they fought for control of the weapon, they stumbled through the hatchway and onto a wing of the bridge.

In the pilothouse, Aldo Arazi pushed slowly to his feet. When the bullet had struck, a blinding white flash had knifed through his groin. Now there was fire in his thigh, and his leg was a minefield of pain. The launch was veering sharply seaward, the deck tilting steeply to port. Beyond the control panel the windscreen was pitted with spray, the runoff blurring the glass. Aldo could see them struggling toward the foredeck, locked in a death grip, each with a hand at the throat of the other, the pistol somewhere in between. For an instant he lost sight of their struggle. Then suddenly there was a shot, a sharp report that echoed over the roar of the engines. In the darkness, Aldo saw an electric blue flash...then another, this one accompanied by a muffled discharge. They were struggling near the bow. He caught a glimpse of something glinting in moonlight. The ship broached a swell and both men dropped from sight, each tugging the other toward the railing. Aldo reached for the throttles. The movement sent shivers of pain through his groin. With a grunt of desperation, he thrust the levers forward. Gripping the wheel, he spun it hard to starboard. Spray showered the deck. As the ship heeled over he heard the shattering of glass, the pneumatic whiff of a bullet in the vicinity of his ear. He spun the wheel and the launch veered to starboard again, skidding as though on ice. The roar of the engines filled his ears.

Minutes later he throttled back. Through a starburst crack in the windscreen, he searched the foredeck. Nothing. He staggered to the hatchway and looked aft. The deck was empty. He looked forward. Nothing. Port. Starboard.

Nothing.

No one.

Dragging his wounded leg, he climbed the ladder to the bridge. Not a living soul, not a breathing living soul, neither German nor American. He was alone, the sea around him heaving, the swells seamed with white, the moon painting a streak toward the lee of the distant island. He looked back at the wake. It silvered in meandering circles before frothing to darkness.

He staggered back to the cabin and eased back on the throttles. He felt dizzy. With the blood beating heavily at his temples, he braced against the wheel and looked blankly at the sky. Night was fading rapidly now; the stars were on the point of demise.

Ste-Anne, the American had said.

The lighthouse at Îlet à Cabrit.

1997

THE VILLAGE OF STE-ANNE

MARTINIQUE

"And the sea gave up the dead
which were in it..." (Bible)

"And?" Rear Admiral Sean Whitely asked. "And then what"

They had moved from the patio to the screened verandah of Madame Rollet's cottage. Whitely was seated at a round wicker table beside the aging white-haired doctor. Across from them sat the men called LeBaron and Harris. The table was topped by a decorous bowl of fruit, empty cups and saucers. Seashells that served as ashtrays were cluttered with snuffed-out butts. It was nearing dusk. To the east the weather was thickening, and squalls were beginning to build over the Atlantic approaches. From the lawn on the bluff Whitely could see shafts of rain arching from bluish black clouds.

They had been at it for more than six hours, having lunched in the garden and taken tea on the patio. Each of the trio had related various parts of the story. What they had not experienced firsthand, they had pieced together from conversations with each other. Of necessity, some of the story remained speculation. Some of it Whitely himself had helped to fill in from his research in Washington's archives, some of it had been be garnered from his grandfather's diary, and some of it would remain conjecture, obscured forever by the narrowing corridors of time.

As the afternoon wore on, the storytellers had become more animated. Each seemed to feed off the recollections of the others. Some of what they related had differed in minor detail, but taken together their versions retained the thread of credibility. Though it had been many years, they admitted, since they had exchanged information, Whitely thought the pieces were feathering nicely to a whole.

As they settled around the table for what would obviously be the story's conclusion, a cotton-haired Creole sauntered slowly from the kitchen bearing brandy and glasses on a tray. He was a tall, loose-limbed man, with a lean physique. As he distributed the snifters, Whitely studied his weathered craggy features.

"Lucien LeClerc?" he asked.

The aging West Indian affected a small polite bow, then smiled and left the room.

When they had paused to adjourn to the verandah, the man called Harris had taken them out to sea in Sambre's launch. With the brandy poured and the man called Le Baron re-lighting a cigar, a re-vivified Madame Rollet picked up the tale. As the story had unfolded, she had become more animated. Re-living those stormy months of 1942, the years seemed to fall away and her eyes took on the luster of youth.

"Father Delon and I returned to Ste-Anne that very morning," she said, nodding to the man called LeBaron, "the morning after the man called Paul had disappeared with the German and the Italian. It was nearing noon. We had taken the girl Lillette to the hospital at Fort de France."

"Then she was not dead." Whitely cut in.

"All but," Nikole Rollet replied. "Her wounds were serious, but not fatal. When I found her in Sambre's villa her pulse was barely detectable. Your grandfather had examined her superficially. When I arrived she was fading fast, but she had a strong youthful heart. The wound was life threatening, but fortunately the bullet had missed her spinal cord. She was unable to speak for weeks, but she recovered nicely."

"Surely there were questions," Whitely said.

"We reported an accident," Madame Rollet continued, "We said that Christopher Delon had been cleaning his gun at his apartment and it had gone off accidentally, that the girl on the adjoining terrace had been hit. Weapons were easy to come by in those days. Soldiers were selling them for souvenirs. I was well known at the hospital. No one questioned my story."

"What if the German had returned? Whitely asked. "Or Sambre?"

"At that point, no one knew where Sambre was," she said. "Even had he returned, he would be unlikely to contradict our story. It was a chance we had to take. I could not risk bringing the girl back here to my clinic. She needed constant attention, something I could not guarantee with all that was going on."

"And me? What did you do with me?" Whitely asked.

She looked at him as though seeing past the man in the naval officer's uniform to the three-year-old of the story. "After hospitalizing Lillette, we brought you to the Consulate. Father Delon pinned a note to your shirt identifying you as the missing son of an American woman on St. Thomas. We rang the bell and left you on the doorstep."

"And my grandfather?"

The aging doctor paused and glanced seaward. Whitely wondered what mental pictures were forming behind those wistful gray eyes.

"I had already phoned the Consulate," she said at last. "From Sambre's villa. Anonymously, of course. I informed them that an American agent was aboard M. Sambre's yacht. I told them to alert the American picket ships. As it turned out, one of your destroyers had been torpedoed that night. The BERKELEY, we learned later. That put the entire island on alert, and, I suppose, the American forces as well."

"Did you know the German was my father?" Whitely asked.

Madam Rollet sipped her brandy. "Your grandfather had mentioned it. After your disappearance from the St. Thomas, he flew at once to console your mother. When he returned to Martinique, he told me the circumstances of your birth."

Whitely looked at the man called LeBaron. He was obviously the priest of the story, though his ill-fitting suit looked anything but clerical. "And you, monsieur. You, no doubt, are Father Delon."

"Bishop Delon," Madame Rollet interrupted.

"I see," Whitely said, trying to fit the aging prelate to the disillusioned priest of Dunkirk. "And you, Bishop Delon. Were you able to keep your promise to help the girl Lillette off the island?"

The Frenchman smiled. "That's for later, monsieur. For now, Signor Arazi should bring us ashore."

Whitely looked at the man called Harris. If the buttery Italian shoes and the European-cut suit had not given him away, his dialect would have, for the more he more he delved into the past the more the Piedmontese idiom leaked into his accent. Despite his Mediterranean features, Whitely was having trouble connecting the gaunt old man in the dark glasses to the swarthy young survivor of the SQUALO's depth-charging.

Aldo Arazi swirled the brandy in his snifter. Whitely noticed he had spiced it with a wedge of lime.

"When I reached the island in the yacht it was nearly dawn," the Italian said. "I was weak from loss of blood, and sitting on a fortune in gold. At the time I had no idea how much bullion the crates contained. All I knew was that I needed a doctor. While we were hugging the coast to avoid the French patrol boats, the American had mentioned Ste-Anne. He had made a point of telling me that Lillette had visited a woman doctor at Ste-Anne, the very same woman who had taken the boy at the pier."

Madame Rollet lay a hand on the Italian's sleeve. "Signor Arazi had been unaware of the plot to steal the gold. Nor did he realize that only a handful of people on the island even knew the gold was missing. For all he knew, the gendarmes were searching for the crates that very minute. If he turned himself over to the French, he ran the risk of being arrested as a conspirator."

"There was no one left to confirm my story," the Italian said. "The German had killed Sambre. He had admitted that on the yacht. I believed Lillette to be dead. Your grandfather and the German were in the sea. Both the manservant Honore and the Creole woman who had nursed me to health had been given the night of the hijacking off. For all I knew they knew nothing about anything."

"And you landed here?" Whitely asked. "At Ste-Anne?"

"Not quite. Before the shooting began on the yacht, the American had pointed out the lighthouse at Îlet à Cabrit. It's south of here, six or seven kilometers. I could see the beam sweeping the sea. I headed for the lighthouse. I had fashioned a tourniquet from my undershirt to stop the bleeding in my leg. But when I tried to move, the bleeding started again. I had little choice but to make for the nearest land."

The Italian paused. He took a sip of brandy then continued with his tale. "I ran the launch aground just south of Ste-Anne. It was extremely dark, a desolate stretch of coast. As the sky lightened, I limped and crawled up a nearby hill. I came upon a village and some huts. A fisherman eyed me suspiciously. I showed him my wounds and asked about the lady doctor. He brought me up the coast in his *gommier.*"

"And you had no trouble finding us?" Madame Rollet asked, as though hearing the story for the first time.

The Italian turned to her. It was obvious they had become close. Whitely noticed that each treated the other with a deference reserved for old friends.

"A few hours later I was out there," Aldo said, pointing beyond the patio, "in your garden. Your housekeeper..."

"Persia," she said.

"...yes. Persia. She took me to the clinic and wrapped my wounds. I dozed until you arrived."

Madame Rollet leaned across the table and patted the Italian's arm. "Signor Arazi told us what had happened on the yacht. About the struggle between the German and your grandfather. He said they had disappeared into the sea. At first Christopher and I were suspicious of him. We knew from Lillette that he had worked with the German. He might have disposed of the German and your grandfather himself. But his wounds were bad, especially the one in the leg. He begged us not to turn him over to the authorities. He had no desire to spend the duration of the war on Martinique. In the days that followed, he related his story. He was young. A victim. We believed him."

Whitely eased back in his chair. "And the gold?"

The Italian resumed his tale. "I could not be sure what or how much Madam Rollet knew. She had been on the pier at Bellefontaine. She had taken the boy. She had seen Sambre's yacht, the crates. I was in need of help. If I lied, I was afraid she would turn me out. I told her where I had left the yacht."

Madame Rollet offered brandy. Whitely nodded and she poured. When the Italian paused to light a cigarette, the Frenchman picked up the tale.

"About your grandfather," Christopher Delon said. "When Signor Arazi told us that the American had gone overboard, I immediately telephoned the U.S. Consulate, again anonymously. I informed them that one of their men had been lost at sea. An agent named Paul. I suggested a search be made somewhere between Forte de France and Ste-Anne. The man who took the message tried to interrogate me. He wanted to know what I knew, how I knew. I told him the information was accurate, that I would have no more to say. He thanked me and assured me they would scour the area."

"And they did," Madame Rollet broke in. "Later that afternoon I went to a point overlooking the sea. I took your grandfather's binoculars. I saw patrol planes, ships of various sizes...." She put a hand to her mouth.

There was an awkward pause.

"They never found him," Whitely said.

"I was certain they had not," the Madame continued. "He would have sent word...."

Whitely squirmed in his chair. They had been at it for hours. He was tired. They were all tired, but their story was nearing an end. He looked beyond the peaks. From the darkening clouds came scratches of lightning. Near the mouth of the bay the sea was choppy, the wave tops seamed with froth. On the beach, trees were yielding to a stiffening breeze and breakers were surging toward the shore.

"And now to the gold," the Frenchman said. "Would you....?" He turned to Madame Rollet.

"Please," the old woman said. "Your memory is better..."

The Frenchman nodded. "Of course, you are correct, monsieur. I am the priest of the story. I am Christopher Delon. What to do with the gold? It was a difficult decision. When Aldo...Signor

Arazi...told us of the gold on the yacht, he was fearful he could be implicated, shot as a conspirator."

"I was anxious to get off the island, the Italian said. Gold or no gold. I was in danger of losing a leg. All the gold in the world would not compensate for a leg. The Americans had a hospital on St. Lucia."

"It was important that he have an operation," Madam Rollet broke in. If he was found here in Ste-Anne, his presence would be difficult to explain. If we returned him to Bellefontaine, he could be implicated in the theft of the gold. Others might be involved. We had no way of knowing. Under the law, we should have turned him over to the authorities."

The priest-turned-bishop continued. "Nikole and I could not decide about the gold. To turn it back to the military could prove troublesome. If Lillette survived, we had no idea what she might say.

We could not be sure the German would not turn up again, or the American, for that matter."

"I can see your problem," Whitely said.

Beyond the bay the storm was intensifying. The clouds were thickening, the palms thrashing wildly in the wind. Ribbons of spume blew from whitecaps on the bay.

Nikole Rollet seemed re-animated now. With the wind stirring her hair and her cheeks suddenly flushed, the decades seemed to fall away.

"We sent the baker Lucien for the yacht," she said. "Aldo had chosen his landing site well. No one had come across it. That night Lucien moved the yacht to a safer place, an abandoned boathouse north of the village."

"And the gold?" Whitely asked.

"It remained on board. For weeks.

"And Signor Arazi? How did you dispose of a wounded combatant?"

"We smuggled him with a defector to St. Lucia."

"The Americans treated me well," Aldo said. "For a time I was in prisoner-of-war camp in Missouri. Toward the end of the war I was shipped to a camp in upstate New York."

"What happened to the girl Lillette?"

The Bishop replied. "I was at her side when she regained consciousness. I told her of the accidental shooting story. She handled it smoothly. I remained with her throughout her convalescence."

"And today? Is she still alive?"

The Bishop nodded. "As of last Christmas she was alive and well. Each Christmas I receive a note. After the war she married a Greek fisherman. Forty years ago I christened her only child. A son."

"What of Sambre? Was his body ever found?"

The Frenchman and the Italian looked to Madame Rollet.

"If he was ever found, we did not hear of it," she said. Immediately after the incident, the assumption in official circles was that he had fled the island. Admiral Robert was rumored to have looked into his disappearance, but nothing official was ever published. Perhaps the Admiral thought it best to let the matter drop. Perhaps be was just too busy. He had his hands full with the torpedoing of the American destroyer, the prospect of an invasion, the incident with the gold. It was a time of chaos, suspicion, uncertainty."

Whitely glanced thoughtfully over the bay. "So none of the islanders knew the gold had been taken from the fort?"

The cotton-haired Creole returned from the kitchen. He was pushing a cart laden with coffee.

Madame Rollet poured as she talked. "It was as though nothing had happened," she said. "We waited, days, weeks, months, for something to slip out, some rumor or report. A scandal about the missing gold, Sambre's yacht, something. There was nothing. Everyone was preoccupied with the war, the mobilization."

Whitely stirred brandy into his coffee. "On that, I can shed some light," he said. "The fact that some gold was missing was not discovered until after the war, five years later. Though inquiries were made, the assumption was that the gold could have been siphoned off at any number of points, just as Sambre and the German had predicted. It was written off as one of those mysteries of war."

"And of course," Christopher Delon added, "Admiral Robert was court martialed after the war; condemned to death. But because his son had been a leader in the French Resistance, they commuted his sentence to house arrest. He was well into his eighties when he died."

"So," Whitely asked, shifting on his chair. "What did happen to the gold on Sambre's yacht?"

Aldo Arazi smiled. "You have waited this long, Signor. A few more minutes."

The Italian seemed more relaxed now. They all did. Apparently their decision to relate their story was well taken. The confession seemed to work a catharsis on them all.

While directly above, the sky was a curdling blue, across the bay it had grown as dark as night. The wind had strengthened and the cove was fretted with waves. Lightning pitchforked beyond the peaks, and there was the rumble of distant thunder. Over Diamant, rain was blurring the dome of the Rock so that its flanks looked flat against the sea. As though drawing strength from the weather, Madame Rollet took up the tale. Her voice seemed like that of a far younger woman, a woman reborn to the past.

"After Signor Arazi left the island, we were torn, Pere Christopher and I. We debated our options long and hard. To return the gold would involve answering questions, questions we were not prepared to discuss. We could risk no perusal. I was SKIPJACK, after all. I was smuggling defectors to St. Lucia. And Christopher was inextricably involved. That alone could get us hanged for treason. It was Christopher who suggested..." She nodded to the priest. "...but why not tell him yourself, your Excellency."

Christopher Delon took a long steady pull on his brandy. He had removed his jacket and Whitely could see the gauntness in his chest, his slender waist. For a man in his seventies, thought Whitely, his features were remarkably striking.

The Bishop leaned forward with both elbows on the table. After much deliberating, we decided the gold would not be returned to bankers, Nazi or otherwise. Or to the military. Remember, in 1942 it appeared the Germans would win the war. We concluded that no matter who got the gold, it would be used to purchase more weapons, to finance more killing. At best, it would serve to feed the scavengers who wreak such havoc. Your grandfather had an impact on us all, Admiral. Madame Rollet was in love with him...."

Whitely looked at the aging physician. There was a softening of her features.

"...and," she smiled, he saved Signor Arazi's life..."

The Italian gestured toward the sea. "Were it not for your grandfather, my bones would be part of that coral reef by now. That's why I agreed to tell his story."

"As for me," the priest continued, "he helped to restore my faith. To assure your own safety, Admiral, he readily surrendered to the German. You were his grandson, to be sure. But still, it was an heroic gesture. Despite one's failings, I had learned, if one prevailed, a single life could make a difference."

Madame Rollet sighed. "Yes, we debated long and hard, Christopher and I. When the war ended, the gold was in a sub-basement of this house. Lucien had carted it in his bakery truck one crate at a time over a period of weeks, always at night. As for the yacht, Lucien took it out beyond the reef one night and sank it."

Whitely remembered the skeleton of the wreck near Diamant. It reminded him of the fisherman he had met on the beach. "There are inconsistencies," he said. "The fisherman Paquet said he saw a submarine in the cove that night. The night the gold was moved."

"Easily explained," said Christopher Delon. Even then Paquet was a heavy drinker. Loaded with crates, the barge could easily be mistaken for a submarine in darkness. It's unlikely he has seen a submarine to this day. Down through the years there have been many stories of submarines coming to the island, some true, most apocryphal."

"But Paquet said there was shooting. That he had fled to the hills."

Madame Rollet looked out to sea. "When they were loading the barge, Paquet was with Lucien above the cove. Lucien reported hearing a shot also. It could have been when the German shot Sambre."

"Yes," Aldo said. "On the yacht, just before the American warship was torpedoed, the German told me he had shot the Frenchman near the cove"

Whitely sampled the coffee. It was coming together. Just a few more strands.

"The officers at the barge. You said the Senegalese troops had left the island. But what of the two officers who were to dump the gold? Why has no one ever heard from them?"

Christopher Delon leaned back in his chair. "To what end, monsieur? As far as anyone knew, it was merely a drill. Only the Senegalese troops knew the crates had been taken to the cove. And they were shipped from the island immediately after the gold was returned to the fort. As far as the officers were concerned, all of the gold was returned to Fort Desaix."

Which explained, Whitely realized, why none of the veterans he had interviewed remembered the gold being moved. He turned to Madame Rollet. "When I arrived on the island two weeks ago, someone telephoned my hotel. The accent was strong, the English broken. He put me on to the fisherman Paquet. I take it that was your man Lucien?

Madame Rollet smiled. "He was at your meeting with the naval veterans. Word had spread through the membership that an American would be coming to ask about the war. We did not know what you sought, or where you would look, or what you would find. When Lucien reported that you were asking about the gold, I decided to interrogate you myself. We were sure Paquet would steer you to Ste-Anne."

"And what if he had not?"

"We would have found another way."

"So when I found you in the church a week ago, you were not surprised."

"I was counting on it, monsieur. And when you left, I telephoned Signor Arazi and Father Delon."

Whitely could not suppress a grin. "So all the time I though I was questioning you, you were examining me."

Madame Rollet smiled.

"Please," Admiral Whitely said, "continue with your story."

Aldo Arazi picked up the thread. "I returned to Martinique after the war," he said, "partially to thank Doctor Rollet for saving my leg and partially, I confess, to discover what had become of the gold. I assumed it had been returned to the authorities by then. I was shocked and surprised when Madame Rollet took me to the basement. The gold was still in the crates, just as it had been when I loaded it onto Sambre's yacht."

"Things had changed considerably by then," Nikole Rollet said. "But there were still problems. Admiral Robert had been arrested, people had fled the island, records had been lost or misplaced, the very status of the island was in question. We frankly had no way of explaining the gold. If we turned it in, it might look as though we had been collaborating with the Nazis. At that point, there was much confusion as to who the real enemy was. Even the Admiral had been taken in chains."

"So I suggested the hospital," Christopher Delon said.

"Hospital?" Whitely asked.

"A children's hospital. For youngsters orphaned by the war. Children who could not otherwise afford treatment. Now it specializes in children with rare diseases."

"And," Whitely asked, though he anticipated the answer.

"We built it," Aldo Arazi said proudly. "We disposed of the ingots on the South American black market. The proceeds were banked in Switzerland. It was not difficult."

"And where is this hospital?" Whitely asked.

"In Italy," Aldo replied. "Near the French border. It's called OSPEDALE SANTA ANNA. In the early years Christopher Delon served as head chaplain. Until I retired six years ago, I served as managing director. I am proud to say my son has taken my place. His name is Dante, by the way. A good Italian name."

They sat for a moment in silence, the trio watching the naval officer's reaction, Whitely toying pensively with his cup.

Finally Madame Rollet said, "So, Admiral. You will reveal our story?"

Whitely sipped the brandy. "And if I do. Then what?"

Christopher Delon leaned back in his chair. "We're reconciled to the consequences, Admiral. We're old. We have far more of our lives behind us than ahead. It's the children who would suffer."

Whitely pushed slowly from his chair. He walked to the patio and looked thoughtfully out to sea. The wind had shifted and the storm was drifting to the south. Shafts of sunlight pierced the clouds, illuminating the waters of the bay. Whitely could sense the eyes behind him. The silence was palpable.

His father.

His grandfather.

The Captain and the German.

In the end, neither one knew if his side had won. In the end, their struggle had been reduced to a personal skirmish in a backwater of the war. Had it been worth the struggle? Given the outcome, would they be pleased?

He looked up the coast, at the massive outcropping called Diamant. The sun was sponging the mist, burnishing The Rock in a halo of light. When he turned to face them, Madame Rollet was standing beside him. He placed an arm around her shoulders and drew her gently to his side.

"So," she said, her eyes glistening, a hand on his hand, "it seems we may escape the tempest after all."

***

Later, when the car bearing Admiral Whiteley was departing the outskirts of Ste-Anne, Nikole Rollet climbed the staircase to the second floor apartment of her cottage. Christopher Delon and Aldo Arazi were on the verandah, discussing the day's work. The Creole, Lucien LeClerc, had been dismissed for the night. The house was silent, the shutters drawn, the remnants of dusk painting slender shadows on the floors and walls. The upstairs apartment overlooked the bay. For some decades now it had been fitted out with special features for special needs.

Nikole pressed the door open quietly.

In the darkened room, a voice cut through the silence. "I heard his footsteps," the voice said. "He has a brisk stride."

"Yes," Nikole replied. "He's quite energetic."

Dante O'Shea stared unseeing through the slats of a shuttered window, the breeze from the bay stirring his hair. "He talks like his mother," he said, a wistfulness in his voice. "With a quiet strength."

The doctor placed a hand on his shoulder. "Perhaps you should have come down."

"No. It's better this way. It has always been better this way."

Nikole Rollet crossed the room and kissed the sightless eyes. "You have always insisted, I know. But it must be painful to have him so close."

"He's no closer than he has been for decades. In my mind's eye, he will always be the gutsy little three-year-old on Sambre's yacht."

"He's makes a handsome officer," Nikole said, brushing the hair from his brow. "Much like his grandfather."

"He has his mother's persistence. I overheard the entire conversation. You and the others did well."

"Aldo and Christopher want to see you before they leave. They're waiting in the garden."

We'll go down in a minute. We did the right thing, Nika. Had I gone back, I would have been a burden to them all these years. I couldn't have lived with that."

"There must have been times when you doubted."

"Occasionally. But whenever I weakened, I thought of what it would mean to them. Had I gone back, I'd have been pitied. Pity is the one thing I could not abide. That and being dependent. At least here, I helped to bring the gold. It was a compensation of sorts. And then there is our life together. I was a dead man when Lucien found me. You nursed me back to life, both physically and spiritually. You are my life, Nika; the Dante of the war is a fossil best left uncovered."

Nikole brushed a finger over his brow. "Those early years were difficult, *mon cher.* Adjusting to blindness, unable to walk, re-learning to speak. You were very brave."

"Perhaps if I had healed somewhat, I might have gone back. But once Casey and the boy left St. Thomas, I was better off out here than in a veteran's hospital."

"You were thinking of your daughter. It was an act of love."

He took her band. "I could never have endured it without you, Nika. Do you think he suspected?"

"Why should he? The story was true, all but the end. There was no need to tell him that Lucien found you unconscious and paralyzed in the salon of Sambre's yacht; that Aldo was in pain and near panic and did not search the ship before abandoning it in near the lighthouse at Îlet à Cabrit. Had we done that, we would have had to fabricate a more complicated story...a story about a burial. Better he thinks you buried at sea. You are both Navy, after all. Besides, you were fortunate not to have bled to death. The reality changed nothing. He had no reason to doubt."

Huddled in the chair, his legs atrophied from paralysis and disuse, he reached up and took her hand. "I wonder."

"I wish you could see him, Dante. He's tall, like you. With lighter hair, but the same strong features, the same easy smile."

"One of the advantages of this", he pointed to his eyes, "is that he'll never grow old. Nor will his mother. Nor will you, my sweet. Yes, we did the right thing. They did just fine without the burden of a blind old cripple. It's not like we didn't keep an eye on them. Had they needed us, we would have been there."

"So what do we do now," Nikole asked. "Do you think he'll relate our story? Betray our secret?"

"I doubt it. He sounds like a man of honor. Of integrity."

"He inherited it", she said, kissing his forehead. "Those things are in the blood."

"I'd like to think so", Dante said, squeezing her hand. "I'd really like to think so."

Finis

Printed in the United States
By Bookmasters